The She-Wolf

BY THE SAME AUTHOR

Anne of the Isles
Bel Demonio
The Black Coats:
    The Parisian Jungle
    Heart of Steel
    'Salem Street
    The Invisible Weapon
    The Companions of the Treasure
    The Cadet Gang
    The Sword Swallower
The Companions of the Silence
Gentlemen of the Night / Captain Phantom (stage plays)
John Devil
Knightshade
Revenants
Vampire City
The Vampire Countess
The Wandering Jew's Daughter
The White Wolf

The She-Wolf

by
Paul Féval

Translated by
Nina Cooper

Annotated by
Jean-Marc Lofficier

A Black Coat Press Book

Acknowledgements: Thanks to Charles Griggs for his reviews of all the drafts and his helpful critique of each.

English adaptation Copyright © 2020 by Nina Cooper.
Introduction and Notes Copyright © 2020 by Nina Cooper & Jean-Marc Lofficier.
Cover illustration Copyright © 2020 illustration by Michel Borderie.

Visit our website at www.blackcoatpress.com

TABLE OF CONTENTS

Paul Féval

Introduction

La Louve, here translated as *The She-Wolf*, was initially serialized in *Le Pays* from 26 December 1855 to 5 March 1856. It was then reprinted as 4 volumes by Hetzel in 1857 and 2 volumes (*La Louve* and *Valentine de Rohan*) by A. Cadot in 1862.

It is a historical swashbuckler taking place near the end of the 17th century, and using as background the tale of the Breton resistance to French conquest. That theme, and indeed the Secret Society of the Wolves featured in *La Louve*, had already been used by Paul Féval in his earlier novel, *Le Loup Blanc*,[1] written in 1843 but taking place later than *The She-Wolf*, in 1720 and 1740, when Brittany had already become part of France.

France, in the 19th century, dominated the art world, and also produced some of the best of the world's western literature. Literacy throughout France had become more widespread, thanks to the Industrial Revolution (1760-1840) which had brought country people into large cities, and to the prevalence of, and competition between, newspapers, both State and privately-owned. Newspapers, to capture and to hold readers, published inserts into each edition, usually published twice a month. The insertions were called *feuilles (leaves)* and those who submitted them were called *feuilletonistes.* Almost all popular 19th century authors were, at one time or another,

---

[1] Available from Black Coat Press as *The White Wolf*, ISBN 978-1-61227-832-2. The introduction to that volume includes a history of Brittany and the French conquest which is essential reading for a better understanding of the historical events mentioned in this volume.

feuilletonistes, although not all are so identified today. Paul Féval was one of the most popular of the feuilletonistes.

A colorful and somewhat imaginative introduction to the work of Paul Féval is the review of his life in *Les Contemporains,* a collection of satiric pseudo-biographies by Eugène de Miracourt.[2] He begins his biography of Paul Féval writing:

"If the firm Alexandre Dumas & Company had interrupted the course of its commercial operation, the writer, still young, whose life this account is going to trace, would have been capable of furnishing, by himself, and without the help of others' pens, a good part of the clientele of that immense novel factory.

"Paul Féval is a literary locomotive, who had Antoine de Joli[3] as a stoker, and who picked up speed, thanks to the coal from the *Courier français* and *L'Époque.*

"But let's not get ahead of our story. The author of *Les Mystères de Londres* was born in the old capital of Brittany, November 28, 1817. His teachers confirm that he had very little taste for books, a great passion for sports, and a firmly established habit of playing truant.

"He was placed when still young in the Rennes secondary school. Féval didn't make a big scholarly splash. He was a puny and sickly child, too weak to stand up under the blows

---

[2] Eugène de Miracourt (1812-1880) (Jean-Baptiste Jacquot) wrote novels, short stories, dramatic works, and biographies. He published 100 satiric biographies of politicians, writers and artists from 1854 through 1858. Frequently sued for slander, he ultimately entered the Dominicans, became a priest, and died in Haiti.

[3] Anténor Joly (1799-1852), he published *Le Loup blanc* in 1843 in his newspaper *Le Courier français* and entrusted Féval with the difficult task of writing *a roman feuilleton* based solely on the title *Les Mystères de Londres* within one month.

brought about by his penchant for mockery. His teachers didn't like him at all; his fellow students beat him endlessly. His memories of that time he reproduced in his works in a bitterly comic tone.

"The story of that good Mister Quandoquidem, author of *Cours de thèmes* and of *Tournures élégantes à l'usage des élèves de seconde,* is an amusing and crazy story.

"Quandoquidem was the father of a dozen blushing children. Disdaining ordinary names, he gave Roman names to those offspring, as numerous as they were ruddy. This noble pedagogue never asked for food or drink with the usual words in such a case. Full of dignity in the exercise of his functions, if he ordered Féval to bend over, he was careful, even for such a simple order, not to deviate from the system of the *Tournures élégantes.*

" 'Prostrate yourself,' he would exclaim, 'into the proper position for a guilty person.'

"And if Paul seemed little inclined to obey, Quandoquidem added:

" 'I'm going to use the help of a servant to force you, and I'll certainly know how to decline you *hors dieu* in the genitive.'

"When the July revolution[4] broke out, Paul was beginning his thirteenth year.

"Seeing his professor and his fellow students wearing the tri-colored cockade,[5] the imprudent student, his head fueled by family inspirations, decided to attach an enormous white cockade to his hat. Up until that point he had shown himself somewhat cowardly in the quarrels the other students picked with him, but this time political excitement inspired him with truly extraordinary courage. Despite the repeated commands,

---

[4] Refers to the July 1830 Revolution which overthrew Charles X, the Bourbon monarch, and replaced him with Louis Philippe.
[5] Tri-colored cockade and white cockade indicating political parties.

followed by a shower of blows, Féval didn't remove his cockade.

"Unable to fight back against the big rascals of the upper secondary school, he showed his heroism by not protecting his back without complaint and to receiving all the clouts they judged proper to administer to him.

"This intrepid Carlist [6] was removed from the school by his mother, without which removal France would have had to weep about the fate of another victim of the July Revolution. Madame Féval took Paul to an old manor house belonging to a member of the family and lost in the depths of Morbihan.

"It was different there.

"Our young adversary of the cadet branch fell into the middle of the clandestine Chouan[7] agitations. The chateau served as a rendezvous for the conspirators. They assembled there at night; they smelted ammunition there. The men seemed resolute, impatient to act, and in that country *Fronde*, the women showed themselves more excited.

"That mystery, those dangers, those alerts, strongly influenced Paul's mind. He obtained the promise of a carbine to go fight the blues; dreaming only of battles, thinking only about massacres, he took into his head one fine evening to insult the police, who had come for a household visit. The good gendarmes seized that snotty-nosed child by the ear, then took him to his mother, who ordered him to behave. None of those Chouan warrior projects came about and the chateau returned to peace and quiet.

"Brittany inflamed its children's imagination at an early age by means of political and religious faith, by the traditions of chivalry, old stories from the chronicles or legends, told by

---

[6] Supporter of Charles X.

[7] Royalist uprising or counter-revolution in twelve of the western départements of France, particularly in the provinces of Brittany and Maine, against the First Republic during the French Revolution. It played out in three phases and lasted from the spring of 1794 until 1800.

the hearth, and to which everyone listened at that hour when the lamp, its oil used up, was about to go out, when the whistling wind outside seemed to strike the high windows with the mysterious wings of ghosts.

"It has been more or less a half century since this strange land ventured into civilized domains, and the number of storytellers that it has furnished to our literature is already considerable. Between Chateaubriand and Paul Féval, God knows how many could be listed here. The hero of this biography, as those who came before him, came to us one day, his head stuffed with native legends. He told us what had been told to him over there under the vast and dark cloak of the fireplace: *L'histoire de la Femme blanche,* that of the *Bonhomme Misère,* of the *Joli Château des coquerelles,* of the *Belles de nuit,* and of the *Maréchal de Raiz,* that implacable and barbaric husband that the fair sex must curse.[8]

"Thanks to Paul Féval, we know that *Barbe-bleue* is of Armorican[9] origin.

"When our thirteen-year-old student left the evening vigil to go up to his bedroom, he had a head filled with terrors and went to bed feverish. If the servant brought up a light, Paul felt a shiver run through his whole body; his teeth chattered; he seemed to see his bed surrounded by candles and sad voices reciting funereal verses from the *De Profundis* at his bedside.

"Paul Féval returned to school in 1831 and remained there until 1833, still puny, still sickly, still a mocker and still beaten. He still kept in his heart the memory of the whacks his comrades had meted out to him. In order to make up in the present for what was due to him in the past, he dreamed that he slapped the face of those he had a complaint against. The

---

[8] The *Maréchal de Raiz* is the notorious serial killer Gilles de Rais, a.k.as. Blue-beard (1404-1440). Some of Féval's folk tales mentioned here are available in the Black Coat Press edition of *Anne of the Isles,* ISBN 978-1-932983-92-0.

[9] From Brittany.

novelist very seriously persuaded himself that he was the chief arm-breaker and scourge.

"He was expected to become a member of the bar.

"His family was an ancient family of barristers; the Baron de Létange, his grandfather, was Attorney General of the Royal Court at Rennes, and his father, an honorable and learned magistrate, died in 1827, a lawyer at the same court. But magistrates of integrity don't become rich. The Féval household was poor, and the young student's mother couldn't afford the expense of her son's education, when suddenly Providence, in the envelope of a letter written by the Chevalier Féval, a banking consultant, sent three thousand francs to pay for Paul's legal studies.

"Except for a prize for excellence, barely achieved in the second form, he hadn't attained any great success in school. His too lively imagination kept him from serious work. Also the dull commentaries of Cujas only dampened his enthusiastic but very slightly; nevertheless he secured a place at the examinations, passed and received a degree, finished his probationary period, and there he was, perfectly free to practice the profession of lawyer.

"Paul wasn't lacking anything else but oratorial talent and a clientele.

"His first case wasn't long in coming, a magnificent case! He was charged with defending a Haut-Breton villager accused of stealing a dozen chickens, complicated by housebreaking and entering. Féval reviewed in his head all that his books had taught him about Demosthenes' harangues; when the great day of the trial arrived, he presented the thief's defense with solemn gravity and in the most pompous language. Quandoquidem would have been delighted.

"Paul's argument was divided into three points; but in the middle of the first one, the judges were suddenly seized with hilarity.

" 'Enough, Master Paul, enough!' said the presiding judge. 'The case is understood.'

" 'Good,' thought Paul. 'I'm making them laugh. They're disarmed.'

" 'What do you have to add in your defense?' the presiding judge asked the village amateur of thefts of other people's property.

"The guilty man, perhaps excited by his lawyer's success, and wanting to amuse the judges in his turn, began a knowledgeable and very complete dissertation on the art of stealing hens without alerting anyone. Féval, from his bench, motioned to him in vain; the stubborn country man didn't understand them or didn't want to understand them. He developed his curious theory to the magistrate, to the audience, to the gendarmes, and paid no attention to his defender's distressed pantomime.

"Marveling at the thief's knowledge, but judging it unfit to let him explain the doctrines thus in public, the court gave him the maximum sentence. Féval tore up his robes in despair, threw his toque to the wind, and turned his eyes toward Paris.

"It was there that he must avenge the humiliation done to his eloquence, and shine in another career, that of literature, for which he felt a decided taste.

"But it was impossible that anyone could come to help efficiently in those new undertakings. Paul had drawn from the bottom of the conscription urn[10] a detestable number. Buying a replacement had exhausted the last maternal resources; and the business consultant at the banking center would not help his second cousin desert the bar for literature. What did that matter? At twenty-years-old, with a Breton head, there are no obstacles.

"Féval quickly wrote to another family member, President of the Business Tribunal of the Seine. He asked him for his help in obtaining a situation. He didn't have to wait long for the answer. The young man was offered a modest employment as a teller in a banking house. He accepted, kissed

---

[10] Military service was then compulsory, usually for a two-year period, and was determined by lot.

his mother, said good-bye to his sisters, took a hundred *écus* they were still able to get together, got into a stage coach and got on the way to Paris..."

A more prosaic, but neutral, version is the following:

"Paul Féval was a member of a Brittany family of lawyers, bankers, and civil servants. His father died prematurely, leaving Féval's mother unable to support her family and provide a suitable education for her son.

"Through the generosity of an uncle he was enrolled at the age of 10 in the Royal Collage. He completed his law degree in 1836. He abandoned the law after losing his first case. He moved to Paris in 1838, entered a bank under the protection of an uncle, but did not take to the occupation and was soon fired.

"He applied himself to literature, but his first submissions to editors were rejected. Introduced to Catholic and Royalist editors, his first work to be published was *Le Club des Phoques* in 1841 in *La Revue de Paris*. The editor of *L'Époque*, Anténor Joly, hired Féval to 'translate' *Les Mystères de Londres*. As translated, the work was not publishable. However, Féval did a total re-write and it was published in 1843 under the pseudonym Sir Francis Troloppe. Immediately popular, it underwent twenty editions and began Féval's long career.

"He is credited with more than 200 volumes: swashbuckler romances, crime thrillers, Breton folk tales, and horror novels.

"While Eugène Sue was born into a wealthy family and lived a life of luxury, travel, and adventure, Paul Féval's life was one of constant work. He married, fathered five children, published a magazine, *Jean Diable,* and twice lost almost his whole fortune in risky financial speculations."

Féval is still published in France and a number of translations of his most famous works are available from Black Coat Press. Some require more of the contemporary reader, who is accustomed to fast-moving, action-packed stories, than they did of the 19th century reader, who read a small portion at a time in newspapers and eagerly awaited the next installment, not minding the frequent digressions.

After all, the newspaper and its reading material were sometimes the only printed matter available to those with limited disposable income, and who got ample value for their five-centime purchase.

Nina Cooper

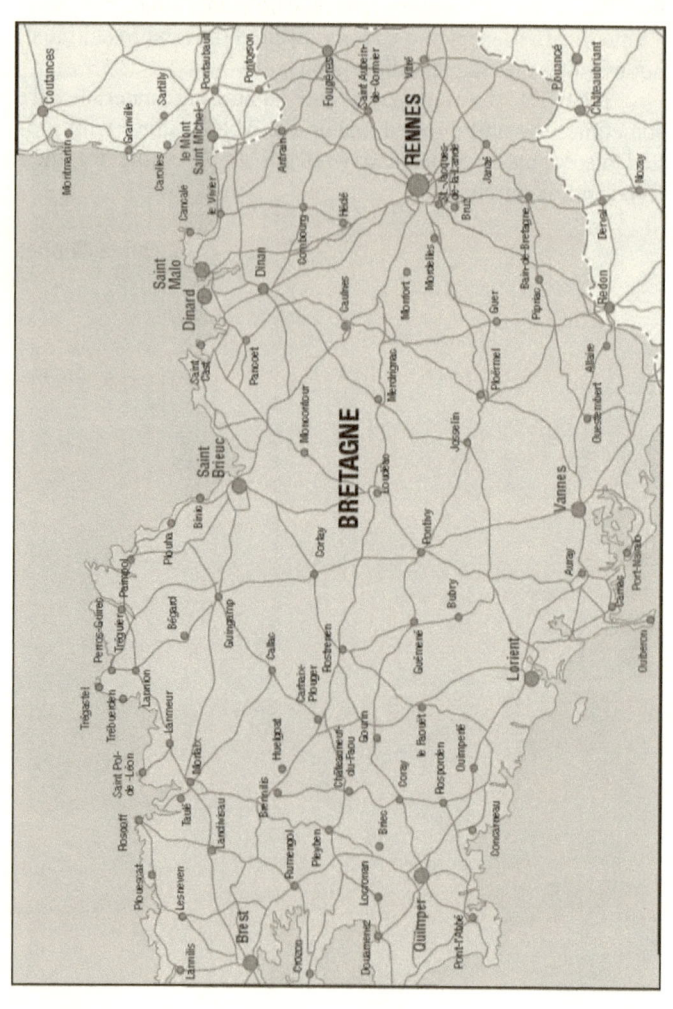

Brittany

THE SHE-WOLF

PROLOGUE

I. The Apparition

The sun was already brightening the pieces of greenery
spread out over the sides of the hill: charming deformed and
gnarled old tree trunks, tall and slim silver birches standing
boldly, wearing with pride their trembling crown of leaves,
robust oak trees, and chestnut trees raising their dense branches like a roof. Above the thick and solid covering, there rose
little columns of smoke that twisted in light spirals, burned
blue by the sun. It wasn't the opaque and thick vapor that the
smoke stacks our factories now put out. It was the timid breath
of the industry at a young age. Each little column of smoke
marked the location of a thatched cottage, the humble factory
of those rosy wooden shoes, curved in the Chinese fashion,
pot-bellied like some tall ships, that are the glory of the
Rennes Forest.

Count Rohan-Polduc,[11] our *Monsieur,* as they called him
in the thatched cottages, said that his manor house had been

---

[11] Also called Rohan-Pouldu. This little-known branch is a
junior branch of the Rohan-Gué-de-l'Isle branch and appeared
around 1500. It was named after the estate of Pouldu near
Pontivy (nowadays Saint-Jean-Brévelay). Its best-known
member is Emmanuel de Rohan-Polduc, Magister Magnus of
the Knights Hospitaller from 1775 to 1797. The branch became extinct in 1800.

built by Saint Guéhéneue. He was a younger member of the Ducal house of Brittany, Count of Porhoët, Viscount of Rennes, and first bearer of the proud Rohan name, in the 9th century of the Christian era. If the good gentleman was mistaken, it wasn't by very much, because the manor house seemed as old as the world, with its narrow turrets piled haphazardly, its little donjon covered by vegetation and its roofs pointed like magicians' bonnets. The slates of the roofs, white with lichen, let joubarbe and moss, resembling long hair, grow everywhere. The walls, composed of blocks of granite, were still strong, but under the black mantle of ivy which enveloped them, there could be seen the wrinkles of old age and the wounds of the soldier. The crevasses, the injuries of time, the breeches, were glorious scars of the sape and the mine.

The large moat, which must have been deep at the time the manor kept up its pretentions to the title of fortress, circled the manor house. It had kept just enough water to be used as a playground for a large gaggle of geese and ducks. However, the portion of the moat facing the avenue situated in front of the moat had been kept full so that the masters, the servants, and the cattle and sheep herds could enter at street level. The moat itself was crossed by a little rustic bridge which ended at a large breach made in the rampart. That breach had its history.

In 1670, when Louis XIV and the Count Rohan Polduc were both young, the Breton gentleman took a fancy to make war against the most powerful monarch in Europe. Rohan was a Protestant, like all those of his race; ducal blood ran in his veins and his genealogy contained more old parchment than was needed to establish his right to the throne of Brittany. But Louis XIV had enough, and more than enough, Rohans at his Court at Paris already: Rohan-Soubise, Rohan-Guéménée, Rohan-Rochefort, as well as the Rohan-Chabots whose comic lives lent themselves so well to the gazetteers of the 17th century. Louis XIV perhaps never suspected that, in the depths of the Rennes forest, there was a deposed prince who claimed to dispute with him a portion of his kingdom. That was the time when Madame the Marquise de Sévigné,[12] the charming Breton woman with so much wit and so little patriotism, scoffed at the poor, savage Bretons. Proud bursts of laughter would have been heard at Versailles if some prophet had predicted that the first thunder clap announcing the Revolution yet to come was already brewing in the distance of that cloudy sky, and that the first cry of "liberty!" would be shouted by those gentlemen with unkempt hair and calloused hands, as good with the plow as with the sword, for whom the very amiable Marquise kept her most disdainful smiles.

But it was still a long way away, the French Revolution. Honoré d'Albert, Duke of Chaulnes,[13] younger brother of the Connétable of Luynes, Governor of the province of Brittany, and the biggest man of his century, sent two companies of soldiers against the Polduc peasants who were entrenched in the moors of d'Auray. There was a battle and Rohan was beaten. The Duke of Chaulnes, taking advantage of that opportunity, confiscated the immense Polduc domain and the Bishops' palace of Tréguier. He set aside that ancient Rohan manor house, whose walls had been breached by the King, as a retreat for the great-nephew of Queen Anne.

But these things had happened a long time ago. That was now 1705; the great Sun King was sixty-seven years-old. The Duke of Chaulnes was dead, and his successor as well, and His Serene Highness, the Count of Toulouse, the second legit-

---

[12] Marie de Rabutin-Chantal, Marquise de Sévigné (1626-1696), French aristocrat, remembered for her letter-writing.

[13] In actual fact, it was Charles d'Albert d'Ailly (1625-1698), third son of Honoré d'Albert, third Duke of Chaulnes, who could not stem the tide of a peasant revolt in Brittany 1675. He demanded intervention from the royal armies and his violence towards the rebels alienated him from his Breton noble allies and gained him the public nickname of "fat pig." He remained in command until 1689.

imate son of Louis XIV,[14] was now Governor of the Province of Brittany. Rohan-Polduc, grown inactive because of age, kept himself aloof in his diminished household. He lived near his daughter, an angel of beauty, the sight of whom very likely inspired him with thoughts of resignation and peace.

To the right of the rustic bridge, the rampart turned toward the west and enveloped some abandoned buildings that flanked a balcony in the form of a turret. There was a legend of love about that balcony. That part of the chateau had a melancholy and a more solitary aspect. Since César de Rohan, the only son of the old Count, had died, no one had gone over the threshold of his living quarters; nevertheless, behind the curtains that the wind moved about, through the holes in the frame, there was very often a light shining all night, a pale light that sometimes showed two shadows on the moving curtains.

The lark awakens from the depth of the shadows of that dark Breton forest just as under the shades of Italy. On awakening, the Breton lark chirps the eternal, sad song which greeted the farewells of Romeo and Juliet. Toward daybreak, a window opened softly. Two human forms appeared on the massive overhang of the balcony. The breeze carried the sound of a kiss. Then the light was extinguished.

Everything was still asleep in the manor house. There was a thick haze over the moats, which had been changed into a marsh. The ramparts and the group of lodgings remained drowned in that darkness, while the fantastic remains of the highest weathervanes were already becoming damp in the pale light that came from the west. That strange beam of sharp keeps, of gables, of gothic turrets, seemed to come out of the night, as in the past Saint Guéhéneue had made them come out of the earth. Usually, at that morning hour, when Rohan

---

[14] Louis Alexandre de Bourbon, Comte de Toulouse (1678-1737), a legitimated prince of the blood royal, son of Louis XIV and his mistress Françoise-Athénaïs, Marquise de Montespan, appointed Governor of Brittany in 1695.

Polduc did not unleash his hunting dogs, everything was solitude and silence around his house. But today, the main road and the paths were filled as if it were a festival like the one held at Bouĕxis-en-Forêt. There was laughter and chatting under the grove. There were people on foot, a holly stick in their hands, carrying full sacks on their shoulders. Others were on horseback, on small horses used for everything, that ambled along, their head lowered, walking in the dust, and letting their riders' wooden shoes trail in the dust on the ground. Others nudged their lazy oxen pulling their carts filled with bundles of hay. All of that moved along in the wide paths between the black hedgerows and the dark thorn bushes where the genet slipped in its golden pods here and there. This was the 25th of June, the day prior to Saint John's day, and the *tenants*[15] of the Rennes country had kept the custom of paying their rent at that time.

People walking, people on horseback, and the rich in carts, met each other in front of the moat, and went together into the open lawn which ended at the breach. No one thought of lifting the door knocker with the head of a ram, suspended on the right panel of the door. They waited. The little girls, who were carrying bouquets of hawthorn, sat down informally on the wet grass beside their flowers made into bundles. The unharnessed carts were arranged in order, while the thin, puny-looking oxen grazed on the lawn, many times cropped already by Rohan's herds. Boys and tenant farmers lit their pipes and gathered in an *idle circle*, as it's called over there, their big hats on their head, their sticks attached to their boutonnieres, serious, taciturn and letting no sign of impatience show. While the female tenants knitted heavy wool, the young girls chatted, looking out of the corner of their eye at the western part of the rampart, around which the haze seemed to be

---

[15] Term used for those who held their land under various forms of land tenure as opposed to those who held it directly from the King or from another nobleman or senior member of the clergy.

condensed to give a final battle to the sun's vanquishing rays. They pointed with their finger at the heavy granite balcony, which extended beyond the walls, and very low. They said, shivering:

"That's where it was!"

In the distance, there was the sound of a hunting horn in the forest. The men listened.

"Steward Feydeau got up early this morning," said Jouachin, a tenant with a gray beard, who added, shaking his head with a sad expression: "I have seen the time when the Rohan domain was so long and so large, that, from here where we stand, the Rohan fanfare could never be heard."

A second, closer sound of the hunting horn came from toward the south. The visage of Jouachin became flushed and there was no boy around him who didn't close his fists, frowning.

"Rohan is asleep," the good man slowly pronounced. "The people of France would do much if Rohan awakened."

The little girls were interested in nothing but the mysterious balcony.

"It's there! It's there!" they repeated, "that a woman in white and a dark horseman… Every day that God gives!"

And those who passed from the other side of the moat heard a horse trot from the depth of the moats.

"The horseman is César de Rohan, the poor deceased young monsieur; that's what's sure! And the woman in white is Jeanne, the beautiful Jeanne de Combourg, his fiancée, dead at twenty."

"And the window which opens by itself?" asked some timidly skeptical voice. "And the horse that trots in the forest?"

"Ah! Lord Jesus! Does anyone know how to explain those things from the other world?"

"The first blast of the trumpet, however," Jouachin said, "came up from the depths of the Sangle. The second came from the Wolf's Den.[16] And I would certainly recognize the sound of the horn of Steward Feydeau. That's not him who is hunting at the Sangle."

"He, or someone else," said a somewhat sharp voice that came out of the fog. "The people of France amuse themselves where they wish and when they wish!"

"Yaumi! Cousin Yaumi!"[17] all the tenants of Rohan shouted at one time. "The handsome cobbler."

Cousin Yaumi, hidden by the fog where every night the phantom horse trotted, could not yet be seen. He finally showed himself on the other side of the moat, which he walked along side. Cousin Yaumi wasn't very tall, but his vest of felt cloth covered large shoulders. A wool cap was pulled down right to his little sleepy and cunning eyes. He had neither a horse nor a cart, and the flat bag that he carried in his hand would have fit in the pocket of his vest. Yaumi, the good-natured Cobbler, went across the lawn, balancing himself on his knotty legs and went right into the middle of the circle. His pipe was out of tobacco. He first lit it, and then said good morning politely to Cousin Jouachin, to Cousin Josais, to Cousin Mathelin, to Cousin Julot, as well as to a half-dozen other cousins whose names haven't come down to us.

He made a protective gesture to young and old, male and female cousins, and gave the closed chateau door a sly look. In another land, that look would have been followed by a question, but the countryman of Northern Brittany is prudent like the Normand, his neighbor. He hardly knows how to speak straightforwardly, nor, ordinarily, how to look you in the face. On important occasions, when once his hat has passed beyond the mills, you'd have to crack his head open right down to his teeth to force him to lower his eyes or to make him be silent.

"You're coming like this from the depths of the Sangle?" Jouachin asked.

---

[16] See *The White Wolf.*

[17] There is a Yaumi in *The White Wolf* who or may not be the same character.

"Yes, yes," the friendly maker of wooden shoes answered. "And isn't that a fog that has chosen its place? On the other side of the moats, you can't even see the end of your nose; over here, the weather is as clear as water running over rocks. All that, you see, it's frost for Saint-Peter's day, and that harms the buckwheat!"

"And the broad beans too," added Mathelin, "that's for sure!"

"Here's what's happening," interrupted old Jouachin. "Don't make us wait. Someone is hunting over there, according to you, in the depth of the Sangle?"

"The Count of Toulouse, our governor, is a handsome young prince," answered Yaumi, who looked around with a cunning glance.

Young girls and peasants had stood up so as to hear better, and the Rohan farmers had instinctively tightened their circle.

"That's the least way that these handsome young princes amuse themselves," Yaumi answered. "It amuses him to hunt, the Count of Toulouse! It's not his fault if he finds the Rohan domain in his path…"

"Then it is the Count of Toulouse who is hunting over there?"

Yaumi's voice became muffled and his eyes turned toward the granite balcony, where the sun, piercing the fog, made reddish reflections.

"There are hunts and hunts," he grumbled. "Hunts in the daytime and hunts at night… Hunts in the forest, hunts in the house… Pray God that the Count of Toulouse limits himself to hunting in the underbrush of Rohan!"

For several minutes a vague and constantly increasing murmur was heard inside the chateau. It was like the awakening of the old manor house. Voices called to each other and answered each other. The paving of the courtyard resounded with the shock of heavy wooden shoes filled with straw. The dogs in the kennel were barking and the Rohan horses, which smelled the little Breton mares, dispersed on the lawn, whinnied at the depth of the stables.

Just at the moment when every mouth opened to ask for an explanation of the enigmatic words of Yaumi, a key was inserted in the lock, then the heavy wooden bar slid outside the notch made into the wall. The right side of the door with the five wolf heads on it rolled slowly on its hinges. A woman about fifty years-old, wearing a round tight bonnet made of black wool, from which there escaped thick strands of her hair already becoming gray, appeared on the threshold and seemed to count the crowd of tenants with a look. There was no tenant who didn't remove his hat, even if it was very little. Tenant farmers and young girls also made the same reverence. And everyone pronounced with one voice this solemn greeting:

"Good Morning to you, Dame Michou Guitan!"

Dame Michou Guitan wore her distaff on one side like a valiant soldier who never took off his sword. She had a camisole worn right up to her chin and to which she had attached an apron of blue material. A skirt with red and black stripes revealed her knitted undergarments, lost in the immense rose wooden shoes lined with sheep skin. She was a beautiful country woman in every sense of the word. Her demeanor was serious and gentle. She had a little beard on her chin and the beginning of a moustache. When she smiled, which often happened despite her importance, on both sides of her mouth, two round gaps appeared which seemed made in her teeth with a gimlet. To know the true origin of these gaps, it was enough to look at the belt of Dame Michou Guitan's apron, where a short and venerably blackened pipe had been hung. Against the ball of that pipe the copper seeds of a long piece of willow branch suspended from her shoulder, and produced very audible music when she walked.

"Good day to you!" she said, bowing her head gravely. "A good Saint-Jean's day to you and for your harvests! Is my boy Josselin with you?"

"We haven't seen him, Dame Guitan," Jouachin answered.

"As to that," said Yaumi with an innocent expression, "it would mean that your boy may have spent the night out, since the door opened only a minute ago."

"I know very well," he said to one side, throwing a rapid glance toward the western rampart, "I know very well that there is a little door that opens onto the willow trees at the end of the moat."

Cousin Yaumi saw nothing but the fog that extended like an opaque tablecloth over that part of the landscape. However, it lifted little by little, and the highest limbs of the willow trees which were swaying in the breeze could be seen. Those trunks came from a piece of land forming the extension of the former pits, turning to the west of the manor and going to disappear behind the ramparts, passing precisely under the famous balcony. The willow trees were separated from the lawn by a hedge of badly tended thorns. It extended for a distance of twenty or thirty feet, bordered by the public enclosure under which the vestiges of masonry could be seen. Then the ground dropped away in an abrupt descent to the bottom of the valley. A hardly visible path ran the length of the moat and followed the slope of the hill through the tufts of brambles.

Dame Michou Guitan, instead of standing aside to allow a passageway for the Rohan tenant farmers, remained on the threshold, unmoving and completely lost in thought. She put her hand over her eyes, and her gaze, passing over the heads of the crowd searched the edge of the forest. Just then, a noise was heard at the side of the moat; it was like a door slowly opened, creaking on its rusty hinges. The high branches of the willow trees were moving about. Everyone saw and heard that. Dame Michou Guitan trembled. No one budged however except the personable Yaumi, who ran behind the carts right up to the hedge of thorns.

"Come in, good people; come in," said the Dame quickly, with a trembling voice. "Rohan would reproach me if he knew that his farmers were waiting at the door of his house."

It was evident that she was trying to divert the curiosity already aroused. But she was too late. There could be seen, passing through the fog that had lifted, a human form enveloped in a long veil. The apparition drifted beyond the willow trees, and it seemed that the breeze carried it to the mountain slopes. At the same time, the gallop of a horse was muffled by the thick grass. It happened as quickly as a thought. Rohan's tenant farmers remained there, their mouths wide open, and the little girls were wondering if it wasn't a dream. But they saw Dame Michou Guitan, very pale, surreptitiously kiss the cross on her rosary. The good woman motioned to the farmers to come in; it seemed she had lost the power of speech. The farmers silently obeyed; each one thinking: *Cousin Yaumi will tell us what it's about!*

What was it? A postern opening from the other side of the rampart? The passage of a human being across the willow trees? The gallop of an invisible horse? But, finally and strangest of all, was Dame Michou Guitan's emotion; that was more than was needed to start conversations. Despite the fog, more impenetrable than even the night, housewives, and little girls, boys and tenant farmers, calculated that the apparition had to have passed ten feet from them, at the most.

When everyone had crossed the threshold of the main door, the closing noise following Dame Michou Guitan, Yaumi rubbed his hands together and began to laugh very softly.

"Yes, good! Very good!" he said, scratching his head under his wool cap. "Master Alain will give me something for that!"

He was very strong, the handsome wooden shoe-maker, and he would certainly have sworn by his great gods that there was no one there to see him or to hear him. So, he let out a frightened cry when he felt himself held back just as he was going to leave his observation post. He turned around quickly. A tall young man, with a pale and intelligent face crowned with long black hair, had stood up to face him from the other side of the hedge.

"Ah! Ah!" said Yaumi, who tried to smile. "Is that you, Master Josselin?"

The young man wore a jacket cut in the fashion of the Rennes forest country people, but made of good black cloth. His breeches were of velvet. He jumped across the hedge and put both his hands on Yaumi's shoulders.

"The good Dame Michou asked about you nearly an hour ago," continued Yaumi, who was trying to compose his facial expression.

Josselin looked straight at him.

"The good Dame Michou was asking about you a while ago," repeated Yaumi, who didn't know what else to say.

"Listen to me well," interrupted Josselin. "I need to talk to you!"

There was nothing at all in those words, but the tone of the young man contained such apparent menace that Yaumi, robust and accustomed to country fights, considered himself warned.

"I'm listening," he said, flexing his muscles and already bending his knees.

"I want to tell you," continued Josselin, "that you are wasting your time coming to spy on this side here. You saw nothing!"

"Thank God!" grumbled the handsome shoe-maker. "I am not blind however!"

"You saw nothing!" repeated the young man, who was frowning.

"I'll say what I saw, young Master," shouted Yaumi. "You don't yet have a fist strong enough to scare me. I saw and recognized the girl."

Josselin's eyes lit up; his cheeks remained pale; his left hand left Yaumi's shoulder to grab him violently by the throat. At the same time, his right hand reached inside his jacket, from which he drew a hunting knife, the blade shining and freshly sharpened.

Cousin Yaumi dropped to his knees.

"You saw nothing!" Josselin repeated for the third time.

28

"That's God's truth!" repeated the handsome shoe-maker, more dead than alive. "I saw nothing at all! Nothing at all!"

Josselin pushed him away with his foot and slowly walked down the road to the main door.

II. Young Monsieur César

It was a long room with vaulted arches supported by four pairs of red slate pillars from Pont-Réau. That room, longer than it was wide, was the vestibule of the armory. The main door led to the front steps of the interior courtyard and was across from the main staircase of the manor, the last step of which was secured in the room's floor. Above the stairway an old silver cloth drapery, mended in a thousand places, descended from the arches right down to the stone floor. A single ogival window with little panes, fixed in place with lead, protected by a grill, lit that room, which was, however, the most frequented of the manor house.

Dame Michou Guitan stayed there willingly under the enormous covering of the chimney; that was her domain and Master Alain Polduc, first cousin to Rohan though he was, had tried vainly to chase her away from it. There had been a compromise between the two rival authorities. Master Alain had taken possession of the intersection and some of its surroundings; Dame Michou had kept the foyer and the surrounding area. Master Alain had light, but he also had the cold wind which slid through the slits in the windows. Dame Michou, obliged to light a lamp at mid-day, could at least keep her feet warm.

The full daylight outside didn't go much beyond the black oak table where Master Alain Polduc laid out his ledgers. One could still however count the shaky ribs of the first pillars and even make out the family heraldry, if you had good eyes, the great Shield of Rohan: *parti de gueules à neuf macles accolées d'or,* for Rohan, and d*'hermine plein* for Brittany,[18] with that so well-known devise: *Potius mori quam foedari*.[19] The two other pairs of pillars were already obscured by the shadows, and despite the resin candle that burned on the foyer wall, the red folds of the silver drapery could be made out with difficulty.

Dame Michou and Master Alain were separated by all the length of the room. They could be compared to the two prime ministers of the Estates of Rohan-Polduc. Dame Michou was the housekeeper; Master Alain filled the functions of steward. He had arrived one evening from the region of Tréguier in South Brittany, with mire right up to his spine, hungry as a wolf, claiming himself to have some kind of distant relationship. Everyone remembered him very well as he was at that time; he had hollow cheeks, a timid and discreet glance, his mouth filled with honey, exhibiting servile behavior. He was then the humblest and the gentlest man in the universe. Now, his cheeks were puffed out; his gaze looked you in the face with effrontery; his voice was cutting. He held his short frame upright with importance; that family squire had hay in his boots. He was already turning toward financial obesity and used Spartan rigidity to rob his poor noble cousin. The bad thing is that, too often, these austere scoundrels succeed in stealing the confidence of good-hearted men. Master Alain spoke five or six times a day about his ardent devotion to the Protestant cause. Rohan wasn't far from considering him a saint. He consulted him in all important matters and blindly relied on him for minor details. But what Rohan called "minor details" was actually the entire oversight of his domain.

That morning, Dame Michou sat, as usual, in her circle near the foyer; Master Alain occupied the center of a group in

---

[18]   See: https:www.theroyalforums.com/forums/f76/the-princely-and-ducal-house-of-Rohan-1885.html;   and http://commons.wikimedia.org/wiki/Category.Coats of arms of Bretagne.

[19] Death rather than dishonor.

front of the casement window. Most of the tenant farmers that we have seen on the lawn, were arranged around him with a respectful attitude. Master Alain, sat in a carved oak chair, consulting the account books and entering the rents paid. But that couldn't be done immediately. Preparation work had to be done before that because of the great diversity of the monies used as payment. Josselin Guitan, the handsome young man with dark hair who, three times in a row, had repeated to our cousin Yaumi: "You saw nothing," was in charge of reconciling the values of the various monies presented: *sous* nantais, *croisettes* of Anjou, French *liards*, Norman and Rennais *piecettes,* and the Laval *gros cuivres.* That wasn't a sinecure, and Josselin Guitan, standing, a piece of chalk in his hand, in front of a board painted black, made a one *aune*[20] addition for the least tax of fifteen or twenty *écus.* What's more, he seemed to give his entire concentration to the task, and you would have searched in vain for traces of his recent violence in his calm and cold expression.

Each time the sum that the tenant farmers paid reached a thousand *livres*, Josselin drew a white cross at the top of his black board. When an argument arose between the farmers and the steward concerning the legality of the currency, their amount and their weight, Josselin crossed his arms over his chest and closed his eyes like a man whose thoughts were far from his present occupation.

In the hearth, two large logs covered with cinders were burning under the rack where was hung a cauldron full of porridge. Dame Michou was seated in the place of honor, to the left side of the fireplace. Her spinning wheel, which periodically made a groaning sound, was supported by two uprights; on one of them a small bottle of oil was balanced. While spinning, Dame Michou found a way to do three other things simultaneously: gently rock a cradle, which was within reach of her hand when her spinning wheel was well underway; smoke a pipe, which was full of tobacco which had never paid the

---

[20] Ancient unit of measure; about four feet.

king's tax; and energetically converse, like the worthy Breton woman that she was. Her listeners were the chateau servants and the tenant farmers who had settled their accounts with Master Alain. Cousin Yaumi and Jouachin, the old tenant farmer, were among those. In the official group presided over by the steward, they spoke in audible voices; here, under the cover of the chimney, they conversed secretly as if it were already sunset.

"So," Dame Michou said, using Jouachin as a witness, "isn't Rohan a great enough Lord for there to be legends about his House?"

"Since the time of Saint Guéhéneue," Jouachin answered with more desire to please than real conviction. "It's a question of that light that passes behind the casement window of the western tower... When I was very young, they already spoke about the woman in white on the balcony and her dark lover."

"Perhaps," muttered Yaumi. "That balcony has been used since the time of Saint Guéhéneue. One knows what one knows!"

The ardently curious eyes of the little girls were fixed on the handsome shoe-maker, who added in a knowing way: "And one sees what one sees!"

"And what did you see?" the good woman asked, shrugging. If our young Monsieur César—may God bless him!— were still alive... But there you are. Those who killed him would very much like to make his sister disappear as well!"

Her spinning wheel, off balance by a sudden movement, began to turn so quickly that its thread broke.

"A bad omen!" murmured Yaumi in a joking tone.

Dame Michou Guitan looked at him askance and made the sign of the cross. The cradle had stopped. An infant's small cry was heard among the conversations. Yaumi gave an ironic wink toward the casement window, and, as he saw that Master Josselin wasn't watching him, he smiled insolently.

"And that," he said, "belongs to your boy Josselin, that beautiful little girl there?"

"And who else would she be?" answered Dame Michou Guitan in a surly tone.

"Do you need help rethreading your spinning wheel, Dame? It is said that your Josselin has taken a wife in the big city of Ernée?"

"Here or there, what does it matter?"

"No one has ever seen her, the wife of your Josselin... Me, I'd like to see her someday."

Dame Michou Guitan became red with anger. Her pipe trembled between her teeth.

"My opinion," murmured the handsome shoe-maker, winking, "is that it would be just as worthwhile to look for a four-leaf clover or a white blackbird!"

The good woman took her pipe out of her mouth and looked straight at Yaumi.

"My boy, Josselin, isn't too far away," she said. "Why don't you talk to him?"

At that moment, Master Alain Polduc's voice was heard responding to the complaints of some tenant farmer.

"My good people, if I were master here, I would take pity on you and your troubles, but I am only the representative of Count Rohan, our Lord."

"Hypocrite!" Dame Michou Guitan thought aloud. "Before his arrival at the chateau, no farmer had ever suffered from poverty!"

"That's the truth!" Jouachin added.

"The trouble came with him," repeated the housekeeper. "Trouble for the vassals, trouble for the master! He was a proud young man, that César de Rohan! And our Valentine, you remember how happily she walked through the forest? Her beautiful hair floated on her shoulders, and not one of you, little girls, could smile so joyfully as the daughter of our master! Now, César de Rohan lies in the cemetery at Noyal, and there is only a poor wooden cross to mark his tomb... Now, and for a long time, we look in vain for a smile on the lips of our Valentine..."

Dame Michou Guitan let her head fall, while Master Alain's voice was raised again at the extremity of the table.

"Vincent Julot," Master Alain was saying with gentle calmness, "if you have not paid by this evening, tomorrow, I shall have your cart and oxen sold at auction."

A murmur arose among the tenant farmers.

"My poor children," Master Alain Polduc gravely repeated, "I am not the master, and I am only doing the business of Rohan, my noble cousin."

"Tomorrow is Saint-Jean's day," said Vincent Julot," and I have kept back a *quartécu* to buy my Saint-Jean's candle."

"Rohan farmers," three or four voices added, "don't have anything with which to buy a candle for the Holy Virgin!"

"If there were only the Rohan farmers in the parish, this year, Saint-Jean's bundle wouldn't be lit."

Master Alain let out a great sigh and wrote in his ledger vis-à-vis the name of Vincent Julot this laconic note: *Farming equipment for sale.*

"Don't you understand?" suddenly burst out Dame Michou, who lifted her head and threw an angry glance about her. "If Rohan no longer sees, except through that man's eyes, it's a punishment from God, because Rohan caused the death of his own son."

The circle moved closer. Then there was a long silence. Jouachin touched the good woman's shoulder, murmuring: "My little chatterbox, don't say more about it that you don't want to say."

"May God keep me from accusing my Lord!" replied Dame Michou, whose emotion made her voice tremble, "but my heart is overflowing. In the past, I have seen Rohan spend entire hours near the crib of his two children... Ah! He loved both of them very much! And I have often heard him say: *I love them twice over, my son, César, and Valentine, my daughter; one time for myself, one time for the saint who was their mother.* Listen! His ancestors sat on the throne of Brittany, and the French took three-fourths of his inheritance. It can't be held against him if he detests the French, even to death. When his son was twenty years-old and his daughter eighteen, he told them:

" 'Now the time to fall in love has come to you. Remember that your fathers would turn over in their graves if Rohan were to become part of France.'

"And he also told them:

" 'The French are the enemies. There are traitors among the people of Brittany who work with the people of France. The French are the enemies; the Bretons who have sold out to the French are vile! My son and my daughter, I would weep over the one among you who would form a misalliance with the French; the one among you who would forget himself to the point that he would enter into a dishonored Brittany family, my son and my daughter, I would curse him or her.' "

"And death came quickly," Jouachin pronounced in a low voice, "for the child that his father has cursed!"

The little girls held their breath. Dame Michou's spinning wheel remained silent; the child in its crib was sleeping.

"Rohan had spoken too late," continued the housekeeper. "Our Monsieur César did not wait until the age of twenty to fall in love."

"Everyone knows that," interrupted the handsome shoemaker.

"He fell in love with Jeanne de Combourg, the daughter of the French King's lieutenant," added Dame Michou Guitan sadly.

"And our young lady?" Yaumi added, "Was it also too late for Valentine de Rohan?"

Dame Michou Guitan's hand searched for the handle of her spinning wheel. She may not have heard what he said, because her gaze, filled with memories, was now lost in the void. She continued, lowering her voice as if speaking to herself:

"Does anyone know where the two young people met? I knew a deacon at Cesson-sur-Vilaine who said that God had a book where the two names were already inscribed side by side... César and Jeanne were married secretly for more than a year; they had a son… I remember that as if it were yesterday; the wind was blowing outside and the rain beat against the windows. It was night. Someone knocked at the front door; it was that man who entered…"

Her finger, extended convulsively, pointed at Master Alain Polduc, whose partially bald head was bent over his accounts.

"He asked for hospitality" continued Dame Michou, "and Rohan took him in like a gentleman. When he had eaten at the table of our Lord and dried his clothing at the chimney fire, he said to Rohan:

" 'But, Cousin, I would speak to you alone…'

"Now understand this, my good people, Combourg is as proud as Rohan. Jeanne de Combourg, in going to Rohan, had gone against her paternal will as well… We hid her and her infant in the cradle in that part of the manor house where no one lived, and every night, our young Monsieur César went there to join her…"

Many knowing looks were exchanged around the hearth; each one thinking of the two shadows that had been seen so many times on the balcony of the west tower.

"Now we're no longer talking about the time of Saint Guéhéneue!" murmured Yaumi, who again put on his mocking smile.

The little girls and the tenant women were saying to one another: "Since César and the pretty Jeanne are no longer there, why is the apparition still seen in the west tower?"

They believed profoundly in phantoms at that time, and even today they still, do in the Brittany countryside. But I don't know why belief in ghosts is always associated with superstitions which have nothing to do with the supernatural.

"They loved each other, however," the housekeeper continued. "They were both beautiful and young. The Chaplain said Mass for them, and we all added an *Oremus*[21] to our

---

[21] "Let us pray" said before short prayers in the Roman Catholic Mass.

evening prayer, so that God would put an end to their troubles. The night that I'm telling you about, Rohan had all of us leave and he remained alone with that man over there. A half-hour went by. Then, in the room where all of us were waiting, worried, we saw Rohan enter, his cheeks pale and his pupils stained with red...

" 'Who gave that stranger entry into my chateau?' he asked in a stifled voice.

"He knew everything! That man over there stood behind him, his arms crossed on his chest, his eyes modestly lowered. It was he who had betrayed the secret of our young master. How had he discovered it? Only God knows! Sp they went in search of César de Rohan and his wife, a poor, beautiful, frail, pale creature who was weeping, with her little enfant in her arms. Valentine, the dear and noble heart, threw herself at her father's feet. Rohan had never refused her anything in her life. But that time, he pushed her away roughly.

" 'You that I did call my son and who has dishonored me,' he said to César, 'leave at once! I curse you!'

"Without that man over there, he would have found no one to open the door. It was *he* who lifted the bar... The storm outside was terrible. It had broken the branches off the mighty oak trees of the forest. The thunder shook the old walls of the chateau. César de Rohan and his wife left. And it was that man over there who shut the door behind them..."

"How many crosses are there?" demanded at that moment Master Alain, who pushed back his register.

Josselin turned back to the black board and counted: "Five, ten, fifteen, twenty, thirty... there are thirty-five crosses," he answered.

"Thirty-five thousand pounds at Saint-Jean's," thought Master Alain, who smiled. "Thirty-five thousand pounds at

Christmas. Rohan still has seven thousand pistoles[22] of revenue!"

There was silence near the casement window, as in the vicinity of the foyer. The sun, advancing in its course, struck the windows brightly. The far-away sound of the trumpet in the forest continued.

Dame Michou Guitan's fingers tightened on the handle of her spinning wheel, that emitted a sharp complaint.

"Oh! That man over there! That man over there..." she said while Master Alain was smiling benevolently at the thirty-five crosses traced on the black board. "I am very old," she continued, "but I don't remember another night like this in all my memories. All the thatched roofs between here and Vitré were blown away. The thunder and lightning set the manor at Tréla on fire. The big pond of Painour overflowed onto the road, and the Vilaine flowed out of its banks, covering five leagues of the road. The lost travelers were too many to be counted. The parish of Noyal buried two poor young people that were found, still clutched in each other's arms, at the bottom of a ravine. The Vicar came to ask Rohan:

" 'Do you want to put a marble headstone on the tomb of your only son?'

"But Rohan refused.

"The priest added:

" 'There is a small infant that Heaven miraculously spared.'

"Rohan had his horse saddled. He went to fetch the child and remained away for two days. Some say he took the child to Rennes; others that he hid it near Quimper. No one is sure of anything—it is Rohan's secret, and Rohan repeats constantly: '*I have no heir.*' "

"Everybody gather here!" suddenly ordered Master Alain, who had just closed his register.

---

[22] French name given to a Spanish gold coin in use from 1537, and also given to the *Louis d'Or* issued by King Louis XIII. One *pistole* was worth approximately ten *livres* or three *écus*.

Little by little, the ranks cleared around the casement window, as Dame Michou Guitan's listeners had become more numerous. They hurried to obey Master Alain, and everyone, retaining the sad impression of the housekeeper's story, marched back toward the Steward's. They looked at *that man over there,* as Dame Michou had called him, and on his detestable face, the tenant farmers of Rohan discovered some kind of dreadful menace.

"The accounts are correct for this year, my dear friends," said Master Alain, who spread his best smile over his lips. "Now, we're going to discuss the arrears."

There was one united shout throughout the room. The arrears had been caused by the great disaster that Dame Michou Guitan had just described: the breaking of the Paintourteau dikes and the Vilaine flooding. The harvests had been ravaged and that unexpected mention of the arrears meant nothing less than ruin for most of the farmers. The tumult mounted, with Master Alain, leaning back in his chair, still smiling, seeming to provoke the crowd. He didn't say a word, letting the clamor increase, peacefully turning his thumbs like a churchwarden in church. There was a concert of complaints; the women were crying; the men soon turned to anger.

"In past times," said old Jouachin, "Rohan helped his vassals instead of wiping them out!"

"If our young Monsieur were alive," a woman tenant said, "he would intercede for us."

"And Valentine de Rohan," asked another. "Does she know how her father's tenants are treated?"

A voice was suddenly raised in the shadows at the opposite end of the room:

"Does Rohan himself know?"

"Dame Michou Guitan is right!" they shouted from all directions. "Rohan doesn't know! Rohan is a good master... Rohan, Rohan! We want to see Rohan!"

Master Alain Polduc made a disdainful gesture to gain silence.

"You will not see Rohan. My noble cousin doesn't have time to take care of you folks."

Dame Michou had left her place under the overhand of the chimney. She walked right up to the steward, leaning on her spinning wheel, which she was using as a cane, and placed herself standing in front of him.

"Have you some reason to lie, Master Alain?" she pronounced, loud enough for everyone to hear her. "Rohan would come if the voice of his vassals reached him."

"Woman," answered the Steward, who frowned, "mind your own business!"

"Everything that regards Rohan concerns me, Master Alain," Dame Michou continued. And turning toward the tenants, she added: "The walls are thick here and Rohan is old. Call him by his name, all of you together!"

The vaulted ceiling shook with the shout of the tenant farmers, who called out three times:

"Rohan! Rohan! Rohan!"

Dame Michou Guitan moved aside the crowd with her spinning wheel and walked the entire length of the room to reach the silver drapery whose folds fell in front the main staircase. She slid back the drapery on its rod, and everyone could see, at the very top of the steps, an old man with a long white beard who came slowly down the steps.

There was immediately a profound silence so that they could hear the horses' hooves beating the pavement, the savage growl of the big dogs in the courtyard, and the noble language of the huntsmen.

Tenant farmers, women and men, made haste, while the young girls, blushing with emotion, lined up at the bottom of the staircase with their big hawthorn bouquets.

That old man with the white beard was indeed Rohan, who had come to see what his vassals wanted.

III. Saint-Jean's Candle

It is said, as a kind of proverb, in Brittany:

> *Strong as Cheffontaines,*
> *Proud as Rieux,*
> *Handsome as Rohan.*

Guy III, Comte of Rohan-Polduc, was then more than sixty years-old. He had had many troubles in his long life, but he carried his old age marvelously well, and, without the white beard that fell down to his chest, he would have been taken for a man still in the prime of life. He was tall and his face had that perfect regularity which was like the privilege of his race. The hunting costume that he wore that morning emphasized the vigor of his members. Neither at Rennes, nor at Nantes, no killer of wolves wore better than he the fitted jacket, the leather breeches, and the strong boots armed with steel spurs. Still, to admire him at his best, one would have had to see him on horseback. At Nantes, at Rennes, even at the Court in Paris, that eighth wonder of the world, you would have searched in vain for a better looking horseman.

He came down the steps slowly, with a thoughtful expression. In the place of a sword, he wore a cutlass on his belt, and held a whip in his hand. His face, between the curls of his long white hair and the white tufts of his beard, seemed pale. He had not yet raised his eyes. Nothing was heard in the room except the sound of held breaths. On the next-to-last step, Rohan stopped, and his gaze glanced over the respectfully bowing crowd.

"Good day, good people," he said. "I heard that you were calling me, so here I am. What do you want of me?"

The crowd moved about instead of answering. No one dared do anything more.

"Well," said Rohan with a sad smile, "do I frighten you?"

"They know very well that they are wrong," Master Alain Polduc said from a distance.

He was standing, his head uncovered, in front of his table. Yaumi, the handsome Cobbler, had succeeded in slipping behind him and had already spoken to him for an instant.

"Mercy! Mercy!" said some timid voices.

The little girls shook their bouquets, whose bittersweet odor filled the room. The women among the tenants held out their supplicating hands and repeated: "Have mercy! Have mercy!" while the men remained motionless, their head lowered even further.

"How pale our Lord is," murmured old Jouachin in the ear of Dame Michou. "I have never seen that dark shadow in his gaze."

"That *man over there* was near his bed when he awoke," answered the good woman, half turning her head toward Master Alain Polduc.

She came out of the crowd and placed her foot on the first step, holding herself upright with her head, facing the old Lord.

"Mercy," she repeated with disdain. "Why mercy? Ask for justice! Then Rohan will hear you. There is only I who knows how to speak to our Master... Rohan! Do you want your vassals to go from door to door to beg for charity? Do you want that?'

The Count trembled and frowned.

"That woman is mad!" shouted Master Alain.

"Do you want it to be said everywhere that," Dame Michou Guitan continued," that Rohan took the last morsel of bread from his servants?"

"No," replied the Count, "I don't want that, my good woman. But what are they complaining about?"

"*Parbleu!*" grumbled Master Alain, shrugging his shoulders. "If you listen to them, they always complain!"

"They are complaining about you. Rohan, my dear Lord," continued the housekeeper, who took the Count's hand to kiss it. "They are poor; their houses are falling in ruins.

42

Their cold hearths no longer have heat. They are so poor that they no longer have enough to buy a blessed candle for Saint-Jean's day."

"They have begun to hunt at the bottom of the Sangle," Cousin Yaumi said at that moment, speaking in a very low voice in Master Alain Polduc's ear. "The Count of Toulouse is having lunch with Feydeau, the Royal Steward. There are tents already set up at Mi-Forêt, the halfway point in the forest, which has been set up as a dining area."

Rohan passed the back of his hand over his forehead. All eyes were lifted anxiously toward him, and each could see that he had, in fact, a strange light in his eyes. A fever probably, because Rohan was not one of those who needed that one last drink when in the saddle preparing to depart.

"Are you there, Josselin Guitan?" he asked suddenly.

"I am here, My Lord," the young man replied.

Rohan stretched out his whip toward the table and pointed to the sacks of money piled up there. "Divide that into two parts," he ordered, "two equal parts."

Master Alain Polduc had not heard this, since he was listening gladly to the words of Cousin Yaumi, who was saying:

"I saw Morvan of Saint-Maugan just as I'm seeing you. It was between midnight and 1:00 a.m. The door which opens there onto the moat was open and Morvan's horse stayed in the forest..."

"Saint-Maugan is the assistant of the Count of Toulouse," murmured Master Alain. "Did he come for himself or for his master?"

"Last night, I met Josselin Guitan, who was riding in a fast gallop on the road to Rennes. The Count of Toulouse was at Rennes yesterday, and Josselin is the confident of the demoiselle."

"Are you sure that she went out this morning by way of the west back gate?"

"Sure? Just as sure that the same Josselin put a knife to my neck and ordered me to stay silent... But I brave everything in order to serve you, my good master."

"Always stay alert and count on me."

And turning around, Master Alain saw Josselin who was separating the farmers' money into two portions. He looked around; hope was shining in every face.

"My noble cousin," he said, approaching Rohan. "God knows where we will find, during the coming season, what we need to pay our debts."

"I know that I am at present a somewhat diminished gentleman," answered the old Count, who seemed deeply preoccupied. "The next season is only a day away. We shall see what we shall see."

"Our income is so small…"

"Then we will sell a mill, or a farm, or a field… As I have no heir."

A smile appeared on the big lips of Master Alain Polduc, who was thinking to himself: *I have one ready-made for you, my noble cousin.*

Rohan continued:

"Valentine, my daughter, will marry a country gentleman who will ask nothing more of her than her good reputation and her beauty."

"And the name of Rohan-Polduc will pass away without splendor…" began Master Alain, who was searching for a sensitive spot to drive his dart into that numb heart.

Rohan seized his arm and lowered his eyes, as if he wanted to hide the light that he felt flooding out of his eyes.

"Do you like to hear thunder?" he suddenly asked. Then he added, trying to smile: "The skies of Brittany certainly deserve an explosion at our last hour, cousin. I had a dream where I saw King Louis grow pale on his throne upon hearing of Rohan's last breath."

"For a long time," Dame Michou was saying to Jouachin, "a long time, in truth, our Lord has not been the same… His eyes are fixed, his pupils are burning. There is some terrible thought in Rohan's mind!"

"May Good keep him, above all, from attacking the people of France," murmured the old tenant farmer.

Working on the share of the tenant farmers' money took the whole attention of Josselin Guitan, who had finished separating the money into two equal parts. Master Alain understood that any further objection was impossible, but he was thinking: *The acts of a madman mean nothing and are of no effect before the law.*

"All right!" he continued, changing tone and tack. "I was going to forget one thing which is important today...Didn't I understand that my noble cousin's property extended up to the cross at Mi-Forêt?"

"Yes. The property line goes around the cross, following the report of my huntsman," the old man replied.

"Well, it would seem that there are establishments there," said Master Alain, "that don't belong to us. You might meet at Mi-Forêt some people you don't frighten at all: our neighbor, Feydeau, the Royal Steward, your nephew-in-law, Morvan de Saint-Maugan, and Monsieur the Governor himself."

"The Count of Toulouse—on my domain!" shouted Rohan, whose pale face became flushed with red.

"As of yesterday, 22 June 1705," Master Alain repeated softly, "the trees of Mi-Forêt, my noble cousin, are no longer part of your domain."

"Sold!" murmured Rohan, whose lips trembled. "It's true! Every day, the circle around my shaking house grows smaller. I will soon see their packs from the windows of my manor. Why should Rohan live when Brittany is dead. God does well what he does. Rohan has no heir."

"There are two piles, each comprised of seventeen thousand five hundred." interrupted Josselin Guitan, who had finished his chore.

Master Alain turned his head away in order not to see. The old Count raised his head so as to see.

"There is half for me," he said, "half for my tenant farmers to make up for their disaster. I want you to share this, good people, and the remainder of your debt should not be mentioned anymore!"

"Bless you, Rohan, our Lord!" was heard from all directions. "May God and the Holy Virgin protect the House of Rohan!"

"Ah! Ah!" said Dame Michou Guitan, who had tears in her eyes. "You are good, like your father, My Lord! May your daughter be fortunate, now that you no longer have a son!"

The old Count seemed for a moment reanimated by those cordial acclamations.

"Now you have something with which to buy those wax candles, my children," he said. "Well! Won't we have a beautiful Saint-Jean's day this year? So, where is Valentine? Hasn't she prepared the Rohan candle, the candle that is as big as a tree?"

"The candle is here," answered Dame Michou Guitan who approached a tall armoire that was situated between the stairway and the chimney.

"As for our demoiselle Valentine," added Master Alain, "she went out at daybreak on horseback."

"On horseback!" repeated Rohan. "At daybreak!"

"Here is the candle," interrupted Dame Michou, who had opened the double doors of the armoire.

The Rohan candle was sixteen feet high, and the old Count hadn't exaggerated in saying that it was as big as a tree. That mass of perfumed wax, was covered with notches, with ribbons and with flowers. But the old Count hardly gave it a distracted look.

"Why would Valentine go out at daybreak on horseback?" he murmured, speaking to himself. "Thank God! I don't suspect my daughter, who is my last love on this Earth... Go back home, good people," he added, taking Master Alain's arm. "Celebrate, if you have a heart for joy, and tell someone in passing to put away our hunting equipment."

The crowd of tenants went away slowly, but not without again lavishing on their generous Lord a treasury of words of thanks and of benedictions. But Rohan was no longer listening to them, and was saying to Master Alain while he was climbing the steps of the great staircase:

"In the forest, at the cross of Mi-Forêt, there is an image of Sainte-Anne, who is the patron saint of the people of Brittany. The grass there is vast and unbroken..."

"Smooth like a piece of velvet," interrupted Master Alain, "so smooth that the Count of Toulouse plans to have a ball there after his lunch."

The old Count stopped at the threshold of the main drawing room.

"What would they say, cousin," he asked in a muffled voice, "if Rohan invited himself to their party?"

Master Alain Polduc tried to answer, but the Count closed his mouth with an imperial gesture.

"And if Rohan appeared in the middle of them," he continued, "with the sword of Pierre de Bretagne, his grandfather?"

He pushed open the door to the main drawing room. Behind him, the face of Master Alain suddenly lit up.

Am I reaching my goal already? he thought, barely containing his joy. *And am I going to start my new life, my noble, rich, and happy life, from this beautiful day of Saint-Jean?*

In the lower room, Josselin and his mother remained alone near the crib where the infant was sleeping. The sounds from the kennels and from the stables had stopped; the last cart had left. Josselin leaned over the crib and placed a kiss on the forehead of the child. When he straightened up, he held out his hand to the good woman, who grasped it in her own in silence. For a moment, they remained looking at each other.

"I remember the expression that you had last year at this time, Josselin, my son," murmured Dame Michou Guitan. "You have become very thin and very pale since then. Young people need sleep. What did you do last night?"

"I searched," Josselin replied, "but I didn't find. May our young lady be more fortunate than I was!"

"Then where did she go this morning?" the good woman asked with curiosity.

"That's my secret, Mother. There is a good angel and a wicked angel in Rohan's house. There is a fight between the two... Me, I do what I can..."

He went toward the armoire holding the candle, and lowering his voice, he repeated:

"I do what I can, but I don't have much hope."

"What are you thinking about, my Josselin, my poor Josselin?" asked the housekeeper, who saw him standing in front of the armoire, whose two doors he kept open.

"I think," the young man replied, "that Rohan is still Rohan. It would take four men to carry that candle to the church."

"At the last Saint-Jean's day," sighed Dame Michou, "our young Monsieur César carried it easily all by himself!"

Josselin violently pushed away the two doors of the armoire, and closed it.

"Our young master César was stronger than four men!" he said.

The old Dame secretly wiped away a tear. Josselin went to sit down at the corner of the hearth. He mechanically stirred the blackened dying embers with the end of his hob-nailed shoe. The cinders fell away; there was a current of air that revived the flame that brightly caressed the cauldron that hung on the rack.

"You see there, my son," said the good woman, who watched all that, smiling through her tears, "so long as there is a spark, the fire can be revived."

Josselin shook his head.

"There is only one daughter in that cradle!" he murmured despondently.

"Then, are you giving up trying to find the son of our young master?" demanded Dame Michou Guitan.

Instead of answering. Josselin asked:

"Mother, do you know what people are saying in the village?"

Dame Michou quickly brought forward her little stool.

"In the village," Josselin continued, "they say the King has made an edict against the people of our religion, the *Edict of Nantes*,[23] they call it. The King is confiscating the property of Protestants and exiling them from France."

Dame Michou Guitan crossed her hands over her breast.

"They say," Josselin continued, "that Rohan has been denounced as a Protestant by a servant in his own house."

"Master Alain Polduc!" interrupted the housekeeper, pale with shame and anger.

"They say, finally, that, without the Count of Toulouse's intervention, the King's soldiers would already be at Rohan's chateau."

"Without the Count's intervention," repeated the housekeeper, who opened her eyes wide. "Rohan is protected by the Count of Toulouse? Then Morvan de Saint-Maugan must have interceded for us…"

"The infant is waking up and smiling at the name of its father," said Josselin, who took an adorable little pink and white girl and brought her up to his lips.

The little girl was awake and her sweet little hands were clinging to the dark curls of Josselin's hair.

---

[23] There is some confusion here. The Edict of Nantes, signed in April 1598 by King Henry IV, granted the Protestants (also known as Huguenots) substantial rights in the nation, which was still considered essentially Catholic at the time. It marked the end of the religious wars that had afflicted the country during the second half of the 16th century. The Edict of St. Germain, promulgated 36 years before by Catherine de Médici, had granted limited tolerance to Huguenots, but was not formally registered until after the Massacre of Vassy in March 1562, had triggered the first of the French Wars of Religion. Féval must be referring here to the later Edict of Fontainebleau, which revoked the Edict of Nantes in October 1685 (still, twenty years before this story), promulgated by Louis XIV, which drove an exodus of Protestants and increased the hostility of Protestant nations bordering France.

"I put her mother in a crib, eighteen years ago," murmured Dame Michou, "but her mother's crib was covered with lace and flowers… Do you know," she continued, while a cloud of uneasiness passed over her forehead, "that they have asked again today where you got that child.?

"Let them talk, Mother."

Josselin's face became serious. He held the enfant against his heart. In spite of himself, his eyes were raised toward Heaven. "Our Valentine is a saint," he pronounced very softly. "A priest blessed the marriage; I would lie to Rohan for the first time in my life. "

"Well!" exclaimed Dame Michou, who held out her arms to him. "I am proud when I listen to you, Josselin, my son, and I thank God for being your mother."

There was silence during which time the gallop of a far-away horse beating the forest moss was heard. Josselin released himself from his mother's arms and listened.

"It is she," he murmured. "Mother," he continued aloud, "Master Alain Polduc, has he asked like the others?"

Dame Michou seemed to try to remember, then she answered:

"Never."

That's because he has already guessed, thought Josselin. *If he has, that's his bad luck!*

"There she is!" exclaimed Dame Michou, who had gone to the window.

A horse in full gallop, jumped the covert and came like a tornado across the grass area. A remarkably beautiful young girl, whose hair in disorder floated in the breeze, jumped to the grass and fell into the arms of Josselin Guitan, who had run out to meet her. Sweat glistened on her temples. She was pale with fatigue and fright.

"Open the door at the edge of the water, Josselin," she said rapidly with an altered voice. "Monsieur de Saint-Maugan is following me."

"In full daylight, our young lady!" exclaimed the young man. "The Count of Toulouse's gentleman in Rohan's house!"

50

"May it please God that is the Count of Toulouse him-self!" murmured the young woman, whose eyes showed a ver-itable distraction. "Hurry and open the door, Josselin Guitan, if you love the daughter of your master!"

IV. A Lost Wager

Deterioration occurs quickly in abandoned living quar-ters. The western wing of the manor house, long since unin-habited, no longer had anything but sad and naked hallways with holes in the ceiling, cracked paneling, on which there fell tapestries in rags, floors mildewed by hail, and rain that the wind blew through the frames without window panes. Rohan servants took care never to enter that part of the chateau be-cause, since the unfortunate end of the *young gentleman,* strange stories were told in evening gathering. Inexplicable noises had been heard at night in the long dusty corridors, without even mentioning that mysterious light that passers-by delayed in the valley sometimes saw shining from the win-dows of the west tower. The frightened servants claimed, mak-ing the sign of the cross over their breast, that they had heard voices from the other world and had seen phantoms.

The bedroom where César de Rohan and the beautiful Jeanne de Combourg had, for a short time, hidden their happi-ness opened onto that granite balcony which projected above the rampart. Nothing had changed since that lugubrious night where the implacable anger of Rohan had surprised the young married couple. The alcove without any curtains revealed the flat, poor little couch behind the willow cradle that had served this poor orphan child, the last male heir of Rohan-Polduc, as father and mother. Jeanne's *Book of Hours*[24] was on a small pedestaled table near a piece of embroidery just begun, and in a corner the hunting carbine of young Monsieur César was still leaning against the wall.

---

[24] Illuminated prayer book used for personal devotion, con-taining scenes from the life of Christ and the Virgin Mary.

The green moat widened under the balcony where the breeze lit up, in passing, the undulating summit of the swaying willow trees. The edge of the moat formed a knoll covered with sainfoin[25] and daisies, where the opposite slope again descended down to the valley among the hawthorns and brambles in bloom. The scattered thickets, where the young shoots of oaks were turning red between the white of the aspens and the dark green of the chestnut trees, began fifty steps from there. To the right were several huts of Cobblers; to the left a great bald rock rose out of the ferns.

Just across from the balcony, the ramp quickly widened, as if a torrent was hidden there, and through that opening could be seen in the distance the little valley of the Vesvre with the velvet of its prairies, its fallow land where the young barley would soon be in flower, and its fields of sarrasin.[26] These were the humble and popular crops of the poor, which provisioned their tables, while giving the sterile soil the pleasant aspect of a flower bed. The winding course of the Vesvre was marked by a line of alder trees, over which grew tall poplar trees. The sun spread its white light generously over all the land. The fog had disappeared. To the sound of the hunting horn, which came from the forest at intervals, now mingled the thousand sounds of the awakened countryside, the bellowing of the oxen, the noise of the farmyard animals, and the melancholy voice of the Rohan mill, lost behind the willow trees , at the foot of the hill.

From the window there could still be seen, half hidden by the profile of the rampart, a small gothic chapel where the poor old chaplain of Rohan, who had recently died, had, trembling, illuminated the candles in an autumn night to secretly marry the son and the daughter of his master: César de Rohan to Jeanne de Combourg-Coëtquen, daughter of the Marquis de Combourg, the King's lieutenant for the province of Brittany,

---

[25] Plant widely grown as a forage crop, with pale pink flowers and curved pods.

[26] Herbaceous plant.

and marry Valentine de Rohan to the Chevalier Morvan de Saint-Maugan, Captain of the La Ferté regiment and *gentilhomme ordinaire*[27] of His Serene Highness the Count of Toulouse.

Valentine was, at that time, sixteen years-old. She was alone during her youth, because she had lost her mother very early, and Count Guy de Rohan, constantly lost in his dreams, had isolated himself not only from society, but also from his own family. At festive gatherings, they spoke of Valentine de Rohan as marvelous. Rennes was a city of pleasures, and the young nobility were given to frivolity, as opposed to the then-austere morals of the court of Louis XIV.[28] But the Rennes nobility scarcely knew anything, except by hearsay, about Valentine de Rohan, who never had crossed the threshold of a ballroom. They spoke about her based on the word of some huntsmen who bragged about having encountered her, by chance, in the forest, and called her a young goddess, more beautiful and more inclined to shyness than Diana herself.

There was, in the Count of Toulouse's court, a twenty year-old captain, Breton by birth, French by political indifference or ambition. Women had spoiled him, because he was handsome, brave and fancy free. Perhaps he was only fancy free because he had been spoiled by women. His name was Morvan de Saint-Maugan and he never remembered having encountered any resistance from any woman.

Among young people, among the military particularly, stupid wagers were sometimes set up. After a luncheon where the officers of the La Ferté Regiment had tasted that evaporative nectar, champagne, Saint-Maugan said boldly that he was going to make the beautiful Valentine leave the forest, and that, thanks to him, Rennes would finally be able to admire in

---

[27] A nobleman privileged to be part of a Lord's retinue in his private quarters.
[28] Due to the influence of Madame de Maintenon who had become King Louis XIV's wife c. 1684 and whose influence was at its zenith in 1700.

full daylight that mysterious fay. The bet was taken and Saint-Maugan was left alone to this different kind of hunt.

The next day, the officers of La Ferté were already regretting their wager. Saint-Maugan, the lady-killer, launched against a poor little sixteen year-old girl! The handsome Saint-Maugan, who had, at the tip of his fingers, all the ruses of amorous strategy, who spouted promises like Don Juan, and who couldn't even be stopped by pity, because he didn't believe at all in women! The battle was lost in advance, it seemed. But, on the contrary, it was won by the opposition. Saint-Maugan was absent two days; after that, he paid the stakes of the wager, to the great astonishment of his comrades. He was asked a number of questions. It apparently was convenient for him not to answer. Despite the fact that duels were forbidden, he gave a sword thrust to the Cadet La Guerche, who had, in his opinion, pushed curiosity a little too far. Saint-Maugan had never been known to dream; he lived in the real world between bottles and bursts of laughter. He was ambitious, that was known, a skeptic in all things; that was rightly believed. His goal was pleasure or fortune, and he was considered to be not at all scrupulous about the choices of the road to take.

What had happened to him during those two days of absence? At his return, Saint-Maugan changed behavior, we would almost say nature; he began to search for silence and solitude. If that transformation hadn't coincided with his excursion into the forest, it could have been thought to be a self-interested calculation, flattery to impress the Count of Toulouse, his master. That prince had, in fact, serious virtues and a private life that defied belief. His enemies could find no other way to slander him than to whisper the word *hypocrisy*. As often happens to people with austere morals, the Count of Toulouse had taken a liking to Saint-Maugan, the brash and dissolute young man. His sudden conversion had astonished and charmed him. Saint-Maugan became decidedly the Count's favorite. But what had happened? The officers of the La Ferté Regiment said, jokingly, that Our Lady of the Mi-Forêt had brought about a miracle.

There is a section of moss wall, a rustic ruin, the debris of some poor chapel where the gentle image of the Virgin Mary smiles at the infant Jesus cradled in her arms. Around the niche hung some wreaths of honeysuckle and some garlands of bright, coral red holly. Above, the hundred year-old chestnut trees made an impenetrable arch.

What the officers of the La Ferté Regiment had said as a joke was, in fact, correct. The Lady of the Mi-Forêt had indeed brought about a miracle.

Saint-Maugan had seen, through the pieces of stone that were lost in the underbrush, a kneeling young girl. His heart, before his lips, had pronounced the name of Valentine. The young girl was praying; Saint-Maugan hid behind the branches and contemplated her, very moved. When the young girl, her prayer finished, jumped, light as a sylphide, into the saddle of the little black horse waiting for her, Saint-Maugan, quivering, had crossed his hands over his chest, but he hadn't dared show himself. He was timid for the first time in his life. He went to kneel down in the same spot where the moss had kept the imprint of the young girl's knees. I don't know if he prayed, but nothing else happened during his two-day absence. Several months went by. The Captain did not see Valentine again, for she was at the bedside of her sick father.

Saint-Maugan was a distant "nephew" of Rohan after the fashion of Brittany, but the post he occupied in the Count of Toulouse's service closed the doors of the Rohan manor house to him. Every night, his dreams showed him the young girl kneeling, with her white dress floating and her brown hair curling on her angelic forehead.

When he was seen sad and fleeing society, many wanted him to marry; that was the accepted remedy. He let it happen because he did not himself want to believe in an impossible and vaporous love. The hand of Jeanne de Combourg-Coëtquen was therefore asked for him by the Count of Toulouse in person. The Marquis de Combourg was too good a politician for His Serene Highness to expect a refusal from

55

him. Jeanne was not consulted, and the public considered the engagement as a fact.

The first time that Captain Morvan de Saint-Maugan went to pay his respects to his intended bride, it was toward the evening. Coëquen house was located on the banks of the Vilaine, opposite the Saint-Yves gardens. Saint-Maugan saw, in the fading twilight, a little boat attached to a weeping willow tree which grew in front of the chateau's laundry. He entered. He was told that Mademoiselle de Combourg was indisposed and he spent the evening with his future father-in-law, who was still, despite his age, a very pleasant companion.

When he left, the bourgeois of Rennes had already shut their lodges. There was a deep silence on the banks of the river. Saint-Maugan had been late in learning to think, and because of that, he was a better thinker. He leaned against a tree and gave himself, in spite of himself, entirely to his dreams. The little boat was still there under the weeping willow. A window in the Coëtquen household opened, and Saint-Maugan saw a shadow balanced against the wall. The shadow came down. The little boat, untied, followed the course of the current, and Saint-Maugan, who rubbed his eyes as hard as he could, believed he recognized his beautiful fiancée. Her indisposition obviously had not kept her for going out for some air, and it wasn't a doctor who was leaving her at that amorous hour!

Saint-Maugan began to run along the river bank. He gave his name and asked the mysterious navigator to do the same.

"I am happy to find you today, Monsieur de Saint-Maugan," replied the mysterious navigator in a gentlemanly manner, "because I would have sought you out tomorrow; I live far from here. In order for us to meet at a better hour, promise me that you will travel halfway. I am giving you a rendezvous at sunrise at the Mi-Forêt."

A cry from the direction of the Coëtquen house was lost in the night and the window was closed again. The little boat landed in front of the old bridge, and as soon as Saint-Maugan had answered, "I will be there!", the pavement of the Vau-Saint-Germain road resounded with the gallop of a horse.

The next day, at the hour stated, César de Rohan and the Captain, met, swords in hands, in the clearing. But their rapiers hardly had time to take an initial swipe at the wind. Two female cries rang out, one from the road to Rennes, the other from the chapel in ruins, the same chapel where Saint-Maugan had seen his beautiful angel kneeling. Jeanne de Combourg and Valentine de Rohan dashed out at the same time. Jeanne, who, the evening before, had heard the challenge. Valentine, who had come to put flowers on the statue of Our Lady. How could the two men continue to fight, and most of all, why would they? The two "cousins" embraced; the two young girls told each other: "We will be like sisters."

A double and gracious love! A charming poem that began in joy, in the sunny rays of springtime, in the hymn of the morning, all the new leaves moved about by the breeze, on the grass where the dew sparkled; a happy poem where the prologue was a song of light heartedness and hope!

But the Breton song says that, on this earth, each smile is paid for with two tears, and that for a dear springtime mornings, winter gives us two stormy nights. Alas! There no longer remains but one of the two couples, secretly united by the old Chaplain. Nevertheless, according to the Breton song, to pay for past happiness, many tears are still needed!

Valentine was going to be nineteen years-old; she was going to be a mother. Her face that, in the past, knew so well how to smile, kept the precocious imprint of sleepless nights and worry. But she had that sculptured beauty with a proud look, with bronze lines that withstood suffering, that often survives youth itself. Valentine de Rohan was beautiful in every way, in both body and soul. Character stood out on every contour of her forehead. Her black eyes showed thought under the bold curve of her eyebrows, and in reverie, her lips took a child-like nobility which was utterly charming. Valentine was tall; her waist had kept that virginal appearance. It could be easily seen that this flower of beauty would develop still more. However, when the wind played with her brown hair that flittered in brilliant curls across the veined alabaster of her temples, when a rosier nuance mounted from her heart to her slightly pale cheeks, a painter, discouraged, might have thrown down his brush and a poet, powerless, would have put down his pen.

Josselin Guitan had carried out the orders of his mistress. The door at the edge of the water, located precisely under the west tower balcony, was opened. It isn't necessary to say that it was in the bedroom of the balcony that Mademoiselle de Rohan usually received her husband. Valentine was seated near the alcove, her head between her hands, when Josselin returned, carrying the crib in his arms.

"Should the signal be raised?" he asked.

Valentine was contemplating little Marie, whose blonde head had halfway disappeared under the swaddling clothes. A tear came to her eyes.

"How peaceful her sleep is!" she murmured. "Isn't there something in that sweet smile that would disarm God's anger!" She passed the back of her hand over her burning forehead. "The son of my brother, César, slept in that same place," she continued, while a shiver ran through her body, "a dear angel who also smiled so softly."

"I see shining out there, through the branches, the uniform of Monsieur de Saint-Maugan," Josselin answered. "Should the signal be raised?"

"In a moment. I have something to tell you... My ride this morning was useless. When I arrived, the Governor had already gone hunting, and Monsieur de Saint-Maugan was riding at his side."

"There is nothing to fear this morning," said Josselin, who lowered his voice. "Rohan is still at the manor."

"Ah!" exclaimed Valentine, astonished.

"He had his hunting equipment brought back."

"Why?"

"Because he knows that the Count of Toulouse is planning to go to the Cross of Mi-Forêt this evening."

"Who told him that?"

"Master Alain Polduc."

Valentine frowned. "There have been many nights," she continued, "that in his fever, Rohan spoke aloud of his dreams. He balanced in his hand the sword of Pierre of Brittany; I know what he wants to do. Has he noticed my absence?"

"Master Alain Polduc told him that you left on horseback at daybreak."

"And what did my father say?"

"Your father is Rohan. He answered: '*I do not suspect my daughter, who is my last love on this Earth.*' "

"Raise the signal!" Valentine ordered in a sharp tone.

Josselin attached a white scarf to the edge of the balcony. The breeze filled and unfolded the light cloth. The leaves on the other side of the moat moved about, and a handsome young man gallantly wearing the uniform of the La Ferté Regiment entered the willow trees cove.

"Listen to me carefully," Valentine said rapidly to Josselin. "You will go to the Prince and you will tell him..." There, she seemed to hesitate.

"I know what you fear, My Lady, "Josselin Guitan interrupted, with emotional respectfulness. "Have confidence in me."

"God will bless you, my dear Josselin. Don't forget to add that you have come on behalf of Mademoiselle de Rohan herself."

There was the sound of the rusty hinges on the door as it was opened at the edge of the water.

"Hurry," said Valentine. "It's a matter of life and death! Before you leave, have your mother stand in the corridor as a guard. Good-bye and thank you!"

She held out her hand to him; the young man took it, bowing.

Boots with spurs sounded on the staircase tiles. Valentine fell to her knees beside the cradle. She was as pale as death and her heart was beating convulsively.

"The infant! The poor infant!" she murmured in a tearful voice, "The son of my brother, César, no longer has a father. The last drop of Rohan blood is in your veins, child, poor child, why did I bring you into this world!"

Someone knocked softly at the outside door. Getting up, Valentine wiped away a tear. She went across the bedroom again with a firm step and presented her calm forehead to Saint-Maugan, who entered.

V. The West Tower

The face of Morvan de Saint-Maugan carried his twenty-two years well; once fatigued by pleasure, he was still a stalwart soldier. His reunion with Mademoiselle de Rohan had left behind the man who, previously, had not yet settled on his destiny. Among women, his reputation had always been that of the most incorrigible seducer. But the ladies were wrong. Saint-Maugan was seriously in love, we can affirm this. Behind his commanding smile, there was worry, and perhaps jealousy. Saint-Maugan was afraid of not being loved!

In the evening, after supper, to kill time, the officers of the La Ferté Regiment had been discussing the question of knowing who among them was the most favored by fate. The votes were unanimously given to Saint-Maugan, a captain since 19, overwhelmed by the favor of beautiful women and possessing the friendship of the Prince. During the scrutiny, Saint-Maugan had his head in his hands. Very pale, he lifted it and said:

"I would trade you my happiness for a paving stone that you could tie to my neck, and throw me to the bottom of the river!"

At these hours of fantasy, he sometimes complained, and at other times he was joyful to the point of madness.

Valentine and he were seated not far from the cradle. Valentine had managed to smile. Saint-Maugan looked at her with a mixture of admiration and sadness.

"I haven't seen you in a long time," he said, taking her hand and covering it with a long kiss.

"Three days," Valentine answered.

"A century! Monseigneur, for the last month or two, has taken, all at the same time, a taste for hunting, dancing and eating. It could be believed that he is in love."

"In love!" Valentine repeated, as if distracted. She added, lifting her eyes to Saint-Maugan: "No one saw you cross the moat?"

"No one. I didn't meet a living soul except that pleasant fellow... You know, the one they call the handsome Cobbler."

"Yaumi?" asked the young woman, who trembled slightly. "Did he recognize you?"

"I don't know. What does that matter? Don't you have anything else to say to me, Valentine, after an absence of three days?"

She took his hand and drew him toward the cradle, saying, instead of answering:

"You haven't yet kissed your child."

Saint-Maugan frowned despite himself and placed a cold kiss on the infant's forehead. Suffering, he opened his mouth two or three times as if he wanted to ask a question, but the rebellious word seemed to stop in his throat.

"Morvan," said the young woman, who was guessing, "you were not mistaken. It was me whom you met in the forest."

"Have you then some secret from your husband, Valentine?" asked Saint-Maugan tenderly.

"Some secrets are too heavy for a weak woman's soul," answered Mademoiselle de Rohan in a low voice. "Why does my father no longer have a son?"

"Valentine! Valentine!" exclaimed Saint-Maugan. "I'm the cause of all your suffering, and you repent that you are mine. Answer me, I beg you, and don't be afraid of breaking my heart. At sixteen—for that was how old you were when you made me the happiest of men—at sixteen, one is almost still a child. Perhaps you were motivated, influenced, by our poor brother. Did he plead my cause to you with too much warmth? Answer me, Valentine. Tell me. Would you ever have become my wife before God, when the Count, your father, had forbidden you to love one of those whom he calls dishonored Bretons. Would you have given me your hand?"

"I have three loves in this world," murmured the young woman, who was avoiding looking at her husband, "my daughter, my father, and you."

Morvan de Saint-Maugan stood up.

"I am only in third place!" he pronounced with great bitterness. "Ah! I demand nothing of you, Valentine. You are my last belief here below, and I respect you even more than I love you… But that's martyrdom, you see, to be in love alone and to see before you either a mother or a daughter, and not a lover."

He took a turn around the bedroom with rapid steps and suddenly stopped in front of the young woman, who had tears in her eyes.

"Don't cry," he continued, trying to alter his voice, which was trembling. "It is said in Italy that fortune is never rebellious toward someone who possesses a strong arm and a valiant sword. If you wish, Valentine, I will leave for Italy and you will be free, and will never again hear from me."

The two tears that were trembling on the eyelashes of Mademoiselle de Rohan flowed slowly down to her cheeks. She took the child from the cradle and put it in Saint-Maugan's arms.

Little Marie, suddenly awakened, put out her pretty rosy little hands and tried to reach her father's shoulder. He seemed to hesitate. A movement of passionate tenderness drew him toward the child, but another sentiment, inexplicable and illogical, a sort of bizarre jealousy, touching on the extravagant, made him right himself, and turn his head away.

"Her! Always her!" he said stamping on the floor and without looking at the frightened little Marie. "Ah! You love her a great deal, that child!"

Marie's blonde head was already under the breast of her mother, who was pressing her lovingly on her heart.

"Do you envy me that joy?" murmured Valentine, stroking the child's soft hair. "Without her, I would be alone here, and the Rohan house is very austere and sad! I don't understand, you, Morvan. Your life is one of victory. You cannot even suspect the discouragement felt by the old, the defeated... If you were unhappy, a whirlwind of pleasures would draw you in and console you. You are in Rennes, in the middle of that brilliant Court which surrounds the son of Louis XIV, while we..."

She stopped as if she had suddenly had an idea.

"He has a noble heart, doesn't he, the Count of Toulouse?" she continued, lifting her eyes which seemed to hide a flame.

"Assuredly," replied Saint-Maugan, astonished.

"His reputation has reached even to our solitudes," Valentine continued, thoughtful. "Our country people, who detest the people of France, speak of him with respect... They say he is good, generous, brave as a lion..."

"Do they say that, Madame?" asked Saint-Maugan with an air of constraint. "I must not find his praises exaggerated, I who am the friend and servant of His Serene Highness."

"Yes, yes," Valentine thought aloud. "I know that the Count of Toulouse is your benefactor."

Saint-Maugan bit his lip. He searched in vain for the mystery of that emotion that Valentine could no longer contain.

"The Count of Toulouse will have his glorious page in history," he continued, "given time. He was still almost a child when he began to win hearts under the eyes of the great king, his father. The Count of Toulouse is a hero!"

Valentine's lips moved as if she had repeated very low that last sentence; but her long black eyelashes were lowered over her eyes, while she murmured still another question:

"And he is very young, is he not?"

"Yes," answered Saint-Maugan, who turned pale in spite of himself.

Valentine was not careful. She was carried away by the irresistible desire to know.

"Those who have seen him," she continued, still questioning, "say that his face is like the mirror of a beautiful soul."

"Have you ever seen him?" Saint-Maugan asked between clenched teeth.

"Never," Valentine answered.

There was something like regret in the inflection of her voice. Saint-Maugan hardly contained his agitation.

"The Count de Toulouse is handsome, Madame. Why should I hide it? The Count of Toulouse is indeed very handsome. But," he asked, suddenly rising, "be kind enough to give me the key to this enigma. What interest could Valentine de Rohan, the wife of Monsieur de Saint-Maugan, have in the kindness, generosity, bravery, youth, and handsomeness of Monseigneur the Count of Toulouse, whom she has never met? I just can't imagine!"

The door to the corridor opened at this moment, showing the frightened head of Dame Michou Guitan.

"Rohan is coming down the main staircase," she said, speaking rapidly. "He has already asked twice for our young demoiselle."

Saint-Maugan's last question had made Valentine tremble. She had just spoken as if in a dream, and, in her preoccupation, was not really exactly aware of what was happening.

"Kiss your daughter, Morvan," she said, seizing the issue. "Leave by way of the willow trees so as not to be seen crossing the moat, and may God go with you!"

Saint-Maugan held her by her arm.

"A lot of things can be said in a few seconds, Valentine," he said. "You have time to answer me, if you want to."

In the look that she gave him, Saint-Maugan saw distress and distraction.

"Listen!" shouted Dame Michou Guitan at the door. "Rohan's voice must reach you. That's the third time that he has called our young lady."

"On my honor. Morvan," Valentine said, disengaging herself, "on my honor, Morvan, you will know everything tomorrow, I promise you!"

She put her daughter in Dame Michou's arms and went running down the corridor. Saint-Maugan let himself fall into a seat and remained absorbed for some seconds. A jumble of thoughts ran through his head.

"The Count of Toulouse has changed a great deal during the last month!" he finally said, without realizing that he was speaking aloud. "I remember now! He's asked me several time if Valentine de Rohan merited her reputation of incomparable beauty…"

A hand touched his shoulder. He straightened up and saw the severe face of Dame Michou Guitan. The good woman looked down at him with a kind of disdainful compassion.

"What?" Saint-Maugan asked in a movement of his surprise. "Did I say something?"

"Yes. You spoke aloud and I heard you," replied the old woman.

Saint-Maugan took out his purse and counted out three or four golden louis.

"Take that, good dame," he said, "and continue to take care of the child."

Dame Michou Guitan recoiled several steps.

"Rohan takes care of his servants," she replied with proud calmness. "I love the infant for the Rohan blood that she carries in her veins. It is a great pity that she has for a father such an insignificant gentleman! Keep your money! I won't tell Valentine de Rohan that you are suspicious of her. Her brother died of sadness. She could very well die of shame."

"On my soul!" exclaimed Saint-Maugan, who hadn't even thought of offending her and had so much passion in his heart. "I don't suspect Valentine!"

"Then you fake it well," the good woman answered drily.

"Tell her," Saint-Maugan continued, begging, "please tell her that I pressed our dear little Marie on my heart. Tell her that I love her... Alas! Tell her that I am a fool!"

He covered with kisses the child whom he had pushed away a moment before. Dame Michou watched that with an impassive eye.

Then, Saint-Maugan rushed toward the door and disappeared through the doorway that carried him to the moat. The old woman put the child back in the cradle saying:

"In the past, Rohan was allied to Rieux, to Goulaine, to Goyon, to Clisson. Neither Clisson, nor Rieux, nor Goyon, nor Goulaine ever suspected their women... Ah! The Count of Toulouse talks about our Valentine! Who then doesn't talk about her? Sleep, child! I would give the five fingers of my hand to have your father be a Bourbon instead of a Saint-Maugan, and that he was the master and not the valet!"

Saint-Maugan at that moment came out through the postern, his head uncovered and his hair in disorder. He walked distractedly, lost as he was in his troubled thoughts. As he turned the angle of the rampart to reach the place where his horse was tied, he heard his name called out.

Master Alain Polduc was walking, his hands behind his back, at the edge of the old pits. Master Alain was austere only with Rohan and had repulsive grimaces only for Rohan's tenants. It was enough to see that fat little man with his full red face to guess that his role as a puritan was weighing on him, but he knew that that role would be his bread winner, and so he acted it out to as well as he could, waiting for the desired time when the curtain would fall on the denouement of the tragedy. We can therefore guarantee that Master Alain had not taken a walk there by chance.

"May God pardon me!" he exclaimed with joyous surprise. "I was hardly expecting to encounter Monsieur de Saint-Maugan here!"

"Monsieur…" stammered Saint-Maugan, "…a hunting accident…"

Master Alain had watched him come out from the willow cove. "Are you wounded?" he asked quickly.

"No," answered Saint-Maugan, increasingly embarrassed, because he was beginning to foresee the possible consequences of that encounter. "Not at all, merely a fall."

Master Alain's gaze was fixed on the scarf which was still floating on the balcony's bars.

"You see me very happy, Captain," he said coming toward Saint-Maugan, whom he greeted with his most gracious smile. "For a moment, I was afraid. But may the chance which brings you here be blessed! I don't at all share my noble relative's prejudices, and I feel myself drawn toward you by natural sympathy."

Saint-Maugan silently bowed. Master Alain continued warming up more and more:

"First of all, it's because of who you are, dear Monsieur, you, who carries, as one should, one of the finest names in South Brittany. I knew your cousin, Maugan de Kermelin, down there at Pontivy… Then, it's because of your master, our young, illustrious and brave Governor, the Count of Toulouse!"

"My master deserves all your praise indeed," said Saint-Maugan, coldly.

"I just thought," Master Alain Polduc interrupted. "Was it in the moat itself that you fell? No! You would have gone down there to rest, since the grass there is thicker. Me, I like this place; you won't believe it; it's so unspoiled. You almost never meet anyone here to disturb you."

Poor Saint-Maugan couldn't share that opinion!

"Then," continued Master Alain, whose smile carried a little bit of friendly teasing, "these old walls have something sovereignly poetic about them. You see that stone balcony where a piece of chiffon is hanging? God only knows who could have put that piece of cloth there... Well, there is no place more popular in our region. Volumes could be written about the dark legends told at the fireside about that balcony. If it were night, Captain, from here, we would see, behind the granite balustrade, the two nocturnal lovers peck at each other like owls in March. But it's about our Governor that I want to talk to you..." he interrupted himself with new warmth. "What glory he's brought to my dear country! May I say that? After all, we're both from Brittany. What exploits! Still so young! Winner of the battles of Mons, and Namur![29] Winner at Messina and Alicante! What more can I say? Many more of his victories are not counted! If the chronicles don't lie, all our ladies at the Court are mad about this generous prince! You, who are very close to him, did he open his heart to you? What do you know?"

"Nothing really," Saint-Maugan answered, making a movement to take leave.

Alan Polduc began to laugh.

"Aloud perhaps," he continued with a mocking expression, "but privately? There is some talk, you understand, that is heard better at a distance than up close... and amorous sighs are among them. Frankly, you see, the hunting parties of the son of Louis the Great have often been seen going across our poor forests for several weeks!"

Saint-Maugan turned his head with difficulty.

"Just today..." Master Alain began.

"Today," Saint-Maugan interrupted in an angry voice, "His Highness didn't think he could turn down an invitation from the Steward Feydeau."

---

[29] During the war of the Spanish Succession (1700-08). However, he was given the task of defending Sicily. In 1704, before Malaga, the fleet the Count commanded inflicted heavy losses on the Anglo-Dutch fleet commanded by Admiral George Rooke.

"Yes, a gallant man, that one!" exclaimed Master Alain. "And he adds to his holdings to the extent that ours grow smaller! As for the Count of Toulouse," he added, putting his hat under his arm and shaking his lace costing twenty-four *sous* per aune, like a boor who wants to imitate a Marquis of the theater, "let's just say that he was in our area just by chance. I don't ask anything better. However, fine pearls are found at the bottom of the Ocean. Diamonds are, they say, pebbles in the desert... We have here, in this little-known country, a priceless diamond, a pearl whose value can't be estimated..."

"Valentine de Rohan and the Count of Toulouse have never seen each other," Saint-Maugan interrupted.

Master Alain looked at him, laughing. "In front of witnesses, perhaps," he murmured, "but otherwise..."

"What do you mean?" exclaimed the young Captain, pale with indignation.

"I?" said Polduc said with gentleness. "Certainly nothing that could offend you, that could hardly concern you, my cousin. After all, you perhaps know better than I why the hunting parties of our Governor so often stray into our forests."

They had come to the grove of beech trees where Saint-Maugan had hidden his horse before entering the manor.

Master Alain Polduc had achieved his purpose: he had found out what he wanted to know, and he had struck the heart of his cousin; a double and precious result which surely would bear fruit in the time and place. So he remained was silent. Saint-Maugan had just stopped some feet away from his horse, which was pawing the ground. He, too, remained silent for a moment. When he finally spoke, his altered voice showed the effort he was making to hold his temper.

"According to public gossip," he said, turning toward Master Alain, "you eat here bread given to charity."

The Steward tried to set the record straight.

"That's enough!" interrupted Saint-Maugan harshly. "If I were acquainted with Rohan, I would denounce to him the beggar who insults his benefactor. If I were not a soldier and a gentleman, I would punish that beggar myself... Be warned, be careful; if not, I'll have my valets deal with you."

He untied his horse, jumped in the saddle, and left at a gallop.

Master Alain was not what is called a coward, because, even before finding out if Saint-Maugan's disdain would shield him, he had not budged an inch. He was a cool, self-contained man, because not a muscle on his face had trembled at that insulting menace. Instead, he watched Saint-Maugan ride away without losing his smile.

"If he had made a move to draw his sword," he said to himself, reasoning like the philosopher that he was, "I would have blown off his head, that's true. I had witnesses to prove his clandestine entry into the manor, and Rohan would have given me half his fortune. That handsome horseman didn't know that I was holding my loaded pistol under my doublet. What use is the sword of gentlemen and soldiers who won't lower themselves to strike anyone but another soldier and gentleman?"

A smile of sovereign contempt played about his lips.

"Me, I'm not proud," he continued. "I would never let an insect that stung me live under the pretext that it was too vile or too little to kill... Where s Yaumi?" he then asked, raising his voice.

The tops of the willow trees were moving about and the handsome Cobbler showed his cynical head at the moat. Master Alain Polduc took his tablets out of his pocket and traced some words with a crayon. He then tore out a page and used it to wrap up a ten livre *écu* and threw both to Yaumi.

"I need this to be given to the Steward Feydeau," he said. "If you bring me back his response within an hour, you will get another *écu*."

Yaumi caught the message and the money on the fly and left quickly.

Master Alain made a tour of the moats and returned to the Manor by the main door. Following his habit, he walked in a measured step, his hands behind his back. On the way, he was saying to himself:

"Half of Rohan's fortune! *Pardieu!* I'm counting on having everything! It's said that those people there throw their secrets to the wind for the first one who comes along to catch them... But what is Rohan? One string to my bow. I have more of them. Eh! Eh! Eh!"

He interrupted himself, with whole-hearted laughter.

"I haven't lost any weight by eating the bread of charity. This beggar will be a millionaire before he dies!"

VI. A Love Rendez-Vous

All the house servants were gathered in the lower room where Master Alain Polduc had calculated the debts of the tenant farmers. Rohan no longer had his house furnished as he had in the great days of his power. But he still had enough officers and valets to fill the hall of his vestibule when it pleased him to come and go in pomp. The squire, the huntsman, the wine steward, the grooms, the gardeners, the laborers and the shepherds, still formed a small army which could be impressive when need be.

Rohan had called three times for his daughter. When he came down the grand staircase, both doors of the courtyard were open and showed his black horse harnessed as for battle. Rohan himself was armed from head to foot, not like the gentleman subjects of Louis XIV, but in the outdated fashion which covered the combatants with leather and iron. To see him, one would have thought he was a Breton soldier from the Mercoeur Companies, during the time of the League.[30] Rohan

---

[30] Named after Philippe-Emmanuel de Lorraine (1558-1602), Duke of Mercoeur, who was the brother of Louise de Lorraine, Queen France, and therefore the brother-in-law of King Henry III. He became governor of Brittany in 1582. The assassination of the Duke of Guise, head of the Catholic League, by Henri III in 1588 enabled the Duke of Mercœur to take

had had himself dressed like that to pay a visit to the Count of Toulouse and his court. Over there, among those aristocrats with immense wigs and plumed hats, he was going to elicit more than one smile and produce at the same time the surprise that reminds us of some austere and bearded portrait by old Porbus[31] surging suddenly out of the middle of those serene canvasses where Vandermeulen[32] grouped the lieutenants of Louis XIV.

In the lower hall of the Manor, the contrast was less striking because the Count's servants did not follow contemporary fashion. Rohan's house systematically retained old costumes; men, furniture, walls, everything had an antique aspect; everything spoke of a past time. That did not seem like a joke at all. There was something venerable in that obstinate immobility which wanted to stop the march of time, turning its back on the hated present to religiously worship the giant figure of ancestors from the distant past. They fell, these living titans, because such is God's law, but they fell with fracas, like the feudal towers that sometimes crumble in our countryside and, in falling, throw the black powder on the white walls of our banal villas.

Rohan wore armor like a true knight. His snow-white beard fell in thick tufts on the steel of his cutlass, and his head, crowned with long white hair, seemed to be waiting for a helmet with a visor. His face was pale, but his eyes were shining, and his exaltation had evidently increased since the morning. It was like a fever. The people in the house were familiar with that fever whose access often returned. Rohan had had that fever the night he had chased his son away. No one had ever

---

advantage of the situation to carve out his own power base in Brittany by taking advantage of local opposition to French royal power.

[31] Frans Porbus the younger (1569-1622), Flemish painter, son of Frans Porbus the elder.

[32] Adam Frans van der Meulen (1632-1690), another Flemish Baroque painter.

given a name to that fever because of the deep respect that surrounded Rohan.

"Here is our young lady," said Dame Michou Guitan, who arrived out of breath.

"Good!" replied the Count with that emphatic calm of people who are becoming drunk. "She will hear my orders and they will be carried out. I want the Fire of Saint-Jean's Day to be lit in the court of honor. I had good dreams and I woke up happy this morning."

There was a coldness in his veins, and everyone predicted, without knowing why, some bizarre tragedy. Valentine de Rohan came in and didn't seem at all astonished at the warlike accoutrement of her father. She approached and bent her forehead forward, where the old man placed a kiss.

"That's my beautiful and good girl," he said, looking at her with admiration. "Don't apologize for your absence this morning, Valentine. You do as you please. I trust you."

"Thank you, father," she stammered, lowering her eyes.

"Today is a festival; it's a feast day," exclaimed Rohan suddenly. "I don't see my cousin Polduc; however, he knows the festival well."

Valentine put both hands over her heart.

"At the moment the bonfire is lit," continued the old Count, "I want the candle to be placed upright; understand that Valentine. And all around it, I want tables set up with food. Why haven't you put on your formal dress, my daughter? By the sacred name of Rohan! I promise you that, since the day of your birth, no one will have = seen such rejoicing!"

A glacial silence followed each word of the old Count. During one of those silences, Josselin, pale with fatigue, slid in through the main door which had remained half-open, and fell, exhausted, onto a stool. Valentine and he exchanged a rapid glance. At the same moment, Master Alain entered from the courtyard.

"Come here, Polduc, my cousin," Rohan said joyfully. "Did you hear a while ago the trumpet of His Highness, as they call him?"

"The *piqueurs*[33] of the Count of Toulouse," said Master Alain, "have just trumpeted that there is a kill in the forest."

"A kill!" repeated Rohan, whose pupils threw out a dark light. "Let them trumpet! Let them trumpet that there's a kill!"

"Father," said Valentine gently, "your hands are trembling and your voice has changed very much."

The Count drew himself up to his full height and motioned to Master Alain, who approached to put around his waist an enormous sword with a guard of chiseled iron.

"When that is in my hand," Rohan said with savage pride, "my hand will no longer tremble... Isn't that right, cousin Polduc? Little fool! Don't you see that I have been rejuvenated by twenty years!"

"Holy Virgin!" Valentine prayed very low. "Have mercy on us!"

The Count leaned toward her.

"If I should by chance die today," he asked her in confidence, "would you be willing to marry our cousin Polduc?"

Valentine made a movement of horror.

"Well! Well!" the Count continued, laughing. "Why should I die today rather than tomorrow? If God pleases, we will rejoice with each other as a family this evening....= Come with me, Polduc! Let's mount up!"

"Why don't you take your squire, father?" Valentine asked, pleadingly.

"Polduc will act as my squire," replied the Count.

Just half way, thought Master Alain, *because today I have a great deal of work.*

Rohan drew his daughter against his heart.

"Your mother is a saint in Heaven," he said. Hugging her in his arms, he murmured with passion: "I have only you, my daughter, and I love you for all those I have lost! If you don't see me return..."

---

[33] Trackers on horseback who followed the hunted prey, laying out the course for the dogs.

"Father!" exclaimed Valentine, falling to her knees, "in the name of God, please, don't go!"

The witnesses of that scene heard, saw, and held their breath. Rohan remained for a moment with his forehead lowered, then he straightened up and reached the door, saying:

"A beautiful bonfire, a brilliant festival and a more beautiful ornament to welcome me when I return, my Daughter! Follow me, cousin Polduc!"

He went down the steps to the courtyard. All the officers and servants accompanied him and made a respectful circle around him while he mounted his horse. It was Polduc who held his stirrup, Polduc who was thinking:

I'm going to know shortly how much, in écus, the life of a son of a King, a Grand Admiral of France, and Governor of the Province of Brittany is worth!

Rohan was now in the saddle. All those in the courtyard took off their hats as he picked up the reins. The black horse responded and lowered his head in front of the vestibule door. Rohan, who seemed a different man since his foot had touched the stirrup, bowed nobly to send his daughter a smile with a kiss.

"That one is a true Breton" said Josselin, who was leaning thoughtfully at the open door.

"Head and heart of iron!" murmured Valentine.

Dame Michou Guitan asked with a sad expression:

"Mademoiselle, should we set up the bonfire and should we set tables around it?"

"Do as Rohan ordered," responded Valentine, who was going up the grand staircase.

Josselin joined her behind the silver drapery.

"Did you see him?" Valentine asked percipiently.

"I saw him."

"Did you succeed in getting to talk to him?"

"Everyone has access to him and can speak to him."

"You told him what it is about?"

"As you told me to, my lady."

"What did he say?"

"Nothing. He started to smile."

"I was afraid of that!" Valentine exclaimed with discouragement. "He is brave, he is proud, and for someone who does not know Rohan, the idea must appear extravagant and mad!"

"Yes," murmured Josselin, "but for those who know Rohan…"

"Terrible!" Valentine finished.

There was silence. On the other side of the drapery, Rohan's valets could be heard talking among themselves and commenting on the Count's mysterious behavior. In the forest, there was an extravagant number of far-away fanfares.

"Then," Valentine continued in a low voice, "the Prince scorned my warning?"

"For whatever it was worth, my lady!" replied the young man, with a kind of repugnance.

"What do you mean?"

"I remember the Prince's very words. If you require it, I will repeat them to you."

"Speak," Valentine ordered.

Josselin Guitan looked down and his cheeks turned a pale red.

"The Prince said," he pronounced slowly, " '*I rend grace to Valentine de Rohan, who is the most beautiful of the beautiful.*' "

In her turn, Valentine blushed and lowered her eyes.

"But," continued Josselin, who was repeating the courteous response of the son of the King of France like a lesson memorized: " '*It is danger that I am warned of, and I know only one excuse for a knight to flee danger…*' "

Josselin stopped.

"Did he specify that excuse?" Valentine demanded without lifting her eyes.

"A love rendezvous," Josselin replied.

A deeper palor took the place of the blush that had spread onto Mademoiselle de Rohan's cheeks. Her breast fluttered; her lips trembled.

"Where is the Prince at this hour?" she questioned suddenly.

"I left him very near here," the young boy continued, "at the Wolf's Den."

"You are going to go back to him, and tell him that Valentine de Rohan will waiting for him here, in the absence of her father, and will give him such a rendezvous."

"A love rendezvous!" stammered Josselin in a broken voice.

"A love rendezvous!" repeated Valentine, who lifted her forehead haughtily.

The young boy bowed and took a step toward leaving. Valentine called him back.

"Josselin," she said with a kind of melancholy and gentle severity, "I have a great deal of pain and I don't expect to win this mortal combat, and your devotion, my poor Josselin, will perhaps never be recompensed as it should. I only ask one more thing of you, Josselin: don't be hasty in judging the daughter of your master."

"For the first time in my life, I am disobeying you, my lady," replied Josselin, kneeling, with tears in his eyes. "My heart is judging you!"

Valentine held out her hand, that he brushed with his lips.

"Go!" she commanded. "Tell your mother to put Marie, my daughter, to bed in the cradle that was used by the late César de Rohan before me. Tell her to carry the crib into the Drawing Room, where she will bring the Count of Toulouse, that is, if His Serene Highness deigns to accept my rendezvous… Rohan ordered me to make myself beautiful today. As you leave, call my chambermaids. I want to obey Rohan's orders. Now, go!"

"One last question," Josselin asked timidly. "Through which entry should the Count be introduced?"

"By the door at the edge of the water."

Josselin Guitan lifted the silver drapery and disappeared.

The next instant Valentine's chambermaids arranged and perfumed her marvelous hair. She was seated in front of a heavy pivoting mirror which, in vain, reproduced the image of her beauty without rival. She did not look at herself. Deep thought put a veil over her eyes, staring without seeing. Her chambermaids turned her and turned her again in front of the mirror; she was docile, as if she was not conscious of their work. She had said: "*I want my most brilliant jewelry.*" Soon the family diamonds from the jewelry box were shining in her ears, on her forehead, on her breast, and among the curls of her coiffure. A silk dress surrounded her supple and narrow waist.

We have said that nothing was modern in Rohan's dwelling. The pretty ladies of the Court would not have wanted Valentine's dress. They would have involuntarily thought of their grandmothers. But, under this attire, somewhat old-fashioned in its magnificence, Valentine's youth remained victorious and proud. There was, among her charming graces, something haughty that went well with the elegant corsage of a type once worn by Anne of Austria.[34] Everything about her was noble. And you would have taken her, when she stood, for a young and radiant queen ready to mount the steps to her throne for the first time. She finally glanced at her mirror and dismissed her women, saying to them:

"That's good!"

Josselin had been gone about a half-hour. Alone now, in front of a prie-Dieu, she tried to recite the orisons for each day, but there was a unique and dreadful thought in her mind. It was like one of those obstinate dreams that comes with high fever. She saw on one side Rohan, her father; on the other, Saint-Maugan, both with a sword in hand: Rohan attacking the Count of Toulouse, Saint-Maugan obliged to defend him.

---

[34] Anne of Austria (1601-1666), Spanish princess and Austrian archduchess of the House of Habsburg, who was Queen of France as the wife of Louis XIII, then regent during the minority of her son, Louis XIV, from 1643 to 1651.

The sun had already passed half of its course, the air was warm, the breeze hardly moving the highest branches of the forest trees. Valentine opened her window. Outside, there was profound silence. All of nature seemed to be taking a nap after the burning mid-day and the thousand noises of the country-side had quietened down. Valentine's glance looked question-ingly at that rustic slope that descended toward the Vesvre Valley, where sheep could be seen in the distance, sprawled on the grass, made languid by the heat. A little dust rose like a cloud above the trees on the other side. The step of an invisi-ble horse sounded dully.

Valentine closed her window and put her hands over her palpitating heart.

"I will have my daughter's crib near me," she murmured, while a sad smile lit up her beautiful pallor, "and God will protect me."

VII. The Ceremonial Room

It was a completely white horse that had raised the little cloud of dust that Valentine had observed. The horse was mounted by a tall, young huntsman whose hunting attire was hidden under an ample azure coat. Josselin, on foot, his hair drenched with sweat, was running in front of the horseman as if to light the road. On coming to the edge of the underbrush, Josselin stopped.

"My Lord," he said, "we are going to cross the corner end of an empty pasture; it's time to walk."

The young huntsman didn't have to be asked twice. While Josselin was tying his horse to a tree, he threw the end of his coat over his shoulder, so as to hide the lower part of his face, at the same time pulling his hat down over his eyes.

Josselin came first out of the covering so as to look down the length of the moat. No one could be seen in the vicinity of the manor. Josselin signaled and the horseman joined him. They both went across the narrow pasture scattered with heather which separated the ditch from the last forest trees, then they entered the willow trees cove, and Josselin opened the postern located under the famous granite balcony.

If the Count of Toulouse had come looking for an adventure, he had gotten his wish. Outside, the slowly setting sun, still lit the wild and solitary surroundings of the old manor, but as soon as the little door was closed, the Prince and his conductor found themselves in complete darkness.

"Rohan looks very far for what he has under his roof," said the Count of Toulouse, whose voice certainly betrayed no misgivings.

"Rohan has grown old and he has suffered much," replied Josselin without turning around. "But we are not here to chat. Come forward, please, My Lord. I shall wait for you at the bottom of the stairway."

Toulouse, groping and stumbling, reached him. Josselin took him by the corner of his coat and, together, they started to climb the steps of the staircase. As they mounted, the shadows became less dark and the Count could soon see the damp walls where the webs of enormous spiders were hanging.

"This must be the road to Paradise," he murmured, laughing.

Josselin put a finger to his lips. There was a noise at the end of the corridor. They stopped near a little gap in the wall. Through its narrow slit, the Court of Honor and the grazing area for animals could be seen.

"What are all those people doing there?" asked the Count of Toulouse, seeing Rohan's servants and farmers gathering as a crowd on the grass.

"They are building the bonfire of Saint-Jean's Day," answered Josselin. "Come on, My Lord, our way is clear."

The Count of Toulouse threw a last look at the lawn, and the idea came to him that that bonfire was being built somewhat for what he intended.

"Old Rohan is celebrating in advance," he thought aloud.

"Rohan has suffered a great deal," repeated Josselin, who was walking into the corridor.

This was a one-story high gallery which went across all the abandoned part of the chateau. Their feet sank into the thick dust. On the right and on the left, the bare bedrooms were open to the wind—a veritable desolation! That touched the heart of the Count of Toulouse and he felt, despite himself, that painful impression which every ruin elicits.

At the end of the corridor, a large tapestry which must have been worthy in the past to decorate a royal dwelling, but was now falling into tatters, hid a double door made of sculpted black oak. Josselin opened it and stopped on the threshold to say:

"Our lady is expecting you."

Then he backed away, leaving the passage open for the Prince, who didn't believe to be so close to the end of his quest. The full daylight that inundated the Salon of Honor dazzled him and pushed his astonishment to the point of becoming a problem. Rohan's Salon of Honor couldn't pass for being splendid in the eyes of this young man who, when a child, had trod the tiles of the Louvre and the rugs of Versailles. Yet, there was something left of its majestic and sad grandeur that seized one when entering that dilapidated dwelling.

The room was vast. Four large windows with a low stone frame let the rays of the setting sun penetrate through their panes decorated with religious subjects. The ceiling, divided into eight compartments, was sculpted from end to end. A line of portraits representing armed knights with all their accoutrements, alternating with their ladies, stiff under their vair[35] or ermine, completed the tour of the room. Below each woman's portrait, there was a brass tag specifying the marriage alliance with what important family.

There were two other doors in addition to the door by which the Count of Toulouse had entered; one went toward the main staircase; the other opened onto a terrace surrounded

[35] Decorative fur made from the bluish underside of the skin of the squirrel.

with giant yew trees shaped into cones which descended by tiled steps to the manor's garden.

Valentine, dressed as we have said, was seated at the other end of the room. The Rohan crib, where little Marie was sleeping for the first time, was hidden not far from her by the curtains of the last doorway. She rose when the Count entered and said in a confident voice:

"Welcome, My Lord."

The Count of Toulouse, the legitimate son of Louis XIV and Madame de Montespan, was in all the flower of his poetic and knightly youth. History hasn't talked a great deal about him because his entire life was spent outside political intrigues. His character was a total contrast with that of the Duke of Maine, his older brother, who had assumed for himself all the grand ambitions of the family. Just as the Duke of Maine was politically active, proud of the equivocal good fortune of his birth, the Count of Toulouse was unassuming, simple, solid and loyal.

What he lacked to reach glory was perhaps some fault, because fame, that madness, turns away from perfect virtue, and never has any exciting fanfare except for the hero who has enough faults. One thing could save the Count of Toulouse: he had a romantic personality and was given to amorous adventures. However, he had married very young, and was, they said, faithful to his wife. What is to be done with a valiant Prince when he wears a plume, who is sincere, faithful, and absolutely lacks any color?

The Count of Toulouse bowed respectfully from the threshold. When he straightened up, he threw back the edge of his cloak and revealed his white hunting attire decorated with small silver and azure braids. The walk that he had just finished, and also the small emotions of his entrance into the manor, had darkened his somewhat pale complexion. His blonde hair, with almost as many tufts as the wigs of his father's courtesans, fell in big curls along his cheeks and right down onto his shoulders. His smiling blue eyes were half-closed, reacting as they were to the sudden light. He held his coat on his left arm, and his hat, filled with plumes, in his right hand.

You may have stopped in front of that odd portrait of Louis XIV as an adolescent which hangs at the end the Rubens Gallery in the Louvre? The King of the Flemish School, while reproducing the features of his model, was also thinking of young Achilles, brought up among women and very proud under the armor which replaced the soft linen tunic for the first time. There was, under the fabulous crest of Anne of Austria's son, a naïve and charming smile; there was nothing in it that was virile, or boastful; he seemed to be like a young girl playing at being a soldier. Rubens's flattery had gotten right to the heart of the matter. Louis XIV always displayed a marked predilection for that portrait. It is said that, in his old age, he liked to repeat: "*When I think that I once looked like that!*"

The Count of Toulouse had all the traits of his father, who was only four or five years older in that Rubens portrait. It was an almost feminine beauty; one could say almost virginal. And certainly, that young man with his slender build, his big, wide and soft blue eyes, looked more like someone too young to have already received a high military rank. However, he had already proved, more than once, that he was an intrepid soldier. Those soft blue eyes had already looked at death in battle.

Valentine, who had risen at his approach, ceremoniously showed him a seat. Toulouse took her hand, which he carried to his lips, and remained standing, while forcing her to be seated. He remained silent a moment, looking at her.

"I was told," he finally murmured, "I have often been told, that Valentine de Rohan was the most beautiful flower in the Garden of Brittany, and gossip, which spares no one, proclaimed her virtues even higher than her beauty."

Valentine didn't reply; her eyelids had lowered their long silk fringes; she remained motionless like a beautiful marble statue.

"When I left Paris," the Prince continued, "to come govern this province, I looked around me, searching for that about which I had been told so many times. I believed I could find it in those brilliant gatherings hosted by the women of the local nobility; but I never found it there. I didn't get discouraged. Should the feeling which drew me on be called curiosity? Should it be given another name? One day, I came to the mansion of Feydeau, the royal Steward, to discuss the Rohan estates…"

"The manor of Feydeau formerly belonged to Rohan, My Lord," she said, frowning.

"I learned that afterward," responded the Prince. "I believe I now know everything that concerns Rohan, but I didn't know it then. That day, I saw the beautiful Valentine. That was in the forest. She passed by on horseback; me, I was hidden by the underbrush; so she didn't see me."

Valentine trembled slightly.

"Since that day," the Count of Toulouse went on, "I still hunt with the royal Steward, who is astonished at that passion. Since that day, I look for certainty; I dream; I am sad or happy. Only one discussion still pleases me; the ones I have with of my subordinates, Captain Morvan de Saint-Maugan."

At that name, Valentine raised her eyes in spite of herself

"Do you know him?" asked the Prince. Valentine bowed as a sign of confirmation.

"And if the discussion with Saint-Maugan pleases me," the Count of Toulouse again continued, his words coming slower and softer, "it's because he sometimes talks to me about you."

Valentine still didn't reply, but the Count saw her change color. He continued:

"It is through Saint-Maugan that I know what Rohan wants. Your father has a lot of anger in his heart."

"My Lord," Valentine interrupted, "my father has a memory, that's all. Rohan's ancestors were princes; Rohan is no longer anything but a poor relative. Rohan's ancestors wore the crown of Brittany on their head, and the Kings of France, your ancestors, took that crown and carried it to Paris, in the language of Duchess Anne… Rohan's rule used to extend over fifty parishes; he had twenty manor houses; he counted ten thousand vassals. Do I have to tell you, My Lord, the small number of servants that remain to him? Rohan, My Lord, was, in those days, rich enough to make sovereigns themselves envy him."

She lowered her voice and her look clouded over while she continued.

"Who knows now if Rohan will still have, for very long, a roof over his sexagenarian head? Please, don't interrupt me, My Lord, because I must finish! Rohan's power, his manor, his vassals, his riches… Who has taken all that away from him if not the King of France? France," she repeated, lifting her beautiful angry forehead, "France, who comes here, into our country, to live off us and drink our blood! My Lord Rohan no longer has anything on Earth but his sword. You are the son of the King of France. Rohan has taken up his sword and is looking for you in order to take his revenge!"

"The King, my father, has other sons," murmured the Count of Toulouse. "By killing me, would Rohan truly assassinate France?"

"Rohan will not assassinate anyone, My Lord," Valentine replied. "I can tell you what Rohan plans to do, because I found out his secret during his sleepless nights, and I heard the confession that he thought he was making only to God. Some people, that you perhaps regard as friends, have told Rohan your plan to put together, this evening, a dinner party at the crossroad at Mi-Forêt, which was, until yesterday, still part of the Rohan estate. There is a poor, ruined chapel where a statue of the Virgin is still standing, dressed with crowns put there by my hands. It was our fathers who built that chapel. Rohan is going to go there to kneel before Holy Mary. He will wait until the son of his all-powerful enemy will have drunk the last cup and give the signal for the dance to begin. Then Rohan will come forward into the middle of your gentlemen, all of whom are wearing a sword. He, an old man, alone against that crowd of young men, will shout to call out the Governor of

Brittany and challenge him to single combat. Cannot that, My Lord, pass for an assassination?"

The Prince had listened to Mademoiselle de Rohan without interrupting her. Fixed on her, his look expressed unlimited admiration. That proud eloquence amazed him and subjugated him. He held out his hand and showed the motto that surrounded the emblem of Brittany.

"*Death rather than dishonor,*" he pronounced very low.

"Death," repeated Valentine bitterly, "because the bodyguards of His Serene Highness cannot answer that outrageous challenge, except with their swords, can they?"

She believed she was dreaming when she heard the Count of Toulouse answer her:

"You are mistaken, Mademoiselle. Rohan was on the Crusades with the ancestors of the King, my father. We are cousins by our connection with Dreux and Valois. Rohan and Bourbon can cross swords."

"They were right when they told me that you were a knightly gentleman, My Lord!" murmured Valentine, moved. "I knew that, and it was the reason that I dared to call on you. I cannot say why I lost, for an instant, my role as a supplicant. I should have knelt at your feet, since I am weak, and you have power. I should have said to you, my hands joined and my forehead bowed: *Mercy! Save my father!*"

She was already almost standing, her knees already bent. Just as the Count of Toulouse took hold of both her hands to force her to sit down again, a shadow passed across the last terrace window. The day was setting quickly. The shadow passed in front of the second window and stopped. If Valentine and the Prince had been paying attention, they would have been able to recognize at the windows which led to the door to the terrace, the worried and curious face of Master Alain Polduc.

That model of stewards seemed mortally disappointed. He was walking up and down, his hands behind his back, not suspecting anything. He was going to turn the key to the door when he had seen, some distance from him, the Count of Toulouse and Valentine. Astonishment had made him draw back, but then he approached again, but this time, he saw little Marie, sleeping in the Rohan crib.

"Oh! Oh!" he grumbled, "things are further along than I had thought. I would not have been surprised if we had found His Serene Highness at the Mi-Forêt! Our dear young lady hasn't wasted her time. It's now matter of modifying my plan slowly! But why make that infant a third party in that tête-à-tête?" He interrupted himself, scratching his forehead. "When you have the misfortune to have a woman as an adversary, you never know what to expect... Ah! It was a great deal easier with young Monsieur César!"

He put his head in his hands and began to think. Meanwhile, Valentine was continuing to speak in the salon.

"Let me make up for my error and plead the cause of my father, My Lord. Reason sometimes becomes shaky under that double burden of old age and misfortune. Bad advice increases bitterness, provides venom for hatred. Just yesterday, my father was told the news of the publication of a new Edict. He doesn't know, as I do, that you have put your clemency between us and those who are going to enforce the law. He shouted:

" 'That is the last straw! Rohan will fall, but he will fall avenged!'

"And he picked up his weapons, too heavy for his trembling arms."

She stopped, repeating at random words she had already spoken. She had thrown at that man, who was there for the possibility of a love rendezvous, words of politics and war. Wasn't it madness to still pretend youth and love?

"You know very well that I am completely yours, Mademoiselle," replied the Prince, as if he wanted to reproach her diplomatically for her useless pleas. "You know very well that no danger menaces your father as long as I am here."

"You are good," stammered Valentine. "You are generous, and my gratitude will endure as long as I live."

"Mademoiselle de Rohan," replied the Count of Toulouse with gentle but firm courtesy, "I don't want your gratitude."

Master Alain Polduc had just left his post. He went down the steps four at a time. His plan was now laid out.

"I know how to get to Saint-Maugan," he muttered, halting the gallop of his short legs. "First of all, to Saint-Maugan, then to Rohan! After that, the King's soldiers... then back to Rohan! If the House of Rohan doesn't fall with that blow, then it can be said that it was solidly built!"

VIII. The Cradle

It is sometimes surprising to see a robust tree trunk, filled with green branches, suddenly fall, crashing down when struck by some mild wind. It is astonishing, until the moment when one discovers a black tortuous trace right at the place where the wood broke. The wind is strong, but under the bark, there is a vile helper without which it would have blown in vain, a patient worm that ate into the wood, fiber by fiber...

Here's what Master Alain Polduc wrote to the Steward Feydeau, a vile gnawing worm under the bark of the old Rohan tree that had victoriously withstood so many storms.

Monsieur, and respected friend,

The fruit is ripe and is going to fall. It will be necessary to wear gloves when it does. If you seek favors from the Court, and I don't mean the one at Rennes, but higher, the one at Paris, from where all favors come, then get together with Monsieur the King's Lieutenant, and send a military squad of the La Ferté regiment to the Cross at Mi-Forêt this evening, at the time of the afternoon dinner party.

For good reason, that squad must not be commanded by Captain Morvan de Saint-Maugan. Let there be, I ask you, one or two of the men who are exempted to carry the legislated abstract of the fortunate Edict. If God wills it, on Saint-Jean's Day, that is to say tomorrow, we will have an empty house.

With this, Monsieur and my most respected friend, etc., etc.

Yaumi, running as fast as his legs would carry him in order to win his second six-livre écu, carried that message to Feydeau, who had his own reasons for not neglecting this warning.

Everything was ready at the time stipulated and one can imagine how sorry that poor Master Alain must have been when he saw his plans so well crafted come to nothing. The main character in that drama, the Count of Toulouse, was absent. Rohan was waiting all alone behind the chapel in ruins. He prayed while waiting. His conscience was at peace, and he sincerely believed that his enterprise was blessed.

Rohan was not the first Breton who had conceived the notion of a judgment of God between France and Brittany. In 1628, on the 29th of October, the day after the day when the city of La Rochelle had surrendered, King Louis XIII received a message from François-Vincent of Châtelaudren, a Huguenot, who had challenged him to hand-to-hand combat as a continuation of the forfeiture of his predecessors, who had traitorously confiscated the liberties and privileges of the province of Brittany. That Seigneur had killed the younger Bryas, who had been sent to arrest him, and he was able to flee to England. Nor was Rohan to be the last.

One of his neighbors from the Rennes forest, Nicolas Treml, Seigneur of La Tremlay, traveled to Paris, in the era of the Regency of Duke Philippe d'Orléans. The Duke was hunting in the forest of Villers-Cotterets. Nicolas Treml, assisted by a poor peasant whom he called his squire, waited for the Regent in front of the gates of the chateau, and the moment the Prince entered, surrounded by his courtesans, he killed him with just one blow of his big gauntlet, thrown as a matter of defiance. [36]

---

[36] A somewhat different version of the events retold in *The White Wolf.*

There may still be found in the Hôtel des Invalides, some old soldier who was witness to the actions of Georges Cadoudal,[37] that other famous Breton, against the First Consul Napoleon Bonaparte!

The people of Brittany didn't usurp their reputation for unshakeable consistency. At the time we are writing, there are still down there, toward the black mountains and along those western shores constantly beaten by storms, some gentlemen laborers, dressed as in the 17th century who still dream, wide awake, of the independence of Brittany.[38]

Master Alain Polduc, seeing that the Count of Toulouse was not there, had slipped away under some sort of pretext. He wandered about like a lost soul among the tents which had been made ready for the dinner party. Luck or instinct pushed him back toward the Rohan manor, where, as we have just seen, he was to find the explanation of the absence of the Governor. His horse was saddled behind the rampart. It took him only a short distance from the Mi-Forêt, where Saint-Maugan, replacing his absent master, was amusing the impatience of the beautiful ladies and was doing the honors at the feast.

Meanwhile, in the Salon, Valentine and the Count of Toulouse were still having their tête-à-tète.

---

[37] (1771-1804). Breton politician and leader of the *Chouannerie* during the French Revolution. He was involved in Pierre Saint-Regen's attempt on the life of the First Consul, in December 1800, and had to flee to England again. He returned in 1803, to undertake a new kidnap or assassination attempt on Bonaparte whilst on the road to Malmaison, which failed. He was caught and executed the following year, but posthumously made a Marshal of France in 1814 by the reinstated Bourbons.

[38] *Author's note*: Just a few years ago, the Viscount of L***, accused of armed revolt, told the Tribunal of Quimper that he was ready to defend, everywhere, armed, the independence of the Duchy of Brittany.

"My Lord," Valentine was saying, "don't ask me for what I can't give you. You must take pity on a young girl who only wants to save her father, and does not have a choice of the means, and must gain some time. I had counted on that delicate loyalty that everyone praises in you."

"Delicacy and loyalty, can they exclude love?" interrupted the young Prince, whose tone was becoming more and more serious.

Valentine tried to smile, but there was trouble in her heart that astonished her. Perhaps she had already guessed, because women guess everything, even the impossible, the strange proposition that he was going to make to her.

"Mademoiselle," continued the Count of Toulouse, who pulled up a chair and finally sat down near her, "I ask you to listen to me carefully. The suggestion that I am going to make to you was not born of the enthusiasm of this moment, when I see you so beautiful. I have been thinking about it for a long time, and if it flatters my heart's inclination, it also satisfies my logic. The Duke of Maine must marry a princess of royal blood, because the law makes him the inheritor of the throne of my father. I, on the other hand, who am not, and do not want to be, anything but a soldier, remain free to choose..."

Valentine wanted to interrupt him, but he silenced her with a gesture, at the same time, begging and commanding.

"Listen to me," he continued, becoming animated. "You talked to me a while ago about your deposed race, about the menaces in the future. All that Rohan has lost, Rohan can recover: power and wealth. Isn't it just that all of it should be given back to him by a French Prince?"

"Please," Valentine stammered, trembling.

"Listen to me!" the Count of Toulouse repeated with fervor. "France and Brittany are no longer anything but one people. However, there is still a feeling of hatred between France and Brittany. Wouldn't it be a beautiful role for the heir of Rohan, a role worthy of her, that of cementing the reconciliation of our two people?"

He stopped. Valentine's beautiful and sad face was resting on her breast.

"That would have been a great destiny!" she said, speaking to herself.

"Mademoiselle de Rohan," the Prince concluded, leaning over her hand, "would you like to become the daughter-in-law of King Louis XIV and the wife of the Count of Toulouse?"

Valentine turned pale. Was there regret in her heart? She was of that proud and strong race that gave companions to Charles VIII, to Louis XII, to Francis I. Was she thinking about the old Rohan throne that could flourish again for her? The Moon, prolonging the evening, lit up three of the salon's windows. The fourth remained in the shadow of some buildings in the background.

Two men who had gone cautiously across the terrace, stopped in front of that last window. The Count of Toulouse's lips were at that moment touching the pale, cold hand of Valentine.

"Answer me," he said, changing his tone and letting himself slip to his knees. "Decide as to my happiness or my unhappiness… For I love you!"

"Well," one of the two men stopped in front of the windows said very low. "I promised you that you would see. Do you see?"

The other man pressed his hands over his forehead covered with cold sweat.

"My wife…" he stammered as if he had been struck by lightning, "…And my master!"

He let his arms fall along his thigh. A moonbeam reflection, striking the windows, lit up the livid and distraught face of Captain Morvan de Saint-Maugan. On the contrary, Master Alain Polduc, who stood behind him, had an excellent happy expression.

"What is to be done?" murmured Saint-Maugan, without knowing that he had spoken.

"Do what you would like," answered the Steward. "That's up to you, since you are her husband."

But Saint-Maugan no longer knew what to do.

To Rohan now! Master Alain thought to himself as he made his way across the gardens.

"Don't you want to answer me, Valentine?" the Count of Toulouse asked tenderly.

Mademoiselle de Rohan trembled and became herself again.

"A dream!" she murmured, rising to go to the crib hidden behind the embrasure curtain.

The Moon passed behind a cloud. Saint-Maugan was leaning against the frame of the window. He could no longer see anything. The Count of Toulouse had followed Valentine, who drew back the curtains and revealed the crib.

"My Lord," she said, "God will surely give you a spouse worthy of you... But I am already married, and here is my daughter."

"Married!" repeated the Count of Toulouse, drawing back.

With her hand, Valentine played with the blond hair of little Marie. The Count, stupefied, said nothing. There was a noise on the terrace. It was Saint-Maugan who had reached the window that opened by leaning on the walls like a drunken man. At the same time there was a grand concert of voices coming from the vestibule.

"What is that?" demanded the Count of Toulouse, who had instinctively put his hand on his sword.

"For you, My Lord, that's the signal of retreat," replied Valentine. "My father has returned to his house, and the hour of peril has passed for him... You don't need your sword; you are under my protection. Follow me."

She took his hand and guided him across the ruined corridor which led to the door at the edge of the water.

"Whatever happens," she said, opening the postern, "Valentine de Rohan will be forever grateful. Good-bye, My Lord!"

There were dull sounds in the countryside. Listening closely, it sounded like the regular marching of a squad of soldiers.

"Married!" repeated the Count of Toulouse, who passed the back of hand over his forehead. "You! Married! Valentine!"

Under the rays of the Moon, which were again shining, Mademoiselle de Rohan believed that she saw a tear roll slowly down the Count's cheek, while he, too, said his good-byes in a low and broken voice.

As she returned to the Salon, she saw a motionless shadow standing in front of the window.

"Morvan?" she exclaimed.

She couldn't see the terrible distress painted on Saint-Maugan's features. He didn't answer.

"Didn't you hear my father's arrival?" she continued.

"I was there," Saint-Morgan finally said. "I saw everything!"

IX. God and His Mother

Saint-Maugan's voice was so changed that Valentine's heart sank.

"If only you could see into the depth of my soul, Morvan!" she replied. "But in the Name of God, go away! I hear my father coming up the stairs!"

Saint-Maugan laughed senselessly.

"I also hear him very well," he said, moving his head as if to hear better. "He's coming upstairs... The sky is clear... We won't have to brave a tempest as your brother, César, had to."

'Why are you talking about my brother, Morvan?" Valentine, more frightened, asked.

"He's coming up!" repeated Saint-Morgan, who seemed to be counting the heavy steps of the old man. He's coming to curse you. Me, I'm leaving and you will never see me again!"

94

"My father!" exclaimed Valentine. "Oh! I, first of all, disobeyed him by loving you; then, in trying to save him... But you, Morvan, what have I done to you?"

Saint-Maugan went across the room toward the corridor to the west. Rohan had only a few more steps to climb. Reddish lights were already shining under the stairway door.

"I will get revenge on my master," said Saint-Morgan. "On my master who has taken my happiness from me!"

"On my honor and on my salvation!" exclaimed Valentine, who rushed toward him, "the Count of Toulouse has done no harm to you, and I am innocent!"

Saint-Morgan pushed her away, saying:

"I don't believe you, but I do pity you. You are going to be cruelly punished... May Heaven forgive you!"

The Salon was suddenly flooded with light. Both of the double doors to the stairwell had just been opened, and Rohan appeared on the threshold, followed by his servants carrying torches. He had a drawn sword in his hand. Master Alain Polduc was by his side. Behind him there were officers and servants, and tenants with their families crowded into the main stairwell.

They had been assembled for the Saint-Jean's Day bonfire, and the tables were laid out on the lawn around an enormous pyre next to which stood the Rohan Candle. Little girls were wearing their Sunday dresses and were holding big bouquets; boys were wearing ribbons. The evening was a beautiful one for drinking and for singing in the light of the Moon, and also for dancing on the fresh grass. But there was no one among Rohan's tenants who was thinking of the bonfire, or of the set tables. The same weight was weighing on every breast. They were breathing the air as if it were the wind of unhappiness.

Dame Michou Guitan painfully climbed the steps, leaning on her son, Josselin, who did not answer any of her questions. The good woman from time to time kissed the cross of her rosary and tried to overhear the words exchanged between Count Rohan and Master Alain Polduc.

"My God! Have mercy on us, My God!" she murmured. "The good Jouachin has seen the King's soldiers going across the forest…"

Valentine came to stand in front of her father, who, instead of greeting her as usual and drawing her to his heart, kept her at arms' length.

"Why would she have wanted to save the Governor?" he asked, speaking to Master Alain.

"Because Morvan de Saint-Maugan belongs to the Governor's household."

"How is that important?"

"Because Valentine de Rohan, your daughter, is the wife of Morvan de Saint-Maugan."

Valentine closed her eyes and crossed her hands over her heart.

"You are lying!" said the Count. "I trust my daughter!"

The trouble in his voice already belied his words. He looked at his drawn sword; then he threw it far away from him.

"Rohan will fall!" he murmured. "And Rohan will not be avenged!"

An infant's small cry came from the doorway where the cradle had been placed. Valentine rushed quickly in that direction. Master Alain began to laugh.

"You accused me of lying, my noble cousin," he said. "But I only wanted to show you the daughter of Saint-Maugan lying in the Rohan cradle."

He drew the Count toward the window. Josselin came toward him and seized his arm violently.

"Look at me closely, Master Alain," he pronounced in a low but distinct voice. "I swear to you before God that night that you will die by my hand."

There was tumult in the major stairwell; confused shouts came up from the vestibule. These repeated words could be heart from every direction:

"The King's Soldiers! The King's Soldiers!"

"My Lord!" shouted Francin, the huntsman, who burst into the salon through the door opening onto the terrace. "The courtyard is full of the King's soldiers!"

Josais, a tenant, making his way through the crowd, showed himself at that moment at the top of the stairway.

"The King's soldiers are entering through the breach!" he exclaimed.

The Count did not hear him; he was looking at the crib. The women were trembling and weeping. On a sign from Josselin, some twenty tenants and servants came to place themselves in the middle of the room.

"My Lord," asked a young boy, "should we take up weapons? These men here are ready, as I am, to defend you."

Rohan did not answer; he was looking at the crib where poor little Marie was moving about in fear.

"These things happen sometimes, when a race is condemned! Valentine, I told that man: '*You are lying!*' Valentine, if I lose you, I have nothing left in the world... Valentine! Valentine! Stand up and face that man and say to him with me: '*You are lying! You are lying!*' "

Valentine's mouth was half-open.

"She couldn't be any paler if she were dead!" exclaimed Dame Michou Guitan with anguish.

Valentine didn't have enough strength to say a word. Then she was seen to fall, kneeling in front of the crib.

"Forgive!" cried the crowd of tenants with one voice; "Forgive our dear young Mademoiselle!"

Rohan straightened up to his full height.

"Forgive?" he repeated. "Forgiveness is given to those who are guilty! But is Mademoiselle de Rohan guilty? Valentine! Valentine! My daughter!" he repeated tenderly. "Speak in your favor and defend yourself. You have only to say one word to refute the charge."

"Mercy, father!" stammered Valentine, overcome.

"Mercy?" the Count repeated. "Ah! We were a proud race," he said. "But God punishes pride!"

He walked with jerky footsteps to the ermine badge, from which he snatched the tag. His foot stood on the gold of the Gothic characters and he pronounced slowly:

"Here is where my two children have twice dishonored the name of my ancestors."

"Soldiers! Soldiers!" shouted Josselin Guitan, who was listening to the sounds from the outside.

The crosses of the muskets hit the solid oak of the outer door and voices could be heard shouting:

"Open, in the name of the King!"

No one budged. Master Alain Polduc's expression showed at the same time hope and concern.

"Since when are the doors to my house closed?" suddenly asked the old Count. "Open! Open! I want to show these people of France how we Bretons do justice at home!"

The door to the vestibule, that had been barricaded at the approach of the soldiers, was opened. During that time, Rohan climbed the three steps to the chair in the form of a throne that rested under the big curtain.

"Come forward, Valentine de Rohan," he said, "and answer your judge. You have disobeyed your father in marrying a traitorous Breton. Have you betrayed your father in working with the Count of Toulouse?"

"Only in order to save you, My Lord!" murmured Valentine, while kneeling.

Dame Michou Guitan passed in front of her and climbed up two steps of the throne.

"Rohan, you killed your son!" she said. "Save your daughter to console you in your exile."

The rattling of muskets was heard on the stairs.

"I no longer have a daughter," answered the old Count, "and I will know how to die well all alone."

Master Alain's expression lit up because the first soldier of the La Ferté Regiment now showed up on the threshold. The servants and the tenant farmers were ranged around the throne. That great family disaster, whose sinister denouement had taken place under their eyes, was a diversion from that other misfortune that came from the outside. It was known, however, that the King's soldiers carried proscription and ruin, but that implacable father was more terrible than even ruin and proscription.

"Take the child of that Frenchman and go,! Rohan said to Valentine, who was hugging his knees. "I am still master here for a few more minutes, and I am banishing you!"

Valentine obeyed. She went to find the infant, whom she, weeping, pressed to her heart.

"Mercy! Mercy!" the distraught crowd shouted one last time.

The officer who commanded the soldiers of the La Ferté regiment stepped forward, holding an open parchment in his hand.

"Count Rohan de Polduc, in the name of the King, you have twenty-four hours to leave the Province of Brittany and French soil."

There was great silence. Rohan stood up. He came down slowly the steps of his throne.

"A sovereign or an outlaw!" he murmured. "Perhaps one day, the accursed Bourbon will learn how slippery the slope is from the throne to exile! Good-bye, my friends!" he said, interrupting himself and extending his hand toward his servants. "Rohan would be uncomfortable in retirement if France were to allow him to live just as a gentleman. An outlaw or a sovereign, there is no middle ground. Rohan should have remembered that."

He walked toward the door of the grand staircase. The servants and the tenants moved to follow him. Only Dame Michou Guitan and her son, Josselin, hesitated to move away from Valentine, who remained as if petrified at the foot of the throne. Master Alain softly approached the officer.

"You will take care, please, to see that nothing is moved, or most of all, damaged, in this manor," he said. "The King's soldiers are respectable people, but they sometimes give way to certain excesses which lead to notable damages."

"But this house no longer has an owner," the officer objected.

Alain Polduc winked and answered:

"My young conqueror, lodgings never lack masters. Over there, in your Court of Versailles, when the King dies, they shout: *Long live the King!* There will soon be here a gentleman wearing honestly the name Rohan-Polduc who will invite you to come enjoy the wines from his cellar."

He cast her out, thought Dame Michou Guitan, *but he forgot to curse her!*

The old Count stopped not far from the doorway.

"Mademoiselle de Rohan," he said in a voice that vibrated like a hunting horn. "I am leaving the house of my ancestors through this door. Leave through that other one so that we will not meet each other, and may you be cursed!"

Dame Michou, who was trembling convulsively, leaned against the arm of her son. The servants of the manor bowed. The soldiers of La Ferté themselves made a movement at the last words of the pitiless old man:

May you be cursed!

Everyone could hear Valentine respond in her sweet voice, broken by tears:

"Bless you, father!"

She left alone, weeping, carrying her daughter in her arms, beautiful as a Madonna. She went down the terrace steps, while Rohan, walking with a solemn step, his head held high, went across the great vestibule in the middle of his respectful vassals. Valentine stopped at the moats and let herself fall without strength into the wet grass. Above her, the Moon lit the granite balcony where the white scarf still floated.

"Child," she said, with heartbreaking sobs, "your father is abandoning you; your grandfather, from the depth of his ruin, pushes you away and curses you! Child, poor child, only God remains for you!"

She placed a long kiss on little Marie's forehead, then she quickly stood up. "God!" she said, lifting her beautiful eyes toward Heaven. "...and His Mother!"

PART ONE: THE WITCH

I. The Pont Joli

Fifteen years had gone by. Saint-Denis[39] had opened its vaults to the royal coffin of Louis XIV. An infant Louis XV played on the throne of his grandfather. Philippe d'Orléans held the Regency. The Bretons respected the memory of Louis XIV; they loved young King Louis XV, a beautiful child that vice was so soon going to spoil. But they abhorred Philippe d'Orléans,[40] who felt the same toward them with all his heart. He had usurped the Regency with contempt for the testament of the late King. The Duke of Maine, dispossessed, shouted vengeance everywhere, and the Duchess, his wife, rose at four o'clock in the morning to have time to conspire before lunch. The head of the police held that couple, who were worthy of the *Fronde*[41] at the end of a tight leash. Their men were given to gossip, thoughtless, vain, open to intrigue, and reported constantly to the Regent. Despite his prudent conduct, the Count of Toulouse participated in his brother's disgrace.

---

[39] The Kings of France were buried at Saint Denis Cathedral near Paris. During the French Revolution, many of the graves were ransacked and their contents were either mixed or destroyed.

[40] Philippe II, Duke of Orléans (1674-1723), served as Regent from 1715 to 1723. His father was Louis XIV's younger brother, Philippe I, also Duke of Orléans. He died at Versailles in 1723.

[41] A series of internecine French civil wars (1648-1653), which arguably strengthened the Monarchy, but weakened the economy of the country.

Dubois,[42] not daring to take the position of Governorship away from him, had him recalled to Paris by a pretext to put in his place Marshal de Montesquiou[43] with the new title *New Commandant for the King.*

That Marshal was as insolent as an executioner's valet. He began by rubbing the Britons the wrong way and their anger knew no bounds. War began between Brittany and the Regent of France, first an open war with scythes and muskets; then, a guerilla war using pamphlets and spies, but always a war to the death!

The ancient ermine banners were seen raised in bishops' territories; rusty swords were taken out of their sheaths, and in an instant, the happy little suppers of the Regent became sad because of their fear of those people with the skin of old hags and wooden shoes filled with straw. The *Companions of the Silence,* as those of Tréguier were called, commanded by

---

[42] Guillaume Dubois (1656-1723), Cardinal and statesman. When the Duc d'Orléans became Regent in 1715, Dubois, who had for some years acted as his secretary, was made councilor of state, and the chief power passed gradually into his hands.

[43] Pierre de Montesquiou, Comte d'Artagnan and later Comte de Montesquiou (1640 -1725) was a French soldier and Marshal of France. A scion of the famous French Montesquiou family, he was the fourth son of Henri I de Montesquiou, seigneur d'Artagnan by his wife. He was also the cousin of Charles de Batz de Castelmore, to whom he lent one of his titles, comte d'Artagnan, on whom the hero of Alexandre Dumas' *Three Musketeers* was based. Montesquiou served for twenty-three years as a musketeer before being made brigadier in 1688, maréchal de camp in 1691, lieutenant général in 1696 and Maréchal de France in 1709 as a reward for his distinguished conduct at the Battle of Malplaquet. He was Governor of Brittany from 1716 à 1720.

Bonamour,[44] the *Brûleurs*, gathered around Vannes, the "Kights of the Good Lord," whose chief, nickamed *Master Pierre,* was in reality the Viscount de Kercaër, and finally the Wolves of the Forest of Rennes, led by their mysterious chief, whom some said was a young woman more beautiful than the day while others said he was a miserable Cobbler from the Sangle, cowardly and cruel as a tiger-cat.

However that may be, those combined associations formed a more and more formidale knot; almost all of the Breton nobility had *gone into the forest* as it was then called in the conspirators' slang. That meant taking up arms against the Court. The mad conspiracy of Cellamare[45] was the pretext. The famous *armada* promised by Alberoni[46] never materialized. They planned on "freeing" Louis XV, but at the bottom of it was hatred against the House of Orléans and the Britons' passion for independence. [47]

---

[44] Louis Germain de Talhouët de Bonamour (1686-1734), compromised in the Cellamare conspiracy (see below) in 1718, refugee in Spain, brigadier of the armies of the King of Spain, then captain of the Walloon Guards.

[45] Conspiracy against Philippe d'Orléans, concocted in Spain. It was the brainchild of the Spanish Ambassador Antonio del Giudice, Prince of Cellamare, and included the Duc of Maine, his wife, Anne Louise Bénédicte de Bourbon, Duke of Richelieu, and others. However, the correspondence between the Duchess of Maine and Spanish Prime Minster Giulio Alberoni was intercepted; on 9 December 1718, Cellamare was arrested and sent back to Spain; Alberoni was arrested on 5 December 1718 at Poitiers. The Duchess was exiled to Dijon while her husband was imprisoned at Doullens in Picardy. The Duke of Richelieu was imprisoned in the Bastille. The conspirators were pardoned by 1720 and allowed to return to their residence.

[46] Spanish Prime Minister (1674-1723).

[47] Féval could have mentioned the subsequent Pontcallec conspiracy which arose between 1718 and 1720. Led by Clément-

At the beginning of the year 1720, before the Chamber of the King, or Prevotal Court,[48] in Nantes, were brought ten Breton gentlemen accused of the crime of *lèse majesté;* among them was the old Count of Rohan-Polduc. He named himself the Eldest of he House of Rohan, Military commander, and Heir to the crown of Brittany. Of those ten, only Rohan was a French prisoner. Four others came the day they were summoned. They had been solemny promised that their life would be spared. They were: MM. du Couëdic, de Pontcallec, de Mont-Louis and de Talhouët. Yet old Rohan-Polduc, held prisoner in the cells of the Lebât Tower at Rennes, was released, it is not known why, the very night that he was supposed to be transferred to Nantes.

Disregarding the Regent's sworn promise, the four gentlemen were instead condemned to capital punishment and were executed in front of the crowd at Nantes. The people made relics of their clothing and noble ladies dipped the embroidery of their handerchiefs into the blood that had fallen under the scaffold. From Saint-Pol-de-Léon right to the Loire, from Belle-Isle-en-Mer to Mont Saint-Michel, a shout of reprobation rose against Montesquiou, the instigator of that judicial murder.

The conspiracies had failed; four thousand French soldiers[49] covered Brittany, and yet, the Regent's Ministers were afraid. Dubois called on the Count of Toulouse, who had returned to his lands, and begged him to please lend the

---

Chrysogone de Guer Malestroit, Marquis de Pontcallec (1679-1720) and a faction of the Breton nobility, it sought to overthrow the Regent in favor of Philip V of Spain. Poorly organized, it failed, and four of its leaders were beheaded in Nantes. Worthy of note, on 15 August, a group of peasants led by Rohan de Polduc forced a group of French soldiers sent to enforce tax collection to retreat.

[48] French Summary Court from which there is no appeal.

[49] In actuality 15,000.

Crown the benefit of his popularity to appease the rage which had overcome the wild beasts of the Breton forest.

So our story beins again in the month of May in the year 1720, a half-league from the old Rohan manor house, which had had a change of master. The road, leading from Saint-Aubin-du-Charnier to the chateau of Steward Feydeau de Brou, passed by the bottom of a ravine serving as a bed for a little nameless stream. There was a place there where the ravine was as wide as the road joined to the width of the stream; the rock seemed bare on both sides, and formed a base of black granite on two parrallell mounds that seemed like a wall sculpted by the hand of man. Above the rock, forty feet from the ground, the banks were still visible and were joined together by throwing an oak tree trunk from one to the other. That was a big, beautiful tree which shook a little when two travelers went across the ravine at the same time, but in reality could have supported the weight of ten men without breaking. It had been laid on its side; most of its roots were still in the earth, and the valiant oak, while serving as a bridge, grew gently and covered itself each year with new leaves.

Things had been like that for some time and the old men who had always seen it hanging there across that empty ravine, said that the oak tree from the Fosse-aux-Loups had increased half of its size during their lifetime. They had pruned its branches and smoothed out the knots from its top part; from above, it presented the aspect of a path bordered with bushes; from below, it was a green arch launched from one hill to the other. That oak tree from the Fosse-aux-Loups was also called the Pont Joli, by way of that green valley of the Vestre, which we have already seen from the window of the old manor house. Beyond the bridge, the road made a detour and began to climb the southern ramp of the ravine. The road, not being able to be be climbed on foot, made a circular arch and turned a hundred and fifty feet from there, toward the summit of the hill.

The opposite ramp had a margin of little heather bushes in bloom, beyond which stretched an ampitheater of stunted pine trees and rare plants, among which there were birds on the silver throne. The land between the main road and the Pont Joli was the most picturesque and the wildest section of the Forest of Rennes. On the right, when looking toward the bridge, there was a ruined windmill, the white roof of which seemed to come straight out of the underbrush. A half dozen thin silver birch trees, which had managed to pierce the rocky earth, did not hide the view of the two hills, opening up like a fan at fifty feet of the narrow pass, to show a good league of forest, an immense ocean of green.

The Fosse-aux Loups, accurately named, which had given its name to the oak tree, could not be seen from there. It hid its black shadows behind the opposite hill. To the left of the bridge, the bare rock rose in terraces right up to the thicket. Some poor tufts of genets could hardly be seen coming up from between the stones. But, as if the vegetation, vanquished, had wanted to take its revenge, the thicket which was an ancient forest of chestnut and oak trees neglected for the last thirty years, offered a mass of follage, opulent and impenetrable to the naked eye. The last trees passed behind the rocks, reaching the spot where the ramp of the hill became gentler and rejoined the road at the border of the Vesvre valley. Across the silver birch trees, on the right, could be seen the weather vanes of the Feydeau chateau, lost in the middle of its magnificent forest. On the left, over the tops of the chestnut trees and the oaks that descended the mountain, the little pointed turets of the Rohan Manor were squezzed together and reached for the clouds.

It was about ten o'clock in the morning. The Breton springtime is more deceptive than the Parisian spring. The sun showed itself at intervalls in the middle of clouds pushed by the northwest wind, and everywhere it had not penetrated, traces of white ice could still be seen. But this May frost, mortal to more civilized flowers, had no effect on the wild flowers. Under the trembling crystal, the aubepine was smiling. The ajone and the genets fearlessly opened their gold-like casks; the verveine showed its purple tufts; and the pentecôte, that gentle queen of the amoricans plains, filled with carmine petals, leaned its soft stalk.

There was no one on the main road, no one in the depths of the revine, nor in the vallely, as far as the eye could see. Nothing moved on that bizarre plateau which formed the border of the Pont Joli. No sound coming from man was heard and that will seem very understandable when one learns that the closest human habitation was as far away as a quarter of a league as the crow flies. The traveler wandering in that solitude, after having looked in all directions, was certainly desperate to find someone from whom to ask his way. Far away, very far away, beyond the clumps of green trees that grew along the shoulder of the opposite hill, the north-west wind carried a soft and almost indistinct song. Shortly afterward a dull noise was heard in the Vesvre Valley. It was a heavy, noisy horse, a drawn coach making its painful way along the rocky road.

A fawn-colored hulk, which until then had remained immobile, blending with the tons of grayish- brown rock to the left of the Pont Joli, made a movement as if to lean over the road. At the same time, the bushes to the right of the bridge moved, revealing the presence of another human being hidden in their depths.

"Can you hear?" asked a hoarse voice from under the bushes.

"Yes, I can," answered the fawn-colored hulk cautiously.

That hulkish mass was a man, even though he didn't seem like one. Looking more closely, one saw two spindly, bony legs bringing their big feet out of the skin of a nanny goat. The man wore a hood, to which was attached a square piece of wolf to hide his face.

A ray of sunshine that slid between two clouds shone on the black barrel of a musket, creating a spark in the middle of the bushes. The little song seemed to be coming from the other side of the ravine, where there could already hear the fresh voice of a little girl.

"Casnm you see her from where you are, Josille?" asked the voice from the bushes.

"Who?" asked the man in the nanny goat skin.

"The little demoiselle Celeste?"

"Our Cinderella?" replied Josille, shrugging. "I don't care about her."

At the bend in the road finally appeared a carriage painfully drawn by four horses. It was a heavy vehicle, narrow below, large at the top, that went bumping along, squeeking on its plaintive axles. The man in the nanny goat skin armed his musket. Also could be heard from the depths of the bushes the dry, double noise of a gun being lifted and cocked. There was silence. The carriage advanced toward the Pont Joli. Josille stretched out his entire length on the rock, letting nothing be seen except his masked head and the end of his musket. He supported his gun against the edge of the rock and began to aim carefully.

"Who is there in the carriage?" asked his mysterious companion, who couldn't yet see because of the branches.

"'Quiet!" Josille answered. "There are two young ladies on one side, and on the other Monsieur Feydeau de Brou, the Steward, and Monsieur Alain de Rohan-Polduc, the Seneschal."

"That's good! We can get them both at the same time!"

Josille didn't ask for anything better. The barrrel of his musket followed the carriage. But his finger on the trigger didn't move.

"Well, what are you waiting for?" asked the voice from the bushes, trembling with impatience."

"Damn!" Josille replied with annoyance, "the French prey is at the end of my sight, but there is over there, at the edge of the water, behind the willow trees, right in front of the carriage, a white dress..."

Before he had finished, the head of a man wearing a fur mask just like his own surged out of the bushes, followed by a body covered with a nanny goat skin which seemed the twin sister of his own attire.

108

"Get down, Vincent! Get down!" Josillle said very low. "They're going to see you!"

Vincent glanced rapidly toward the bridge.

"I certainly recognized her voice!" he said to himself. "That's the poor little demoiselle Celeste. Don't fire, Jossille, and get over here."

Josillle obeyed and went around the roots of the big oak tree and into the brush. The carriage had just come under the arch of the leaves. The four persons that it contained could be heard laughing and chatting. Josille and Vincent, side by side, put their muskets back in play.

"Which one will you take?" asked Josille.

"I will take Polduc."

"Feydeau is mine, then!"

A white dress was no longer there to block their sights, and no poacher in all of the Forest of Rennes could brag of being a better shot than Josille or Vincent. The latter aimed at Polduc's head; Josille aimed at the Steward's belly. These two eminent personages were separed from death by only a hair's breath.

"We're going to fire at the same time on the count of three... Do you agree?"

"I do!"

"One!"´counted Vincent, "two..."

They turned around at the same time, stifling in their throat a cry of fear. A hand had just been placed on Josille's left shoulder, another on Vincent's right shoulder. Behind them stood a tall man wearing, like them, a nanny goat's skin uniform and a mask made of wolf fur.

"Not this time," the newcomer said, lifting both of them with the strength of his arms.

"Mordienne!" said Josille angrily. "I had mine!"

Vincent had turned to be face to face with the man.

"Why are you meddling in this?" he asked between his teeth and in a menacing tone.

"Going about my business," the unknown man replied coldly.

"Who are you?"

"A former acquaintance."

Josille and Vincent looked at each other. The carriage was beginning to climb the mountain and would soon be hidden behind the trees. At the bottom of the ravine, among the willow trees, the white dress had disappeared, but at intervals, carrried by the wind's caprice, the echoes of the her song could still be heard.

"Alain Polduc is the reason that my two children lied in the graveyard," murmured Josille, convusivley grasping the barrel of his musket.

"I know that," said the unknown man.

"Alain Polduc and Feydeau, his father-in-law," said Vincent in a voice stifled by rage, "sold the very mattress of my poor, dying mother!"

"I know that, too," repeated the unknown man, who remained impassive. He added in a tone of bitter joking: "Feydeau owns half of the countryside between Rennes and Fougères; and Polduc is Count of Rohan and the King's Seneschal for the province of Brittany!"

"Is that the reason why you stopped us from killing them?"

"No."

"Then, why

The newlcomer held out his hand toward the high pitched roof of the windmill in the distance. Through the fissures of the cracked roof, small spirals of smoke were escaping.

"Because there is someone there," he answered, "that would have heard your musket shots."

"Who is that?"

"The Witch."

"Oh!" said Josille, without hiding his fright. "Our score would have soon been settled."

Vincent shook his head with a disbelieving look.

"But the Witch lives down on the moor," he muttered.

"No. The Witch is here!" pronounced the unknown man, whose extended hand still pointed toward the windmill.

Josille shivered under his nanny goat skin and Vincent, too, trembled.

"Besides," continued the unknown man calmly, "those people there, the Seneschal and the Steward, must still stay alive. It's not the time to be finished with them."

"Are you the one who will decide when the hour will come?" asked Vincent mockingly.

"No, not me, but the woman whom I serve."

"Then, my friend, you must serve a very great lady!"

The unknown man took off his fur mask and answered:

"I serve the She-Wolf."

Under the mask was a handsome man whose head was crowned with black, curly hair. Vincent and Josille stepped back in awe, uttering the name of Josselin Guitan.

II. Triumfemina

There was then, in the region of Rennes, three women who occupied a very high position, and attracted much public curiosity. These three women will play such important roles in our story that we must introduce them to our readers.

The position of each was very different. The first led at Rennes the veritable life of a Princess. Noble youths paid court to her. She was the queen of the festivites of the new Marshal, and, with a sign of her beautiful hand, they said that the Royal Steward had thrown- the rich contents of his strongbox out the window. That one was the Countess Isaure of Porhöet.

The heroic house of Porhöet had not existed for centuries; everyone knew that; but no one had thought of checking the genealogy of Countess Isaure. She threw away gold with both hands. She was marvelously beautiful and all of Rennes, panic-striken by the magnetic regard of her large black eyes, worshipped her as if she were an idol.

The second woman was known under the nickname of the Witch. Everyone who was a woodcutter, a coalman, or a Cobbler in the Forest of Rennes trembled at her name. No one would have been able to say if she was beautiful or ugly, young or old, because she always wore one of those homespun hoods that peasant folks of Northern Brittany wore in rainy weather. Some people had seen her toward dusk at the doorway of an abandoned hut at the depth of the Sangle. Others said that she lived in a shepherd's hut on the moor at Saint-Aubin-du-Cormier. A pale face, almost invisible in the shadow created by a black hood, such was her vague portrait made by those who claimed to have spoken to her. She had delivered oracles that everyone knew. She had predicted the death of the four unfortunate Breton gentlemen at Nantes, and even on the scaffold, the leader of the rebellion, the Marquis of Pontcallec, had murmured, according to common belief: *"The Miller Woman had truly preducted it."*

The Miller Woman was one of the euphemistic sobriquets given to that fearsome prophet by the good people. What's more, that sobriquet had its reason. The Witch often chose as a retreat one of those abandoned windmills so common on the Breton moors. She lived alone. Those bizarre and almost supernatural beings never have a family. However, for a month, there had been a new story about her circulating throughout the countryside. Sheep shearers, from the other side of Saint-Aubin, had seen, in the rubble of a ruined farm dating back to the tobacco revolt, some pine resin fire alight past midnight. They were careful not to approach too closely, but from a distance, running fast, they had spotted two silhouettes in front of that fire: the Miller Woman, with her big hood, and an old man whose face disappeared among the ruffled tufts of his white hair.

What was to be believed? The next day, there was not a soul living in that ruined farm. Those people who run across the moor after midnight are most often drunk and don't have a clear mind. However that may be, the Witch was, for the poor country people of the forest, what Countess Isaure was for the noble youth of the Breton capital: the subject of evey conversation.

The She-Wolf, the third person of our mysterious female trinity, had this advantage over Countess Isaure and the Witch, that she occupied the attention of both country people and city gentlemen. The She-Wolf was spoken about in the forest, which was her true domain, her camp, her place of power, but she was also discussed in the Breton Parl;iament, and the ears of even the French Regent had heard her name mentioned more than once.

The She-Wolf was powerful. She reigned over *The Wolves,* a vast association whose primitive neucleus had been formed by the former vassals of Rohan and which controlled at present the entire forest and a great part of the countryside of Rennes, on both sides of the Vilaine. Some years later, when Monsieur Bechamel, of gastronomic memory, replaced Steward Feydeau, the Cobblers, the coal mercants, the woodcutters, again took on their wolf mask and, under the leadership of the man who called himself the White Wolf (his real name was Pelo Rohan of the town of Bouëxis-en-Forêt) got away in one fell swoop with five carts filled with three pounds of ecus stolen from the new Steward.[50]

The She-Wolf had, therefore, an army, and it could almost be said that the fate of the civil war was in her hand. What legends recounted about her, not only in the poor thatched cottages of the moor or the forest, but even in the brillant salons of the ladies of the Breton Court, was beyond all belief. Nothing positive was said, however. They had tried to find out, following the eternal custom, the unknown truth about her, but failing, they had replaced it by tall tales made up at one's pleasure. They said the She-Wolf was a man disguised as a woman, a big, wicked Cobbler thirsty for massacres or pillages; or perhaps, a gentleman instead, because a simple peasant could never have acquired such absolute authority over those like him; or perhaps, a real

---

[50] See *The White Wolf.*

woman, but an old surly and bearded one, who roasted the feet of the King's soldiers while smoking her pipe; or perhaps, a beautiful, proud and sad creature like Milton's archangel, whose face radiated a somber light in the middle of an endless night.

There was in the forest a deep underground area hollowed out by the Druids during the time of their supreme fight against the triumphant Christians. These caverns had been used to shelter revolts from the time of the League by the fearless men holding on to the idea of an independent Brittany united around Rollan-Pied-de-Fer at the beginning of the reign of Louis XIV.[51] The King's men had made many attempt to find the entry to those grottoes, which had always escaped their search. Tradition maintained that the principal opening was not far from the Fosse-aux-Loups. Five hundred feet around the terrain had been sounded, but only a half-dozen fox burrows were found.

Now, just imagine an immense underground gallery, held up on columns of porphyre or jasper, crystal that hangs on arches and throw their bizarre garlands along the walls cut out of the rock. Imagine torches that are shining as far as the eye can see, perspectives that are dying in the distance in a mysterious half-day; a great murmur of human voices, a crowd moving about like a sea, and what a crowd! Men, masked with wolf fur hiding their features, dressed as savage beasts! Over there, on a brilliantly lit platform, is a golden throne; and on that throne sits a woman, radiant with youth and beauty, a crown on her forehead, a bare sword in her hand

---

[51] *Rollan Pied-de-Fer* (Ironfoot Rollan) was Paul Féval's second published work, a short novel serialized in 1842 about the eponymous hero who fights for the independence of Brittany and to avenge the death of his nursing brother Julien d'Avaugour during the early days of the reign of Louis XIV. As he did with the saga of the *Black Coats*, Féval retroactively incorporates several earlier Breton novels into a single continuity.

in lieu of a scepter, her shoulders covered with a long and magnificent ermine cloak, straight from the imagination of some Breton poet. The crowd that filled those fantastic caverns was the countless army of the Wolves. The woman in the ermine cloak was the She-Wolf!

From the point of view of a war between Brittany and France, the position of the She-Wolf was well known: she naturally made common cause with the rebels. The Witch, on the other hand, was suspected of espionage to the profit of the French King. And Countess Isaure, courted equally by both the servants of France and the discontented gentlemen og Brittany, remained steadfastly outside and above the political sphere.

There was assuredly no probable point of contact between these three woman: Countess Isaure, the She-Wolf, and the Witch. Yet, some shadowly link united them in public opinion. Society sometimes has that inexplicable and accurate premonition. Many people, without knowing why, had the notion that those three women maintained some hidden rapport; that they saw each other, although no one would have been able to say where; that they had a common interest, but no one would have been able to say which one; and that the power each one held derived from the mystery of that strange association. We will certainly see if society was mistaken, and we will do whatever is possible to surprise them together some day, or rather some moonless night, in the place chosen for their secret conferences.

Josselin Guitan was now a handsome man of thirty-five or thirty-six with a calm, open and resolute face. He no longer took out his hunting knife, filed as sharp as a razor, for just any reason. Instead, sharper than ever, it hung on the reverse side of his goat skin jacket.

Josille, also known as Josais or Joso, because all three names were used at the borders of the Vilaine, was a former Rohan farmer that we have previously seen at the manor house. When Vincent, the third wolf, took off his skin mask, to imitate his companions, he revealed the face of a young man, hardly twenty years-old, whose red fuzzy hair reached the edge of his forehead, falling on his thick eyebrows.

"May God bless you, Master Josselin!" Josille was the first to say. "You must come from far away, because we haven't seen you in a long time."

"I do come from far away... You, Vincent, my friend, little Celeste meets you too often across her path. You frighten her. Consider yourself as warned!"

"The road is free," murmured the young man. "Was it the young lady who complained about me?"

"Going down over there, under the bridge, lookat yourself in the stream, friend Vincent, and you will see that you shouldn't clutter up the path of young girls."

Josille began to laugh and Vincent became very pale.

"Was it the She-Wolf who ordered you to speak to me this way?" he asked, trying to smile.

"Perhaps."

"They said that the She-Wolf was dead," murmured again Vincent, who looked down in spite of himself.

"When the She-Wolf dies," Josselin Guitan pronounced with emphasis, "her last breath will shake the forest!"

"If she isn't dead, where is she hiding?"

Josselin was silent. He glanced toward the windmill where the roof was no longer letting out any smoke.

If the Witch is there, as I've been told, he thought, *and if she is a real witch, I'll know more about it shortly.*

"Vincent, my boy," he continued aloud, "the She-Wolf makes her retreat wherever she chooses and she doesn't have to give an account to anyone. The proof that she is not dead is that the Fosse-aux-Loups is full, and the Lebât jail is empty... The proof that she is not dead is that, right now, as you and I are talking, they are distibuting, just as in the good old days, tobacco and brandy."

"Tobacco!" exclaimed Josille avidly. "Tobacco and brandy!"

"Quiet!" said Vincent, who placed his ear to the ground.

"I have heard walking for the past five minutes," said Josselin, shrugging. "Go back to your holes, Wolves, if you want to have something to put in your pipes and to fill your goblets!"

Josille had already turned around to reach the chestnut trees and go down into the valley.

"Aren't you coming with us, Master Josselin?" Vincent asked suspiciously

"No, I'm staying here."

Vincent approached him.

"You are here for the Witch, aren't you?" he asked.

"What does it matter?"

"After the She-Wolf, it is my father who commands down here, and my father doesn't like you, Master Josselin."

"That's because the handsome Cobbler has his own reasons for that, my boy."

"The Witch has sold out to the French."

"So they say."

"You, who know everything, Master Josselin, what face does she hide behind her mask?"

"In my opinion, that of a tigress!"

Vincent gave him with a defiant and hate-filled look.

Suddenly, a trembling voice was heard from the direction where Josille had just disappeared, behind the forest of chestnut trees. One might have almost guessed that the song belonged to a coward who was singing to hide his fright. The song was:

> *The Baker Moman has money*
> *That she didn't earn*
> *She has it; I saw it*
> *Just as I saw*
> *The Baker Woman*

Josselin and Vincent quickly reattached their masks. Almost at the same time, the song ended with a long cry of distress. Evidently, the singer had encountered Josille. The view of the nanny goat skin and the wolf mask had pushed his song down his throat.

"Good bye, friend Vincent," Josselin, always calm and pleasant, said at that moment. "When the handsome Cobbler wishes to talk to me, let him bring you with him. I will try to be strong enough for the two of you."

He turned around and started toward the windmill.

As Vincent moved off to take the road followed by Josille, the chestnut tree branches moved and a poor, pale boy fell head-first onto the rocky platform. For a head dress, he wore a cotton cap. His attire consisted of white breeches, and white stockings, covered by a long camisole of the same color. His physionomy, at that moment, when terror controlled him, could hardly be judged, but his white-as-snow costume showed hardly gracious shapes, and the strands of light yellow that escaped from his cap surrounded a comic face that certainly would not have attracted a baker woman and her money.

"I saw the Devil!" he shouted, running straight ahead of him blindly. "A hairy face; I didn't notice the horns! Aie! Aie!" he interrupted himself with the double cry of a man who is being choked.

He had just collided with Vincent, who had roughly pushed him away. That made two devils he'd just met! Keeping the speed he had, the poor wretch continued his run across the rock, and, without Josselin Guitan, whose kindly hand stopped him at the edge of the ravine, he would have fallen, head first, under the arch of the Point Joli.

"Mercy!" he said upon seeing a third wolf's head. "A third Devil! Ah! Magloire! Poor Magloire!" and he fell exhausted on the grass, his forehead, between his hands, bathed with cold sweat.

Meanwhile, Vincent had rejoined his comrade Josille in the bushes.

Josselin Guitan had entered the massive bushes that surrounded the ruins of the old windmill. The carriage had not been in sight for a long time. A deep silence reigned on the surrouding area. Magloire stayed with his face against the ground, holding his breath, listening with all the strength of his ears. After three or four minutes, he began, in such a sweet and lamentable voice that even a heart of stone would have been touched by his words:

"Gentlemen, dear friends, I beg you to take pity on me. I have no malicious intentions against you, and if it pleases you to visit my pockets, I swear I will not give you any resistance."

He stopped talking to wait for the effect of this straightforward discourse. There was no response. However, he had seen three men: one in the thicket, one in front of the rock (who had given him a rough shove), and a third one who had seized his arm not far from the bridge. That was nice. But why hadn't he heard them move? Why did they not speak? Magloire asked himself these questions, but he didn't dare to take away his hands that were glued like a bandana over his eyes. Perhaps the three scoundrels were still surrounding him and spying on his first movement waiting to slay him?

Magloire was a young boy, a baker, located rue Vasselot in Rennes, and God knows that in the back streets of Rennes, they told terrible stories about the Wolves that walked on two legs in the forest.

"Gentlemen, my good masters," he continued with growing humility and trembling a little more. "I want you to consider me as the most submissive among your servants. If you need a valet, I may be the man for you... But I ask you, don't let me languish, and tell me at what price you will let me live."

There was still no respose. That was terrible! Magloire's teeth were chattering. Something told him that the three scoundrels had all drawn their swords and were leaning their terrible faces over his shoulders, which were trembling convulsively. He committed his soul to God, feeling in advance the sensation that three cold blades entering his flesh would produce.

119

"Ah! Sidonie! Sidonie!" he murmured. "At that supreme moment, your Magloire loves you passionately, but he would gladly give you to just anybody to get out of this predicament!"

That invocation should have moved the god who presides over faithful lovers. If poor Magloire had thought to lift his fingers cautiously and to look furtively around, he would have seen that there were no big scoundrels moving around him. There was only the head of a naïve and smiling young girl showing herself among the branches of the Pont Joli.

The young girl had not yet seen Magloire; her big blue eyes were fixed on the path that ran along the water in the valley. There was there, along the stream, a nice-looking young boy, dressed poorly, but in the fashion of a gentleman. His hat, which dated from the time of the late King, was atop the fullest mop of hair in the world. He wore his worn doublet with charming grace and he went alone, sometimes running as fast as his legs would carry him, sometimes beating the bushes like a handsome young greyhound on his first hunt.

The little girl was wearing a white dress and the straw hat of the forest peasants. She wore little wooden clogs, like Cinderella's slippers, on her small feet. In her hand, she was carrying a big bouquet of pentecôte flowers. One could see that, when looking at the boy beating the bushes, she said to herself:

"He's looking for me…"

And her cheeks became as red as a cherry, and her heart beat very quickly under the chaste corsage of her white dress; her pretty, half-opened mouth stammered, in spite of herself, the name of Raoul!

Just as Raoul passed under the arch of the greenery, he accidently lifted his head.

"Celeste!" he murmured, putting his hands to his lips.

The young girl fled across the bridge and ran to hide in the brush on the opposite hill. But, before fleeing, she had made divided her big bouquet into tow parts; one of those went between the branches of the Pont Joli and fell at Raoul's feet.

III. The Short Straw

Magloire still had his face on the ground; he saw nothing of all that, neither the handsome young boy, nor the delightful little girl, nor the bouquet of pentecôte flowers split into two parts. Here is, however, what the god of faithful lovers did for Magloire: fright caused him to fall asleep!

When he awoke, he rubbed his eyes and looked around. The sun was lighting up the countryside. The breeze gently shook the top of the trees. Magoire felt a strange feeling inside himself; it was like the fatigue left after a nightmare.

"Ah, well!" he said to himself. "Let's think back a little. My noble friend, Master Raoul, left me here, in the Vesvre Valley, to run after this nymph in wooden shoes. Who should have such tastes! I walked through a thicket black as ink, and I went to sleep in this place, where I dreamed that three Wolves wanted to kill me…"

He looked around him worriedly.

"But what if it wasn't a dream?" he continued.

And, in fact, some of the objects surrounding him gave weight to his recollection. He shivered.

"Let's think of Sidonie," he murmured. "This solitude is picturesque and lends itself to sentimental thoughts…"

His voice took on an unusual note of tenderness while he continued:

"What a nice lunch someone could have here on the grass! A little cold meat, a quart of black pudding, just a little something! My stomach is empty, but my heart is full of Sidonie!"

He stood up and struck a noble pose:

"Echoes of this deserted place!" he shouted, throwing his head back proudly: "I am telling you my dearest secret… I am Sidonie's lover!"

He had taken off his cotton hat, and the breeze played with his tow hair. His right hand was on his heart, while his left executed different gestures which all came out reluctantly.

The echoes from thoses deserted places retained the name Sidonie, and Magloire went on, carried away by his passion:

"She is as beautiful as Love itself, and not the slightest word can be said against her behavior! Economical and as hard-working as an ant, not greedy, not a drinker, an angel of divinity! My attraction for her draws me out of my my native city, and my profession, by which I live; I am looking for a fortune in order to be worthy of her hand. I go through dark forests; I stop in strange and wild places; I endure hunger and thirst without complaining, having no other recreation but to carve her name with mine in a heart on the barks of trees."

Magloire yawned and changed tone.

"Ah! Well!", he said, "it's not worth the trouble to talk for two when one is always alone! Where has my friend, the gentleman, gone?"

He leaned over the ramp and let out a cry.

"Raoul! Monsieur Raoul!" he called out.

But Raoul didn't hear. He was climbing like a squirrel along the ledge and didn't stop except to throw kisses toward the chestnut forest. Magloire looked in that direction and saw a white form disappearing behind the leaves.

"Good! Good!" he murmured with disdain, "the little lady in wooden clogs! Me, I can't understand how anyone could run after a country girl in that way."

"Did you call me?" asked Raoul, showing his face drenched with sweat out of the bushes. "Did she pass by here?"

"No," answered Magloire with bad humor.

Raoul jumped down on the mound. His very young face, with delicate and proud traits, was on fire; his magnificent blond hair fell spread out on the worn material of his doublet; his out-of-style hat had almost no shape any longer; his shoes were so covered with dust that it would have been hard to tell their color.

Magloire looked at him with disdain, but, in truth, he was wrong. Despite his shabby get-up, Master Raoul, with his slender and well-formed physique, his gracious presence, his strong, and, at the same time sensitive, face, shining with juvenile gaiety pierced with a small amount of reflexion, was certainly the most charming cavalier that could be seen.

"She was there a while ago," he said, pointing to the trees. "I'm sure of it!"

"Word of honor!" Magloire replied sternly. "You are starting to worry me."

Raoul wiped his forehead and let out a great sigh.

"I believe I see her everywhere," he said. "It's true; it's driving me mad!"

"That's been so for a long time," Magloire interrupted.

Raoul listened to the faint noises that came from the thicket. He hesitated an instant between wanting to continue his pursuit and his overwhelming fatigue. Fatigue won out. He let himself fall down, worn out, on the grass.

"It seems she runs better than you do," said Magloire.

"A fairy!" replied Raoul, "a passing vision, a flying bird…"

Magloire took on an important air:

"I've had some of them here—some visions!" he said very low. "I've seen some vicious birds, too! Ah! If I told you about all that…"

Not listening, Raoul continued:

" Her song always attracts me; her sweet voice makes my heart beat! I have been more than once on the point of reaching her, while she was gathering her pentecôtes in the clearings. But when I was a child, I also chased after beautiful butterflies that went from wild rose to the queen of the fields to the stems of the chèvrefeuillles, hanging and balanced by the breeze. I thought I could could catch them."

"I wish you could!" Magloire interrupted. "But the butterfly always flies away, and the beautiful girl did the same… That's flattering for you!"

Raoul put his hand inside his doublet.

"She ran away, that's true," he thought aloud, taking out his hand from his doublet full of half-opened pentecôtes. " But she threw me half her bouquet!"

"What effrontery!' grumbled Magloire.

"With a smile," ended Raoul, who pressed the beautiful little flowers against his lips.

"Ah!" said Magloire. "What a smile!"

Raoul held his dear pentecôtes against his chest.

"You don't understand!" he said with disdain.

"You bet I don't!" exclaimed Magloire. "I don't spend days looking at the towels that Sidonie puts to dry on her clothes line."

"Are you daring to compare…?"

"Compare to what? Everyone knows your Celeste! A little foundling brougt up on charity!"

Raoul became pale with anger.

"They call her Mademoiselle Cinderella…" continued Magloire.

But he didn't finish. Raoul, who had jumped up with one bound, grabbed him by the throat and shook him violently.

"I didn't mean any of it, Monsieur Raoul!" stammered Sidonie's lover. "Your Celeste is a true princess."

Raoul released him.

"But she is a very well disguised one," added Magloire with a touch of sarcasm.

He readjusted his white camisole and recoiled two or three steps.

"I believe I must forgive you this time, Monsieur Raoul," he said with a dignified air. "But if you again happen to try to strangle me again…"

"Peace!" the young gentleman interrupted sharply. "Enough foolishness. Let's talk business. I have left Rennes to seek adventure; that's my vocation."

Oh! My Sidonie! thought Magloire. *My vocation would be to have a good meal on your lap!*

"I am allowing you to follow me," continued Raoul.

"A great favor!

"I have projects that you don't know anything about… If I left the city…"

"My word!" interrupted Magloire. "You left because you feel the Law nipping at your heels. You allowed yourself to draw the sword agaisnt the watch, and on behalf of a still unknown person."

"A proud cavalier."

"Who wouldn't tell you either his name, or where he came from. Further, you have left the city because you no longer had any credit there."

Raoul shrugged.

"What a pity! " he said.

"The word is well chosen. But to live off love and fresh water, a loaf or two of bread is sometimes required."

"I left Rennes," Raoul corrected him, "because I no longer saw Celeste, because I knew that she lived in the Rohan-Polduc manor with the Demoiselles Feydeau."

"Yes—as a chambermaid," Magloire insinuated.

"You're lying!" shouted the young gentelman who blushed right up to his eyes. "Yes, Celeste is poor; I know that very well, and I am glad about it, because, if it pleases God, I will make her rich; but she is as free as the sky. Listen to me, if you can, without interrupting me. I have something serious to tell you. There's a mystery in my life!"

"Really?"

"Be quiet! I didn't come here by accident… Either I will become a soldier, following my vocation, or, if I choose another vocation, I will need a valet."

"You need a lot of other choices, Master Raoul."

"Probably, but…"

"You also need new socks; yours have holes in them. You need a new doublet and a new hat; and new shoes, too."

"Probably! Probably!"

"In addition, you needed to eat this morning, and since you abstained, you likely have doubly need of diner."

"Friend Magloire, 1 have thought of you to become my servant."

The former bakery boy drew himself up to his full height.

"In society," Raoul continued in a persuasive tone, "the main thing is to cut a figure. If I could say, pointing to you, 'This is my valet…' "

"Well!" retorted Magloire, who was looking over his shoulder, "I could say that just as well as you, 'This is my valet.' "

"You are forgetting the fact," Raoul said, laughing, "that I am a gentleman."

"And I am Sidonie's lover," retorted Magliore, putting his hand over his heart.

"You don't want to become my valet?" Raoul asked.

"No."

"Then let's separate. I don't need you."

Magloire hesitated; The forest seemed to him more savage, and he had as a kind of aftertaste from the nightmare that the three Wolves had shown him.

"Master Raoul, wait," he said. "I had never tought of becoming a valet. But you have given me the desire to be one. We will trust it to chance, if you agree."

"You will cheat, you scoundrel!"

"I am not capable of that."

"Let's trust it to the short straw, and let me choose."

"All right!" said Magloire.

Raoul snatched two pieces of straw. At his age, when you begin a game, you always believe you are going to win. He placed his two pieces of straw carefully while Magloire obediantly turned his shoulder.

"Ready!" he said, with some emotion.

IV. A Meal on the Grass

Magloire turned around and reached out to choose a straw. But, changing his mind, he asked:

"Which one wins, the long straw or the short straw?"

"The short one."

Magloire chose one of the straws at random. It was the long one. Raoul let his hands fall against his hips.

"Me! Me!" he exclaimed as if he had received a blow to the head. "Me, valet to a former apprentice baker!"

"A gambling debt!" shouted Magloire, triumphant. "That's sacred."

He began to march around shaking the reverse side of his camisole where he still had a little flour, his head held high and his chest puffed out.

"I have a valet, I! And a valet who is also a gentleman."

Raoul remained kneeling in the same place, still holding the piece of straw that had condemned him. Magloire threw his cotton hat in the air to catch it on the fly, and then he began to do a dance from South Brittany.

"Palsambleu! Palsambleu!" he repeated, "When Sidonie learns that I have a valet! " He stopped, out of breath. "Let's see," he said to himself seriously, "what am I going to call my new valet? Raoul is not a name to wear livery. Could it be Frontin? Champagne? Champagne is nice. But what if I named him Lafleur? I like Lafleur... Let's go with Lafleur!"

Raoul listened with a stupid expression.

"Lafleur, you scoundrel!" continued Magloire, who had dropped his cotton cap on purpose. "Hurry up and pick that up for me!"

Raoul, confused, thought aloud:

"He's already calling me scoundrel and speaking to me familiarly."[52]

"And what are you waiting for?" asked the apprentice baker. "Since when do you cause trouble? If I speak to you in the familiar '*tu*,' that's a mark of confidence. If I call you scamp, yokel, scoundrel,, that's a sign of affection. Pay attention to that, Lafleur. When I speak to you formally, that means that I am not happy with you!"

Raoul peered at a certain branch of a chestnut tree that hung outside the brush, and which would make a good, long pole. He pulled it down.

Magloire has stuffed his hands in his pockets and he asked himself that very natural question:

"What am I going to do with my valet?"

He hadn't read the story of good Hidalgo Don Quixote de la Mancha, but nevertheless he had the idea of sending Raoul to Sidonie, his Dulcinea, with the mission of saying to that washerwoman: "I am the valet of Magloire, who is dying of love for you."

Meanwhile, Raoul reflected. The chestnut tree branch was certainly a means to correct his predicament, but he had gambled and had lost, and Raoul was honesty personified. Beside, using the branch might give him his freedom back, but not his valet.

"Do you know something, my dear master," he said without laughing, after some thoughts, "I would gladly eat a bite."

"Yes!" replied Magloire. "Me, too."

Raoul unbuckled his belt without seeming to do anything. "Did you hear something?" he asked with a worried expression.

"Hear what?"

"Footsteps, here, in the thicket…"

---

[52] In the original French, which has two words for "you," the more formal "*vous*," and the familiar "*tu*," Lagloire has switched from the former to the latter.

Magloire quickly rushed to Raoul's side. He didn't have any courage at all. His cheeks were already pale.

"You didn't want to listen to me earlier," he said in a trembling voice. "I have even seen some strange things in this forest."

"Well, yes," said Raoul, imperturbable in his seriousness, "this place is known for being very dangerous! My dear master, please, I beg you, take this sword that now belongs to you rightfully... If we are attacked, as that seems to be likely, use it to defend us."

"If we are attacked? God help us, I have legs to run!"

"Legs?" Raoul repeated, scandalized. "To run away? Is that how you understand your new job, master?"

"My word," replied Magloire, "I see no malice in it. I could claim that my valet is helping me..."

"And feeding you too, perhaps?"

"Yes, that would please me very much."

"And clothing you? And paying you?"

"And most of all, defending me!" added Magloire, without being disconcerted.

The sound of horses' hooves was distinctly heard between the ruins of the windmill and the edge of the ravine, in the little covered path that led there.

"Well, Magloire, old friend and presently my lord," said Raoul, "I think we can conclude out bargain. I agree to clothe you, feed you, pay you, and defend you, but as all that is the proper function of a master, I will have the right to call you my valet out in the open."

Magloire, in his turn, began to reflect.

"If it is also agreed that I won't do any work with my ten fingers..." he began.

"Agreed!" Raoul interrupted.

And, as the apprentice baker still hesitated, Raoul added, pointing at the start of the little pathway:

"God knows what's going to happen to us there in a little while! We are very close to the Wolf's Pit."

"It's a deal!" exclaimed Magloire. "You will be the master and do all the work and I will be the valet and not do anything!"

He prudently got behind Raoul because a tall cavalier wearing a hat with black plumes and wrapped in a dark cloak had just appeared at the top of the path. Magloire noted that his rapier was unusually long and that he had enormous pistols in his belongings.

"What a terrible expression!" he stammered.

"A handsome and adventurous chevalier," Raoul murmured from his side. "He is marvelously attired for day or for night!"

"I beg your pardon, friends," the cavalier asked, greeting them with a slight motion of his hand. "Which way is the manor of Viscount Rohan-Polduc, Seneschal of Brittany?"

Magloire looked at the stranger over Raoul's shoulder. He was a very tall and apparently strong man, despite his slight build. His face, proudly formed, lacked a little flesh. The bones of his nose, curved like those of an eagle, were almost cutting. He had a tanned complexion, a moustache as black as a crow's feather; his eyes were shining under the deep arcade of his eyebrows.

"Friends!" grumbled Magloire, not pleased with his examination. "I don't like people who call you friend right off like that. What the Devil! We haven't done anything together."

Raoul, answering the stranger's question, said:

"This road goes around the hill straight to the chateau of the King's Steward. To go to the Rohan manor, you must turn at the forest and take the road to Bouëxis-en-Forêt."

The chevalier bowed; but, instead of spurring his horse, he put his hand in front of his eyes so as to look more attentively at the two young men.

"Insolent man!" said Magloire between his teeth. "It seems to me that I have seen that brute somewhere!"

Raoul was smiling and happy to wait.

"Well, well!" exclaimed the cavalier, who dismounted quickly and threw the bridle over the shoulder of his horse. "If I am not mistaken! That's my young defender of last night!"

He came toward Raoul and held out his hand.

"My valiant champion," he continued. "I knocked at your door this morning to thank you, but the bird had flown away and left the cage empty! This is, on my word, a fortunate coincidence, and if there were only an inn in this god-forsaken country, we would toast our encounter with a glass of brandy in our hand."

He must be a Gascon,[53] Magloire thought. *He is saying that because he knows there isn't any inn!*

Raoul, however, cordially returned the man's handshake.

That business with the night watch wasn't a very complicated story. The watch had encountered in the old city, toward the extremity of the old Place des Lices, where Bertand du Guesclin[54] once learned to fight, a man who was climbing the terrace of a hotel. It was an ungodly hou, so the watch tried to arreste the man, who wasn't in a mood to let that happen. There was an argument. Swords were drawn. Then young Master Raoul, who had been wandering about under the light of the Moon near the Feydeau town house, arrived. There were three night watchmen against a single man. So Raoul joined the party on the side of the lone cavalier; that was not an unusual thing. Magloire, awakened by the noise, watched the fight taking place under his window.

The night watchmen lost. That, on the other hand, was usual; all the vaudevilles will confirm it. The cavalier thanked his liberator and again began peacefully to continue his climb. He had, it appears, a great interest in climbing that terrace of the hotel neighboring the Place des Lices, but he wasn't a

---

[53] Gascons were noted for telling tall tales and being poor.

[54] Bertrand du Guesclin (c.1320-1380), nicknamed "The Eagle of Brittany" or "The Black Dog of Brocéliande," was a Breton knight and an important military commander on the French side during the Hundred Years' War.

thief. The hotel next to the Place des Lices belonged to Countess Isaure. Raoul didn't know that detail. If he had known it, perhaps he would not have meddled in that affair.

"In the absence of an inn," continued the cavalier, "we're going to make do, as at war. When I travel, I always carry some provisions because I don't like to accept hospitality from just anyone."

"That's wise," said Magloire.

Since the stranger had spoken of provisions, he no longer found him to be so unpleasant.

The black horse, docile, had remained at the head of the pathway. The stranger put Raoul's' arm under his own and drew him along saying:

"I have been riding since the morning and I have a good appetite. Would you share my meal?"

As Raoul didn't answer immediately, Magloire pinched his arm from behind. The stranger opened the contents of a little valise that was on the croupe of his saddle. Magloire hurried to help him take out a firm, crusty bread, a sausage of a respectable length, and some additional food items.

Magloire put the place setting on the grass, not forgetting a beautiful, completely full, big canteen.

"Let's eat!" said the stranger, sitting down first.

Raoul imitated him, repeating:

"Let's eat."

Magloire devoured that improvised menu with his eyes. No one thought of inviting him. He began again to think that the stranger had an unpleasant face.

These adventurers don't know how to behave, he thought.

He approached very quietly and sat down in his turn, saying in a honeyed tone:

"Like this, I will be closer to serve you, masters."

The stranger snatched two or three handfuls of fresh greens and put them on top of a piece of ham that he offered to his guest.

132

"I would finally like to know the name of the brave cavalier who rescied me last night."

"Did you forget it?" asked Raoul, blushing slightly.

"I know your baptismal name," the stranger continued.

"That's all I have," interrupts Raoul, somewhat abruptly. "My baptismal name is, until further notice, my full name, but that doesn't keep me from being a gentleman."

V. Information

Magloire had procured for himself by his industry a third of the beautiful soft bread and a notable morsel of sausage.

"Just Raoul," he said with his mouth full. "That doesn't really sound as good as Rohan or Montmorency! Me, my name is Magloire, a native of Vasselot Street... And you?"

Raoul tried to shut him up.

"Let him be," said the stranger laughing. "I didn't want to say my name before those scoundrels yesterday, but I don't have anything to hide from you, my young friend. My name is Don Martin Blas, and I am Castillian by birth."

"In that case, you did well to not tell me your name," Raoul responded. "Since the Cellamare Conspiracy was exposed, it's not safe here for Spaniards."

"That's what I'm told... But I am only a poor gemtleman traveling for his business, and I hardly concern myself with that of the Government."

He uncorked his canteen and started again as if to change subjects.

"Here's to your loves, my young master."

Raoul took the canteen, lowering his eyes.

"Because you are in love, I wager," finished Don Martin Blas, whose smile became dreamy.

Magloire had eaten so fast that he was already stuffed.

"I'm very much in love, too," he said, thinking that was a way to have a go at the canteen.

"That's youth!" slowly pronounced Don Martin Blas, who threw his hat on the grass and thereby uncovered his magnificent, black hair, where one could count, here and there a few strands of silver. "What's the use of saying to the young, *Be careful!* Man would be equal to God if his will could balance destiny. One loves just as one dies, necessarily and fatally. Fortunate are those who die before they have loved!"

He took the canteen from Raoul's hands and drank a large swallow.

"I'm making you sad, my young companion," he continued, shaking the brilliant curls of his hair. " I'm wrong, but such as you see me, I loved like a fool, and like a fool, I believed that I was loved... That was a long time ago... A very long time ago. But it feels the same; it sometimes seems to me that I am still in love."

"You are still young, sir," said Raoul, who considered him with astonishment.

"Over there," Don Martin Blas answered, "our sun matures us quickly, but our looks remain young for a long time. I could be your father."

He drank a second large swallow, closed the canteen, and threw it on Magloire's knees; the valet let out a grunt of pleasure.

"I drank to your good fortune, my young master," the Spaniard continued. "You seem to be traveling the world seeking fortune. Have I guessed right?"

"Perhaps," said Raoul. "And you?"

"Me, I'm looking for something different."

Magloire had put the neck of the canteen into his mouth and was drinking voluptuously.

Martin Blas seemed to reflect.

"I knew at the Court of Madrid," he said, choosing his words carefully, "a man who would pay pounds of gold for certain information... Wasn't there in the past, in this region, a Rohan-Polduc family who claimed to descend from the sovereign Princes of Brittany?"

"Certainly."

"Does that family still exist?"

134

"You should talk to the Seneschal," replied Raoul. "He carries the title of Viscount Rohan-Polduc."

"He is not that," said Martin Blas, shaking his head.

"What do you mean, *He's not that?*"

"The man I am talking about, the one from the Spanish Court, is not looking for information about the Seneschal, but about the person who carried the name of Rohan-Polduc before him."

"You might as well say, before the Deluge!" grumbled Magloire, who clacked his gourmand tongue. "That was some wine—as good as a sweet cider!"

"Thst was fifteen years ago, perhaps even more," said Raoul, searching his memory. "The Rohan-Polduc manor was inhabited by an old Lord, whose name the peasants of the forest still pronounce with respect mingled with terror. That old Lord had a son and a daughter. A sad and long story is told about them... The Edict came; the old Lord was a Protestant and so, he was evicted from his lands. One of his relatives, who is now the Seneschal, married the elder daughter of the Royal Steward Feydeau and had himself vested with the large holdings of the exiled man. I am telling you the outline of the story, as it was told to me. The old Count went into exile alone. His son was already dead, and he had cursed his daughter..."

Martin Blas was listening with unusual attention.

"...The beautiful Valentine de Rohan!" Raoul continued. "I don't know how the Count of Toulouse, who was Governor of Brittany at the time, and very young, got mixed up in that adventure. It seems there had never been a more perfect beauty than that of Mademoiselle Valentine."

"What became of her?" the Spaniard asked.

Magloire moved to get the ham, which was out of his reach.

"My word!" replied Raoul. "I don't know any more than that. The old Count maybe left France? Nothing more was heard of him, nor of his daughter, until the time when our gentlemen *went into the forest*, as they say here. Do you need that expression explained to you?"

"No," answered the Spaniard. "When your gentlemen *went into the forest*, was Valentine talked about?"

"Her father was talked about. All the former Rohan vassals revolted and took up arms, from Vitré right to Rennes. In the battle that took place below the town of Liffré, the King's soldiers seized a poor old man who seemed insane. At Rennes, he was identified as Count Rohan-Polduc. He was put on trial and condemned to death, as were a number of others."

"And his daughter saved him?" the Spaniard quickly asked.

"His daughter?" Raoul repeated with astonishment. "You know more about that than I do, sir."

"I don't know anything," Martin Blas said. "I am groping and I am searching. Go on, I conjure you."

Raoul had stood up; the Spaniard had done the same. Magloire, who had not stopped eating for one instant, gobbled up the remainder of the food, exclaiming unashamedly:

"Finally, my turn at the table!"

"It is known," Raoul continued, "that a woman came into the Tower of the prison of Labat, where old Rohan was a prisoner. The guard was a man of the forest; the doors were opened in the middle of the night…"

"And right on the threshold of Rohan's cell," said the Spaniard, completing the sentence, "a sign was later found that carried in big letters the words: *The She-Wolf*!"

"Ah! Ah!" exclaimed Raoul, laughing. "But our Brittany is the country of Fairy Tales, sir! I warn you about that. Beware of what people say, or you will go astray."

"Nevertheless, the She-Wolf exists," objected Martin Blas, who remained serious.

Meanwhile, Magloire made the debris of the lunch disappear inside the pockets of his camisole.

"I don't believe that she exists," exclaimed Raoul with mockery. "She'd be a six-foot-tall woman with a beard like a Muslim!"

"But I was told…" Martin Blas began.

"I know! I know! The diadem of pearls in the silky curls, the throne surrounded with girandoles, the famous ermine cloak, and so on and so forth... Before reaching the age of reason, all those fables gave me a fever, and I would have sacrificed ten years of my life to see the marvels of the Wolf's Den."

"But now that you have reached the age of reason," Martin Blas interrupted, changing tones, "you have become skeptical. "Then let's leave those stories that don't have anything to do with us, and let's talk a little about you, my young master."

He took Raoul's hand affectionately and added:

"Would you like to *go into the forest,* to use the current vernacular?"

"On the contrary," replied the young man, "I want to become one of the King's soldiers."

"Are you looking for recruiters in these bushes?"

"If I told you my history, you would mock me, sir."

"No! On my honor!"

"But you would perhaps be right," said Raoul, pensive.

"There is no *perhaps* between high and low," Magloire corrected him. "But even so, he's going to tell his story."

Raoul began:

"I am poor; I never had any parents. I live in a small bedroom in Rennes, whose window looks out on the Rohan-Polduc house."

"Where the two young Feydeau ladies live," murmured Martin Blas.

Since he was no longer eating, Magloire was very jealous of the attention given by Martin Blas to his traveling companion.

"The young Feydeau ladies are much in demand," he said, winking in the direction of the Spaniard.

"In the big Rohan town house." Raoul continued, "there was a young girl, an orphan like me, whose tiny room, lost in the attic, faced exactly across from my small room. Feydeau and Rohan-Polduc will soon be just one family because the Seneschal is getting ready to go before the Parliament to adopt the two sisters of his dead wife so that they will have the right to carry the name of Rohan. I don't know what legal difficulties the Parliement faces, but Steward Feydeau has millions... The poor orphaned girl has been the childhood companion of the young Feydeau ladies."

"Brought up by charity!" grumbled Magloire.

"Have you heard about," Raoul continued, suddenly lifting his head, "a noble lady who came from Paris last winter and who has brightened like the sun the parties of the young Breton nobility?"

Martin Blas didn't answer, but his eyes took on a strange expression.

"Countess Isaure!" said Magloire, "a good for nothing!"

"Countesse Isaure," Raoul repeated, "Queen of Enchantments, to whom the Royal Steward would give his entire fortune for a smile."

Martin Blas frowned. "I have spent only one night in Rennes," he said in a low voice, "but I already know that Countess Isaure is Feydeau's mistress."

"That's all about the streets!" Magloire said with self-importance.

"Me, I don't know that for a fact," Raoul continued. "I know that I have often seen a crowd of our young gentlemen follow her and make her a cortege of honor. I know that I have seen the streets filled with flowers after she passes. I know that the proudest, noblest, and most beautiful ladies are jealous of her radiant happiness..."

"From that enthusiasm," said Martin Blas, whose voice for the first time took on a nuance of bitterness, "I am guessing that my young friend's heart is in a very embarassing position. In one direction, there is that triumphant siren, Countesse Isaure, and on the other, the nice little orphaned girl whose name I don't know."

"It's Celeste!" said Magloire, pulling him by his sleeve, "a country girl, a Cinderella, an orphan!"

Raoul lifted his glance toward Martin Blas.

"You are not guessing anything, sir," he said almost severely, "and I am not telling you my story."

"Why not?"

"Because you wouldn't understand it."

Raoul turned his head and took some steps toward the ravine. Hours had gone by; the sun had begun to set behind the walnut tree forest.

It's time! thought Raoul. *Countess Isaure told me*: *At the sunset...*

"If you would like," Magloire wispered in Martin Blas' ear, "I will tell you his story—and mine in the bargain—and a great number of others..."

For the first time, Don Martin Blas looked at him with attention. The look of that face, half simpleton, brought a smile under his mustache.

"You really know a lot of stories?" he asked

"All the nobility of Rennes shops at my master's," replied Magloire.

Martin Blas approached Raoul, who was standing, his arms crossed at the edge of the ravine, looking steadily at the roof of the windmill.

The Spaniard was thinking: *If I had not interrupted him, I might have found through him the girl that I am looking for.*

"My young master," he continued aloud in an affectionate tone, "I am afraid that I have offended you."

"Not the least in the world," Raoul replied, with a touch of coolness.

"Give me some proof of that. I will no longer ask you your little secrets. I hope to learn them in the future by becoming your friend. What I need is some information."

"I am listening!"

"You were speaking a while ago of Countess Isaure. I come from far away and I am charged with very serious business. Do you know Countess Isaure well enough to know where she goes when she does not spend the night in her townhouse?"

"Have you come from Spain specifically to see Countesse Isaure?" asked Raoul, who, in his turn, had a hint of irony in his voice.

"Yes, I have come for that," Don Martin Blas answered seriously.

"Well, sir," replied Raoul, tit for tat. "I need to be alone here. Find a pretext to get this boy away from me for an hour and I will tell you where I myself would go this evening if I needed to speak to Countess Isaure."

VI. A Christmas Song

According to all appearances, Don Martin Blas was not lying when he said that he had come from Spain in order to see Countess Isaure. That had been, at least since the evening before, his only business. He had arrived late and had gone to stay at the Hotel on the Place des Lices bearing different messages from Madrid and Paris.

The Countess was not available.

Don Martin Blas should have left at the end of a short time, but as a besieger who wishes to look over his target carefully after a first useless overview, he had wandered around the townhouse all evening. The ramparts of Rennes still partly existed at that time; an old piece of wall holding to the Mondelaise Gates existed behind the townhouse.

From that observation post, Don Martin Blas could, at midnight, see the interior rooms of the townhouse suddenly lit up. Moving shadows were outlined on the muslin of the curtains. That wasn't a ball, because there was no music, and the projected shadows moved with grave slowness. There were only men there—conspirators perhaps. God knows that in Brittany, at the beginning of the 18th century, there were conspirators everywhere. But any place where two conspirators met, there was a curious eye to watch them. Conspiracy very naturally draws espionage, just as war does vultures and wolves.

Don Martin Blas didn't at all look like a spy; however, he watched with all his ability, cursing the inopportune curtains that screened his excellent view. That mysterious assembly that he had partially observed as through a cloud went on for an hour more or less. After that the Spaniard only saw two human shadows outlined on the curtains: a man of certain corpulence and a woman with a supple and gracious physique.

He descended from his observation post, hoping to find a place closer and more convenient. Steps were heard in the street in the distance, and he saw a dozen persons wrapped in their cloaks, their hats pulled down over their eyes, pass successively in the dark.

As for the townhouse, its remained silent and dark; down below, nothing was heard or seen. It was then that the Spaniard, reverting to the customs of his country, had the idea of scaling the terrace, and when the night watch surprised him half-way.

After he was freed, thanks to Raoul's opportune intervention, Don Martin Blas returned, and was more fortunate that time. He was able to reach the terrace. At the end of some steps, he recognized the same salon that he had seen from the ramparts. It was again entirely lit up, but no shadows stained the rich muslin of the curtains any more. It was empty. Poor Martin Blas had no luck!

At the moment when he was looking at that well-lit but deserted room, he heard the outside door of the townhouse open. He leaned quickly over the balustrade and could see a woman on horseback who was going back up the slope of the Rue des Lices. He would willingly have given fifty pistoles to be in the street at that moment. But in the time it took for him to descend, the Amazon had disappeared in the maze of little streets that separated the Lices from the Place Sainte-Anne.The hooves of her mount could no longer be heard on the pavement.

Don Martin Blas had wasted his time.

Early in the morning, the next day, the Spaniard knocked for the second time at the door at the townhouse. He was answered, just as the day before, that the Countess was not seeing anyone.

"Would Madam the Countess be on a trip?" he inquired.

The valet, scandalized at that indiscreet question, shut the door in his face.

If we now again find Don Martin Blas on the Pont Joli, asking the way to the chateau of the Seneschal, that may be because he had some other business to conduct in Brittany in addition to running after the beautiful Countess Isaure.

"A pretext won't be hard to find," he said, responding to Raoul's last words, who had begged him to send Magloire away. "I'm going to give something to this boy for him to take the bridle of my horse and lead him through those bushes."

But he thought to himself: *I wouldn't mind chatting a little with this droll young man later.*

Raoul approved and continued:

"If I wanted to talk to Countess Isaure today, I would go where you are going, sir."

"To the Rohan-Polduc manor?" the Spaniard asked, astonished.

"Precisely," Raoul replied.

"But how do you know…?"

"I don't know anything, but I am guessing… Yesterday, when I left you, I went back to my lodgings to prepare for my trip, since I intended to leave at daybreak. .Suddenly, I heard a horse behind me, and I saw the light from the lantern that burns at the foot of Notre-Dame des Lices. I recognized Countess Isaure at once…"

"As a matter of fact," murmured Martin Blas, "I know she left her townhouse at that hour."

"I followed her, because the outskirts of the city are not safe, and if some evil-doer had approached the Countess, it would have been up to me to defend her… So I followed her right to just beyond the Convent of Saint-Melaine. Then I saw her steer her horse into a trot at the Croix-Rouge Road. Now that road only leads to the place where we are now, to the Wolf's Den and the Seneschal's manor."

"Hola! Boy! Do you wish to earn a three livres écu?" shouted the Spaniard to Magloire.

"If there's not too much work involved," replied the valet, who put his hat in his hand.

"It's a matter of taking me to the chateau of Rohan-Polduc."

I don't know the way very well, thought Magloire, who added aloud: "I could take you there blind-folded."

"You will find me in an hour at the cross of Mi-Forêt," said Raoul.

Don MartinBlas mounted the saddle again. Just as Raoul exchanged a handshake with him, the Spaniard leaned over the withers of his horse and said in a low voice:

"My young friend, since your loves are in the Rohan-Polduc manor, remember, I ask you, that in a short time, I shall have some credit in that house, and you will be able to call on me as you like. En route!"

He started without waiting for Raoul's answer.

Magloire took the horse by the bridle and led him into the brush that rejoined the Northern road. He turned around from time to time to measure the distance covered. When he judged that Raoul could no longer hear him, he restarted the conversation in a capable and assured tone.

"Yes," he said, "I can tell you Monsieur Raoul's story and amy other stories you might want to know. There are stories and stories. That of Monsieur Raoul doesn't mean very much, but my own is astonishing! I am Sidonie's lover; her mother was first married to…"

"What relationship exists between Countess Isaure and this young Raoul?" asked Martin Blas, interrupting him.

"I couldn't care less!' Magloire answered. "Sidonie's mother married…"

Don Martin interrupted him again:

"The Seneschal of Rohan-Polduc doesn't have any children?"

"No," said Magloire, "since he wants to adopt the young Feydeau ladies, his sisters-in-laws… I was just telling you about Sidonie's mother…"

"Tell me more about that Rohan-Polduc family instead," Don Martin Blas interrupted for the third time. "Also tell me about that young girl, Celeste… If I learn something useful, you will be rewarded."

Decidedly, the Spaniard didn't want to know anything about Sidonie's mother's first husband. Magloire spread out as well as he could his string of gossip. At first, Don Martin Blas listened to him with attention. Then his mind began to wander. After several minutes, they were in the thickest part of a beautiful thicket of young oak trees. Magloire stopped, not knowing which road to take.

"Give me the bridle," the Spaniard said to him. "Take this six livres *écu* and go to the Devil. I know the forest of Rennes better than you do!"

He disappeared behind the foliage. He indeed knew the forest better than his guide, because he rejoined the Northern road without making a mistake and stopped only at the top of the hill. From there, the Rohan-Polduc manor house was only a quarter of a league away, roughly. Martin Blas measured the height of the sun and seemed to hesitate.

"I still have time," he murmured, spurring his horse.

Instead of going toward the manor house, he went down the road at a gallop, made a tour of the two hills joined together by the Pont Joli, and dismounted on the other side of the stream, at the bottom of a dark ravine that we have already mentioned several times: the Wolf's Den.

During all that, poor Magloire compared himself to Hop-o'-my-thumb stranded in the forest by his wicked parents. Fate was multiplying trials in his path in order to make him more worthy of Sidonie. He sat down at the foot of a tree and began to cry. Then he took the remaining scraps of bread and ham out of his pocket and sadly began to eat.

Raoul had remained alone sitting on the ground. When the steps of the horse were muffled in the brush, he took the little path by which Don Martin Blas had arrived. After about a hundred steps, he left it and turned into the thickest of the bushes. The terrain went upwards abruptly. Raoul soon found himself in the center of a little open space that dominated the mound. On his left, very near him, the ruins of a windmill were half hidden by the brambles. He looked at the mound, which was deserted and silent as a tomb. He had a discouraged smile on his lips.

"Why would he mock me, that man," he murmured, "since I am tempted every moment to mock myself! It is useless for me to tell myself that life is not a fairy tale. I find that I am losing myself, despite myself, in the land of extravagant visions! The Witch," he interrupted himself, stamping his foot. "I have come looking for the Witch, I who am nineteen-years-old and a grown man! Who is the Witch? Some ignorant but cunning peasant woman! And what do I need the Witch for if I want to wear the uniform of a soldier?"

Following such beautiful logic, he should have gone backto the city and let the Witch, at her leisure, abuse the credulity of the forest peasants. But this wise reasoning never stopped anyone on the road to madness. Raoul was looking for a way across the bushes to reach the ruins of the windmill. What stopped him was the soft and clear voice that we had already heard that morning; the voice of a child naively singing far away the naïve song of the Chandeleur.[55]

Raoul turned around quickly; he had recognized the voice. The Witch could wait. At first, he saw nothing on the mound that he had left, nor anything on the opposite hillside, but the Pont Joli balancing gently. Then he could make out Celeste hidden behind the foliage of the big oak. Through the branches that crossed the two sides of the bridge, he soon spotted her white dress.

Celeste was walking slowly, and, head lowered, was singing:

---

[55] Catholic holy day celebrating the presentation of Baby Jesus at the Temple.

I saw from Holy Paradise, Its gates wide open;
Baby Jesus wore, His most beautiful garland;
The blessed Virgin on her knees, Was smiling and joyous.
My sweet and gentle Lord, Will accept my offering...

At the end of that couplet, Celeste was in the middle of the bridge, that oscillated under her weight. The last rays of the sun played about in her blonde hair. She didn't even know that she was singing. Her dreamy head was inclined and her fairy fingers arranged the stems of her pentecôtes.

Raoul had put both his hands over his heart. In his dreams of love, he had never seen her so beautiful. The breeze made the curles of her haid and the floating pleats of her dress ondulate.The old oak that formed the arcade of the Pont Joli rocked her between two ramps of greenery.

The sound of her wooden clogs could be heard in the woods, because Magloire hadn'd lied: she did wear clogs.

For an instant, she leaned over the chasm to look at the road; then continued her walk and her Christmas song:

I saw the Evening Star, Gaze upon our Land;
Baby Jesus sees all, Through His Mother's eyes
The Blessed Virgin's eyes, See all the Unfortunates.
Baby Jesus in Heaven, Will receive my prayers.

VII. Raoul and Celeste

When she finished the second couplet of her song, the young girl jumped over the head of the bridge.

She walked over to the hill, going toward the covered pathway. Raoul no longer saw her, but he felt her coming. Just as he came out of the pathway to enter the little clearing before the ruins of the windmill, he hid behind a bramble bush. He knew by experience that she could run faster than a doe, and he didn't want to miss her that time.

Celeste stopped. She thought she was alone. She said:

146

"I don't regret the flowers that I put at the foot of the Lady of Mi-Forêt, but the Witch will certainly know that I gave away a part of my bouquet to someone else."

The Witch! thought Raoul, who was listening.

"She knows everything," Celeste continued, thoughtful and a little concerned. "I was wrong to give away half of my flowers… very wrong. And if the Witch asks me why I did that, what can I tell her?"

Raoul smiled in his hiding place; he heard the dress of the young girl rubbingagainst the rough stems of the bush.

She made a detour to approach that terrible windmill that she didn't dare look at. The bushes stood out silhoueted in black against a sky that was the color of fire. The sun no longer threw out red lights across the leaves; the evening was coming. Celeste was late.

"How frightening those ruins must be after sunset!" she murmured. "Not a soul in the vicinity! If only I saw someone down there, on the road, it seems to me that I would be less afraid."

For she was afraid.

Raoul believed the opportunity was a good one and wanted to take advantage of it. He took a step out of his shelter and said in his softest voice:

"Mademoiselle Celeste…"

The young girl let out a loud cry and almost fell over backward.

"Lord God!" she said, making a movement to flee. "Monsieur Raoul! That was all that was missing!"

"Then my presence here doesn't reassure you, Mademoiselle Celeste?" Raoul asked sadly.

He didn't dare advance any further. The young girl turned toward him , still angry, but ready to smile. A painter would have wanted to capture her wild little face shining with naïve coquetterie. She was delightfully attractive that way, and Raoul wanted to fall to his knees.

"Well," she said, with a mischievous expression, casting a devious glance toward the poor man in love, "it was precisely because I was thinking of you that I was afraid."

"You were thinking of me?" repeated Raoul, who, in his turn, saw the door to Paradise wide open.

"Yes, and all the way, I was saying to myself, I hate that man!"

Raoul lowered his head and felt a tear at the edge of his eye.

"Why is he constantly in my way," continued Celeste, whose tone wasn't matching her supposed indignation. "Why do I always see his two big eyes following me? He must have cast a spell over me!" Her voice soften as she added: "It must surele be true, because, in spite of myself, I spend entire hours watching him from behind the curtains of my little room…"

Raoul placed both his hands over his heart.

"It's in spite of myself," she continued, "that I answer with a smile the kiss that he sends me every morning."

Saying that, she was stilll smiling, so much that Raoul gradually raised his head. But she suddenly frowned.

"Have you no shame, sir?" she interrupted herself with real anger. "Whom do you take me for? Answer!"

Raoul did not answer, but again looked down. A rosier nuance appeared on her forehead, and she looked at her beautiful pentecôte bouquet.

"It's still against my will," she said, letting her words fall one by one, "that I gave you half of my flowers."

Raoul took out of his doublet the flowers already wrinkled by the heat of his chest. He held them for an instant pressed against his lips.

"I would have paid for them with my life," he said, with deep passion, "but if you regret doing that, Celeste, I'm going to give them back to you."

"Now that they have been there," declared the young girl disdainfully, "on your heart and your lips! No, Monsieur Raoul, I don't want them anymore!"

"Oh!," said the poor man in love, "you are right; you must hate me!"

Celeste began to laugh again; then she became thoughtful.

"Countess Isaure, however, does say that I love you…" she murmured.

"So you know Countess Isaure?" Raoul quickly asked.

The mischievous little girl replied:

"What is that to you?"

Then, giving in to a new caprice, in the place of an answer, she told a story:

"One evening last week," she started, without looking at Raoul, "our young ladies were at a dance given by the King's Lieutenant… They were very happy! I, as usual, was left at home. I had gone to sleep under the treillis in the garden of the townhouse when I felt that someone had kissed me on the forehead, so I woke up. The beautiful Countess stood there, near me. I rubbed my eyes; I thought I was still dreaming.

" 'Was it you who kissed me?' I asked her.

"She began to laugh and answered me:

" 'Were you already dreaming of kisses, little fool?' "

Raoul was listening, his mouth agape. He was thinking: *That's why I love her so much, the beautiful Countess!*

"She said something else to me," Celeste continued. "She said, still laughing: 'Little girl, there are shepardesses who marry Princes.' "

"Alas!" sighed poor Raoul, "if only I were a Prince!"

" 'That has appened before,' the Countess continued. 'Go find the Witch of the Forest, who is also called the Miller Woman, and ask her to tell you your past, your present and your future.' "

"But you said," Raoul interrupted timidly, "or at least I thought you said…"

"You are so curious!" said Celeste. "Well, yes, Countess Isaure did mention you. Here's what happened: Without being aware of it, I was looking at the opal medallion that she wears in her beautiful hair. Suddenly said to me:

149

" 'Would you like to have it, little girl?'

"I answered:

" 'What would I do with it?'

"She smiled very gently; her hand caressed my cheek and she continued:

" 'You're right, girl; he would not find you any prettier.'

"I was startled and I asked her:

" 'Whom do you mean, Madame?'

"Just then, you passed by on the rampart;. She extended her white hand toward you, nurmuring:

" 'The one you love.' "

Raoul raised himself to his full heigth and, his head red and his eyes flashing, proclaimed:

"The first person who henceforth insults Countess Isaure in front of me, even if he were a Duke or a Peer, or a Prince of the Realm, will make the acquaintance of my sword!"

The young girl looked at him with admiration.

"I don't know," she murmured, "if the beautiful Countess is mistaken, but she left too early, Monsieur Raoul... or too late! Why did she tell me that I was in love, since she didn't have the right to tell me if I was loved?"

"If you were loved, Celeste?" exclaimed Raoul, who was kneeling on the grass. "You are not loved, but adored!"

He took the young girl's hand, that was trembling between his fingers. Celeste's charming head leaned down and touched his shoulder. Raoul's heart was full, but he could not speak. They sat down beside each other on the grass burnished by the sun. Their silent lips left eloquence to their eyes. The evening breeze played in Celeste's beautiful hair; her caressing curls moved around Raoul's head. The last rays of the setting sun gave a golden reflection to their happpy faces.

Above their heads, the oak trees were softly swaying, chanting the vague harmony of the sunset: the mingled scents of the honeysuckle, the broom plant and the heather flowing through the air. Time could move on; Celeste and Raoul had forgotten the Witch.

After a long silence, Raoul said:

"She knows it very well, however! I talked to her once; I spoke to the beautiful Countess Isaure. It was at the Commandant's Royal Review. She motioned me to approach the window of her carriage. I didn't know who she was, but an unknown instinct compelled me to obey. Countess Isaure looked at me for a long time, then said to me in a voice I will never forget even if I were to live a hundred years.

" 'To love her will bring you happiness.' "

"She didn't say my name?" asked Celeste, who wanted to be certain.

"You were at the window of the Rohan townhouse. My regard had not left you. Countess Isaure had followed my eyes and her smile pointed at you out as clearly as her words.

Celeste didn't take the trouble to hide her joy.

"Oh! The good Countess!" she exclaimed. "I would die for her with all my heart. And didn't she tell you anything else, Raoul?"

"Oh, yes, she did. But that won't interest you anymore. She showed me the serried ranks of the King's soldiers and said:

" 'Gentleman, that is where your place will be.' "

Celeste had a movement of fright.

"A soldier," she murmured. "But soldiers go away."

She withdrew the hand that Raoul wanted to carry to his lips.

"She told me finally," he added, " 'Go find the Witch of the Forest.' "

"Exactly the same as she told me," the young girl interrupted.

"Not quite, Celeste. The Witch is supposed to tell you your past, your present and your future. You will find out everything that you don't know. You are very fortunate. Me, no one will clear away the darkness that surrounds me. The Witch is only supposed to give me a talisman to help me make my way in the army."

There was a little skeptical smile under his nascent moustache.

"Do you believe in the Witch?" asked Celeste, her head lowered.

"No," answered Raoul without hesitation.

"And yet, you came…"said the young girl.

"I came somewhat to obey Countess Isaure, but a great deal mpre to be near you, Celeste. But if I tell you everything, you'll make fun of me."

"I won't! Tell me everything!"

"I don't believe in the Witch, that's true, but I was hoping that she would give me a potion that would make you love me."

"And I," replied Celeste, smiling, very moved, "I want to ask her for a potion that would keep me from loving."

"Oh! Don't do that!" exclaimed Raoul, begging.

"You see that you do believe in the Witch," said the young girl, looking at him with playful, but moist eyes.

There was a slight noise from the direction of the windmill. Celeste's fresh color vanished as if by magic. Raoul himself couldn't hold back a worried movement. They both stood up and listened. The noise happened again.

"Is it possible," said Raoul "that a human creature could live in those ruins?"

"But is it a human creature?" answered Celeste, whose voice trembled.

She listened again. Then, coming close to Raoul, she whispered in his ear:

"The Witch is not alone down there."

"What?"

"Hush! I have often heard a grave and muffled voice that seemed to come from the ruins… One time, at dusk, I saw a tall phantom appear out of the rocks."

"A phantom?"

"A very thin and pale old man, with long, white hair. I wanted to run away, but I couldn't. My eyes stared at him in spite of myself… He walked with unsure steps; his beard flowed down right to his chest. His eyes lost themselves in the void... He saw me and stopped right in front of me. He said to me, in a voice that chilled my blood in my veins:

" 'Go away, young girl! I am on my land. I am waiting here for the Regent of France so I can kill him in hand to hand combat.' "

"The Regent of France?" repeated Raoul. "A hundred leagues from Paris! There is something strange here."

"In this place where we are," said the young girl, whose arm trembled under that of Raoul, "everything is mysterious and strange! But night is coming quickly, and you are pale... If you are trembling, you who are a man, what will happen to me, a poor little girl?"

"I am not trembling," said Raoul, standing up straight.

"Then you do have courage! As for me, I will never go into these ruins alone."

"Do you want to come with me?"

Celeste didn't answer, but she leaned confidently on Raoul's arm.

"Through that way," she said, pointing with her finger at the eastern angle of the little clearing.

Raoul pushed aside the growth of brambles with his sword, and they both went into the thickest of the undergrowth. The windmill in ruins stood right at the center of that inextricable thicket; only its roof was above the growth of the greenery. The body of the building remained in the shadows. Here and there, scattered among the dark thorn-filled bushes, great white stones resembled tombs.

Deep silence reigned in these ruins. Raoul and Celeste, whose eyes had become accustomed to the obscurity, could make out the door of the windmill and, in front of it, a dark mass that remained immobile. Poor Celeste's body shook.

"Near me you have nothing to fear," said Raoul to reassure her.

"Near you, no," stammered Celeste, "but what if the Miller woman is going to separate us?"

She was very careful not to call her the Witch at that terrible hour. The dark mass in front of the door moved. The two children could hear a grave and sweet voice which said:

"Why separate those that the Providence of God has reunited."

VIII. Past, Present and Future

Celeste clung close to Raoul. That dark mass was, in fact, the Witch.

The words that she had uttered were not frightening, but nevertheless the poor little girl felt that her heart was going to stop beating. Raoul was supporting her. By the light that still came through the leaves, he saw a very tall woman walking slowly. She was wearing with a kind of majesty the attire of the forest people: a dress of black homespun cloth, a short cloak, the hood of which was adjusted front and back, and pulled down like a monk's hood. Even if the obscurity had been less, it would have been difficult to distinguish her features under such a hood; at that hour, it was impossible to see anything clearly.

"You have been very slow, my children," said that same grave and soft voice that had spoken before. "Come forward; I was waiting for you."

Celeste and Raoul remained motionless. We wish, for the honor of the stronger sex, that Raoul had been the less frightened of the two. However, it was Celeste who took the first step forward.

"Good Lady," she said timidly, "I wanted to bring you an offering and since I did not have anything, I stopped in the valley to cut a bouquet."

"Give me your bouquet, daughter. I love pentecôte flowers and children who fear to tell lies."

Lowering her head, Celeste held out her flowers.

"And you, Raoul," the Witch continued, "do you also bring a present?"

The young girl, astonished, thought, *She called him by his name.*

"Me," said Raoul, "I've come because I was told to come. If I had known that it was necessary to bring something…"

"You have nothing on you that you can give me?"

"Nothing."

The voice of the Witch took on a tone of severity.

"One who calls himself a gentleman," she pronounced slowly, "and who wants to be a soldier, must never lie."

"Lie?" repeated Raoul, offended.

The Miller Woman stretched out her arm and put her finger on the young man's closed doublet.

"There is something there," she said.

Raoul stepped back. '

"Those are also flowers," the Witch added.

Celeste had reason to be afraid; the Witch knew everything. She trembled like the guilty person that she was.

"Those flowers," Raoul said quickly, "I hold them dearer than my life!"

"Ah!" said the Witch, whose extended hand still pointed at the young man's chest. "And are you as much attached to the golden cross that rests under the flowers?"

"How do you know?" exclaimed Raoul, stupefied.

A golden cross, thought Celeste, already jealous, without knowing it, but curious most of all.

"A woman's cross," the Witch added.

Celeste joined her beautiful little white hands across her wounded heart.

"My good woman," Raoul continued after a short silence, "I have been cold; I have been hungry; I have suffered in my life everything that a poor child without a family can suffer, but I have never parted with my mother's cross!"

Celeste took a deep breath and, from the botton of her soul, ardently thanked God.

However the Witch replied:

"You are arranging things to your taste, young man. That cross was on your neck; someone other than your mother might have put it there. You never knew your mother."

Raoul opened his doublet and took the golden cross to his lips.

"This tells me about her," he said with profound emotion, " and makes me worship her memory!"

"Poor Celeste!" murmured the Witch, whose voice was filled with melancholy. "You don't even have a golden cross that tells you about your mother and makes you love her memory!"

"Oh! I don't need that, good lady," the girl exclaimed. "Something tells me that God will give me back my dear mother... If you would let me know..."

The Witch suddenly changed tones.

"I will pay you for your bouquet, little girl," she aid. Then, turning toward Raoul, she added, "You, boy, since you are a miser and want to keep these two treasures for yourself, I will be satisfied with your gratitude."

"It will be worth something in time and place, good woman," Raoul replied.

"In time and place; we'll see about that, boy!"

The Witch broke off the conversation with a gesture and took Celeste's trembling hand.

"It's between the two of us now," she said. "Here is the Moon that has come to see us. Open your pretty fingers so that I can read your destiny."

The evening breeze was increasing, and the thicket, becoming agitated, let in the white rays of the full Moon. The poor debris of the windmill took on a certain grandeur under that discrete and noble light. When a stronger light passed over the long stones, one would have said they were ghosts turning over in their sleep.

Raoul made a movement to go to one side.

"Stay, I beg you!" said Celeste, very pale.

Raoul hesitated; he was searching for the invisible features of the Miller Woman under her hood.

"Stay, if you like, boy," said the Witch. "I do not need my science to see that there is a strong bond between the two of you. You can very well share your secrets today, because tomorrow, you will no longer have but a single heart."

"True God!" Raoul exclaimed enthusiastically. "These are good words! I would wish to have the fortune of the Royal Steward so that I could give you your weight in gold, good woman."

Celeste lowered her eyes, smiling.

"Stay, if you wish," the Witch repeated, "but if you do, remain silent!"

She leaned over Celeste's hand to examine it attentively.

"Past, Present, Future!" she murmured. "The Past: a noble dwelling, a great heritage… The Present: abandon, poverty, innocent love… The Future: power and riches."

"Don't make her too rich for me!" exclaimed Raoul.

"Power! Riches!" repeated the young girl, shaking her blonde head laughing. "Power and riches for poor the Cinderella! I don't believe it!"

"Silence!" commanded the Witch, who stood up to her full heigth.

She drew Celeste toward one of the big rocks that rose out of the soil and made her sit down near her. Raoul remained standing a few feet away.

"Young girl," the Witch continued, almost solemnly, "I'm going to tell you your present as it is, so that you will have faith in me when I tell you your past as it was, and your future as it will be. You are unhappy in the household of the Seneschal."

"I am not complaining," murmured Celeste.

"You are unhappy and you pay too much for the hospitality that you are given. The women who want to buy tomorrow the right to call themselves Demoiselles of Rohan, the daughters of the Royal Steward, sometimes make you cruelly feel your poverty."

"I am not complaining," repeated Celeste, who had tears in her eyes.

"And you are right not to complain, because you would be turned out! In the past, Agnes and Olympe Feydeau treatedyou almost like a sister. Now, they are afraid of your beauty, I believe, because they have put your little feet in clogs and have hidden your fine figure under ill-fitting clothes. You are smilling, proud one!" the Witch interrupted herself with some complacency. "But they did that in vain, didn't they? Raoul guessed about your small feet in their heavy shoes and your gracious figure under your crass clothing. Your present—isn't it like what I have just described?"

"Yes!" replied Celeste. "You have told the truth, good lady."

"Listen to me, then," said the Witch, who passed her hand over her forehead to gather her thoughts.

Raoul and Celeste were all ears. The Witch started again in a slow and slightly altered voice:

"You were born in an ancient manor that carries the most noble name in Brittany, Your mother was the daughter of a great Lord, and the wife of another. But misfortune inhabited that proud chateau where you were born. Many tears were shed over your cradle. One day, your mother was abandoned by her husband and cursed by her father."

"My poor mother!" Celeste interrupted. "My heart cries out to me that my mother wasn't guilty."

"Disowned and cursed," finished the Miller Woman, gloomy with discouragement.

A sad sob rose from the Celeste's breast.

"Your mother took you in her arns," continued the Witch. Then, she interrupted herself suddenly. "But I didn't answer you, child," she added. "You are right; your mother wasn't guilty. She was innocent vis-à-vis her father; innocent vis-à-vis her husband. Your mother took you then in her arms and carried you away, putting her confidence in God alone. She never knew, before that day, what strength there was in her suffering! After leaving the chateau, she sat down on the grass on the edge of the road and, trembling, warmed you against her heart. She wept, because she was a woman; but her tears soon dried.

" 'Child,' she said to you, to you who couldn't yet understand, 'you no longer have anyone on Earth but me. Those who are strong and should protect you have deserted you. Well, I shall protect you! They have disinherited you, but I shall know how to conquer an inheritance for you. They have thrown you naked and weak into life, I shall cover you and support you.' "

The voice of the Witch resonated under her homespun hood. Raoul and Celeste trembled to the depth of their heart when she added, leaning toward the young girl:

"Child, you will be loved! Child, you will be happy! And all that you will have, child, dear child, your wealth and your happiness, after God, you will owe only to your mother!"

"That was a noble mother!" said Raoul, wiping his tearful eyes.

Celeste, on her knees, stammered:

"My mother, my poor saintly Mother!"

The Witch fell silent. In the intermittent rays of the Moon, her breast could be seen beating under the rough fabric of her cloak.

"But," said Raoul, who had just had a thought, "did you see all that in her hand, good woman?"

Celeste stood up and threw a suspicious look at the Witch, who didn't deign to answer the young man's question.

"So much for your past, young girl," she said as all her gravity returned. "As for your future…"

"Oh! I believe in you, good lady!" exclaimed Celeste. "Tell me again about my mother! If she loved me so much, why did she abandon me?"

"She has used her entire life to work for you"

"Is she very far from here?"

"Too far, because she cannot hold you against her heart that calls to you."

Celeste thought, in spite of herself, of Countess Isaure and the curious kiss that had awakened her in the Rohan gardens.

"Have I ever seen her?" she asked again.

"Yes, you have seen her," answered the Witch.

Celeste thought back and said to herself: *But Countess Isaure is too young to be my mother.*

"Give me your hand, little girl," the Witch continued, "and don't interrupt me anymore if you want to know the future... The hour grows late..."

After some seconds to collect her thoughts, she continued with that solemn and confident voice that all prophets use:

"Young girl, you will see your mother when the days of happiness and glory come, when she has clawed your noble inheritance back from the hands of the despoiler, when you become the wife of a Count!"

"The wife of a Count," Raoul exclaimed, trembling. "That Count had better be careful," and instinctly his hand was already searching for his sword.

"All this is a dream," Celeste thought aloud.

The Witch crossed her arms over her breast.

"I have spoken," she pronounced drily. "I am not the one who makes destiny!"

She rose and walked toward Raoul, adding:

"Your turn, young man!"

Raoul held out his hand to her, half smiling, half fearful, skepticism fighting with emotion.

"Good woman," he said, trying to joke, "examine these hands of mine well. If you discover the crown of a Count somewhere in there, I promise you will have half of my domains to come."

The Witch pushed his hand away and answered:

"It is not at all a question of that between us."

"Won't you tell me my future?" Raoul asked, disappointed.

"No."

"You won't talk to me at all about my family?"

"No."

"At least, won't you let me know…"

"Nothing!" said the Witch in a preemptory voice. "I have my task laid out for me."

She drew a paper from her bosom.

"You were sent to me to look for a talisman," she said. "Here it is!"

Celeste open her eyes wide. Raoul took the paper unwillingly; it was a letter. He tried to read the address by the moon light.

"*To the Viscount of Rieux*," he read, "*Colonel of the Conti Huntsmen.*"[56]

"I have the correct height," he interrupted himself. "They could have hired me without that."

"You are going to return to Rennes immediately," continued the Witch. "You will put that letter in the proper hands tomorrow at the first light; the Viscount needs a new *cornette*."[57]

"Officer? Me?" said Raoul, astounded.

"Oh!" stammered Celeste. "If he becomes an officer, he will see noble ladies, and he won't love me any more."

Raoul laughed whole-heartedly.

"If you had said to me," he reasoned, "that the Viscount needs a *fourrier*,[58] that's one thing, but to becan officer right off, in the Conti huntsmen! My good woman, you're making fun of me."

"When the Viscount grants you your commission," she said calmly, "you will need some equipment."

---

[56] First cavalry regiment created in 1651 and renamed after Armand de Bourbon, Prince of Conti (1629-1666) in 1733.

[57] Military rank roughly equivalent to that of under-lieutenant in the French light cavalry of the *Ancien Régime*.

[58] The man in charge of arranging for housing and food in a Company; usually a sergeant or a corporal.

"I certainly think so!" exclaimed Raoul. "Let's think about this a little! I hadn't thought about equipment."

The Witch kept her very serious tone.

"You will go to the townhouse of the Royal Steward with this letter," she said, "and the cashier will count out to you the sum of three thousand livres."

"Better and better! said Raoul.

"What if it were true," the sweet voice of Celeste whispered in his ear.

Raoul shrugged, but he was beginning to believe.

"Now, girl," the Witch continued, "you must retirn to the manor, where your absence has been noticed. You, young officer, go find your valet, Magloire, who is waiting for you at the Cross of Mi-Forêt. I have nothing more to tell you."

Raoul tried to pull her back as she was leaving.

"Wait, good woman," he said. "I don't believe much in soothsayers when I am in my right mind, but right now, I am like a child who has been rocked to sleep with fairy tales. I don't know if there is somehing serious in all this, and if it's necessary to thank you."

"Thank her nevertheless," whispered Celeste, who nudged his shoulder.

The Witch was already at the door of the windmill; she stopped.

"I forgot," she said. "Tomorrow, in the evening, even if you are otherwise occupied, you must go to the chateau of the Seneschal of Rohan-Polduc. You will be needed there."

"I will go there, if I am an officer," Raoul responded. Then he added very low to Celeste: "And if I am not, which seems very probable, I will go there in the morning. "

The Witch rejoined them.

"See," she said, almost gaily, "you are both embarking unknowingly on the great journey that will decide your fate in this life. Kiss each other again, nicely and innocently, like the children that you are. For soon," she continued while she herself gave the young girl's forehead to Raoul's lips, "you will learn to offer your hand as is proper for the daughter of a nobleman, Celeste… And you, my little gentleman, you will brush it coquettishly with your lips."

Raoul deposited three kisses instead of one. He felt Celeste tremble in his arms.

Suddenly, a rasping and hollow voice came out of the ruins:

"Saddle my horse! Bring me the sword of Pierre of Brittany, my ancestor! This is the hour when Philippe of Orléans, Regent of France, is going to pass by!"

"Go on; this is your path," the Witch said quickly to Raoul, pointing out the path by which the two young people had approached the ruins. "Yours is there, child," she added, gesturing Celeste toward an another road which led back to the manor.

Her accent and her gesture were so commanding that the two young people went away immediately, one to the right, the other to the left. Just as they disappeared behind the trees, the voice from the ruins was raised again, crying out:

"My horse! My horse! My weapons and my horse!"

The Witch reached the door of the windmill and stopped on the threshold.

"Father," she said, "the Regent of France passed by a long time ago."

"Then," replied the voice, which seemed to fade away, "it will be necessary to delay again the great combat until the morrow!"

IX. The Wolves' Camp

At the very bottom of the ravine where the Pont Joli was balancing its arch of leaves, the road and the little tributary stream of the Vesvre shared the space between them for about a hundred feet. The angle of a meadow that rejoined the forests of the plain soon became a sharp, green corner. The stream, bordered by old willow trees, moved slowly to the left, and to the north. The road, on the contrary, made a circle, to climb the southern hill, forming a half-circle that contained the ruins of the old windmill.

Instead of following its course in the plain, the stream made a sudden bend at the end of the valley and remained at the base of the hill, the contours of which it traced faithfully. In the distance, one could see a thin thread of silver rolling among the dark green, then suddenly disappearing among the trees. That was another ravine. The place was known in the country as the *Fosse-aux-Loups*, or Wolf's Den, and began precisely at the spot where a traveler on a chariot on the road lost sight of the stream.

The hill, covered with enormous oaks, was much taller than usual, and rose toward the North. Here and there were gray boulders, littering the ground.

There were no trace of cuts in these secular woods, and no road had been laid out to penetrate their depths. At the time when the Breton peasants revolted against the governorship of the Duke de Chaulnes,[59] under Louis XIV, to trade timber and tobacco freely, the French soldiers came to camp some five-hundred feet from there in a beautiful prairie located near the great pond of Muys.

So long as there was daylight, not a single rebel was spotted in the area. When night came, the French turned the spit and boiled the marmite, like the good soldiers that they were.

Some of them could hear something like a dull fracas that seemed to come down from the dry stones of the old dike built in front of the pond, but they thought that it was water hitting against the edge. They ate their supper gaily, then went to sleep on the grass. But a harsh awakening in the middle of the night was in store for them.

That dull noise that they had heard was that of the pickaxes of the men from the Wolf's Den busy destroying the dike. The rush of the cold water snatched them out of their sleep. The prairie became a lake. Those among them who

---

[59] See Note 13.

knew how to swim could see on both side of the demolished causeway, joyous fires around which men dressed in nanny goat skins and wearing wold fur masks danced like devils incarnate.

Since then, no one had rebuilt the causeway. The pond of Muys formed a large, half-dry basin where big trees were already growing; in its center an oblong-shaped puddle of water lay dormant in a muddy bed.

Level with the former dike, the stream formed a thin cascade and fell foaming on the little stones down to the inferior level where the Duke of Chaulnes had been defeated by the peasants. The beautiful prairie had regrown; young trees grew haphazardly, intermingled with tufts of reeds measuring fifteen feet in heigth. Once lost in the middle of that crater, an unwary traveler could believed himself to be a hundred leagues from all civilization. As far as the eye could see, there was nothing there but wildness and chaos. It was a virgin forest of Druidic Brittany, with its bald grey rocks staining the green spaces, and its purplish swamps made of the viscous waters imhabited by plaintive, crying birds.

And yet one had only gone around the little hill planted with green trees at the extremity of the Pont Joli. On leaving that fearsome crater, one only needed to walk for ten minutes across the trees in the direction of the west to find oneself at the edge of the forest and see the friendly surroundings of the Vesvre Valley.

It was abandon that had thrown a thick veil of sadness on that place, which in the past had been inhabited and fertile. That section of the forest no longer had a master since Rohan-Polduc had left his manor. It was also perhaps the memory of that terrible night, but, most of all, it was the closeness to the Wolf's Den...

But where exactly was that Wolf's Den, whose fantistic name had for so long been the topic of conversation during the long winter evenings? There was a prairie changed into a forest there, a dried-up pond, two hills covered with woods... Was the Wolf's Den there? Yes and no. That spot was topographically the place in the Forest of Rennes designated with the name *Fosse-aux-Loups,* but that strange and mysterious underground kingdom was assuredly not comparable to the galleries hollowed out by the giants of green Ireland; comparable to those dark retreats where Galgacus[60] sheltered barbaric England against invading Rome; comparable, finally, to the grottoes of King Pelagius,[61] to the Caves of Hercules at Toledo,[62] and to the famous underground Caves of Montesinos that Miguel Cervantes did not invent.[63] That was not that somber city of a thousand unknown voices, that, according to popular belief, extended under a good half of the forest.

That was only the entrance. Common belief held that the underground of the Wolf's Den had three entrances: the first one at the pond of Muys, the second one at the Two Windmills on the domain of Treml, and the third one in the vicinity of the Rohan-Polduc manor. The Wolves themselves had not been able to find those two last entrances; as for the first, there was a proverb that said: *So long as an armful of* blosses *can be cut in the forest, the King's men will search in vain for the Wolf's Den.* Now the *blosse,* a kind of wild plum tree, is as common

---

[60] Galgacus (or Calgacus) was a chieftain of the Caledonian Confederacy who fought the Roman army of Gnaeus Julius Agricola at the Battle of Mons Graupius in northern Scotland in AD 83 or 84. His name can be interpreted as Celtic calg-ac-os, "possessing a blade." Whether the word is a name or a given title is unknown.

[61] Pelagius (c.685-737) was an Iberian Visigoth nobleman who founded the Kingdom of Asturias in 718. Pelagius is credited with initiating the Reconquista, the Christian reconquest of the Iberian Peninsula from the Moors, and establishing the Asturian monarchy, making him the forefather of all the future Iberian monarchies.

[62] A subterranean vaulted space dating back to Roman times located in the alley of San Ginés in the city of Toledo.

[63] *Don Quixote*, Part II, Chapter XXIII.

in the countryside as heather is on the moor or sainfoin on the prairies.

At the time our two lovers left the ruins of the old windmill, the pond of Muys and its borders presented an unusual spectacle: fires had been lit here and there on the edge of that puddle of water which reflected their red light at the same time as the pale rays of the Moon. Other fires were lit along the former causeway; they could be seen even lower in the prairie thicket that had become a forest. It was like a camp and the eye could see, not far from each crackling foyer, one or two huts made of *calfeutres*, tree branches recovered with *janique*.[64]

Men wearing nanny goat skins were crouching on the ground, watching marmites boil. There was a continual dull sound. The Wolves were chatting while waiting for their supper. Hardly a week passed without Marshal de Montesquiou[65] dispatching spies to that suspicious part of the forest. They sometimes didn't return to give him their report.

The night before, some French spies had climbed, trembling, some of the local inclines, and, from the height of some old oak tree, their view had plunged right to the bottom of the crater. They had seen nothing. The pond and its surroundings were a desert. They had left and reported to the Marshal that all was quiet at the Vesvre Valley. And the Marshal no doubt had slept well, not remembering, perhaps, that that devilish country thrived below as well as above ground, and that the phantom they called the She-Wolf could, at a snap of her fingers, raise an army out of the ground.

There was nothing that night; and still nothing the morning of the next day. But about an hour after noon, the thickets became full of people. Hatchets were used. Cabins were erected and fires were lit after sunset. Men, with wolf skin masks on their faces, muskets on their shoulders, had

---

[64] Small thorny reeds. *(Note from the Author.)*

[65] See Note 43.

come from all corners of the forest. Why? No one knew. The She-Wolf had assembled her army, that was all.

Near Le Mené, there is a moor where witches and warlocks from all over Brittany gather to hold their annual court. Everybody knows that during he night of Toussaint[66] they erect a city, not with weak branches or with cut reeds, but with beautiful stones cut from Penmarch granite whose quartz is dotted with little rosy flakes; a real city, as big as Quimper, with a Cathedral even higher than that of Paimpol. But when the sun rises on the moor of La Mené, one would search in vain for such marvels; everything has disappeared.

It could be said that the camp of the Wolves was almost as fantastic as that of the Court of Breton warlocks, because at dawn, it, too, would disappear.

Looking around one would have recognized most of the former tenants of Rohan.

"The last time I saw him," said the old tenant Jouachin, who had brought there his three sons and five grand-sons, "he was walking near Antrain to reach the coast and to go across to England. My Lord is seven years older than I am. That makes him very old, and when you go across the big sea at that age, you don't always return, I tell you!"

"But you didn't actually see him board a ship, did you, Jouachin?"

The old man shook his head.

"Do you remember what a proud checalier Count Guy of Rohan was? The evening of the day he was chased away from his manor by the soldiers from the La Ferté Regiment, I saw him following a deer in the woods of Boislevé. His huntsman was five hundred feet behind him, and since the wall of my farmyard barred his passage, I took off my hat in order to say to him, laughing:

" 'Jump one time to enter, one time to leave, my Lord!'

---

[66] Halloween, or All Saints' Day.

168

"He jumped one time to enter as easily as I open my petuniere.[67] He threw an écu of six livres to the children who were playing in the courtyard and jumped a second time to leave, shouting:

" 'God Bless you, you and your little house, Jouachin, my good man.'

"There was a big bottle of brandy there. We all drank a swallow, and all those who had known Guy of Rohan repeated:

" 'As for that, he didn't have his equal!'

"Well," old Jouachin continued, "when I saw him down there, neat Antrain, he was weaving on his saddle. His body was bent double and his poor head was shaking, putting his chin against his chest. Here or there, my poor children, in France or in England, our Lord didn't have long to last after the day that I saw him!"

"And his daughter?" several voices asked.

"There was no one with him," replied Joachin, "except a young, bare-footed boy to whom I showed the road."

"Our young lady has disguised herself more than one time as a young boy," said a voice in the circle.

The good man Jouachin remained silent and the bottle was passed around.

"I see a man in a black coat wearing a hat over his face," interrupted Josais who sat at a neighboring foyer. "His horse is tied to a tree on the back side of the path."

"When did he come?"

"Late."

"Did the handsome Cobbler know him?"

"I don't think so, because he didn't show him the path to the Wolf's Den."

"And no one knows his name?"

"No one."

---

[67] A box made from the horn of a bull where Breton peasants keep their tobacco. (*Note from the Author*)

Having said this last word, Josais pointed toward the end of the path, where an isolated fire was dying out.

Two men who were walking and chatting came out of the darkness. One of those two men, who was very tall, wore indeed a black cloak, which was lifted at the end by his sword. His hat was pulled down over his eyes and hid his face. The other man was a bumpkin dressed in his Sunday best who carried his nanny goat skin attire across his arm and displayed his big uncovered head wearing a wool cap. That one was short and stocky; his litle legs seemed to need help to support the weight of his large shoulders.

They walked as far as the abandoned fire, which was turning into cenders. The group led by Josais kept silent so as to catch at least a few words as they walked by. But the handsome clog- maker was talking too low and his companion hardly opened his mouth.

When they had passed by, Josias asked:

"Has anyone seen tenant Julot who went to Paris with Master Josselin Guitan?"

"He is over there with Dame Michou, at the edge of the water," one Wolf answered.

"You, who answered, can you tell me the name of the bourgeois woman who tok care of their business at the Court?"

The peasant hesited, thought, and finally answered:

"Madame Saint-Elme."

Josais clapped his hands.

"Well," he exclaimed, "it's that same name I overheard... That man in the cloak struck me as a French spy. I hid myself in the bushes so as to know what they were talking about, the handsome Cobbler and him... I could only hear this: *Madame Saint-Elme.*"

The handsome Cobbler and his companion had gone back into the shadows. They were walking side by side to the end of the pathway.

"I am master here," said Yaumi, straitening himself up with importance on his short legs. "Something is needed to amuse the good people. So we talk of the She-Wolf."

He shrugged instead of finishing his thought.

The man in the cloak stopped and crossed his arms over his chest. As he stood that way, his head raised, a moonbeam slid under the edge of his hat, revealing the proud traits of the Spaniard, Don Martin Blas.

"Then one might waste his time looking for the She-Wolf?" he asked.

"Not at all!" exclaimed the handsome Cobbler, laughing. "In order to please you, sir, I'm going to show you the She-Wolf!"

At the end of the pathway there was a little drop that looked out over the entry to the ravine from the direction of the Vesvre Valley.

Yaumi moved aside some reinforcing material, and uncovered a small steel cannon mounted on a pivot, whose black mouth was pointed toward the entrance to the ravine. That was the pride of the arsenal of the Wolves.

Yaumi knocked on the cylinder head, that sounded full, because the old cannon was charged right up to the mouth, and said emphatically:

"Here is the She-Wolf!"

X. A Wolf's View of Paris

Hours passed ; a number of fires had been extinguished around the great pond and along the road. The aspect of the camp had changed; everything that was not directly under the Moon' rays retreated to shadows. The countryside was soon going to look forlorn again. There was hardly any more talking. The cooked marmites had transferred their thick contents to the Wolves' stomaches. Many of them were already snoring, stretched out on the grass, their feet toward the warm coals.

The Moon was ascending toward Heaven and its lights became clearer as the campfires died and its pale disc was mirrored in the sleeping water. The hills sketched their profiles all around on the milky firmament. A warm breeze ascended from the plain. A profound silence reigned in the forest. Nothing was heard, but the heavy and lazy footsteps of the watchen posted at the edge of the camp. However, there was still, toward the center of the pond, a fire burning and a few people prolonging the evening under a beautiful leafy tree.

That circle was presided over by Dame Michou Guitan, who had herself put bread into their bowls. Her hair was completely white, and her rosary with its big brass beads made music at her belt just as it did when she was in charge of Rohan. But now, one would have seen something more belligerent in her, even a little savage. Dame Michou was no longer entirely the discreet matron turning her spinning wheel and smoking her pipe all day long under the shelter of the fireplace of Rohan. In the past, she had only made war on Master Alain Polduc, the cunning and deceitful steward. At present, it was easy to see that she had put aside her once peaceful habits. Still, she did not reach the level of tragedy despite her dignity, the way she carried herself, and her expression. She was a venerable woman, capable of, if needed, of providing enough soup for an entire army, and afterward throwing the marmite at the head of the enemy.

The element of honesty overflowed in that worthy woman. She remained a good Christian, devotion incarnate, exhibiting total fidelity. She was seated on her folded mantle to avoid the cold grass, which is not good for old people. She held herself upright, as in the past, and her face still showed good health.

She was the only woman there; some thirty peasants were seated around her. Some of them had been at her meal; others had left their fires to finish the evening with her.

"Brandy is good for men," she said, carrying to her lips a large bowl of hard cider, adding: "And as for that, Josselin

172

Guitan, my son, is going on thirty-five years-old. I can't very well keep him on a lease!"

She looked around with solemn courtesy and emptied her bowl with one swallow.

"Still," replied the forner Rohan huntsman, who wore like the others the nanny goat uniform. " If Master Josselin has returned since this morning, he certainly could have found the time to say hello to his old mother."

"What do you know about it?" the old woman replied with sharpness. "Those who are on the same side as Josselin Guitan know thy can count on him. Who are you to judge him? Every day that God gives me, I say an *Ave* to Holy Mary to thank her for having made me his mother."

Then she added, turning to a boy was lying nonchantly near her:

"So is that Madame Saint-Elme then like a fay, Julot, my boy?"

At the name of Madame Saint-Elme, Josais and old Jouachin, who had just arrived, listened closely. Fat Julot raised himself to his elbow.

"Who knows?" he said. "We saw a lot of odd things over there! Paris is bigger than from here to the end of the parish! There is a river large enough for the Vivaine to dance with the Vesvre, the Vanve, the Couësnon, the Ille, the Schiche, the Mayenne that runs through Laval, and the Orne, and many more too."

"Really?" said the circle, impressed.

Travelers are always lying, but they are still listened to. That boy Julot, with his little thin face and full red hair, was a traveler.

"You shouldn't laugh," he continued as a man sure of his facts. "To cross the river I'm talking about, there are stone bridges that are so huge you can't see the other side. The King's palace is five hundred meters-tall! I heard Mass at Notre-Dame, whose towers are so high that from the top, men are like ants.That's the God-given truth!"

"But," Dane Michou Guitan interrupted, "what about Madame Saint-Elme?"

"Madame Saint-Elme ?" Julot repeated. "Well, under the Pont Neuf, I heard a carillon that played music. They called it the *Samaritaine...*[68] And one day, as I walked by there to listen to the carillon, my purse, where I had five pieces of six liards, was stolen. Master Josselin had told me not to go see that comedy, but it was so nice, and so funny! It told how a father wanted his daughter to marry a rich man. She tells her troubles to her maid, a clever gossip, who tells her not to worry. The maid meets a valet who is a little scoundrel, but good-natured, whom she orders to not try to kiss her, but he kisses her all the time. Anyway, the valet goes to look for his master and a ladder. The master has a mandoline; he sings; the girl goes to the window. The ladder is put in place. The young girl dries her eyes with her apron and goes down on the ladder into the street, saying that it is not proper conduct to have her elope that way! But she does elope. Then, the father comes in with the old man; you could die laughing seeing them lament! But the valet soon brings everybody together again. It turns out that the girl and her new beau, who is the only son of a Spanish Lord, are richer than the King! Everybody starts to

---

[68] The *Samaritaine* was a pump that brought water from the Seine to the Louvre Palace, the first of its kind in Paris. It was built on the second arch of the Pont-Neuf by Flemish engineer Jean Lintlaër for King Henry IV. It was a three-story mill on stilts, whose pump could draw 700 cubic meters of water per day, with its impeller nearly 5 meters in diameter. It was able to raise the waters of the river in a reservoir, and from there to take them to the Louvre and the Tuileries. Until then, the Louvre had only been supplied with water from a small fountain of the Croix-du-Trahoir located at the crossroads of the rue de l'Arbre-Sec and the rue Saint-Honoré. The *Samaritaine* later become the name of a large department store built near the Pont-Neuf in 1869.

dance, except for the old miser, whose face, under his wig, is very angry. That's what the comedy was all about."

"That's amazing!" said a few voices in the circle where everyone had listened with gaping mouths. Julot the traveler was well aware of his success.

"Pass me the bottle, he said, throwing a look of superority around. "Paris is Paris! You can't stay at home when you want to know the world!"

"But do you actually know," old Jouachin asked, "why Master Josselin and you went to Paris?"

"As for that, not at all!" answered Julot without hesitating. "Madame Saint-Elme needed to see Master Josselin; that's all I gleaned. But look up there and see how many stars there are. Master Josselin and I once went into a house, decorated all in gold, where all the women were dressed in something, I don't know what, that left them almost naked; and there were ten times more candles in that house than we see stars over our heads."

"Don't make fun of us, Julot," Jouachin interrupted severely.

"Twenty times more," exclaimed the traveler, "and velvet, and flowers, and violins! Everything there was bright and like Paradise. That's as true as the fact that I was baptised! Ah! Dame Michou! You can certainly not believe me, because that seemed to me as if I was dreaming. There was a handsome Lord who approached our Master Josselin and said in his ear:

" 'The Regent has discovered everything. Pack your bags, and get on your way.'

" 'Another man took me by the arm and whispered in my ear very softly:

" 'If you will tell me where Madame Saint-Elme is hiding, I'll give you fifty gold Louis.' "

Julot stopped to light his pipe. His listeners didn't understand too well that confused story, where Julot himself seemed to walk as in a maze. But curiosity about it was even greater. No fairy tale had ever excited such interest.

"Fifty gold louis," Julot repeated. "A hundred and twenty pistoles, neither more nor less. I missed getting a fortune! It would have done as much good to ask me in what hole on the moor the *corniquets* hide, or the *chats-courtels*...[69] Well! The next day, Master Josselin had me get into a carriage and we came to a place that you could never imagine, with a garden you accessed by climbing up a hundred steps of white marble; flower beds where all the bouquets of the world were growing; yew trees sculpted to resemble ferocious animals; statues that vomited water out of their mouths and through their nostrils, so much that, looking at those sprays in the sun, I was more astonished than by all the gold in that house that they called the Opera... [70]

"Where we were then is called Versailles. They wanted to keep us from going into a pavillion where there were guards at the door. Master Josselin told them that he came on behalf of Madame Saint-Elme and, right then, the guards winked and let us pass... It's not often you who will ever see a Cardinal! There was one inside that pavillon, a skinny man with a red robe and a red hat, a big cross on his chest, a half full bottle on the table beside him, and an empty glass. I could have heard what rhey said, but Master Josselin ordered me to stay outside. Pass me the bottle!"

Julot had sweat on his forehead; he was telling the story as well and as much of it as he could.

"No!" he exclaimed with sudden fervor. "I remember! It was in the Cardinal's pavilion that I stayed in the kitchen! My head was a little warm when we reurned to Paris. I said to Master Josselin on the way:

" 'What business are we conducting here exactly?'

---

[69] Breton goblins. (*Note from the Author*)

[70] The Paris Opera was founded in 1669 by Louis XIV as the Académie d'Opéra, and shortly thereafter was placed under the leadership of Jean-Baptiste Lully and officially renamed the Académie Royale de Musique, but continued to be known more simply as the Opéra.

"But Master Josselin only speaks when he wishes!"

"However, when he wishes, he does speak well," said someone in the audience.

Everyone gave a flattering glance at Dame Michou. It seemed decidedly that Master Josselin was a power to be reckoned with.

"Toc ! Toc ! Toc !," Julot continued, tapping his medium finger against the bottle. "It was Josselin who knocked like that at a little door located in the Court of Fountains behind the Palais-Royal."

" 'Who's there?' someone answered.

" 'I come on behalf of Madame Saint-Elme,' Master Josselin replied.

" 'Good!'—and they let us in.

"We were now in a dark corridor at the end of which was a small staircase. After that, there was another corridor, and then—my word!—yet another corridor, and thena series of never-ending corridors, all full of ladies and gentlemen laughing so much that they had to hold their sides when they saw our big hats and our round jackets. I heard someone say as we passed by:

" 'Those are the two clumsy oafs of Madame Saint-Elme—a fantasy of his Royal Highness.'

"With one blow of the big end of my stick, I could have knocked over a half-dozen heads, but Master Josselin didn't want me to... In the last room, we found five or six gentlemen and as many ladies who were eating out of golden plates and drinking white wine as full of bubbles as our little cider. The Cardinal was there, too, quite untidy, I tell you, and also a handsome gentleman more than half- drunk, that the others called *My Lord.*

" 'There they are,' said the Cardinal, laughing.

"The ladies looked at us and one of them put her bouquet under Master Josselin' s nose. Me, I received a good slap with a fan on my left eye, and the smallest and most delicate of the princesses spoke to me."

"What did she say?" someone asked, curious.

" 'Oh! Such a commoner!' " Julot replied. "The Lord sat in a corner with Master Josselin. The princesses had me drink out of their glasses and me, who am talking to you, sang them the *Boys of Locminé.*"

"Then," interrupted the old tenant Jouachin, "you don't know what that man they called their Lord said to Master Josselin?"

"It's quite good, their little bubbly white wine," Julot continued, "but I like our Noyal Cider better. The Lord was saying what he wanted; me, I was drinking and I only heard words about Madame Saint-Elme and the Bastille. When we left the palace, I must tell you, I could scarcely see ten steps ahead. I must tell you that they have put lanterns everywhere throughout Paris so that gentlemen can see clearly when they cut each other's throats after nightfall. I certainly was not looking for a fight, but suddenly, Master Josselin shouted:

" 'Saint-Maugan! Alone against three men!' "

"Saint-Maugan" repeated old Dame Michou, whose voice trembled. "You met Saint-Maugan in Paris!"

For all those in Julot's hearing who were of age, that name was like an echo of a time already long gone. Josais, Jouachin and others wanted to ask questions.

"I am telling what I know," interrupted Julot, "and don't ask me any more than that. There was sword fighting and some blood on the pavement. The night watch arrived to take away a man pierced through and through, and they put us all in the Châtelet Prison. I forgot to tell you that I recognized among those who were fighting the man who had offered me fifty gold louis if I would tell him the lodgings of Madame Saint-Elme."

"Was that one the same man that my son Josselin called Saint-Maugan?" asked Dame Michou.

"I don't know," replied Julot. "Pass me the bottle."

In the middle of the deep silence that now enveloped the pond and the neighboring thicket, one suddenly heard the hooves of a horse on the rocky terrain.

"I hope," grumbled Jouachin, "that the handsome Cobbler and his comrade have had time to chat."

"But where are they going together at this hour of the night?" thought those listening to Julot.

XI. Inside the Windmill

That long conversation that the handsome Cobbler had had with his unknown guest had excited general curiosity. The two men had left the pathway a half-hour before and kept together in the thicket so that they couldn't be overheard. They were soon seen to move into the darkness with slow steps, the handsome Cobbler his hands in his pockets and his pipe in his mouth, the stranger holding his horse by the bridle.

"Don't breathe a word!" Josais said very low. " I promise you that we are going to see his face."

He picked up a piece of tree stump and approached the fire that was smoldering under the ashes.

Julot, all too eager to empty his sack all at one time, and not to omit any of the marvels of Paris, had started to take up, from his point of view, a description of the rue Quincampoix, where there were feverish buyers of Mississippi shares.[71]

---

[71] The Mississippi Company (Compagnie du Mississippi; founded 1684, renamed the Company of the West from 1717, and the Company of the Indies from 1719) was a corporation holding a business monopoly in French colonies in North America and the West Indies. When land development and speculation in the region became frenzied and detached from economic reality, the Mississippi bubble became one of the earliest examples of an economic bubble. In May 1716, the Scottish economist John Law (1671-1729), who had been appointed Controller General of Finances of France under the Duke of Orléans, created the Banque Générale Privée. It was the first financial institution to develop the use of paper money. It was a private bank, but three quarters of the capital con-

What had struck him most of all in Law's business was that famous hunchback lending his shoulder in the middle of the street to be used as a desk and earning in that original profession an honest livelihood.

But the circle surrounding Dame Michou weren't in the mood to listen. General curiosity was concentrated on the stranger. Julot, reduced to silence, was shaking on his pedestal.

Josais was lying in wait for the approach of the handsome Cobbler and his companion. Everyone in the circle understood his plan. They waited. Just as the stranger, who was walking a little ahead, passed in front of the campfire, Josais threw a piece of wood into the middle of the ashes, which raised a spray of sparks. The stranger shook and quickly put his hat over his eyes; but there was no longer enough time.

"Jesus God," shouted Julot, dropping his bottle. "It's that man from Paris who wanted to give me fifty gold louis!"

Dame Michou Guitan , trembling and confused, crosssed herself several times.

"This is not possible," she stammered. "No! No! This is not possible! I have grown too old and my eyes have given out!"

Josais laughed in his beard at the success of his stratagem.

"Ah! The aristocrats from the Paris Court are now coming to talk to our Yaumi! We're going to see something new, that's for sure!"

---

sisted of government bills and government-accepted notes. In August 1717, Law bought the Mississippi Company to help the French colony in Louisiana, and conceived a joint-stock trading company called the Compagnie d'Occident. Law was named the Chief Director of this new company, which was granted the trade monopoly mentioned above. Its chaotic collapse has been compared to the early-17th century tulip mania in Holland and was contemporaneous with the South Sea Company bubble in England.

The shadows had returned; the horse's hooves stopped pawing on the grass for a moment. and everyone knew that the stranger was ready to mount into his saddle. The handsome Cobbler and he were exchanging handshakes and taking leave of one another.

"No one in the country knows you, sir," said the Cobbler. "Our boys' curiosity can't be prejudicial to you."

The stranger didn't answer. He put his hand on his horse and said, very low:

"Tomorrow, an hour after sunset at the Mordelaises Gates."

"They will have paid the violins for us," muttered Yaumi, laughing.

The horse left at a fast trot.

"Put out the fire and go to sleep, good people," said the handsome Cobbler as he passed in front of Dame Michou's camp.

A few minutes later, the pond of Muys became something like a great black hole between the partially lit hills. Nothing more could be heard, except the night wind that murmured in the oaks. Through the biggest parts of the woods, stars could be seen shining in the cloudless heavens. The Moon occasionally sent a bean as far as the interior of the old windmill in ruins. The moss had eaten away the tiles. It would have been for the Miller Woman and her *old lion*, as Master Josselin Guitan called him, a bad retreat on winter nights, but in that season, it made a passable shelter. Besides, the Miller Wman and her *old lion* were not too demanding as to the choice of their nest. The floor forming the first floor of the windmill no longer existed. There remained only the walls of the tower and the worm-eaten frame supporting it.

The soil was strewn about with a thick covering of joists half-hidden by leaves and dust. In a corner, someone had spread out several sacks of straw. The owner of that hoarse and deaf voice that had been heard from inside the ruins when Raoul and Celeste had left the Witch, was asleep on that stack of straw. The Miller Woman was keeping watch, seated on a huge beam that leaned against the wall. Behind her, a thin resin candle, stuck between two stones, slowly died out.

The old man was restless in his feverish sleep and mumbled some confused words. Except for that sound, the ruins were silent. In the great silence that reigned all around, a slight sound was heard in the bushes. The Miller Woman, until then as still as a dark statue, stood up slowly. She listened and walked toward the door.

"Josselin Guitan," she said in a loud voice, "you are very late!"

The bushes stopped moving, but Josselin didn't answer.

"I know that you are there!" the Witch continued with authority. "Come forward and show yourself, if you have the heart of a man!"

In the demi-obscurity that reigned under the coverage of leaves, a shadow passed by. The Witch recoiled a step or two as the shadow crossed the threshold of the windmill. It really was Master Josselin, such as we had seen him in the morning, except that his face, worried and pale, no longer wore a wolf skin mask. He glanced around him rapidly. The old man turned over. The dying candle silhouetted the Witch against the light.

"You searched," she said, "and didn't find. You will search again and not find anything more."

At the sound of that voice, Josselin trembled throughout his whole body.

"Aren't you Dame Barbe, the Miller Woman," he murmured. "Old Dame Barbe told me my fortune more than once when I was a child. But I don't recognize her voice…"

"You came right up to my door, but stopped," the Witch said, instead of answering. "Why didn't you come in?"

"I took a horse on the moor, Barbe, my good woman, and I galloped all the way to Rennes to find the woman that you well know… And I didn't enter because of the gossip about you, Dame Barbe…"

"What are they saying?"

"There are some that accuse you of taking money from the French and of being their spy in our country."

"Money is good, whatever hand it comes from," growled the Witch under her big hood. "If you have some money, I will tell you the location of the woman you are looking for."

Josselin plunged his hand into the deep pocket of his sheepskin and took it out full of six livres écus that he placed on the stool where the Witch had been sitting.Then he took out his good hunting knife and stuck it into the wood in front of the écus.

"That's all I have. Understand me, Dame Barbe, my good woman. You know that I have never lied... The money is yours if you tell me where I will find our young lady; but if you tell others..."

He didn't finish his words, but his extended finger pointed to the shining, sharpened blade of his hunting knife.

The Witch snatched up the stick holding the resin candle and started toward the stack of straw, making a sign for Josselin to follow her.

"You are a good servant," she said, suddenly throwing a light on the face of the old sleeping man.

It was a large face, pale and thin, framed by thin, white hair. There was on those features, deeply shrunken by age, fatigue, and sadness, some kind of chevaleresque exaltation. That old vanquished Breton, couched as he was on the edge of his tomb, must have still been dreaming of battles and victories. An exclamation came from the chest of Josselin, who knelt on the floor.

"Our Lord is very changed since the last time that I saw him," he said, with respectful pity.

Then, suddenly having an idea, he lifted his head, exclaiming:

"Our young lady never leaves her father; she must be here!"

These last words were stifled in his throat because, when he turned around, he saw, right where the Witch had been standing only a minute before, a woman of serious yet gentle beauty who was looking at him, smiling. Her head was uncovered and she had pushed away the hood that was henceforth useless. Her black silky hair flowed in waves along her admirably contoured face. The resin candle that she had lifted put a shining light on her big pale blue eyes. That was the beauty of a queen which borrowed some mysterious splendor from the shadows that served as a frame for her.

Jossselin Guitan bowed his head and joined his hands; it would have seemed that he was worshipping a Madonna.

"Valentine de Rohan!" he stammered.

With a gesture, the young woman commanded him to be silent because that name could awaken terrible echoes in the forest of Rennes.

"They have put a price on my father's head," she said. "Old Dame Barbe died not long ago, down there on the moors of Saint-Aubin-du-Cormier. I took her cloak and the hood that she wore over her face to frighten the superstitous peasants. The French pay me as they paid her, and I give them information about the Wolves. With their money, I have prayers said at the chapel at Bouëxis for the salvation of my father's soul and the happiness of my daughter..."

She interrupted herself, then presented her hand to Josselin, who brushed it with his lips.

"My friend," she continued, "I am glad to see you again. Have you accomplished your mission?"

"I have done my best, and I believe I have succeeded. The Count of Toulouse is en route for Brittany."

"He is arriving tomorrow," said Valentine, who seemed preoccupied. "I know that, and I rejoice because of that. What do you have to say about Madame Saint-Elme?"

While she was posing that question, there was something like a smile around her beautiful, pale, lips.

"I have looked for her in vain," Josselin replied. "But her name was enough to open all the doors, to push aside all the obstacles. That woman is more powerful than a princess! I believe that if I had demanded, in her name, the key to the

184

room where all the finances of the kingdom are kept, the Regent would have given it to me!"

"Perhaps…" murmured Valentine de Rohan, while a rosier shade came into her cheeks.

"Isn't it time now?" suddenly asked the old man, who raised up on his bed and gave a confusded look around him. "I don't want to be told again today: *Philippe d'Orléans passed by sometime ago.* I want to stay awake and wait for him."

Valentine de Rohan had drawn Master Josselin toward the darkest part of the ruins. After an instant, the old man tottered and fell back on his bed of straw.

When Josselin Guitan had made his report and given an account of his mission, Valentine remained toughtful.

"You followed this Don Martin Blas?" she asked.

"From Paris right to Rennes, where he arrived yesterday evening," replied Master Josselin.

"And with your own eyes, you saw him wandering around the townhouse of Countess Isaure?"

"With my own eyes."

"Do you know what he has come to do in Brittany?"

"He has come to assassinate the Count of Toulouse," Josselin answered without hesitating.

Valentine trembled and her look was astonished.

"For the King of Spain?" she asked.

"No."

"For Dubois, or for the Regent, his master?"[72]

"No."

"For whom, then?"

"For himself."

"So this Don Martin Blas is the enemy of the Count of Toulouse?"

"His mortal enemy."

"Do you know why?"

"Yes."

"Why are you hesitating to tell me why?"

---

[72] See Note 42.

Josselin Guitan was, in fact, hesitating. He passed the back side of his hand over his forehead where there were pearls of sweat.

"This Don Martin Blas," he finally said, with visible repugnance, "had a wife whom he adored…"

Valentine's eyelash quickly raised, then lowered.

"The Count of Toulouse." Josselin continued. " was then very young. Calumny, aided by appearances, misled Don Martin Blas. He suspected his wife, who was a saint on the Earth, and he swore to revenge himself on the Count of Toulouse."

"The Count of Toulouse then lived in Spain?" stammered Valentine, whose cheeks had a darker pallor.

"The story that I'm telling you didn't happen in Spain."

"Where did it happen?"

"In Brittany."

There was a long silence.

"This Don Martin Blas, at that time, wore another name," Josselin continued.

"What name?" asked Valentine in a sinking voice.

She put her hand on her beautiful sad forehead and her eyes filled with silent tears as Josslin answered:

"He called himself Morvan de Saint-Maugan."

PART TWO: THE LITTLE CINDERELLA

I. The Boudoir

As much as could be restored had been done in the old Rohan manor. The Seneschal of Brittany, that in the past we called Master Alain Polduc, was now an important Seigneur and a man much in demand. That antique manor with its gaunt pointed towers did not go well with his rotund belly wrapped in taffetas cloth.[73] The Seneschal really wanted a more modern house, all white and completly square, like that of his father-in-law, the Royal Steward, but Monsieur Feydeau kept his dwelling for himself.

We say for himself only, but in fact, it was a temple of easy love, where the wealthy financier, who displayed *moeurs galantes* to the excess, allowed only himself in the position of god, and in guise of priestesses, certain ladies indifferent to gossip. At least, that's what he claimed. He was happy that it was believed, or repeated about him. Everyone takes his glory where he finds it.

During the lifetime of his oldest daughter, the wife of Viscount Alain of Rohan-Polduc, Seneschal of Brittany, Steward Feydeau, in order to be freer and have less control over his life, had sent his two youngest daughters to live with their sister. Now that the Seneschal was a widower, Agnès and Olympe Feydeau remained in the Rohan manor, with the consent of their mother. They were like the Seneschal's adopted daughters, who had petitioned Parliement to grant them the right to wear the name of Rohan-Polduc.

---

[73] A fine lustrous silk with a crisp texture.

It is not necessary to tell those who remember Master Alain and his excellent character that he certainly hoped to gain something for himself in that scheme.

What's more, the Seneschal and the Steward were like two fingers on the same hand. Pythias and Damon[74] could not have loved each other more. For twenty years, they had dealt with extremely delicate affairs together, and they had never quarreled in front of witnesses. That is the sublime proof of friendship between speculators.

When Master Alain was still only the steward of the household of his noble cousin, Rohan-Polduc, we have seen how he contributed to the ruin of the old man and facilitated the expansion of Feydeau's domains.

Thanks to him, in the exercise of his functions, Rohan's property, his farms, his fallow land, were transferred, little by little, for very cheap prices, into the hands of the Royal Steward. But to seize the manor itself and its adjoining property, they had to play a subtler game. The Steward and his future son-in-law had increased the hatred of the old man for Catholic France, and the recent Edict had come out from Heaven to bring about a propitious denouement, like a deus ex machina.

The scheme was simple, although cleverly managed. All went according to plan. Once Old Rohan had been exiled, Master Alain Polduc was amply recompensed for his efforts. Thanks to his father-in-law's credit, he was made Seneschal, and Feydeau himself, having been assigned the task by the

---

[74] The story of Damon and Pythias is a legend in Greek historic writings illustrating the Pythagorean ideal of friendship. Pythias is accused of and charged with plotting against the tyrannical Dionysius I of Syracuse. Pythias requests of Dionysius to be allowed to settle his affairs on the condition that his friend, Damon, be held hostage and, should he, Pythias, not return, be executed in his stead. When Pythias returns, Dionysius, amazed by the love and trust in their friendship, frees them both.

King to judge conflicts of titles amongst the Breton nobility, could put him down in the register as the Viscount of Rohan. That was certainly a great deal for a simple squire from Tréguier who had arrived in Upper Brittany with his clogs full of straw. But the new Seneschal demanded even more. Feydeau was eight or ten times richer than he. That made him want to emulate him. He made claims to the Lieutenancy of the King and he wanted to fish once more in troubled waters to grab one or two more millions before he died.

It would have been hard at first glance to recognize the once austere and almost primitive Rohan manor. The moats, filled in, had been changed into carefully maintained flower beds and formed a mass of little symetrical and pretty designs; an alley of linden trees parted the lawn in its middle and came out on the repaired breach. The trunk of each tree was surrounded with a bush of roses to which the pruner had given the shape of a vase.

The walls had been replastered; the venerable moldings on the main door had been covered a triple coat of green paint. The section of the manor that had been falling in ruins had been restored as well as one could, and on the western facade only the old granite balcony had been kept intact as a curiosity.

The same changes had been made inside. The great salon of honor, now split into two parts by a wall, had kept nothing of its once severe magnificence. Feydeau's elder daughter had found it too long, too large, and too dreary. The two rooms that replaced it were not completely in the style of the Court, but their Louis XIV furniture made, none the less, the most unfortunate contrast with the gothic architecture.

Through the restored bay windows, one could see the retiled and whitened terrace, as well as the newly-pruned trees. All that could have been done had been done. There was between that well-kept house and the manore that we saw fifteen years ago the same differences as there was between the noble and sad face of the old Count and the rubicond and freshly shaved face of the Seneschal.

189

The western part of the manor, because of its more modern look, had been chosen by the young Feydeau demoiselles to be their living quarters. The last bedroom, located at the end of the corridor, the one that opened onto the famous balcony from where one could see the entire Vesvre Valley, was used as their shared boudoir.

They were young and rich; there is always some hint of taste among the young for whom nothing is too expensive to satisfy their caprices. The favorite retreat of Agnès and Olympe was charming. You would have called it a gracious and well-lit boudoir, where the two beautiful and lazy girls came to stretch on their velvet sofa among rosy curtains, coquettish paintings, and big Chinese vases overflowing with flowers when they returned from admiring the splendors of the countryside.

It is in that boudoir that we will first take our reader. Only, on the velvet sofa facing the window, we will find neither Agnès, nor Olympe, nor even their poor little companion, Celeste, the Cinderella of the Rohan manor. She was presently in her own bedroom, hurrying to put the last touches on the dresses of the two young ladies who had to be elegantly dressed that evening, to attend at the Palace of the Governor in Rennes an official reception for the new Governor, His Serene Highness the Count of Toulouse.

Celeste had the delicate fingers of a fay. Olympe and Agnès could count on her. While waiting, th two girls were in the drawing room, doing the honors of the chateau to the numerous guests, letting themselves be called, with anticipated flattery, Mesdemoiselles of Rohan. In the boudoir, the Steward and the Seneschal were having a tête-à-tête. Master Alain Polduc had not changed noticeably, except that he was fatter and shorter. His plump shoulders filled out his velvet jacket. His flat, sparse hair had hardly begun to turn gray.

His pretentions to good breeding had naturally increased; that could easily be seen from his outfit. Under his velvet jacket, he wore a heavenly blue satin vest attached by diamond buttons to a pair of light green trousers. The buckles on his high-heeled shoes were dazzling. Under his double chin and around his wrists were torrents of lace.

As can be imagined, all that formed a most satisfying ensemble from the point of view of comedy. However, the Seneschal didn't give in much to laughter, because his large face, intelligent in its ugliness, bore an expression of cunning in his brilliant little piggish eyes, in which a wise man would have read the experience and knowledge of a highly skilled thief. The attractive smile that played around the glowing stoutness of his cheeks didn't hide the cold-blooded determination of a villain.

Next to him, charming, complete, made all of a single piece, was Achille-Musée Feydeau, Lord of Brou and La Muette, Royal Steward for the province of Brittany, former disciple of Apollo, and grown old in the service of women.

Achille Feydeau could well be sixty years-old, but thanks to the combined efforts of his barber, his dentist, and his valet, he reached for the promise of eternal youth. Considered closely, his face offered all the attraction of a work of art. His dark blue eyes, a little glassy, had eyelashes reshaped with a mascara brush, lengthening them and giving them character. On the right and left, level with his temples, thick make-up hid two layers of wrinkles. Another brush, coated with a sooty pommade, restored each morning the arrogant curve of his eyebrows. A few carefully arranged curls came down from his noble wig à la Louis XIV to hide the folds of his forehead. His lips, painted with carmin, showed off the whiteness of thirty-two savoyarde teeth, purchased for good money. Some pearls, mounted to perfection, gave a childish charm to his entire person.

Achille Feydeau had taken care not to fall into the same barbarisms of dress as his son-in-law. His outfit was irreproachable and truly resembled that of a courtier of the Court. He had just the proper number of ribbons and lace, and his jewels, of enormous value, were in small quantity. This favorite of beautiful women couldn't choose dull colors for his dress, but the pale nuances of his shoes, his trousers, and his

191

doublet were perfectly matched. Thanks to the prodigious amount of padding added to his pectoral muscles, his hips and the place where calves ordinarily become rounded, Achille Feydeau, who never had possessed the opulent form of an Antinoüs,[75] could reasonably pass for an ancient Adonis.

He had long legs, like the sacred birds on the Memphis hieroglyphs; his torso was somewhat stooped and very short. Seated nonchalantly on a sofa, as we find him today in the boudoir, he had his knees crossed almost at the level of his chin. In his left hand, paited white with cream, on the finger of which shone a most beautiful solitaire diamond, he held a gold box enriched with pearls, fingered by his right hand, equally daubed in white makeup. To find a financier touched up more competently, all of Paris would have to be searched thouroughly.

"I brought you here, Mr. Steward, because my house is full and we need to talk in peace," said the Seneschal.

"Eh! But you don't need an excuse," replied Achille Feyeau, whose almost transparent nostrils flared spryly. "A boudoir; I'm familiar with that! Flowers leave perfumes behind them. Women are like living flowers."

He took two or three deep breaths as if to wake up his embalmed nose.

Alain Polduc pretended to look at him with admiration.

"You are positively the man of the century," he exclaimed, "and the Regent is only a novice compared to you!"

"Eh! eh!" sniggered the financier. "The Regent has had, however, many good buisness deals, and I do not flatter myself that I am at his level. But if I had been, as he is, the father of Madame the Duchess of Berry... eh! eh!..."

"There has never been seen anything like this," interrupted the Seneschal. "I ask you to believe that I am not referring to the talks going around about Philippe d'Orléans

---

[75] Bithynian Greek youth (c.111-130) famous for his beauty and a favorite of Roman Emperor Hadrian.

and his family. I am alluding to our own situation. Hostile elements pursue us into this very chateau with such doggedness that we are reduced to talking privately in the boudoir of your daughters."

Feydeau rumpled up the end of his lace collar like an ardent conversationalist ready to embark on a new subjct.

"My dear son-in-law," he replied, "private talks and boudoirs don't go badly with each other. Just consider the *Fronde*.[76] Ah! How I would have liked to have conspired at that time! I wrote some bad poetry in the past," he added, sitting back, "when I spent my free hours with the liberal arts. I rimed, so-so, a little tale in the Italian style intitled, The Boudoir Conspiracy. The title is rather intriguing, don't you think so? I'm not asking if you ever heard of it, but it made quite a splash at Versailles and the Duchess of Chevreuse-Lorraine, with whom I was not on too bad terms, had the spirit of a demon, the temperment of a tiger! And toenails that resembled the petals of little roses! The Duchess was kind enough to tell me once that, on reading my light poetry, the ghost of Boccacio[77] was going to dry up with jealousy on the Elysian fields..."

"That's a nice compliment!"

"Isn't it? My memory is full of these delicate and flattering words. But I believe that we did not come here to chat about poetry or conspiracies, my dear son-in-law."

"Indeed. We are here to agree on a set of facts. It's about time we had a frank tête à tête, my dear father-in-law. We are

---

[76] A series of civil conflicts in France between 1648 and 1653. King Louis XIV confronted the combined opposition of the princes, the nobility, the law courts (*parlements*), and most of the French people, and yet won out in the end. The dispute started when the government issued seven fiscal edicts, six of which increasing taxation. The parliaments pushed back and questioned the constitutionality of the King's actions.
[77] Giovanni Boccaccio (1313-1375), Italian writer, poet, correspondent of Petrarch, and an important Renaissance humanist.

being threatened bya series of pernicious events, and there are days when I think that when one straddles fences too much, one risks ending up impaled."

"We aren't stranddling fences, dear son-in-law. We stand on the contrary on very solid ground, thank God!. We have one foot at the French Court, and another at the Spanish Court!"

"Dear father-in-law, it is said that little gifts preserve friendship. It's been a long time since we've given the Regent any such gifts..."

II. The Royal Steward

The Steward threw a worried look at his son-in-law.

"You're right," he said, "quite right. You were telling me, I believe, about a little girl, as beautiful as spring?"

"Have you noticed her?"

"As a general rule," the Feydeau replied, opening his gold box, "I notice every young girl."

"It astonishes me that a connoisseur of your stature hasn't been struck by the sight of that one."

"A brunette, correct?"

"Hair as black as jet."

"Short?"

"The size of Hébé."[78]

"A rebellious nature?"

"A pensive and dreamy expression, that's true, but knowing well how to smile."

"The devil! The devil!" said the Steward. "What a portrait! But I shall admit to you that I have been somewhat off the peasant girls lately."

"Yes, when they have big feet, big hands and suntanned cheeks. But this one's complexion is all lilacs and roses. She

---

[78] In ancient Greek religion, the goddess of youth, daughter of Zeus and Hera.

has the feet of a child and hands..." He made a circle of his fingers and blew a kiss to finish his sentence.

The Steward sighed while raising his eyes to heaven.

"Since I have given myself totally to the adorable Isaure..." he began.

"True! True!" interrupted the Seneschal. "I always forget that you are the luckiest lover in the universe! But let's leave your good fortune there, I beg of you."

"Alas!" exclaimed Feydeau, "it has made me a number of enemies!"

"Let's talk business while you count them on your fingers. I must tell you about the Wolves, who spent the night armed at the pond of Muys. I must discuss Countess Isaure, purely from the point of view of your cashbox. I have to talk to you about the old Cobbler, Yaumi, and some witch who's alleged to make miracles at the old windmill near the Wolf's Den. I must tell you that the She-Wolf has again been seen in the forest, and that Madame Saint-Elme, a fierce protectress of Rohan, is better placed at Court than ever; so well in fact that our colleagues attribute to her influence the return of the Count of Toulouse. Remind me also, in case I forget it, to add a little word about a handsome cavalier who showed up last night at my house."

"Don Martin Blas?" the Steward interrupted with a slight yawn. "Didn't I share with you the little conversation I had yesterday with Countess Isaure? We were having a private moment when she suddenly said to me in a melancholy voice:

" 'Dear Achille, it seems to me that you don't love me anymore.'

"I immediately answered:

" 'I swear to you by all the gods that you are mistaken, Madam!' "

"This Don Martin Blas," continued the Seneschal, who nodded, instead of shrugging, as he really wanted to, "has come to Paris with a message for Countess Isaure."

The Steward straightened up, becoming more attentive.

"Ah! I see that you're now paying attention, my dear father-in-law," exclaimed Polduc. "Listen to me carefully; and believe what I say. The game has started, in spite of us. Our cards have been shuffled, all by themselves, and it is not up to us to step away from the table."

"Explain yourself, please, about the subject of that message to the Countess..."

"Later," the Seneschal interrupted. "First of all, we have to take care of the *little gift*, as they say in parlementary language, that we are going to offer to the Regent of France. I am only a poor gentleman, and for my part, I shall furnish that beautiful young girl, who is the eighth wonder of the world, for the single and honest purpose that the Paris Court may have one more pretty ornament. You, my dear father-en-law, will furnish the rest; that is to say, a sum of five or six thousand livres, so that His Royal Highness has something suitable to offer to said eight marvel of the world upon her arrival in Paris."

The Steward moved about on the sofa and the blood rushed to his face.

"And I'm not talking," the Seneschal continued calmly, "of the little nothing of twenty or twenty-five thousand écus for the indispensible Dubois, who loves little gifts almost as much as his master does."

There was another violent movement by the Steward, who calculated the total loudly in a desolated tone:

"Six hundred seventy-five thousand livres."

Then he added, looking at Alain Polduc:

"My dear son-in-law, have you gone mad?"

"My dear father-in-law," replied the Seneschal, who assuredly had his reasons for having the conversation follow that circuitous road, "let's not talk about this anymore; that would be premature. Before going into the question in depth, let me appraise you of certain details that you surely don't know."

"Six hundred and seventy-five thousand livres," Feydeau repeated.

The gold box was turning between his fingers like a spinning top from Germany.

Alain Poulduc got comfortable at the other end of the sofa and began thus:

"There was in the past—I'm talking to you about a dozen years—in the city of Pléchastel, between Quimper and Chateaulin, in Southern Brittany, a peasant named Thurien le Bozec. He had a nice farm on the banks of the Bénaudet, and, as his wife, Julienne, had not given him a child, he adopted an orphan boy. I have read this maxim in the New Testament: *Seek and ye shall find.* I have been searching for fifteen years. Forget for an instant your six hundred seventy five thousand livres, my dear father-in law, and learn that one day, I recognized a man, seating on the ground on the threshold of Thurien le Bozec's house, playing with the little orphan boy on his knees. That little orphan boy was smiling."

"Of what importance is that?" growled Feydeau, giving entirely to his bad humor.

"That matters a great deal to you. You possess about two thirds of the former domains of Rohan, and that's the best feather in your cap... That matters a great deal to you. César de Rohan and Jeanne de Combourg, united in legitimate marriage, left a son, whose birth was authenticated by the chaplain of this very manor..."

The Steward began to understand and opened his eyes wide.

"All that matters a great deal to you," Alain Polduc continued, "because you know, like everyone else, that after the tragic end of César and Jeanne, his wife, old Rohan mounted a horse one morning to go and search for their son who was said to be in the parish of Noyal. Old Rohan was several days without returning, and it was said at the time that he had gone as far as Quimper... All that matters a great deal to you, I repeat, because I recognized that man who was playing with the little orphan boy on his knees at Thurien le Bozec's house. He had been searching for this boy and had found him before me."

"Who then was that man?" Feydeau demanded.

"He was César's friend and Valentine de Polduc's henchman—Josselin Guitan."

They say that every passion has its sad moments and its triumphant moments. The passion that moved Achille-Musée Feydeau, Royal Steward, was gallant pride and romantic bluster. He had spent his life trying to be a true Don Juan. If the masses appeared to believe in his amorous successes, Achille-Musée Feydeay was actually proud. Public opinion was enough for his happiness. Despite the fact that he was rather economical, he had spent foolish sums to simulate the enthusiasm of successful seduction. One evening, his valet, pretending to be drunk, earned twenty louis by just calling him a libertine. Of all the good fortunes that he had given himself, and on which he counted to assure his reputation as a ladykiller, the most flattering was certainly his liaison with Countess Isaure. Countess Isaure reigned over the cream of Brittany youth. All that there was noble, handsome and vaillant was at her feet.

What glory, therefore, for Achille Feydeau, who was no longer twenty, by his own admission, and who was, after all, only a man of finance, was there to dance and mingle with all that nobility! Countess Isaure was dipping into his till; that was a fact! But Feydeau would have been willing to write it in large letters on the carriage entrance of his townhouse. Countess Isaure had private meetings with him night and day. On those occasions, Feydeau would have gladly flown a flag at the top of his highest chimney to let the entire city know the delights of his tête-à-tête.

He had, those days, indiscrete reveries. He let escape, as if in spite of himself, some revealing words, and pretended to forget, in front of the whole world, little perfumed notes that he had scribbled himself.

But see the wickedness of people! Because despite all this, few actually believed in the good fortune of Steward Feydeau. What does it usually take to start malicious gossip? A gesture, a look, less than nothing! Well! Malicious gossip was cruel in not believing all these serious clues left by the Steward. Yes, people talked, it's true, because the province would have died if gossip were to stop, but they talked to make fun of Achille Feydeau, his efforts and his good fortunes. High Society seized on his ridiculous behavior. The world made fun of him so much more because he was richer, more powerful, and more highly positioned. Only those who needed his purse and his influence condescended to regard him as an old libertine.

The Seneschal was, naturally, amongst the latter, first because of his position as Feydeau's son-in-law; then, because he always needed the Steward. For him not to humor Feydeau eben a little, there had to be some serious circumstances. The Steward had vaguely sensed it from the beginning of their conversation. The Rohan Estate was the foundation of his immense fortune. So he put to one side for a moment his amorous mania and determined to listen to the Seneschal.

"Don't worry, dear father-in-law," Alain Polduc said as if he wanted to play with the financier's concerns. "We are going to return soon to the beautiful Countess. But before telling you what Josselin Guitan was doing there, I first need to establish clearly with you what our respective situation is as to the subject of the Rohan Estate."

"*Parbleu!*" exclaimed Feydeau, "the situation is very clear. I have bought almost three quarters of it."

"Bought?" repeated the Seneschal, who shook his head. "God alone and we two know at what price!"

"And as to the fourth quarter," Feydeau continued, "you had it given to you after the confiscation."

"And I would very much like to keep it, dear father-in-law!" Polduc pronounced with a great sigh.

The Steward's gold box stopped between his fingers, and his face took on an expression of real concern.

"Since it wasn't necessary," continued Polduc, "I didn't bother you with all the details. You did buy most of the Estate, that's true, but that transaction was subject to Articles 7, 22, and 23 of Appendix II of the Edict of Union.[79] To make your possession definitive, the absence of a rightful heir or a Royal Decree was necessary. That Decree, you haven't been able to obtain it from the late King, and until now, the Regent has neglected to grant it to you."

"It's been fifteen years now that things have been like this," Feydeau objected.

"But there remains the absence of a legitimate heir," Polduc interrupted. "The most problematic condition, in my opinion, one over which we have no more control than on the other. The double marriage, performed by Father Sidoine, the Rohan chaplain, produced double fruit; you know that as well as I do. César had, with Jeanne de Combourg, a male heir. Valentine brought into the world a daughter, the father of whom was Morvan de Saint-Maugan..."

"Who has disappeared since," objected the Intendant.

"Who has disappeared since," Polduc repeated. "That adds nothing new to the situation, except that people who disappear can certainly return when other people no longer expect them. In the terms Breton Law, which governs all of the nobility estates, Valentine is as much to fear as is César's son."

"Are they both alive?" demanded Feydeau.

"I have reason to believe so," Polduc responded.

III. Two Heirs

At that categorical and menacing reply, Achille Feydeau squirmed on his sofa.

"They are alive... They are alive... but there is neither paper nor proof..."

"César and Valentine de Rohan could have all that."

---

[79] Francis I of France incorporated the Duchy of Brittany into the Kingdom of France in 1532 through the Edict of Union between Brittany and France, which was registered with the Estates of Brittany.

"Still, their births..." the Steward began.

"Their births," the Seneschal interrupted, "were certified by the same Father Sidoine who died when Saint-Maugan and Valentine's daughter was already three months-old."

"You have seen the legal documents?" demanded Feydeau.

"If I had seen them, dear father-in-law," Polduc answered very low, "we would right now be talking about more pleasant things. But at least, now you know everything about my story, and why I am taking it up where I left off, with the certainty of being carefully heard. So after Master Josselin Guitan left, I went into the farm of Thurien le Bozec. I questioned him as adroitly as I could. But he was a true Southern Breton, taciturn and rude, and I got nothing of value from him. It was necessary to wait until next day. When it was time for him to go to work, Thurien sent into the fields and I wasleft alone with his wife, Julienne..."

"Ah! Ah!" said Feydeau, "if I'd been in your place, dear son-in-law, the gossip would have started very quickly!"

"I don't pride myself as having your skills with women, dear father-in-law, but I took Julienne's dirty hands, I opened them, and I poured a handful of big sous... In Southern Brittany, a handful of big sous has the same effect as a rain of gold. Julienne told me everything that she knew. Unfortunately, she didn't know very much. Apparently, three years before—pay close attention to that date—Julienne had seen, coming on the road from a distance, a tall gentleman mounted on a big Normand horse. This gentleman held himself very upright in the saddle, although he was an old man. A long white beard framed his stern face. As he was approaching, Julienne tried to see what kind of the burden he was carring. It was a child. The old man stopped in front of Thurien le Bozec's house and said to Julienne:

" 'My good woman, would you give food and shelter to this orphan? You will make him an honest and God-fearing peasant. For your trouble, you will receive each year a dozen écus of three livres at Christmas.'

"On that basis, the bargain wasn't difficult to make. Julienne called her husband and pocketed the dozen écus. The old man had not gotten down from the saddle; he turned his bridle and left without even kissing the infant. Time passed; they never saw the old man again seen, except once at the following Christmas. Julienne remarked that his face was more pale and that his eyes were shining with the light of madness. He asked if the child was still alive, paid, turned around and left.

"But without his knowing it, someone had followed him, and as soon as he had turned his back on the road, Julienne saw another man approach, a man who took the child in his arms, called him his young Lord, and covered him with kisses..."

"And you said that Julienne didn't tell you anything!" exclaimed the Steward, who was sweating under his Louis XIV wig.

"I love to see you this way, dear father-in-law," the Seneschal replied smiling. "The interest you take in my story flatters me, and I don't need to tell you that, from this moment, I was sure that I had found the son of César de Rohan. As you can certainly understand, I thought about it, and here are the results of my reflections. So long as the child is at the Le Bozec farm, I told myself, reared like a good little peasant, according to the wish of his grandfather, who made us his accomplices without knowing it, there is nothing to fear. The bad thing is those visits from Josselin Guitan. Something had to be done. The child was six or seven years-old; I was already Lord of Rohan-Polduc and I believed that my noble cousin had already taken refuge in England.

"You perhaps do not remember this next detail: We had Josselin Guitan arrested under some pretext or another, and he was put under lock and key at the Lebât Prison. Every year at Christmas, I sent from my own funds a dozen écus to Le Bozec so that he would continue to lodge and feed the child."

"And the child has become a young man?" demanded Feydeau, whose impatient curiosity pressed for the denouement of the adventure.

"The child must now be around twenty years-old," the Seneschal responded.

"Is he still at the Le Bozec farm?"

"Alas, no, my dear father-in law, and that's the devil of it! I was some time without going to see him, because of my important political work. That scoundrel, Josselin Guitan, managed to escape frm Lebât when our troubles began, but I didn't worry about it, because his old mother starting wearing black after the battle of Château-Bourg and went about everywhere weeping for her son, telling people he'd been killed by the French soldiers. When I went back to the Le Bozec farm, the bird had flown the coop."

The Steward let both his arms drop to the sides of his body.

"I understand, I understand!" the Seneschal said. "Your opinion is that sterner measures should have been taken. You are right, dear father-in-law, but facts are facts. Besides, that son of César and Jeanne de Combourg hasn't reappeared so far. He doesn't figure into our problems, except as a nagging memory. I point out to you on this occasion the rather curious fact that we have ascertained rather accurately the identity of the Rohan male heir, but we don't know where he is; we know, on the other hand, where the Rohan female heir is, but we have only very uncertain information as to her identity."

"What Rohan female heir?" exclaimed the Steward, confused.

"The fruit of the other marriage conducted by Father Sidoine," Alain Polduc explained. "The daughter of my dear cousin Valentine de Rohan and the handsome Morvan de Saint-Maugan."

"You haven't told me anything!" , exclaimed Feydeau.

"I was going to come to it. What made me wait is the extrordinary way these two stories cross, dating from a certain moment. There's something there to reflect about, dear father-in law, and you're going to be surprised to see a new character—one whom you know very well—enter our stage soon—politically speaking. You don't have to be told that the will of the Regent was transgressed in the execution of the four Breton gentlemen at Nantes.[80] Marshal de Montesquiou kept the royal message of pardon in his pocket, and these four severed heads shall weigh heavily on his conscience at the Last Judgment."

"Agreed, dear son-in-law," said the Steward, "but aren't we getting away from our subject?"

"No, we're not. Do you remember a certain romanric adventure that immediately preceded the exile of Count Guy of Rohan, my noble cousin, fifteen years ago? A rendezvous Valentine had given to the Count of Toulouse under the pretext of love? A revelation...?"

"I remember all that, dear son-in-law, but what is the connection?"

"It's said that the Regent, who, like you, is very gallant, dear father-in-law, fell in love all of a sudden with a marvelously beautiful woman whom he noticed in the half-light of a box at the Opera. The gallant messengers who followed did their job well..."

"By Jove, son-in-law," interrupted Feydeau, who was on pins and needles, "I know how affairs of that type unfold."

"This is the first time, dear father-in-law, that I find you reluctant to hear a nice boudoir story. You must, nevertheless, listen to this one, which is not at all a digression... The lady in question was contacted again and decent propositions were made to her in the name of His Royal Highness. Do you know what she answered? She replied:

" 'This is marvelous. I have come from far away precisely to have a conversation with the Duke of Orléans.

"That was ike a repeat of the fake love rendezvous between our Valentine and the Count of Toulouse. The lady in question, introduced into the Palais Royal, cut short the

---
[80] See Note 47.

galantries and—*ma foi!*—spoke about Affairs of State. When she left, the Cellamare Conspiracy had been exposed, and the Regent had given his word, as a Bourbon and as a gentleman, that not one head would fall because of this in Brittany."

"Ah! A contract à la La Châtre![81] You are telling me the history of Madame Saint-Elme, my dear son-in-law!"

"Precisely, my dear father-in-law, and you are going to discover why. Let us assume, for the rarity of the fact, that the Regent was not able to obtain any favor from Madame Saint-Elme and thus remained her passionate devotee; that Madame de Parabère[82] was jealous of her; and that her occult power was great at the Court. Will you grant me these premises?"

"I don't see any reason why not."

"Well, dear father-in-law, when I returned to Thurien le Bozec's farm where our little orphan boy no longer resided, I began, naturally, by throwing fire and flame. Here is what I learned then: Josselin Guitan had returned, but not alone that time. He had come with a beautiful young woman whose face showed signs of sufferings. Josselin Guitan and his lady friend asked for hospitality at the farm. The farms of Southern

---

[81] Expression allegedly coined by the famous courtesan Ninon de l'Enclos (1620-1705). The Marquis Louis de La Châtre (1695-1734), her lover, demanded that Ninon, fickle by trade, remain faithful to him while he went to war, and obtained a written promise from her swearing her attachment to him until his triumphant return. But no sooner had he rejoined his unit than Ninon again plied her trade and was reported by another lover to have exclaimed several times during intercourse "What a good contract La Châtre has!" The expression spread and came to embody the notion of a contract of dupes. From then on people who jeered at a man cheated in love or stupid in business said that he had "a contract à la La Châtre."

[82] Marie Madeleine de La Vieuville, Marquise of Parabère (1693-1755), was a French aristocrat. She was the official mistress of Philippe d'Orléans during his tenure as Regent of France.

Brittany have only one bedroom. To make room for their guests, the Le Bozec couple made a bed for themselves in the stable. When they awoke the next day, they found neither Josselin Guitan, nor the young lady. The child, then eight or nine years-old, had also disappeared. On the table there was a well-filled purse. In the linens of the bed where the young lady had slept, Julienne found a piece of paper that, not knowing how to read, she carried to the Parish priest. It was the address on a letter and it was thus written:

"*To Mademoiselle de Rohan*?" broke in the Steward, sure of his fact.

"No. *To Madame the Baronness Saint-Elme in Paris*," the Seneschal corrected.

A blush spread on Feydeau's pale cheeks and he remained as if stunned. After a silence, he asked:

"Do you think that...?"

"I'm sure of it," the Seneschal answered.

"Have you met her?"

"Never!

"I have, however, a vague memory of letters exchanged between you..."

"She wrote me only once, dear father-in-law, and we are here entering the part of the story that concerns the daughter of Valentine de Rohan and Morvan de Saint-Maugan."

The Royal Steward opened his eyes wide. Until then, he had believed that the Rohan-Polduc house, fallen and stripped, had faded quietly into oblivion. If sometime the idea of the old Count and his daugher, Valentine, crossed his mind by chance, it was a memory so far away and so vague that his digestion was not at all troubled. He felt that he was rich; he had some ambition that all those écus could be used at Court. He told himself that, in becoming even richer, he would buy, someday, political power, as he had bought the small satisfactions of his vainglorious love affairs.

It couldn't be said that the Seneschal, his son-in-law, had drawn him into the tragic comedy of Cellamare. The Steward was very naturally a friend of troubled waters and shady intrigues. What's more, he wanted to appear in control of the situation as he played at being a Don Juan. He was an old misbehaving child. A padded cell at the hospital for the incurably insane, that's what human justice should give to those modern-day Catilinas.[83] The passion *sui generis*[84] that he nourished for Countess Isaure had drawn him far into the plot He was, due to his position, the King's cashier. He had secretly made himself the cashier of the conspirators, which meant that he would pour the sums owed to the King into the Countess' beautiful hands, on condition that he could sometimes leave his carriage parked in front of her town house and cross her threshhold from time to time after nightfall, wearing a cloak. Such were the serious preoccupations of Achille Feydeau. It could certainly be thought that he hardly had the time to think of the Rohan-Polduc Estate.

The reader would be mistaken if he compared the position of *Intendant Royal*, Royal Steward, to whatever employment having to do with public finances exists today. The Steward was then an officer and magistrate of the highest rank. He was an officer of the State in that he was responsable for the paymant said State of a certain sum in taxes determined by mutual consent between him and the State. He was a magistrate in that he had the power to judge any disputes related not only to taxes, but also to contested cases of nobility. That gave him enormous influence. There was no appeal from his decisions, except to the King's Chamber. The reason for that authority was easy to understand. Since gentlemen did not pay tax, the Royal Steward therefore had to have the right to demand proof of their noble status in order to

---

[83] Lucius Sergius Catilina (108-62 BC), a Roman patrician, soldier and senator best known for the second Catilinarian conspiracy, an attempt to overthrow the Roman Republic and the power of the Senate. He is also known for several acquittals in court, including one for the charge of adultery with a Vestal Virgin.

[84] Unique, in a class by itself.

exempt them from taxation. One could have compiles a curious book just from their decisions in that respect.

It was therefore a completly new horizon, a dark and menacing horizon that had just opened in front of Achille-Musée-Feydeau. Tha morning, he had thought that he would only chat about anoying little political hassles. But now he had been shown something like a mysterious hand that had the power to grasp his millions acquired thanks to legally dubious decisions.

Those Rohans seemed to be reborn from their ashes. He had been told about a son of César and a daughter of Valentine. An occult protection obviously surrounded that son of César, last heir of Rohan; that protection must also extend to the daughter of Valentine. And that protection had a name: Madame Saint-Elme.

Achille Feydeau made every effort to avoid thinking about a new thought that had just occurred to him. Could that Madame Saint-Elme be Valentine de Rohan?

However, the Seneschal continued:

"Madame Saint-Elme did me the honor of once writing to me, as I told you. I would not need any great mental effort to recall her letter, because it contained only a single line:

" '*Paris is far away, but I have a long reach. Saint-Elme.*' "

IV. Madame Saint Elme

Upon hearing that laconic message, the Royal Steward shook his head and frowned.

"That's a threat," he said.

"I took it for that, my dear father-in-law," replied the Seneschal.

"But what is that threat about?"

"I have always had a tender heart, you understand, and my leanings are charitable. I had just taken into my house that young girl we were talking about a while ago."

208

"The future odalisque?"[85]

"Yes, and one of my valets told me I don't know what romantic story about her. She was sleeping down there in the bushes near the Pont Joli and a beautiful lady was leaning over her to kiss her, weeping."

"So that Saint-Elme woman," interrupted the Steward with a real effort, "would then have come into the region?"

"I have reason to believe that she is here now, my dear father-in-law. Our delightful little Celeste went to consult the Witch at the old mill, and she promised her that she would one day be a Countess."

"You don't believe in eitches, do you, Seneschal?"

"I believe in the Devil. Let's sum up: Paris is far away, but the woman capable of resisting the Regent of France has a long reach. You and I could lose in this business much more than money."

Achille Feydeau, as if he had been a pretty marquise, felt a fainting spell coming on. He closed his eyes and saw the four gentlemen in Nantes pass by without their heads on their shoulders.

"Why didn't you tell me about this sooner?" he murmured plaintively.

"Things happen, father-in-law," replied Polduc calmly, "and their allure, which varies, determines our conduct each day. Perhaps, yesterday, I had some good reasons to let you ignore all that."

"Then our interests are not the same?"

"Oh, yes, they are, dear father-in-law; yes, they are, at least in general terms."

The Steward threw a suspicious look at his son-in-law.

Polduc began to laugh. "I am weak; thus, I have an advantage over you," he continued. "The weak moss attaches itself to the powerful oak and doesn't worry about choking it."

---

[85] A chambermaid or a female attendant in a Turkish seraglio, particularly the court ladies in the household of the Ottoman sultan.

"Choking me! Monsieur de Polduc!" exclaimed the Steward with real horror.

It was truly a pity to keep such a poor man in the dark. Polduc judged that he had led him to a sufficient degree of terror and could continue, changing his tone.

"With a devoted worshipper of the muses like you, my dear father-in-law, I thought I could allow myself a rhetorical allusion. What's more, you know my devotion to your person. Everytime I could help you without harming myself, I did it with all my heart. But the Christian Gospel and the Pagan Fable come together to agree on the same principle: Help thyself! I have said all I have to say concerning the Heirs of Rohan... Without any other material proof than that brief letter from Madame Saint-Elme, I am certain that young Celeste is the daughter of Valentine de Rohan and Monsieur de Saint-Maugan."

"According to you," the Steward interruped, "that Madame Saint-Elme would be Valentine herself?'

"I didn't say that! Only that that Madame Saint-Elme had César's son reared by the Le Bozecs, and that same Saint-Elme seems to take a very great interest in Valentine's daughter. I will let your excellent mind draw from this twin set of fact all logical consequences."

The Steward began again to play with his gold box and pretended to reflect deeply. He knew very well that his son-in-law would spare him the trouble of drawing every kind of consequences.

"Let's come now," continued the Seneschal, "to an even great danger—one much stranger still. Without a doubt, you have heard about the witch known as the Miller Woman?"

"That soothsayer? My intelligence finds these stupidities repugnant."

"I understand that very well. I don't want to talk to you about miracles that frighten those who wear wooden clogs. I want to tell you that, last week, someone found the body of the Miller Woman under a heap of branches not far from a hut in which she lived on the moor of Saint-Aubin-du-Cormier."

"May God bless her!"

"Amen! But notwithstanding that, the same Miller Woman continues to give oracles in the forest."

The Steward inhaled a pinch of Spanish tobacco with that carefree smile of the skeptic.

"How do you explain that?" he asked, shrugging.

"At the hour we are now," replied the Seneschal, whose glance had changed, "it is perhaps arranged. Don't you smell an odor of smoke, father-in-law?"

Feydeau's nostrils expanded.

"Oh, yes I do," he said.

"The wind is coming from the east," continued the Seneschal, lowering his voice. "Yaumi will have done his job."

"What job?"

Alain Polduc stood up and reached the balcony. A column of smoke rose in the distance among the forest trees, in the direction of the east.

"Where do you think that fire is?" he demanded.

"Near the Pont Joli," answered the Steward, orienting himself.

"Yet there is nothing to burn in that direction, or so it seems to me."

"Some brush," the Steward said again, "and the ruins of the old windmill."

Alain Polduc came back and sat down.

"It was from these very ruins," he said in a low voice, "that the new witch put out her oracles."

"Ah!" said the Steward, stupefied, "It was the…"

"She had with her an old lunatic," continued Polduc.

"And that fire…?"

"Fire often happens accidentally in dry leaves."

Achille Feydeau remained with his mouth open, stammering.

"You mentioned Yaumi doing a job for you?" he said.

"My dear father-in-law," Alain Polduc, said slowly, "that smoke, which is going away, is perhaps taking with it Madame Saint-Elme and Valentine de Rohan."

The Steward was livid, but his little blue eye suddenly cleared up.

"If that is true, my dear son-in-law," he said to Polduc, who was biting his lips to the point of drawing blood, "why should we send the Regent six hundred seventy-five thousand livres?"

"Well, scoundrels!" shouted someone in the corridor. "Ddo I have to break a half-dozen skulls to get in?"

The son-in-law and the father-in-law started to listen.

"Don Martin Blas!" Alain Polduc murmured.

"Do you think that he followed us here?"

"Don Martin Blas is not among those who wait, father-in-law."

"Is he then a very important important person?"

The Seneschal struck his forehead.

"Didn't I tell you who that Don Martin Blas really is?" he said, like a man who seriously regretted having forgotten something important.

"You didn't say a word to me about him."

"That is annoying! Extremely annoying! So such more so since I don't have any more time."

In fact, the back of a valet hit the closed door heavily. He had to have been pushed by a very strong hand.

The Seneschal got up.

"When I think," he said," that I had you come here precisely to tell you... Ah! It is enough for you know, dear father-in-law," he interrupted himself on reaching the door, "that this Don Martin Blas has been sent by Alberoni..."

"Ah! The Devil!" said Achille Feydeau, hastily reattaching the curls of his massive wig.

The Seneschal opened the door.

You idiots!" he said to his people. "The instructions were for everyone, except for this gentleman... Come in, Don Martin. You are welcome!"

212

Achille Feydeau turned his head and saw the tall silhouette of the Spaniard in the half-light of the corridor. He didn't like these adventurers. Very rarely do people of that sort appreciate the charm of a wig arranged symetrically. They are savages who let their hair go to the devil and their mustache to the wind, look at their betters insolently and showing no respect to gentlemen of the nobility. However, he sketched a pleasant greeting and a smile. That was wasted. Don Martin Blas didn't see it at all. He stood on the threshold and his glance looked around the room with an unusual expression of astonishment.

Could he aleady be in love with Olympe or Agnès? Alain Polduc wondered.

As for that, the idea had nothing that was unlikely. Don Martin Blas, silent and immodile, looked at everything. Sometimes men in love act that way, showing too much emotion when they enter the living quarters of the adored one for the first time. They are seen with their mouth agape and their hands over their heart, savoring the delight of their silent transport. Agnès and Olympe were beautiful. The Seneschal wondered what he could get out of that sudden passion.

Don Martin Blas took a few steps into the room. The sofa, where Feydeau sat, sad and discontent about the little effect of his greeting, was located in a small alcove, under a tapestry. It was the same place where Valentine had once sat. When the fake Spaniard looked in that direction, he lowered his eyes and became pale.

Is it Agnès? Is it Olympe? wondered the Seneschal.

Don Martin Blas, however, recovered and went out on the balcony as if to breathe more easily; a deep sigh rose from his chest. He took a long look at the countryside.

"These ladies have a charming view from here," Alain Polduc said.

"These ladies," the Spaniard repeated, distractedly.

He crossed his arms and again contempleted the Vesvre Valley. While he had his shoulder turned, Alain Polduc shook the Steward's hand.

213

"Look very carefully at that man there," he said in a low voice, "and search your memory."

"I am perfectly sure that I have never seen him before!" Feydeau replied without hesitating. "When you have met, even if it was only once, a person with such bad manners, you remember him forever."

Don Martin Blas's conduct, since he had entered the boudoir, certainly deserved that reproach; it was absolutely lacking in courtesy. Not only had he badly received Achille Feydeau's pleasant greeting, but, even more, he had scorned Alain Polduc's eager greeting. If he was not in love with Agnès or Olympe, what other tyrannical preoccupation could be bothering him?

Suddenly, the Seneschal and the Steward saw him tremble and pass his hand over his forehead. He looked at both of them as if he had not yet seen them.

"Viscount," he said, addresssing Polduc in an almost severe tone, "it was a private conversation that I wanted to have with you."

Polduc, smiling and obsequious, took Feydeau's hand.

"I have the honor to introduce to your Lordship," he said instead of answering, "Monsieur Feydeau de Brou, my father-in-law, Royal Steward of Brittany."

Don Martin Blas bowed to him coldly.

"That's different," he said.

And while Achille Feydeau, in spite of his bad humor, became confused, while bowing, he added:

"Monsieur the Royal Steward is well regarded at the Court in Madrid."

Without contradicting him, Feydeau replied:

"I am much honored."

He thought to himself: *That must mean that I am in a detestable position at the Court in Paris!*

"I will speak then," said Martin Blas, "openly before the Steward, as if I were alone with the Seneschal... My trip to Brittany had a double purpose: first, the interest of the State, and in second place, a personal business. Let us talk first of all about the business of the State..."

Don Martin Blas took a seat and appeared to meditate.

"Yesterday, on arriving at the manor of Rohan-Polduc," he began, "I gave the Seneschal proofs of my political misssion…"

The Seneschal bowed.

"We had a conversation," continued Don Martin Blas, "that dispenses me henceforth from going into the details, but before leaving this chateau, where I was greeted with the most courteous hospitality, it behooves me to summarize the situation and to lay out the facts... The Steward's experience might even help clarify the facts. Events have gone on as usual for some weeks, contrary to public opinion. Appearances are against us; facts help us. The misadventure of that poor Prince of Cellamare has put the Regent of France off guard. He believes that he has won the war because he seized some insignificant documents and put an eccentric diplomat under lock and key. He triumphs; he cuts off a few heads; he loses all caution. This is the moment to act!"

Achille Feydeau gravely shook the pommeaded curls of his wig.

"I believe that I have told Your Lordship," risked the Seneschal, "that such was never our opinion here."

"Please allow me!" replied Martin Blas. "We are still discussing my instructions. Youb will have time to respond afterward. I am summing up our conversation of last night. The Spanish fleet is ready; Flanders has risen; Austria awaits our signal; and the Court at Rome only asks to give it. I have come from Paris; the Parisian nobility, without its laughable leader, the Duke of Maine, has formed the most beautiful army one has ever seen. The plan of campaign is laid out. In the event of war, we remembered the griefs of the valiant Breton Nobility who was the first to move, and I was asked to bring them this word, this command: Forward!"

The Steward became agitated on the sofa. The Seneschal raised his eyes to heaven and let out a plaintive sigh.

"That's what I had to say," continued Don Martin Blas. Now, here is what the Seneschal told me: The desire for vengeance provoked by the unfortunate end of the four gentlemen is beginning to quiet down, according to him, while the fear generated by that display of great severity grows day by day. The author of that judicial murder, the Marshal of Montesquiou, Commandant of the King's army, has taken upon himself the united hatred of all the noble Bretons. Just yesterday, thanks to the aversion that that man inspires, one might have stated that all the Breton Nobility was readty *to go into the forest*. But things have now changed. The Marshal of Montesquiou is in disgrace, and the Count of Toulouse has been recalled—and he is the idol of the Breton nobility. His presence is an absolutely insurmontable obstacle. From that, it follows that the opinion of the Seneschal is to abstain."

"At least until we see..." interruped Polduc.

"I think that my memory was faithful?" asked the Spaniard.

"You have reported my very words," replied the Seneschal.

"Now let us have the opinion of the Royal Steward."

"Abstain! Abstain!" exclaimed Achille Feydeau.

"Because of the Count of Toulouse?"

"Yes, because of the Count of Toulouse."

"Gentlemen, if you please, I shall now summarize our discussion," continued Don Martin Blas. "The Spanish Court, to whom you have given guarantees, is counting on you in this serious circumstance... The Count of Toulouse must be made to disappear through your actions."

Achille Feydeau almost fell backward and Alain Polduc looked at the Spaniard as if confounded. Don Martin Blas finished with a calm tone:

"To do that, you are given twenty-four hours, and I am especially charged with seeing that you do it quickly."

V. The Will-O'-The Whisk

Don Martin Blas fell silent. He coldly contemplated the confusion of the Royal Steward and his son-in-law. Achille Feydeau opened and closed his gold box with frenetic activity. Alain Polduc fixed the ground obstinately.

"I am waiting for your answer, gentlemen," said the Spaniard after two or three minutes.

"*Palsambleu!*" exclamed Feydeau, abandoning the pretenses of his character. "You will wait a long time! Assasinate the Count of Toulouse! I already sleep with difficulty and lightly. If I had that murder on my consience, I wouldn't be able to sleep at all. Now, slumber is sanity, Don, and sanity, you can't ignore it, is the most important of all things. I suggest that you go and talk to someone who is in need of such a mission. I am rich enough to want to hold on my sleep."

Having pronounced that discourse full of philosophy, Achillle Feydeau looked at his son-in-law, who still had his eyes lowered.

"Seneschal," said Don Martin Blas in his most flegmatic voice, "please spare me the trouble of explaining to your father-in-law how he is not at all in a position to resist our demands."

"Father-in-law," Polduc, obeying immediately, said, "a result of my last and confidential conversation with Don Blas is that he is in possession of your encrypted letters."

"And yours as well?"

"And mine as well," the Seneschal confirmed with a great sigh.

"Only we, and the Abbot of Porto-Carrero,"[86] continued Achille Feydeau, struggling like a devil, "possess the key to that cypher."

---

[86] The whole plot of the Cellamare conspiracy, the names of the conspirators, the models of the letters that the King of

"The Abbot of Porto Carrero is in prison," Polduc pronounced sadly.

Feydeau lifted again the reverse of his doublet and threw his gold box in its pocket.

"I will risk the consequencies," he said, almost resolutely.

"Father-in-law!" Polduc objected.

"I digest badly, very badly. If my sleep is taken away from me, I am a dead man!"

"That's still not all, father-in-law," Polduc continued. "I don't know how all that came about, but your name is in Don Martin Blas' notebook, evidencing the sums that you poured into the hands of Countess Isaure."

"A lover's prodigalities!" Achille Feydeau tried to stammer.

"Father-in-law," said Polduc, discouraged, "please, keep those lies for your judges."

The Royal Steward let his arms drop down.

"My judges! My judges!" he repeated. "Are we there already?"

And as no one said anything, in his bitter distress, he thought aloud:

"I clearly see that one slides, fatally, in spite of oneself, down the slope of the conspirators! I have lost my appetite. From now on, a mere chicken wing will be enough to cause me great stomach pains. My father had good digestion right up to the age of seventy-four. He ate, I remember, at his last meal, a pork roast with remoulade sauce; but, then, he hadn't assassinated anyone! But, listen to me, Spaniard," he said suddenly, "I will only provide the funds, since you have my

---

Spain was to write to the King of France, to the States-General, to the Parliament, to the intendants and to the clergy; instructions and letters signed by Cellamare had been given to the Abbot of Porto-Carrero, nephew of the cardinal of that name. But he was followed closely by agents sent by Cardinal Dubois, and was arrested in Poitiers.

letters, but you will have to find a reliable scoundrel who is not too expensive to do the deed. That's my last word!"

"I have another solution to propose to you," said Don Martin Blas,

Alain Polduc had been expecting that for ten minutes. Was he going to talk about Agnès or Olympe? One thing was certain; one or the other was going to be discussed.

"Let's hear it!" said the Steward with a languishing air.

"I had the honor to tell you at the begining of this conversation," continued Don Martin Blas, "that my trip to Brittany had a twofold purpose: first of all, the interest of the State; next, an entirely personal business. Without putting the State after my own, I can nevertheless offer you some concessions if you help with the latter. Do you know the Baroness of Sainte-Elme?"

That question was asked point-blank, and still more commanding with the eyes than with the mouth.

The Devil! thought the Seneschal. *So he isn't interested in either Olympe or Agnès?*

That name of Madame Saint-Elme, pronounced suddenly, brought back all the threads of that skein so painfully untangled earlier. Could any conversation, no matter its topic, be entertained without the mention of the name of Madame Saint-Elme? And what had Don Martin Blas had to do in that shady story?

"Just by your silence, gentlemen," continued the Spaniard, whose bronzed face cleared up, "I see that you do know her. I left Madrid just to see her. So I gather we are going to be able to work with each other."

"Just to see her?" asked the Seneschal, smiling mechanically. "For no other reason but to see her?"

Don Martin Blas glanced away. The Seneschal continued:

"You have probably heard it said that Madame Saint-Elme sold the secrets of the Prince of Cellamare to the Regent?"

"Sold, no," replied the Spaniard. "Gave, instead."

219

"Gave, if you like that word better," Polduc replied with a wink.

Don Martin Blas shook his head.

"I knew that and it id of very little importance to me. I tell you again, Seneschal, that we are no longer talking politics. The reasons that make me follow the footsteps of Baronness of Saint-Elme are totally personal, and you do not need to know them."

"They say that she is very beautiful," murmured Polduc.

Achille Feydeau smiled and took advantage of the moment to suck on a stomach gumdrop because the conversation did not require his active cooperation.

"What you do need to know," Don Martin Blas continued, "are my actions, because they will help yours. You don't have a choice, gentlemen; you can only be my allies. I hope that is settled?"

The father-in-law and the son-in-law bowed with the same movement.

"I began my search in Paris, the same evening I arrived," the Spaniard continued. "I had no trouble picking up the language. Everyone at the Court knew the Baroness of Saint-Elme, or, rather, they all bragged that they knew her. That was the latest name in fashion. Some told me that she lived in an isolated townhouse behind the Minimes.[87] Others, in a bizarrre, old chateau in the plains of Biçêtre. According to one man, she had a little house in Grange-Batelière.[88] According to another, she took a carriage every night to go and spend the night at the Trianon. Some affirmed that she had an apartment at the Palais-Royal. I went behind the Minimes; I explored the plains of Biçêtre and the Grange-Batelière; I visited the Trianon. There were no traces of Madame Saint-Elme! I questioned the valets of the Regent, who laughed in my face like the insolent scoundrels that they are. Tired of this fruitless

---

[87] Near the Place des Vosges.
[88] Near Montmartre.

investigation, do you know what I did? I asked the Regent himself."

"Really!" exclaimed Polduc and Feydeau at the same time.

"And he didn't do the same as his valets?" asked the Seneschal.

"He would not have dared," Don Martin Blas replied drily.

Achille Feydeau opened his eyes wide.

"The Regent," the Spaniard continued, "answered me this way: when Madame Saint-Elme wishes to see me, she knows where to find me. That's the advantage that she has over me."

"What a strange creature," grumbled Polduc.

"And you didn't think to go and speak to the Lieutenant of Police?"

"Oh, yes I did. I met Count Voyer d'Argenson[89] in Spain when he eas your Ambassador there. He received me well; he had his reasons for that... but when I questioned him about the Baroness Saint-Elme, he answered me: 'I have in this drawer three hundred thousands livres in gold for whoever will find where she lives for me.'"

"Oh, that woman is really a willl o´the wisk,!" exclaimed Polduc.

---

[89] Marc-René de Voyer, Marquis de Paulmy and marquis d'Argenson (1652-1721). In 1697 d'Argenson became lieutenant-general of police. It not only gave him the control of the police, but also the supervision of the corporations, printing press, and provisioning of Paris. During the twenty-one years that he exercised the office, he was a party to every private and state secret; in fact, he had a share in every event of any importance in the history of Paris.

"Saint-Elmo's fire,"[90] murmured Feydeau. "Forgive me if I couldn't help making that ingenious connection."

He began to laugh alone.

"We Spaniards," continued Don Martin Blas, "do not easily lose our patience. So I renewed my search. I found a furnished house in the Saint-Denis quarter, where Madame Sainte-Elme had occupied an appartment for three days. The trail was still warm; I followed it, right to Versailles, then from Versailles to Dreux, from Dreux to Prez-en-Pail, where false information led me to Mortagne, on the trail of another Madame Saint-Elme, a local tradeswoman selling earthenware, may God confound her! It was necessary for me to go back to Alençon, where Madame Saint-Elme had spent twenty-four hours, during which time she had met Beautru, the Duke of Maine's valet, and the Abbot of Kergrist, Montesquiou's confidant."

"Do you see that!" interrupted Polduc, very curious.

"I took up her trail again, and I started toward Mayenne, where Madame Saint-Elme had just passed through. I missed her by half an hour in Laval. And, without my devil of a horse, which was exhausted, I would have caught her on the road to Vitré... But here is a different affair: at Vitré, no one had heard of Madame Saint-Elme. The whole city was excited because a certain Countess Isaure had just passed through on her way to Rennes..."

The Steward and the Seneschal both trembled. The piercing glance of the Spaniard searched their expressions, but he was disappointed. Ploduc's wily face, like that, self-important and stupid of Feydeau, showed only one expression: surprise.

Suddenly, great clouds of smoke appeared above the trees and, when the wind died down, even reached the valley. There was agitation at the chateau. On the other side of the

---

[90] A weather phenomenon in which luminous plasma is created by a corona discharge from a sharp or pointed object in a strong electric field in the atmosphere.

moat, a half-dozen peasants were running, carrying their shoes in their hands, shouting in a breathless voice:

"Fire! Fire! It's near the Wolf's Den! It's the old windmill of Pont Joli! Fire! Fire!"

The Seneschal, holding back a nervous movement, went to look at the balcony. He glanced toward the forest. The rays of the setting sun mingled with the billowing clouds of smoke.

That Yaumi is a valuable rascal, he thought.

"What do you think of that, gentlemen?" asked Don Martin Blas, who wasn't at all concerned with the fire.

"Seneschal!" called Feydeau. And when Polduc had turned around, he added: "Don Martin Blas is doing us the honor of asking what we think of his story."

"Assuredly," said Polduc, "appearances seem... I would lean toward... Well, would Don Martin Blas like to be introduced to Countess Isaure de Porhoët?"

"Yes, I would. Which woman is she?"

Polduc turned immediately toward his father-in-law, who began to speak.

"Perhaps I am less qualified than anyone to answer such a question," he pronounced with modesty,. "My honorable relations with the Countess have long been the subject of malicious gossip throughout Rennes..."

"Which woman is she?" Don Martin Blas, who had shrugged, repeated.

"I was going to have the honor of describing her to you..."

"Is she young?" the Spaniard again interrupted.

"She is adorably beautiful."

"Brunette or blonde?"

"Blonde."

Don Martin Blas bit his lips. Polduc, who had been watching him attentively for several seconds, smiled imperceptibly.

"Women can be clever," he pronounced in a neutral voice. "Had someone told you that Baronness Saint-Elme was a brunette?"

223

VI. The Watchword

Steward Feydeau looked from the Spaniard to Polduc. He no longer understood anything.

"Have you studied a little, Don Martin," he asked him, "the various shades of women's hair? I have, in that regard, a certain expertise. I have seen so many adorable hair styles, and some up close! I can paint for you verbally the exact color of Madame Isaure's hair. It's not ash blond, which is charming; it's not lager blond, the superlative of ash blond, which diminishes the face somewhat. It's not fawn-colored blond, nor very fair blond. The little Marquise of Kermelan, who made me duel in '87 that big fool of Pacé, had hair of that same shade. I still have a curl of it. But I have so many others, and the proverb says: 'Try not looking for a needle in a hay stack!' It isn't olive blond, either. Take the Countess of Montmurant, a beautiful creature who died of sorrow when I went out with the Councilwoman of Septeuil... It's not honey blond either, nor the blond that resembles the plumes of young turtledoves and even less the Scotch blond that is the color of fire and that running dogs can follow by smell. It is celestial blonde, M. Martin Blas, the blond that makes a luminous halo around a charming forehead, a blond that shines like a diadem of gold with a reflection from the sun.

Achille-Musée stopped to catch his breath. Don Martin Blas, who hadn't been listening to him for a while, tapped on the Seneschal's shoulder.

"You have something to tell me, Monsieur de Rohan-Polduc?' he asked very low in his ear.

Cast pearls before swine, thought Feydeau.

"I must protest...." replied the Seneschal.

But the Spaniard squeezed his arm and Polduc didn't even try to look straight back at him.

"It would seem as if Countess Isaure isn't her real name," Don Martin Blas continued, staring at him with blazing eyes.

"I didn't know; I absolutely didn't know," stammered Polduc.

Don Martin Blas turned him loose and walked around the room.

"Isn't she the one who lives in that apartment?" he suddenly asked, while a bright red surfaced under the bronze of his skin.

"No. Those are the Rohan-Polduc demoiselles, my two daughters," replied Feydeau.

"Your daughters!" repeated Dn Martin Blas, who stopped in front of him. "Then that name of Rohan fits everybody like the coat of a used clothes dealer."

"I am the one, Don Martin," the Seneschal hurried to answer, "who is going to adopt my two young sisters-in-law and give them my name."

"In our country, in Spain," Don Martin Blas replied, frowning, "road-side thieves give charity to monks from the money they have stolen." Then, in a harsh and commanding tone, he added: "I must see that woman! I must!"

"With your name, Don Martin, and the mission with which you are charged, Countess Isaure's townhouse will open wide its doors."

It was the Seneschal who spoke thus. Feydeau merely waved with his hand, smiling, and said:

"If there were still some obstacles, a word from me would remove them."

"There are obstacles," replied the Spaniard. "I have been in Brittany forty-eight hours. During that time, I have looked for Countesse Isaure, who is fleeing from me just as in the recent past Baronness Saint-Elme did."

"Señor Don Martin Blas," said Feydeau, rising up, "it is an honor and a pleasure to offer you my feeble help: The Countess is at the chateau and..."

"You're wrong, my dear father-in-law," interrupted Polduc.

"What?" exclaimed the Steward.

"The Countess left this morning."

"Without telling me?"

Involuntarily, Polduc looked again toward the clouds of smoke outside that were diminishing.

Even if she made a pact with the Devil, he thought at that moment, because he was a man capable of managing several pieces of business at the same time, *there is still a way to deal with her. If I can have Countesse Isaure, the She-Wolf, and the Saint-Elme woman handled in the same manner that I did the Witch, I'll wager my head that we won't hear anything more about Valentine de Rohan.*

"Don Martin," he continued aloud, "Countess Isaure has a vagabond nature, and doesn't honor the same lodging very long with her presence. We had her an instant yesterday. At daybreak I saw her horse already saddled in the courtyard..."

"Ready to leave?" asked Feydeau.

"To return home, dear father-in-law."

"A horseback ride, at night?"

"Parbleu!" exclaimed Don Martin Blas, "it was actually at night that I saw her leave Rennes, alone and also on horseback. What a strange life that woman lives!"

Achille Feydeau had no longer but one thought: that was to play with dignity his role of jealousy. He struck his gold box violently.

"Jarnibleu!" he exclaimed. "I will have some explanation from her and clear this matter at once!"

"I don't have the same reasons as my father-in-law to pay close attention to the comings and goings of the beautiful Countess Isaure," added Polduc, "but I'm astonished that an envoy from the Court of Spain in Madrid doesn't know what her activities are."

"Be astonished, my good Seneschal," said Don Martin Blas, smoothly. "There are many things like that which I don't know. But what does matter," he said, suddenly giving his language a provocative and rough accent, "is that I know enough to have you both hanged."

Feydeau straightened at that blow; he was almost a gentleman. On the contrary, Polduc lowered his eyes after having thrown a dirty look at the Spaniard.

"We are not accustomed," he said very low, "to such behavior."

"Habits can be acquired," the Spaniard responded. "I am not happy with you two. Listen to me carefully. Both of you are gorged with wealth dishonestly acquired. If you prove to be useful, you will be tolerated... If you don't, beware!"

He put on his hat and pushed the door open with a kick of his foot like an angry commoner. On the threshold, he stopped to say:

"You will bring Countess Isaure to me this evening at the Governor's Ball. We will also talk again about the Count of Toulouse business. Until then!"

He left.

Steward Feydeau let himself drop down on the sofa.

"I prefer the grand airs of the French!" he exclaimed. "The tyrannies of these Spanish boors are intolerable!"

"Intolerable!" repeated the Seneschal like an echo. He reflected and said to himself: "He reminds me of someone... But in the past, it was all about courtesy and elegance, a true chevalier... Why is he running after that woman... and why those troubled glances as he looked around the room?"

"What are you thinking about, dear son-in-law?" asked Feydeau.

"No," said the Seneschal, still talking to himself, "that couldn't be him."

On leaving the boudoir, Don Martin Blas had gone down to the stable and had had his horse saddled. Before leaving, and despite Ploduc's formal assurance, he entered the salon to check if Countess Isaure wasn't there just in case.

As soon as he was in the presence of the two Demoiselles, you wouldn't have recognized him. It would have been impossible to meet a more perfect gentleman. Evidently his brutal behavior before the Seneschal and the Steward had been an act.

Thus, Agnès and Olympe Feydeau, soon to be called the Lladies of Rohan-Polduc, didn't share their father's opinion of that gallant Spaniard. They had discovered in him something mysteriously romantic, and the bronze tone of his skin pleased them. We must state here that they had taste, and that they were generally drawn toward handsome cavaliers.

Countess Isaure wasn't in the salon. So Don Martin Blas took his leave, promising to see the two ladies again at the Governor's ball.

As he was going down the main staircase to reach the courtyard where his horse was being held, a young girl came up, singing. They met each other face to face.

The young girl was clothed in a simple cloth dress. Her hair escaped from her headband in a profusion of beautiful dark curls. She wore little wooden clogs on her feet, with the apron of a servant falling over her skirt.

She just passed by, carrying in her hands a beautiful rose silk dress. The Spaniard stpeed aside to make way for her. She thanked him with a smile.

Don Martin Blas remained motionless; his mouth wide open. He put his hand over his heart, which was pounding. For an instant, he was on the point of going back up the steps of the staircase, but he changed his mind and slowly descended into the vestibule.

He mounted the saddle without saying a word and spurred his mount. The ride from the forest to Rennes was long. For the duration of the journey, Don Martin Blas forgot to push his horse. An irresistible reverie seemed to draw him in.

On arriving at the city gates, he shook himself like a man who had just awakened. Was it a dream? he asked himself. Then the name of Valentine came to die on his lips.

In the boudoir, Achille Feydeau repeated
"What are you thinking about, my dear son-in-law?"
Instead of answering, the Seneschal asked:

"My dear father-in-law, what is your opinion about all of this?"

"Hum... Er..." replied the Steward. "He's a brute. I admit I don't fear such a rival. My adorable Isaure has too much delicacy both in her mind and in her heart to pay him much attention."

"Good Lord, father-in-law," interrupted Polduc, indignant, "have you suddenly gone mad? Do you have the heart to joke when it is surely a question of our fortunes, and perhaps of our very lives?"

"I'm not joking... The Countess..."

"Let's stop talking about the Countess, please! We will talk again about her when it's time for us to explain how she, the heroine of conspiracies hatched in Rennes against the Regent, is connected with Baroness Saint Elme, a shady operative at the Court."

"Would you like for me to tell you, Alain, my boy?" replied the Steward with a knowing air. "That man was trying to scare us, that's all."

"Well, then, he's succeeded, my dear father-in-law," Polduc seriously replied. "I am afraid of that man."

VII. Profits and Losses

The Steward straightened up and took on an offended air.

"Afraid of that man!" he repeated. "Come now! Speak for yourself, my dear son-in-law!"

"Then you are very brave, my dear father-in-law, and I admire you!"

Achille Feydeau de Brou began by caressing his chin lovingly. Then, when he saw that the Seneschal remained immobile in front of him, his forehead wrinkled, his head lowered, his facebegan to show, under the expert whitewash that covered him, a worried expression.

"It's not that man who frightens me," he said, finally. "It's you!"

"Mr. Steward," Polduc began with a note of discouragement, " a great writer of antiquity pronounced these words: '*It is more difficult to keep a province than to conquer it.*'[91] We are rich; you, powerfully so; me sufficiently so. We have good reputations and honest positions. I don't know if all that means very much to you."

"What! Of course, it does!" exclaimed Feydeau.

"That's very good. The same goes for me. In that case, let's play it close to the vest, believe me, because all that can be snatched away from us today or tomorrow."

"Come now! You're exaggerating the danger, my dear son-in-law."

"And the day that all that is snatched from us, my dear father-in-law, our heads will be shaky on our shoulders."

"That's it! You see us being beheaded! Why not hanged!"

"Only because your own actions have made us gentlemen. When the Count of Toulouse was recalled to Paris, remember, my dear father-in-law, that his attention had become focused on your actions. And he isn't one of those who can be bought."

"No," replied Achille Feydeay, who put his fingers into his wig, an idiotic smile spreading on his lips. "But he comes back to us married, my dear son-in-law. The beautiful Madame de Noailles[92] is a daughter of Eve. I know a serpent that will tempt her!"

Polduc stamped his foot angrily.

"On my word, he exclaimed, "that passes the limits. There are instants when I feel like reaching the bank all alone, Mr. Steward, and leaving you struggling in the middle of the

---

[91] Publius Annius Florus (?-130 AD).

[92] Marie Victoire Sophie de Noailles, Countess of Toulouse (1688-1766), daughter of Anne Jules de Noailles, the second Duke of Noailles, and Marie-Françoise de Bournonville. Her second spouse was Louis Alexandre de Bourbon, Count of Toulouse.

river. By theDevil! Will you be practical for once in your life, yes or no?"

"La! La! Seneschal, I know that I cause the persons of my sex a painful feeling each time that I allude to my frequent successes with the ladies.... Let's not talk any more about that! Let's talk seriously. I believe that I can say that, when it comes to business, my outlook is accurate and sharp... If you fear the Count of Toulouse, would you like us to enter whole-heartedly into an alliance with the Spanish Court?"

"Whole-heartedly?" repeated Polduc. "Bah! A conspiracy can't get reheated any more than a good dinner can. The Spanish have staked everything—and lost."

"Do you want us to side with M. de Montesquiou?"

"Worship the setting sun? Never!"

"Do you want us to denounce that Spaniard to M. de Toulouse?"

"I have considered that, but his papers would be seized, and we would be compromised."

"The Devil! The Devil!" said the Steward, "Then tell me what you want."

"I want to barricade myself with you behind your fortune, my dear father-in-law. What threatens us? The new Governor, the Wolves in the forest, and the Spaniard Martin Blas. As for the Governor, the Rohan-Poldue young ladies are going to attend the Governor's Ball tonight. I have solicited for them, in your name and in mine, the honor of presenting the keys to the city to His Serene Highness, the Count of Toulouse."

"Our names... Inseparable from Marshal of Montesquiou!" murmured Feydeau, who blushed under his make-up.

"So we remain the Marshal's faithful friends while we also become the Covernor's new friends. It's very simple. As for the Wolves, I have Yaumi, who has just today rendered me a great service. And speaking of that, I see that smoke is no longer coming from the direction of the Pont Joli."

"The fire must have been extinguished," said Feydeau.

Polduc went to the balcony and put his hand above his eyes so as to shade them. He took a long and careful look toward the forest.

"The fire extinguished itself. Theold windmill of the Pont Joli no longer exists... My dear father-in-law, I will ask you for a small subsidy: The Wolves are poor, and we need Yaumi."

"Later, my dear son-in-law; my cash box is empty."

"God knows I don't want to rush you, but Yaumi needs to be paid before tomorrow morning... Now, let's come to Don Martin Blas... Just as he surprised us by his brusque entry, I was about to paint you a moral picture of his character. Have you heard of those Castillan beggars who ask for charity with a musket and a cross?"

"That proud Hidalgo..." the Steward began...

"Everyone in Spain is proud," the Seneschal interrupted, "even beggars... Don Martin is a scoundrel of that type. But he can be bought; and that's up to you."

"If he's not too expensive...."

"He *is* expensive. We talked last night. He's a strange character. He brags that he has neither faith nor law, and that he respects nothing in the world."

"A free thinker?"

"Quite. Drawn to women like Don Juan, althoughthrough hatred rather than love, searching for forgetfulness in drunkenness... One of those madmen, my dear father-in-law, who was once brazenly deceived and who is seeking revenge!"

"Women have never deceived me," said Achille Feydeau.

"Just a moment," continued the Seneschal, whose voice had become dreamy. "I thought... I thought... But you know how I am, always seeing resemblances? Didn't I imagine one night that Valentine de Rohan was hiding under the name of Countess Isaure?"

The Steward made a disdainful grimace.

"Valentine de Rohan was very beautiful, but that was fifteen years ago," he said. "You are not a connoisseur of women, Seneschal. Could seven or eight lusters[93] have passed over the fresh lips of my adored one?"

"Enough! So be it!" said Polduc. "I see phantoms everywhere, but I don't complain. about it. That forces you to stay on your guard. For a moment, I had the notion that the ferocious Martin Blas wasn't any more Spanish than you or I. Do you remember Morvan de Saint-Maugan, the former friend and aide of the Count of Toulouse, and secret husband to Valentine de Rohan?"

"I have probably seen him, but I don't have any recollection of him."

"Eh! Eh!" said the Seneschal, sniggering. "That's because you weren't busy cospiring then. Do you know that I risked four inches of steel in my stomach more than once by shoving my finger between the tree and the bark so strongly?"

"That metaphor doesn't make any sense," said Achille Feydeau, who prided himself on being a grammarian.

"It's been fifteen years since then," Polduc continued. "Fifteen years can change a face a great deal. Besides, it's said that Morvan de Saint-Maugan died in 1707 at the battle of Almansa.[94] Let's say that it wasn't he, but following my system, let's act as if it was he. And if it is, then we have something better than a tiger to throw at Valentine de Rohan."

"Your conclusion?"

"It is this: During his stay at Rennes, that man needs something with which to lead a good life. Martin Blas doesn't want any women that are bought. But women who are not bought cost an insane price."

---

[93] A luster is five years.

[94] It took place on 25 April 1707 between the forces of Philip V of Spain, Bourbon, claimant to the Spanish throne, and his Habsburg rival, Archduke Charles of Austria. The result was a decisive Bourbon victory that reclaimed most of eastern Spain for Philip.

"Well, my dear son-in-law," said Achille Feydeau, "he will be given what he would prefer."

"Very good, my dear father-in-law. You're starting to understand!"

"So much the better," continued the Steward, "since I no longer see the necessity of sending to the Regent the money..."

"On the contrary, father-in law, on the contrary!" exclaimed Polduc. "Let's take care of what surrounds us. Bribing the Wolves is good. Let's be generous with this Martin Blas so long as events won't put a rope around his necks... Good sense demands it... And thus, let's send some nice things to the Regent, my dear father-in-law. Let's do it!"

"Easy for you to ay so, my dear son-in-law. It isyou're your purse. And the Wolves have big appetites."

"With fifty thousand écus, you will be left in peace."

"And that Spaniard?"

"A hundred thousand livres. Think of the fact that we are in his hands. Do you prefer that he turns on you as he seeks to do to the Count of Toulouse?"

"Plus five hundred thousand livres to the Regent..."

"Six hundred seventy-five thousans livres, including the good Abbot Dubois."

"That makes more than a million."

"Not a great deal more."

"I can't..."

Alan Polduc took the Steward's hand and squeezed it strongly.

"Listen, my dear father-in-law," he said, lowering his voice suddenly. "You risk more here than I do, simply because I have less than you do. Don't bargain away the head that is on your shoulders."

Feydeau couldn't keep from shivering. He felt the Seneschal's cold hands between his own.

"Are you hiding something from me, my dear son-in-law?" he stammered.

"I not hiding anything from you," Polduc replied, "but am I sure of seeing everyhing? There are, I don't know how many, mysteries and terrible menaces around us. This is a time of crisis. I sense that, but I cannot explain it more clearly to you... It's the type of crisis that saves or that kills."

Achille Feydeau saw beads of sweat trickle down from his son-in-law's forehead.

"You are as pale as a corpse!" he stammered, catching the contagion of the fright. "I have never heard you talk this way"

Polduc tried to smile.

"My eyes and my ears are awake all the time. I am active. I stay awake. I do not rest, day or night."

His voice was as frank as that of a good father proud of his daily work.

"Thank God, my dear father-in-law," he continued, "you see that I work like a beast of burden, and I am not ashamed of it! Every task is good for me, but the road is slippery... very slippery! It is useless to stand up straight, because one might lose one's balance. Philippe d'Orléans is still the master, and Paris is still the last refuge in case of misfortune... So let's send him that money, father-in-law, do it!"

"I'll do it immediately!" exclaimed Feydeau, touched to the bottom of his soul. "Eventually, it will be the Province of Brittany that will pay, anyway. Have one of your servants be readied to go out."

Polduc took his hand away.

"The Spaniard is here to spy on us," he said.

"That's right. Do you have a messenger?"

The Seneschal rang a little bell.

"Bring in that young boy who is waiting in the vestibule," he ordered the servant who answered.

The servant left. Achille Feydeau.

"Those ladies must be deploring my absence," he said while rearranging the symmetry of his wig in front of a mirror. "I am leaving you to arrange all that... Without a good-bye!"

Polduc stopped him just as he started toward the door.

"Stay, please, father-in-law," he asked.

"Do you still need me?"

"Absolutely!"

"For what?"

Polduc took him back to the sofa.

"Sit down," he said. "In these kinds of operations, I like to keep my friends very near me. That doesn't disengage me, that's true, but that engages them. Sit down, please."

Achille Feydeau took a place on the sofa with bad grace. At that moment, the door opened and our friend Magloire appeared on the threshold.

"That's enough, you rascal!" he shouted behind him to the servant who had brought him. "Have you ever seen such a thing! This fellow calls me his friend as if I were some flat footed idiot of his kind! Get lost, you wretch! And don't forget the respect that is due to me if you want to keep your ears!"

Achille Feydeau put on his pince-nez. Polduc himself stared to examine the new arrival. Magloire had completely renewed his costume. He was wearing a somewhat used doublet, but cut in the fashion of gentlemen. His vest was too tight for him and his trousers too long. The lace on his shirt, no longer of its first freshness, had been arranged so sloppily that one would truly have taken him for a young comedian from the provinces. He was coiffed casually, and his hat, thrown negligently under his arm, let fall a half foot of braid.

What had that Magloire done with his white shirt, his white jacket and his white cap? We must declare that these simple clothes looked better on him, but that was not at all his opinion. He found himself superb, and his feet no longer touched the ground figuratively.

He took some steps forward; his feet turned outward as in ballet; his hand was kept on the lace, his fist on his hip. He said, looking his world in the face:

"Good day Mr. Steward. I'm your servant. Good day, Mr. Seneschal... How are you in this beautiful weather?"

VIII. The Interrogation

Both the father-in-law and the son-in-law began to laugh. Magloire did the same and took his hat from under his arm to fan himself.

"Not bad, and you?" he said before there was any response to his question.

"Where the Devil did you fish up this character?" grumbled the Steward.

"The fact is that he is priceless."

"Don't disturb yourself," Magloire continued. "The young ladies are well? Good! So much the better! So much the better!"

He saw a mirror with his reflection from head to toe. It looked grotesque, including head and toe. Nut he thought:

What would they give, these two old men, to have my looks! With all the gold that they have wickedly acquired, they can't acquire the attraction of my youth. That's what's chaffing them.

"Are you looking for employment?" the Seneschal asked.

Magloire put his nose in the air, his hat under his arm and made a pirouette.

"Yes, dear sir. At the moment, I want to use my diverse talents and make myself a position in society. It's time; I have the age and the capabilities."

"He's a simple-minded person," Feydeau whispered in his son-in-law's ear.

"We don't need a genius," Polduc answered, also in a low voice. And he said aloud: "What do you know how to do, my good fellow?"

Here is another one who is much too familiar! thought Magloire. *I must display self-assurance, or I'll miss my career!*

"Sir," he answered in a stentorian voice, "I'm a jack of all trades... Yes, a jack of all trades! Without that, you can be sure that I would never have come to see you."

237

"What?" said Achille Feydeau, who thought that he had misunderstood. "What did he say?"

"A jack of all trades," Magloire repeated for the third time, lifting his head proudly. Then, with an ineffably stupid smile, he added: "You're both scoundrels, they say. So you need a cunning fellow! Well, I'm your man. You would look a long time before you could find a rascal as cunning as I am!"

"He doesn't look the type," Feydeau observed.

"Appearances can sometimes be deceptive," Polduc murmured.

Magloire gave the Steward an irritated look.

"Me, not looking rascally enough? My good man, you don't know what you're talking about! It's the most cunning rascals who don't look like it. I hide my game. Is that so clumsy? But in my soul, I am as scoundrelly as you!"

Feydeau and Polduc looked at each other. The Steward wanted to get angry.

Magloire told himself: *I've stunned them.*

"Send that lunatic back, son-in-law," said Feydeau.

"I want to keep him," Polduc replied. "He's a lucky find."

Feydeau remained stunned.

Magloire continued with warmth:

"Proofs! Do you want some? Do you know what base acts I did despite my age when I was still very young? Primo and first of all, I fornicated with my Sidonie!"

"Really?" said the Steward, who suddenly became attentive.

The Seneschal lent his ear.

"He's our man!" he said.

"Because he fornicated with his Sidonie?"

"Because no one could seriously believe that we could choose such a tool."

"As for that, you're right! But what if the tool proves worthless?"

"What is the story of this Sidonie, my boy," the Seneschal asked.

Achille Feydeau offered his gold box.

Magloire stuck two fingers inside, saying:

"I normally don't, but on this occasion...."

He sneezed and continued in a solemn voice:

"Far from the Courts, far from the shiningt palaces where shamelessness thrives in the golden halls of opulence, there lived a young virgin whose innocence was only equaled by her naive candor. Her name was Sidonie, and her family name, I shall keep secret out of respect for her aunts... You could say that she was well known in her neighborhood, because she was honest and sober, and a washerwoman by trade. Before chance, or rather fate, had led her to the road where I passed by, she had the purity of the dove! Well! I had the effrontery of staining her honor, coldly and without remorse. I made it a barbaric game to abuse her with all my empty promises, and finally, having mingled her in all my farces, I dropped her there one fine morning, neither seen nor known, to go and dazzle other women...

"Poor Sidonie!" said Feydeau.

"You are indeed a scoundrel," Polduc added.

Magloire rubbed his hands together enthusiastically.

"Isn't that so? Isn't that so?" he exclaimed. "You are forced to do me justice. You deplore the fate of that girl deflowered by my hellish breath. And, in passing, didn't you find that I expressed myself rather nicely... isn't that true? That's necessary to seduce them! That's not all... I did something even better..."

"Not possible!" said Polduc.

"Let's hear it," added the Steward.

"Do you know Monsieur Raoul?" Magloire asked.

"No, I don't think so."

"Tall, blond, a good physique, like me... See, I'm wearing his clothes..."

"His clothes!" Feydeau and Polduc repeated at the same time.

When Magloire saw that they were looking at him with a kind of fear, pride and joy almost made him faint.

"Yes, his clothes!" he exclaimed, "his very own clothes! Because Raoul was my master, and I threw him out; I kicked him out the door without pity."

"Ah, young man," Achille Feydeau said sternly, "that's too much! Do you think that you can make fun of a man of my age?"

"I see I've startled you... The notion of seeing a servant fire his master is shocking to you? I will tell you much more... Raoul was my master, but he was also my friend.. It was agreed between us that I would carry his things, that I wouldn't do any work and that he would take care of me. But this morning, when I woke up, he had already left. And how did he manage to go, leaving behind his bed, his doublet, and his shoes? That's what's astonishing, but that's none of my business."

"That young Monsieur Raoul," the Seneschal interrupted, "doesn't he live across from the Feydeau townhouse?"

"In an attic, yes, which he rents for six sous a year. For some time now, I have wanted to try on the clothes of a gentleman. These are torn, that's true, but you can see the effect... Taking advantage of my master's absence, I put on his abandoned clothes, and I took to the open fields. There's my proof!"

"And afterward?" Polduc asked.

"Don't you find that this is enough?" Magloire replied, sadly.

"I find that you were very wrong, my boy," Polduc said with menacing irony, "to come and report this to me, me who puts thieves in prison!"

"And to me, who assesses fines!" added the Royal Steward. "What a fool!"

Magloire looked at them askew.

"Do you believe that you two are going to make me fee frightened?" he shouted.

"Silence!" Polduc rudely commanded.

240

"C'mon, c'mon, my good gentlemen," Magloire continued. "I am young... Have some indulgence. I can't yet be as strong as you are in chicanery as you are. With time, I will manage to do better!"

"Let's deliberate, Mr. Steward," said Polduc in a serious voice.

Magloire started to tremble.

"Listen! Listen!" he said. "They say in Rennes that you are two damned good-for-nothings, my good masters; that you believe neither in God nor in the Devil! That you are stealing with both hands."

"You insolent man!" both the father-in-law and the son-in-law, cut to the quick, shouted at the same time.

Into what trap did I stumble? Magloire wondered. *It didn't seem to please them when I said they were scoundrels!*

"My good masters," he continued in a begging tone, "I would very much like to be a rogue like you! My former boss said, when he was talking about you, 'They are two clever rogues.The only stupid ones are the honest folks.'"

Feydeau and Polduc deliberated.

"This boy seems rather dangerous to me," Polduc gave his opinion, winking.

"Dangerous to the highest degree," continued Achille Feydeau. "*Ad gradum supremum.*"

At that, Magloire turned pale.

"Ah! dear sirs," he cried out with distress. "Have I been misled: are you not rogues?"

"My opinion," said the Seneschal, "is that we should make an example of him."

"*Exemplum facere,*" Achille Feydeau translated.

Magloire fell to his knees and cried out, weeping:

"Have Pity! Have Pity! I lied to you, my good judges! Is it a sin to look at a young girl who is drying her laundry? When she looked at me, I lowered my eyes. I never dared to ay a hand on her. I was bragging, sirs. I can only hope that Sidonie may be as faithful as I am, because I have often seen some boors frm the Conti regiment smoking their pipes at her window. Me! Seduce a young girl! Good Lord! Everything that I said was to make you think well of me!"

Polduc spoke in a low voice to the Steward.

"Do you believe him?" said Feydeau, with all the appearance of profound astonishment.

"It's a suspicion," Polduc replied, "a very vague suspicion... I will do my best to clarify it."

Magloire's teeth chattered because he was now very frightened.

"And the business with your master?" the Seneschal suddenly asked him.

"A lie—like the business with Sidonie, my dear sir. My master gave me his clothes."

"Is that really true?"

"As true as that the sun shines on us. Steal Monsieur Raoul's clothes! Never! He would have broken my ribs; I know him!"

"But you don't know him under any other name except Raoul?"

"No, my good master."

"What is his occupation?"

"He doesn't have one."

"What are his resources?"

"I don't know if he has any."

"Is he not in love with one of the Rohan young ladies?"

"Yes, Celeste."

"Then, in order to give you his clothes, he must have gotten new ones?"

"Ah! Sir, there are some people who have all the luck in the world. Raoul is, since this morning, an officer in the Conti regiment."

"An officer!... That Raoul!" exclaimed the Seneschal.

"Yes. Yesterday, he went to consult the Miller Woman, and she gave him an amulet and there he is."

"What do you make of that, Seneschal," the Steward asked.

Polduc reflected:

"This is no longer a farce."

With a commanding gesture, he pushed poor Magloire aside and took the Steward to the other end of the room.

"Who is forcing us to tremble before the first person who comes in, father-in-law?" he pronounced in a low voice. "Who is pushing us to hedge our bets constantly, to keep a foot in both camps, and to try to please everyone... What is our stumbling block, our sword of Damocles?"

"What are you getting at, my dear son-in-law?", Achille Feydeau interrupted, fearing another demand for money.

"It's the existence of César's son," Polduc replied. "It's the existence of Valentine's daughter. Without that double living menace, we could lift our heads high; we could avoid wearing masks, and deal frankly and openly with all these intrigues which are only good for desperate rogues. In a word, we would be unassailable."

"What is your conclusion?"

Polduc thought again.

"Suppose, my dear father-in-law," he said so low that the Steward could barely hear him, "that Valentine's daughter left for Paris tonight—an elopement. Suppose that César's son fell in love with her... There are bizarre things like that in life that make the inventions of poets pale by comparison. Suppose now that the man in love is told about the elopement of his flame. What would he do?"

"He would despair."

"No, not a Rohan! He would pick up his sword and jump into the saddle."

"That's true... And then....?"

"Suppose now that, in the dark of night, our Yaumi is taking a walk with a dozen well-armed Wolves..."

"I hate to compromise ourselves with that Yaumi!"

Polduc wore a superior smile.

"Tsk, tsk, my dear father-in-law! Think! Our man in love wears a French uniform. The Wolves will naturally attack a Conti soldier just like a bloodhound will attack a deer..."

At that moment, bursts of laughter were heard in the hall.

"My daughters!" said the Steward, who rose.

The door opened almost immediately. Agnès and Olympe Feydeau de Brou, also known as the Demoiselles de Rohan, made their entrance into the boudoir.

IX. The Demoiselles Feydeau

Agnès and Olympe were accompanied by two female servants.

"We have come to reclaim possession of our domain, gentlemen," said Agnès, a beautiful blonde with provocative eyes and a too seductive smile.

"Are you chasing us away immediately, my beautiful ladies?" Polduc asked.

Olympe, desperate to be as casual as her sister, had taken being languorous as her specialty. She had dark blonde hair, a somewhat stocky figure and a dark complexion.

"We only have an hour to get dressed," she said, drawling her words, "and our Cinderella is so clumsy!"

"Since we have been dismissed, my dear father-in-law," said Polduc, who was in a hurry to go somewhere else to continue the conversation, "let's obey with good grace."

Feydeau kissed his daughters' hands with that gallantry that made him such a likeable man. Polduc bowed; he was less attentioned.

"Can I leave?" asked at that moment Magloire.

"What's that?" Olympe and Agnès, who hadn't even noticed him, cried out at the same time.

"Oh! Beautiful young ladies," said Magloire, tears in his eyes, "you buy your cakes from us. My Sidonie's the one who does your laundry! Take pity on a poor unfortunate man, led astray by love, because it was to make myself a position from which I could marry her that I put myself in the position where I am now..."

The two sisters looked at each other, laughing.

"Follow us!" Polduc commanded.

Magloire joined his hands, imploring the attention of the two sisters. When he saw that he got nothing but a burst of pitiless laughter, he straightened his back.

"That's all right," he said. "I have my business! Still, that doesn't keep people from the neighborhood saying that the two Feydeau ladies aren't waiting to get married to change they names, because otherwise, they'd have to wait for a long time!"

He hurried after the Steward, who was the last to leave. From the threshold he shouted again: "

That's how it is, my beautiful ladies, that's what they say, and more... That you make eyes at any gentleman who pass under your balcony, and that gentlemen have only eyes for your Cinderella."

He slammed the door.

Agnès and Olympe, red with anger, remained motionless.

"Father-in-law," said Polduc, in the corridor. "All this must be done tonight."

"But what about the money for the Regent?" observed Achille Feydeau. "What if the Wolves attack the escort..."

"The Wolves will attack," answered the Seneschal, "but we will send the money by another way."

He turned around.

"Where are you, boy?" he asked.

"Hang me if you want," replied Magloire. "I cut them down to size, those two uppity lasses."

"Do you want to become someone important? I have a job for you," the Seneschal asked.

"For real? What job?" asked Magloire, who was suspicious.

"A government courier—almost an ambassador?"

"I'm cut out for that," answered Magloire, who had suddenly returned to the excellent opinion that he had had of himself. It had taken him only a second to say to himself:

The two old fellas only wanted to test me... They wanted to see what mettle I'm made of.

"What's the salary for being an ambassador like that?" he asked aloud.

"Enough to marry your Sidonie," the Steward replied."

Magloire swallowed.

"Maybe,"he said, smiling a little, "maybe if I will still want her when I'm rich. And what's the risk?"

"None."

"Then, that's the job for me!"

"Go down to the kitchens," Polduc continued. "Eat well, drink better, then lie down and take a nap. You will be awakened when it's time for you to start to work."

Agnès Feydeau de Brou was twenty-four years-old; her sister, Olympe, was twenty-two years-old. In the 18th century, people married young. Agnès and Olympe were already old maids. That was not because they lacked a desire for marriage. The Steward was rich and his daughters had some beauty, but that wasn't enough, The Breton, by his nature, is as proud as two Spaniards. There, a wrong marriage is almost a failure, and Achille Feydeau was, after all, only a civil servant. So little thought of as Alain Polduc was, his marriage to the elder of the Feydeau daughters had displeased the whole province, because of the title of Viscount de Rohan that he wore.

Olympe and Agnès were thought to willingly look for the small adventures that lead to marriage by the shortest and most picturesque way. They had a reputation for not being cruel to the excess. Navailles,[95] the friend of the Regent, had jokingly accused them, during his passage through Rennes, of wanting to compromise him.

On a walk, at the church, at a ball, everywhere there was a crowd, Agnès and Olympe were seen. Always overdressed, always doing what they could with their eyes behind their sparkling fans.

---

[95] Philippe de Montaut-Bénac, Viscount then Duke of Navailles (1619-1684).

They were like wax dummies; nothing in their heads, nothing in their hearts, pretty dolls, talkative, vain, and cold. They were bitterly jealous of the nobility above them; but those below them, the honest bourgeoisie, they crushed with their stupid contempt. Add to that, a good dose of scandal-mongering, curiosity, coquetry, a great deal of impudence, little wit, and a tiny layer of varnish over their learning, uselessly covering a thick coat of ignorance, and there you will have a rather accurate portrait of the two daughters of Royal Steard Achille Feydeau de Brou.

They ruled over four slaves, who had a hard job there. In the first place, there was Annette and Mariolle, their chambermaids; then there was Celeste, nicknamed Cinderella, that gracious little girl who was cutting bouquets of pentecote flowers in the valley. Finally, there was Zoé des Étangs du Ronceroy de Kerméléon, their former governess who had grown to be their lady companion. She was from a good household. Her mission was to accompany the two girls and to chaperone them. Just imagine a little woman with a dull face, a poor physique, always dressed in dark wool like a Spanish Dueña stuck between two girls showing off their frills. Agnès and Olympe counted a great deal on that contrast. Poor Zoé earned her living by that martyrdom.

On entering the boudoir, Agnès said to Zoé, who was showing her thin face at the door:

"Go away, des Etangs, go get dressed!"

"And try," Olympe added, "not to be too ridiculous today!"

Zoé went back, sad and cold, to her little bedroom, and when she entered it, she closed the door. She took out from the bottom of a chest a famous silk puce dress that she had been given when the oldest of the two Feydeau girls had taken her first communion. Zoé respectfully unfolded the napkins filled with camphor, pepper and lavender, that kept the cloth from worms, and began her solitary dressing.

Then, Olympe said to Mariolle:

"Hurry! Be quick!"

"Hurry up, Annette," Agnès, said at the same time.

And then both exclaimed:

"But where is that lazy Cinderella?"

That lazy Cinderella had been given orders to prepare the outfits for each of the two girls in secret. Agnès hoped very much to eclipse Olympe that night, and Olympe was certain she would crush Agnès. Annette and Mariolle set up the preparations for each to be dressed for the occasion. While the ladies' hair was being coiffed, it was a competition where the most beautiful of the two would have the honor of presenting the keys to the city to the son of Louis XIV.

While leaving the preparation of their coiffures to the cares of the chambermaids, they examined each other on the sly. Agnès was thinking: *Poor Olympe, I am sorry for her; this will be such a disappointment.* And Olympe was telling herself: *Poor Agnès, Can anyone be so blind? I am sure she is counting on being the most beautiful.* That was without diminishing the stream of reproaches made to the chambermaids. Both Olympe and Agnès were in a detestable mood. That fool Magloire had stirred up their anger. The pride of the Feydeau young ladies was cut to the quick by that recent wound.

"I am a fright," exclaimed Agnès, the first to push Mariolle away.

"I am horrible," Olympe said in her turn.

"We need Cinderella!" they both exclaimed.

"Cinderella is running around the woods, as usual," Annette replied.

Mariolle added:

"No. I bet she is still in the main stairwell being admired by some gentleman."

"Who looks at her?"

"It happened only a short while ago," Mariolle answered, "but a handsome foreign gentleman..."

"Don Martin Blas!" the two sisters interrupted at the same time.

"Yes! Don Martin Blas, that's his name," Mariolle continued. "He was just standing there, looking strangely at Cinderella, who was begging his pardon for going past him."

Olympe and Agnès had a moment of forced laughter.

"The manners of our Cinderella!" they exclaimed.

Then Agnès added seriously:

"The effrontery of that girl will end up compromising our reputation!"

To which Olympe answered without laughing:

"It's a mistake to keep such bad subjects in our household."

It was at that moment that the gracious Celeste entered the boudoir. She was very pale and seemed to have trouble standing. Her forehead and her hair were bathed with sweat.

"Why do you keep us waiting like this, lazy girl?" the two sisters said in a sharp voice full of rancor.

"Is my dress finished?" added the elder.

"Is my corsage ready?" asked the younger. "And the embroidery for my petticoat?"

"And the lace for the dickey?"

While they were talking, the two daughters were looking at each other in a manner that was anything but friendly. Just imagine two enemy armies successfully unmasked as having managed to keep several batteries secret. Agnès had a dress that Olympe didn't know about; Olympe was having a corsage secretly prepared! And that embroidery for the petticoat...

Celeste arrived with an arm full of chiffon.

"What you asked me for is ready," she responded.

Her legs were trembling. She let herself fall into a chair.

"What does this mean?" Olympe asked severely. "You now take a seat in our presence?"

"When you are too kind to these people..." began Agnès in a sententious tone.

Celeste tried to stand up, but she fell back again.

"Was it that foreihn gentleman, Don Martin Blas, who put you in such a state, girl?" asked Olympe.

At that, Annette and Mariolle burst out laughing.

A tear rolled down Celeste's cheek.

"Good ladies,"she said, in a voice that was strangled by the irregular beating of her heart, "I don't know what you want me to say. There was only one woman in the whole world who'd told me to take courage and to hope—I, whom nobody loves and everyone rejects..."

"The Witch, was it? People pay that creature to listen to her tall stories. Since when did you have enough money to do that, girl?"

"She won't be paid again," murmured Celeste instead of answering. And, among her tears, she added: "Ah! I beg of you, let me weep for the one who spoke to me about my mother!"

There was an emotion so touching in that cry that the two girls, Annette and Mariolle, were astonished and could no longer laugh.

"Her mother!" repeated Olympe, looking at Agnès, who looked away in disdain. "These foundlings can be made to believe in anything."

Celeste heard. She dried her eyes, and became paler.

X. The Gun Shot

Celeste stood up. She untied the package containing the chiffons she had prepared. Then there was great movement in the boudoir. The open armoires spat out torrents of silk, tulle and velvet. A large armchair was put in the middle of the room. To its right extended the domain of Olympe; to its left the camp of Agnès. There were certainly many rooms at their disposal in that vast manor, and it wasn't their mutual affection which brought them into contact in the important work of their toilette; but the two sisters liked to watch each other, to criticize each other, and above all, to mock each other. Each of them admired her dear sister with one eye and mocked her with the other. That was a pleasure that well compensated for the clutter and the inconvenience.

Each on one side, Annette and Mariolle began their difficult work. The young ladies had turned their wardrobes upside down in the wink of an eye. Capricious and lacking a little of that exquisite taste that even the most perfect beauty knows how to borrow, the two Fedeyau girls foraged in that mass of chiffons, choosing this, discarding that, picking up again what they had discarded in the kind of blind panic that seizes any coquette an hour before a ball.

They both had the fever. They found a way of being contemptuous and jealous at the same time. Annette was accused of being dull-witted, Mariolle of being clumsy, and Celeste of clumsiness, which was manifestly unjust. What a fairy that Celeste was! In the middle of work that fell back to her, she left Agnès to take on Olympe, repairing in one turn of the hand the stupidity of Annette, and the mistake of Mariolle. And if you had seen her, between the two heavy chambermaids and their mistresses held upright by too tight corsets, she was alert and lively, smiling now because her work occupied her, giving a slight turn to Agnès' hair, loosening the row of pearls that was badly placed on Olympe's forehead, draping coquettishly that fold, replacing that flower, readjusting, amending, giving to everything she touched a sudden and inimitable grace. One would have thought that the two young ladies were fortunate to have found in the depths of the forest of Rennes a chambermaid without peer.

The two young ladies, however, were far from being grateful, but one might have guessed the reason with a glance. Celeste, with her little round bonnet, her camisole and her cotton skirt, showed to their disadvantage, the toilettes of the two sisters.

"How much prettier she is than Agnès," thought Olympe.

"How ugly Olympe appears beside her," Agnès thought in her turn.

And by ricochet, even though they wouldn't have wanted to admit it, Olympe and Agnès, happening to take their eyes

251

away from the mirror, found there the radiant and unadorned face of that poor child of nature.

Everything has an end, even the toilette of the two badly brought up young ladies. Olympe and Agnès stationed themselves at the same time in front of their respective mirrors, adjusting the folds of their dresses, and throwing that supreme and triumphant look that every woman gives to her psyche and that serves as a farewell.

"What do you think of me, Agnès?" Olympe asked.

"And you, Olympe?" Agnès questioned.

As a response, Olympe let out this reply in a half-joking voice:

"Let's hope!"

And Agnès:

"Damn!"

Read into that whatever you will.

"Ah," Mariolle said to her colleague, Annette, "I have never seen our ladies look so attractive!"

"For sure," Annette agreed. "They are like stars!"

Celeste stood immobile, looking at her work with naive pleasure, because she was the one who had put on the ensemble of those toilettes, a perfume of good grace and beauty. One might wonder: Where did our little Celeste learn that difficult knowledge? She had learned nothing. Do poets learn how to sing? The pretty woman was born complete, like any other masterpiece of God.

"You will see," Agnès said, pinching her lips together, "that our Cinderella will say nothing!"

"I certainly think so," Olympe added. "Jealousy is choking that little girl."

Celeste blushed, then smiled. Why would she be jealous? Her smile shone a great deal brighter than all the shimmering silk reflections, all the flowers, and than all the pearls.

"Let's see which of the two of us will carry away the prize for this evening, which of us will give the keys to the city to the Count of Toulouse."

Which of the two of us? she had said, because she never thought that the victory could leave the family.

"Well!" said Mariolle, Olympe's chambermaid, "it will be you, Mademoiselle Olympe!"

Stupid woman, thought Agnès.

And Annette, Agnès' chambermaid, answered:

"Of course, it will be you, Mademoiselle Agnès!"

And Olympe, to herself, thought: *Fat idiot!*

"And what is our Cinderella's opinion?" they both asked at the same time.

"You are both very beautiful," Celeste answered.

"Coward!" they both shouted. "She's afraid of compromising herself!"

Horses were snorting in the courtyard of honor. Several times it had been announced on the part of the Seneschal and the Royal Steward that the carriages were ready. There were three carriages for the ladies and their noble fathers, as they say in the theatre. The other gentlemen who were not too old were to ride horses. There were not very many ladies. Without the noble fathers, three carriages vould have been plenty. On the other hand, there was a crowd of young horsemen.

As a general rule, one might note that money is enough to attract men, while women, the superior half of the human species, sometimes require something more. It is superfluous to be informed aboit a household where there are as many honest women as honest men, even if there is some deficiency among the latter. The presence of an adventurer doesn't prove anything more than that of a gallant man. The latter sneak in, the former go astray. But the presence of beautiful ladies does not lead us astray.

It is with difficulty that one would have counted in the courtyard of the manor more than half a dozen women of quality, including two wives of local bourgeois and three Counselors. There was, however, one marquise, Madame de Bourgueil, but she had dragged her heraldic insignia around for the past forty years.

As for the men, they were, for the most part, true gentlemen. The local nobility needed Feydeau. There is no bad turn that an angry Steward can't do to a gentleman. And then there is the cashbox, and also the experience which proves that our masculine habits pass intact into those suspicious places that would deplorably stain the while toilettes of our wives. Montbourcher was there, Talhoët also, and Guébriant, and Carheil and Derval, descendant of dukes, and Kersauzon, son of the Saxon kings, and Huchet, grandfather of the unfortunate La Bédoyère,[96] companion of Ney,[97] and Bussy-Rabutin, and Chantal, and others, but without their wives.

When a valet appeared at the top of the steps with two torches and announced the Rohan-Polduc ladies, all those people started to move about and become festive. The Marquise de Bourgueil came forward to embrace the dear beautiful girls. The three Counselors clapped their hands and the two bourgeois ladies were in raptures. Those gentlemen testified as to their admiration in keeping with the others.

Then, Olympe and Agnès, having taken their place in the first carriage, the caravan departed. It was a dark night, but Feydeau was a little Fouquet;[98] and had had lanterns hung in the forest trees so the caravan rode for three leagues in the middle of brilliant illumination.

---

[96] Charles Angélique François Huchet, Comte de la Bédoyère (1786-1815), French General during the reign of Napoleon I who was executed in 1815.

[97] Marshal Michel Ney (1769 -1815), French military commander who fought in the French Revolutionary Wars and the Napoleonic Wars. When Napoleon was defeated and exiled for the second time in the summer of 1815, Ney was arrested tried and (allegedly) executed.

[98] Nicolas Fouquet, Marquis de Belle-Île, Vicomte de Melun and Vaux (1615-1680), Superintendent of Finances from 1653 until 1661 under Louis XIV. He had a glittering career, and acquired enormous wealth. He fell out of favor, and was imprisoned from 1661 until his death in 1680.

The Breton peasants, who paid for all that luxury, had gone to bed with the sun so as not to have to burn their candles. Mariolle and Annete were with the group leaving; Cinderella remained alone in the chateau. She was lying down on the old stone balcony that looked out over the valley and extended over the ancient moats. In front of her, the road that led to Rennes traced in the night a long and winding furrow of light. For a few minutes, she heard the happy noise of the cavalcade in the courtyard, then the gates opened noisily, and the cortege, turning to the south appeared, preceded by the torch bearers. That was beautiful. Poor little Celeste sighed when looking at those proud young gentlemen on their lively horses and leaning gallantly towards the open windows of the carriages.

My mother was the daughter of a count, she was thinking.

The splendors of the life of the fortunate appeared different to her today than it did yesterday. Until then, she had admired without hope or envy. The idea was now being born in her head that these pleasures should belong to her, and that she, too, was made for these magnificent things.

That evening, the bad treatments and the jokes of the two sisters had wounded her even more. She had no resentment, but an unknown sadness persisted and clutched her heart. She analyzed vaguely her suffering. She had been humiliated and as if murdered in her pride of that day.

We are saying this, but Celeste wasn't able to express it; she didn't yet know how.

Only, while her eyes followed the caravan, that was already becoming lost in the distance, Celeste dreamed as she had never done in her life, and that thought came back to her in spite of herself.

My mother was the daughter of a count!

The light from the torches soon became part of the illuminations on the road. Dull noise was prolonged in the evening silence, telling the fact that the gates had been closed. Celeste remained immobile, always in the same place, but her reverie changed. She was now thinking of her mother, no longer remembering that she was the daughter and the wife of a gentleman. She was thinking of her mother and saw her as good and beautiful, weeping perhaps because of the absence of her daughter. Her heart was trembling with love; her eyes filled with tears. Oh! How, at that moment, she no longer envied those Feydeau ladies who no longer had a mother!

The chimes of the clock sounded. The lights on the road dimmed little by little after the passage of the cavalcade. Celeste, continuing her reverie, had returned to her point of departure. Thoughts of her mother had brought her back to that mysterious woman who had first spoken about her.

Horrible event! Charitable souls drawn to the Pont Joli by those cries of "Fire! Fire!" had watched the destruction of the windmill without being able to help in any way. The windmill, as we have already said, was surrounded by a mass of bushes, half of which were dry and dessicated.

Here is what had been recounted at the Rohan manor, in front of Celeste herself, who was returning with her package of chiffons:

In the morning, some Wolves had been spotted on the hill. One of them had climbed to the top of a walnut tree to try to reconnoiter the inside of the windmill, that no longer had a roof. A shepherd, hidden in the underbrush, had heard that man say to the others:

"They are there!" Then an instant afterward: "They're asleep!"

The shepherd had not been able to see that man's face, but he would have sworn that it was Yaumi, the handsome Cobbler, who had come with his gang of Wolves, the previous year, to loot his master's farm. In any event, the man who had climbed the old walnut tree, had come down without any noise. He motioned to his men, about a half-dozen, who were running across the hill and going into the bushes.

In his turn, the little shepherd had climbed a tree to see what they were going to do. He saw them silently roll away some big rocks to the threshold of the windmill, and pile some dead wood and dead bushes on top of them. Then the leader had used a flint to start a fire and a light spiral of smoke arose, turning about the tower.

The Wolves and Yaumi, the handsome Cobbler, were armed. They hid in the brush and waited. The spiral of smoke grew larger. Crackling sounds were heard among the bushes. An indecisive light appeared, followed by a high jet of flame. At that moment the Wolves, without exchanging a word, got ready to descend, running, into the ravine, under the arch of the green leaves. Their work was finished. An instant later, in fact, the windmill was surrounded with flames, and the ruins of the tower soon disappeared in the middle of the conflagration.

In the midst of that Hell, the little shepherd, who had been the first to raise the alarm, had heard the loud cry of a woman—only once! Then a deep voice had dominated the other sounds like thunder. That voice pronounced the name of Philippe d'Orléans, Regent of France, and called him out to combat three times.

XI. Cinderella's Toilette

There ended the story of the little shepherd, who had left running to go and look for help. On the way, other children had joined him, crying out in the most plaintive way that turned the blood cold: "Fire! Fire!"

When the help arrived, an enormous fiery blaze was surrounding the old windmill. A human chain carrying water from the ravine to the hill was created, but what could those few drops of water do against such a fiery furnace!

The fire expanded so long as it was fed, that is to say, so long as there was rubble that, in the past, had masked the ruins. When the flames died down, the old tower was still standing, but blackened, calcinated, and showing large crevices. There was no effort to enter it; it was impossible for a human creature to be alive in that place. Such was the main story, in its authentic version. But in Brittany, the marvelous clings to every tragic event as moss does to a tree.

People claimed that, at the strongest moment of the conflagration, when the smoke was still burning hot, spread by the wind, blinding every attempt at gazing through it, a white form had appeared behind the burned ruin. Others, going even further, gave as the companion of the white form, the shadow of a giant, black, like a statue of iron. Perhaps, they were already saying, it was the soul of the Miller Woman and her mysterious companion. That hadn't lasted but a moment, when the gust had dampened the smoke at sunrise. Then, the gust had passed, the fire had broken out again, crowned with flames, and the strange vision had disappeared.

Celeste knelt and said a prayer for the one who had put Raoul's hand in her hand. That was a prayer for the dead.

The valley was mute and dark. The night wind blew, whistling, over the roofs of the Rohan manor after having snatched from the forest trees a large, low murmur. Those committed to guard the chateau had doubtless gone to bed because no noise was heard from the interior. Toward the east, light vapors began to turn white. The confused mass of gothic architecture that made up the manor came out of the obscurity little by little. The towers became visible, carrying behind them deep shadows. The windows, struck by the Moon that showed over the bushes, sent out white reflections. At that moment one could have seen Celeste's face, pensive, but smiling. Do sad dreams last a long time at that age?

Celeste, still leaning against the granite balcony, had done the same thing as the Moon, that, victorious, had come slowly out of its ocean of clouds. She was thinking of Raoul. She had not seen him again since their visit to the Witch. And he had promised to be at the Rohan-Polduc chateau that evening. It was no longer possible to enter the Seneschal's dwelling. Celeste had heard all the gates close a long while ago; the hounds had been let loose, and one heard the bells on their collars from time to time in the courtyard.

Once, however, Celeste thought that she heard the gallop of a horse on the path coming from the Vesvres Valley. But she had been mistaken. The Moon brightly lit the place where the dry, powdery path came out of the high bushes, then proceeded quickly across the dark fields. Celeste opened her eyes wide and looked as hard as she could, and saw a bizarre vision.

Perhaps it was a vague echo of the shepherd's story and the fright caused by the fire, but she saw00or believed she saw—two ghost-like figures, completely dark, glide alongside the path: a woman, whose head disappeared under the ample folds of a tenant farmer hood, and a very tall man, straight and stiff, who held, while walking, the pommel of a gigantic sword. They soon left the lit area. Celeste knew she had not been dreaming! She saw the tops of the bushes move. She heard the stalks rustle for an instant when the wind was not blowing. Then, there was a sound like thar of a key being inserted into the lock of the postern gate under the balcony. The door opened. Celeste, frightened, leaned over to get a better look. The grass was high and thick in front of the postern gate, which hadn't been opened in years, and the foot of the rampart was solitary as far as the eye could see.

I am asleep standing up, Celeste thought, going back into the boudoir.

She felt reassured by the brilliant clarity of the lamps that had lit up the toilettes of the Feydeau young ladies. But she had another fear. She found herself faced with the chores that remained for her to do that night. She heaved a big sigh on seeing the mountain of chiffon thrown in disorder in the boudoir. All of that had to be put in order before going to bed. If she failed, she would incur the wrath of Agnès and Olympe

There was a lot of it! A lot of it! The entire contents of the armoires were laying on the floor. Poor Celeste joined her hands, feeling tired and discouraged. However, she began her work: folding here, putting things together there, doing her best so she could quickly retire to bed after having said her prayers.

I don't know, in truth, how the thing happened, but it is certain that during folding, arranging, and hanging up, she had the idea that she would look very nice with the discarded chiffons. Do you know a child capable of resisting such a fantasy? Just as she had that idea, she was holding in her hand a red satin dress on which she herself had put some chiffon. A real gem of a skirt that Agnès had worn only once, but discarded because the new fabric had let her get a sun burn.

Celeste became rosier than the satin skirt. She lowered her eyes and her smile became mischievous. She hesitated. She did not dare look at herself in the mirror that was in front of her. Her hand gently untied the strings of her cotton dress that fell off. The top went to join the skirt. Celeste was blushing, but what better opportunity to satisfy an innocent fantasy? Who could surprise her? So she put on an embroidered undershirt and the famous dickey that Agnès had found too simple. Over that she tied the rose satin skirt. Its folds began to sparkle, The top came next, like a light and gracious cloud to soften the too brilliant colors.

All of that was too large, but Celeste couldn't be embarrassed by such trifling detail. When she shortened the waist to adapt it to her size, she threw a disingenuous look at the mirror. Her eyes were sparkling with pleasure. She had not thought that she would find herself so pretty. However, a blouse was still missing.

But I ask you this: Can a ballroom dress be put on while keeping one's hair, even if it is the most beautiful in the world, in disarray under a little cotton bonnet? So there went the bonnet on the floor. Her hair, once free, fell in long, heavy, prodigal curls, running from the forehead to the shoulders, from the shoulders to the waist.

Celeste picked up the curls with full hands, twisted them, plaited them, and that admirable hair, always a captive until then, made a splendid crown. She then tied it together with a piece of clematis picked at random from the jumble of flowers.

Ah! she said to herself, looking enviously at the box of powder, *I have everything but that.*

The foolish girl! She would have wanted to tarnish the black enamel of her hair. She, at least, put a dab on the cheekbone of her rosy cheek, then another near the little dimple that a smile placed at the corner of her lips.

She jumped for joy.

"Now for the bodice! On to the bodice!" she exclaimed.

We will be pardoned for omitting the stockings and the shoes that the Feydeau young ladies were not wearing.

On to the bodice! Here is the history of the bodice, which was in white velour decorated with Flemish lace.

Olympe drank, morning and evening, some vinegar in order to lose weight. A councilor from south Brittany had also advised her to drink beef bouillon and extract of hickory for the same purpose. At the end of three months, she was supposed to be as thin as the fairy Diffo who spent the night on the Gallic countryside without bending the trembling stalks of maize. Anticipating that result, Olympe had ordered that divine bodice three month before but when it arrived, it was too tight by half. That's why the bodice remained there, unworn, waiting for Celeste. She put it on without any effort.

That's impossible! she thought, shamed at admiring herself. *I am mistaken. I am not that pretty!*

Occupied as she was, Celeste didn't hear a slight noise from the direction of the balcony. One might have supposed that it was some spying page who stifled a burst of laughter. She had tried to fasten the bodice in the back. She was very adroit, but one of the fasteners, placed just between her two shoulders, resisted all her efforts.

"Decidedly," she exclaimed, stamping her foot, half laughing, half annoyed, "it's very annoying not to have a chambermaid!

A shiver passed through her whole body because she had just felt a hand gently pushing hers aside and tried to fasten the difficult fastener. She didn't dare turn around, but the mirror was there. It showed her something so prodigious that she fell backward. Fortunately, there were two arms there to catch her.

There is a saying in the county of Vitré, an austere region where women flee coquetry to the extent of fearing water itself; it is this: *When a young girl is alone, and she looks at herself in a mirror, she sees the Devil.*

Poor Celeste must have believed in that proverb for a moment. She had seen the Devil! In the mirror behind her, she beheld not a hideous and hairy horned demon, but an officer with his rank embroidered in silver, a sword at his side, and a hat with a plume.

Wasn't one as prodigious as the other? An officer of the Conti Regiment at ten o'clock at night in the boudoir of the Feydeau daughters!

Celeste, feeling herself caught in his virile arms, tried to cry out, but a hand was placed over her mouth and a well-known voice said to her:

"What's wrong with you? It's me, Raoul!

So it was!

Raoul put his lips on those white shoulders that were gently trembling.

Celeste, awakened, fled to the other end of the bedroom. She didn't know how to hide. Her dress was burning her.

"Don't you love me anymore, Celeste?" murmured the young man in love.

"I was no longer expecting you," replied the young girl.

"But," said Raoul, in order to excuse himself, "I have been here a long time.

Celeste hid her face in her hands.

"Where?" she asked, speaking so low that the new soldier had trouble understanding her.

"There, on the balcony."

Celeste's eyes filled with tears.

"On my honor!" exclaimed Raoul. "My look did not offend you. Don't I know that you are as pure as you are beautiful.... and would I love you otherwise, Celeste?"

"But to surprise me this way!" stammered the young girl, who didn't yet dare look at him.

That was too bad, because if she had, she would have seen a face so repentant, so contrite, that her anger would not have lasted.

"Everything happened by chance," Raoul continued, in order to prove his innocence. "I carried out, point by point, everything that the Miller Woman ordered me to do. I went to see Monsieur de Rieux, Lieutenant Colonel of the Conti Regiment. I gave him my letter of introduction. He read it smiling. After that, he looked me over from head to foot and I heard him say:

"A handsome soldier, on my faith!"

XII. The Cornette [99]

Celeste found her mischievous smile again and, imitating Raoul, said:

"A handsome soldier, on my faith!" Then, she added: "We know very well that modesty doesn't hold you back, Monsieur Raoul."

She was really delighted to see him, so handsome in his rich uniform, but that made her want to tease him. She wouldn't have taken that mocking tone with the poor little gentleman of yesterday who was wearing a torn doublet, a crushed hat and dirty braid.

"I am only repeating what Monsieur de Rieux said," Raoul replied. Then he added: "But my life doesn't interest you at all, Celeste, and I can see that you don't love me anymore."

The girl turned her eyes away.

"I can certainly promise you, Master Raoul," she suddenly said, defending herself of a crime that she had not been accused of, "that if I put on those beautiful clothes, it was without a wicked thought... I was here all alone. I wanted to

---

[99] See Note 37.

see how that skirt would look on me... and then one thing led to another... I don't know how that happened: there I was, in elegant clothes, as if I were a princess... You must have been astonished."

"It seems to me," Raoul interrupted in good faith, "that I have always seen you like that, Celeste. These gracious surroundings are certainly made for you!"

"Oh!" the little Cinderella, blushing with pleasure, wanted to protest.

"You are as beautiful," Raoul continued with passion, "as beautiful, believe me, wearing your poor clothes, but this finery suits you. The cotton dress and the round bonnet seem to be a disguise under which your proud line and noble blood are apparent. I can't say that I like you any better that way. I see you from below and I admire you!"

She frowned in earnest.

"Go away! You're making fun of me!"

Raoul came forward a step.

"Don't you remember any longer what the good woman at the windmill told you yesterday?"

Celeste' beautiful color vanished. Her voice became soft and trembling, while she made the sign of the cross:

"You have just spoken of a dead woman," she said.

Then, she told the young stupefied soldier about the fire in the tower and what happened afterward. Raoul listened to her, serious and somber.

"Celeste," he said, while the young girl dried her moist eyes, "I don't yet believe in witches, despite the fact that some of her strange predictions came to pass. But I believe in God, who protects us, and I also believe that there is a Supreme Being who watches over both of us."

Celeste involuntarily approached Raoul, and sat down near him on the sofa where Achille Feydeau, not long before, had swaggered. He took both her hands, but didn't try to get a kiss.

"Between the two of us," he said, giving his voice a sound of deep conviction, "because we are tied to each other, something at the bottom of my heart tells me so, even before we met... If someone put to death that poor woman, I swear God to avenge her!"

"You would attack the Wolves!" Celeste, frightened, interrupted.

"I would attack something more powerful than the Wolves," answered Raoul, who lifted his young, handsome face, shining with courage.

Celeste lowered her eye lashes under his look.

"Do you know something more than you did yesterday?" she murmured

"About my own history, I know nothing," Raoul answered. "About yours, I know what the Miller Woman wanted to tell us. But when Monsieur de Rieux held out his hand to me, after having read my letter, he murmured as if talking to himself:

" 'By the help of God, here is at least one face that carries the expression of a Breton of the old stock. That one, if they put the whip in his hand, will be able to chase the enemies from the house of his father.' "

"And you didn't ask him...?" Celeste started.

"Oh! Yes, I did, but Monsieur de Rieux has an unusual character. He rang to have me brought tea and he had me drink a full cup as a welcome. Each time that I wanted to question him, he gave me a big clap on my shoulder, and told me, laughing as hard as he could:

" 'My pretty fellow, when you have the whip, strike! Strong and firm, and don't hold back! ' And also: 'My boy, have you heard about that mythological serpent that had, I don't know how many heads, and who was called the Lernean Hydra? That good woman had only three heads, four counting the one in Paris, but they stand firm on her shoulders.' "

Celeste opened her eyes wide.

"Do you understand any of that, Raoul?" she asked.

"Not a lot," he answered, "but I have thought, since this morning, three times more than I have done in all my life, and I am sure that he was talking of the Miller Woman. What's more, I am also very sure that the Witch and Countess Isaure have the same plans. Finally, I would bet that those plans have something to do with the two of us."

"What plans?" asked Celeste.

Raoul shook his head and replied:

"I will find out. Meanwhile, I have faith in my destiny because it is linked with yours, Celeste. I will serve those who love you wuth my life, and will fight their enemies to the death."

"But do you know who they are?" the young girl asked.

"Monsieur Rieux pronounced three names between two bursts of laughter: that of the Seneschal..."

"My protector!" Celeste interrupted.

"That of the Royal Steward," Raoul continued, "and that of a man fate made my friend for a day, the Spaniard Don Martin Blas."

"A handsome gentleman!" exclaimed Celeste, "and someone who stared at me this evening on the stairs, so long and hard that I didn't dare lift my eyes. But I beg you, Raoul, tell me all at once, so that I don't diè, everything that passed between you and the Lieutenant-Colonel!

At the age when the two Feydeau young ladies began to be bored with their dolls, and the when the now dead wife of the Seneschal, Feudeau's elder daughter, after two or three years ofa childless marriage, despaired of ever bcoming a mother, under the main door of the Rohan manor, there was found a little girl asleep in a walnut crib.

She was taken in. She was delightfully pretty and she replaced in an advantageous way the dolls that Agnès and Olympe no longer wanted. She was what the two girls would love most passionately. They gave up everything for her; for her, they left their favorite dog and even their white cat.

The little girl was Celeste.

About that time, the wife of the Seneschal, who was a good creature, was already suffering from the illness that put her in the grave; one day, she met an unknown woman in the forest who told her:

"The orphan means safery for the chateau."

Then, the Wolves began to be talked about. Josselin Guitan had been seen in the vicinity of Saint-Aubin-du-Cormier. The country people said that Valentine de Rohan went about the countryside, at night, disguised as a beggar. For some time, in the dwellings of the forest, the mysterious name of the She-Wolf was uttered for the first time.

So long as the wife of the Seneschal lived, Celeste was happy. She was brought up beside Agnès and Olympe as if she were their younger sister. It was the Seneschal's wife who gave her the name Celeste, because they had found no information in the crib.

Celeste was so sweet that the two Feydeau young ladies loved her. It was when she was twelve or thirteen years-old, the year after the death of the Seneschal's wife, that her martyrdom began. The gentlemen who came to the chateau found her charming, and said so. That was enough to make her horrible in the eyes of Agnès and Olympe. Their aversion made such progress that, in a few months, they went so far as slapping her. Celeste resolved to run away. But toward that time, the conduct of the two tyrants changed somewhat. The Seneschal had stepped in openly.

If the reader remembers the last conversation of Alain Polduc with his father-in-law, and a certain letter signed Saint-Elme mentioned in that conversation, he will easily guess the motive for the Seneschal's intervention. Up until that time, Celeste had seldom been mistreated, except in words. But the hatred of the two Feydeau young ladies grew daily with all the signs of admiration lavished, even in their presence, on their "Cinderella," as they called her.

Celeste did her best to side-step them. She forgot the rebuffs and the sarcasms of the day to only remember the caresses of another time, and her gratitude toward the Seneschal was as strong as it was sincere.

Nothing, right up the last days, had thrown the least light into her mind as to the secret of her birth. She believed herself to be the daughter of some poor village woman who had been seduced, then abandoned. The first suspicion that came in her mind was the mysterious kiss bestowed on her forehead by the beautiful Countess Isaure. The words of the Witch had changed that suspicion into a fever. But that little drama, whose prologue had seemed so full of promises, had, just met its sad and silent denouement. That day

The Miller Wman was dead, having taken with her that secret that only she probably knew. But now, Raoul, who had been, until the evening before, still a stranger, had just brought her other hopes and other ideas. She resolved to henceforth love him more than a brother. But she also wanted to know the truth. The words of the new Conti soldier had violently increased her curiosity, without satisfying it. She was there, near him, on the sofa. Her beautiful wide-open eyes shone with naive intelligence. Her mouth breathed slowly and very low.

"I was saying just now," Raoul continued, after having collected his thoughts, "that if the Miller Woman is dead, I will avenge her. I also say that, if she is alive, I will defend her. Those savages from the Wolf's Den were accustomed to trembling before the Witch. They wouldn't have attacked her retreat of their own volition. On the other hand, that good woman who served France in secret must have taken her precautions... France has a long arm and, this morning, I took an oath of fealty to the King of France. Until Countess Isaure tells me: 'She is dead,' I won't believe it. And I am to see Countess Isaure tonight."

"But what about your conversation with Monsieur de Rieux?"

"Well," Raoul replied, "Monsieur de Rieux, after having forced me to drink to his health, got up from his seat and took my sword out of its sheath without asking my permission.

" 'Cadet,' he asked me, 'do you at least know how to use this?'

" 'Rather well,' I answered.

"I didn't believe I needed to tell him that my old friend, Caderasse, had kept me four years in his fencing school, giving me instructions.

"Monsieur de Rieux, however tested my sword on the floor.

" 'There is mine, over there,' he suddenly told me, pointing to his sword hanging on the well. 'Take it down, Cadet; we're going to see.'

"I obeyed. Even before I was on guard, he gave me a thrust. I parried with a firm foot and so strongly that he transferred his sword into his left hand to spare the fingers of his right hand, that were swollen. And he was laughing, the worthy man, with such good heart!

" 'Your name is Raoul, isn't it?' he asked. 'That's a valiant name. *Palsambleu!* You have a good wrist!'

"Without seeming to do anything, he gave me a thrust with his left hand, so strong that I believed I was blinded by the blow. I parried again as well as I could. The sword jumped out of his hand.

" 'Ah! Ah!' he said, holding his sides, 'Beautiful, my boy! Pick that up for me, Cadet. You are now a Conti officer. Go buy your *cornette*!'

"Saying that, he put a fistful of gold coins in my hand. I told him that I had a requisition form to present to the treasurer of the Regiment.

" 'Good, very good, my little Raoul,' he said, laughing heartily. 'You are proud. You have the right to be. I am allowing you to call me cousin.' "

XIII. The Fairy Godmother

Raoul continued:

"I thought I was dreaming... and as I was giving my overwhelming thanks, Monsieur le Viconte de Rieux took my hand and shook it warmly.

"For a moment I thought that he was going to stop laughing. In his expression there seemed to be a nuance of soft emotion.

" 'What am I going to have to do in the service of the King of France?' I asked.

" 'When you are equipped, Raoul, my nephew,' he answered, 'I order you to walk about in the streets of Rennes. This evening, you will come and tell me what the weather was like... Wait!' he added suddenly, 'be sure to pass by the Place des Lices, under the balcony of Countess Isaure.'

"He then waved to me with his hand and I left. I was as if I were drunk. The treasurer counted me out a thousand ecus. An hour afterward, I had my uniform and I rode on horseback through the city on the service of the King."

Raoul had told all this in one breath. He stopped in order to take a breath."

"Is that all?" asked Celeste, who had expected something very different.

"Just about," Raoul replied, "except that, obeying his instructions, I passed by at least twenty times under Countess's Isaure's windows, but she was not there. But it was only much later, just as the sun was about to set, that I saw her carriage coming in the distance. I approached and she smiled at me. You are the only one in the world, Celeste, who is more beautiful. And there are moments when I find that you resemble her...

" 'Greetings, young officer,' she said to me.

"A dozen gentlemen accompanied her carriage. She motioned to me to come up close to her carriage window. I obeyed. They looked at me, stupefied and jealous. I heard them murmur from all directions:

" 'Who is that man?'

" 'Tonight, be at the chateau,' the Countess whispered to me.

"And as I bowed respectfully, wanting to say that I had not forgotten, she added:

" 'This evening, at the Governor's Ball, I will have something to tell you.'

"She sat back on the cushions of her carriage, and I went to tell my Colonel the events of my day.

" 'By Heaven!' he exclaimed when he saw me, 'here's the most valiant officer in my regiment. I know what the weather's like, my nephew. Are you eager to begin your duties?'

" 'I am burning up with impatience, Colonel,' I replied.

" 'Very well, Raoul, you're going to go to work immediately. I am turning over to you the command of the night station at the Mordelaises gates. They fear a surprise attack. I don't think it will happen, but you will have thirty horses and a brigadier of your age. Don't spend the night drinking.'

" 'I was about to tell him about the rendezvous that Countess Isaure had given me, but was that secret mine to share? Besides, several gentlemen entered at that moment, and Monsieur de Rieux greeted them with a burst of laughter so frank and so loud that they all imitated his confidence.

" 'Why are you laughing, Viscount?' Monsieur de la Bourdonnaye asked him.

" 'Eh ! Eh ! my good fellow,' the Colonel answered, 'I have no idea, and you?'

"Then he offered me his hand before I took my leave, adding:

" 'Gentlemen, here is a budding Marshal of France and who won't be the first of his name.'

"You can judge how they looked at me!

" 'What name does that young man have?' they all asked.

"Monsieur de Rieux burst out laughing.

" 'Go away, nephew,' he said to me. 'And keep your mouth closed about the State secrets I have confided to you.'

"There was nothing left for me to do but to say good-bye and depart.

"Toward seven thirty in the evening, I took command of the men assigned to guard the Mordelaises gates. At a quarter to eight, I had become my sergeant's best friend and promised him my patronage at the Court. He was a handsome little young man whom I thought would not betray me.

"At eight o'clock, I said to him:

" 'Sergeant, I would really like to go and say good night to my mistress, who lives over there, on the other side of Saint-Martin bridge.'

" 'Well,' he answered, 'by all means, do it. We're here just as a show for the Governor's Ball, and inside the gate, we have a whole company of those scoundrel soldiers of the Stewardship... Unless the English come, I don't see what we have to fear.'

"I jumped in the saddle. I used both spurs, and in the time of a gallop, here I am."

"You have abandoned your post!" said Celeste, a little frightened.

Raoul laughed somewhat constrained and answered:

"Alas! Yes! That's my first exploit!"

"But how does the military punish soldiers who abandon their post?" the little girl asked.

"They are punished with death," Raoul replied.

Celeste's very heart ran cold.

"Bah!" Raoul continued gaily, "who will be aware of my absence?"

Then, letting himself slide down to his knees, he continued, covering her hands with kisses:

"I have come to see my mistress, the mistress of my entire life, the queen of my destiny. Everything that happens to me is like a walking fairy tale. I know that well and I wouldn't believe it if I didn't adore you, my beautiful love. You are my faith and my hope. I have confidence in that voice that said to me one day: 'Loving her will bring you happiness.' "

"But what do you intend to do here, Raoul?" Celeste demanded.

272

"How do I know? I am waiting for the order of the woman who told me to come."

"The woman who gave you a rendezvous yesterday," the young girl said very low, "is no longer of this world today."

"I will wait an hour! I tell you, my dear Celeste, witches don't die like that. At the end of an hour, I will again mount my horse that is grazing over there, then I'll ride it back to the Mordelaises gates!"

The little girl reclined a little on her sofa. Her expression had new signs of timidity.

"An hour... with you..." she murmured, "alone. That's a long time, Raoul!"

"What are you afraid of, Celeste?"

"I don't know... but at least promise me that you won't talk to me of love."

Raoul, still on his knees, placed his lips on her beautiful little hand.

"What would I tell you on that subject that is more than you already know, my adored Celeste!" he exclaimed. "No! I won't talk anymore about love. I will leave the care of that to my hand that trembles, to my heart that beats, to my whole being that quivers delightfully near you."

"Is that the way you no longer talk about love?" asked Celeste turning away her eyes. But she couldn't hide her smile.

"Well," Raoul continued, "to shorten the time that seems so long to you, let's tell stories. Have you heard about the beautiful gallant adventures that took place here, in this very place where we stand?"

"Beautiful?" Celeste repeated. "Mostly tears, I was told."

"But after many smiles," Raoul interrupted. "Can happiness cost too much? In climbing up this granite balcony a while ago, it seemed to me that I could again find traces of that unfortunate gentleman, César de Rohan, who had taken that road more than once."

"César de Rohan and the noble Jeanne de Combourg took another route to go to their death!" murmured Celeste.

"And that bold soldier," Raoul continued, "Morvan de Saint-Maugan, who came to visit Valentinede Rohan..."

Celeste shivered.

"I have often thought about all that," she said again, in an altered voice, "when I was alone here, after my mistresses left. There is grief in this room that seems to weep under its new tapestries. The balcony looks out to the forest. It was in the forest that spies were hidden..."

Suddenly there was a noise outside and Celeste became very pale, listening. It was not the wind that had thus shaken the tree leaves.

"Don't be afraid," Raoul said gaily. "That's my horse down below who is growing impatient. We are not grand enough personages that anyone would take care to spy of both of us... While I was listening in the moat to see if you were alone, I believed that I had already heard some movement in the walnut trees. The Steward and the Seneschal are poor hunters. Game must come very near their dwelling."

"Listen!" stammered Celeste.

Their ears now caught something like an indistinct and far away murmur.

"I must tell you, my beautiful Celeste," Raoul continued in a more serious tone, "that there is in fact something out there. The forest is sleeping with one eye open tonight. Down there toward the Pont Joli, I heard, in passing, Wolves walking on two feet along the road, rustling the dry leaves."

"But since you have successfully climbed the balcony..." Celeste began.

"For you," Raoul interrupted, "I would climb the Towers of Saint-Pierre.[100] If someone has followed the same road that I took, he will find someone to be reckoned with here."

Raoul slapped his sword. The noise ceased.

Celeste looked at that proud young man. Her fear went away. But how could an hour go by without talking about

---

[100] Rennes cathedral.

love? She didn't want to talk about that. Here is how she found a way to avoid that dangerous pitfall.

"Monsieur Raoul," she said, "let's be practical. When you came in, I was in the process of trying in vain to fasten my blouse in my back. Do you know how to do it?"

Loop and hook are the technical terms for the two parts of a fastener. She stood up. Raoul stood behind her in the position of a chambermaid. He made several attempts, we must admit, to accomplish that simple task. Finally, not succeeding, he had to use both hands—which were too large for the task—to grav Celeste's wait and force the hook into the loop; but at least, they didn't talk any more about love.

Then Raoul moved three steps away to contemplate his work. They looked at each other. We don't believe much in little country girls who have the feet and the hands of a duchess. You don't go into the fields without receiving some injury from the sun. The immortal author of the fairy tale *Cinderella* didn't make his heroine a country girl.

Our own Cinderella, the second of that name, wasn't a girl of the fields either. She lived in Rennes in the winter with her mistresses, and in the chateau during the summer. Her only work was to help Agnès and Olympe. At this work, the complexion remains white and the hands do not become rough. It is true that Celeste was wearing wooden clogs, but that good beech tree wood from the forest of Rennes could make shoes as comfortable as the famous glass slipper.

Celeste was a true gem in her borrowed finery. As for Raoul, the Viscount of Rieux, that merry man, was right in saying that the Conti Regiment hadn't his like among its officers. He wore that uniform, new for him, with a grace, an ease, and in such a charming way that he must have been the darling of all the Rennes ladies. In fact, Celeste was already afraid of that. Raoul, for his part, told himself: *If the other gentlemen could see me!* And he thanked fate for having tucked away that treasure for him.

They were there, facing each other; they naively admired each other, their eyes shining. But they did not talk about love.

"How handsome you will be, tonight, at the Ball, Monsieur Raoul!"

"If you were there, Celeste," answered Raoul, "there would be no one there as beautiful as you!"

"Me, at the Governor's Ball!" exclaimed the young girl, "among so many noble ladies!"

She shrugged and laughed. Then she put her hand over Raoul's mouth as he was going to reply.

"Be quiet, she said, "flattering a young girl is also talking about love."

She glanced in the direction of the mirror and draped the folds of her dress.

"They go like this..." she murmured, flirting a little, "and then like this, and then like this again... Oh, my! How clumsy I am!"

"You are adorable," Raoul protested.

"Be quiet! And when they dance, they pose this way."

She made a bow with a noble and serious look.

Raoul answered her with another bow that is the traditional debut of a minuet.[101]

"What a pity we have no violins," Celeste said.

"I am going to sing the minuet of the Prince," continued Raoul.

And there they went: passes, contrepasses, sisols, demijeté, battements, glissé, assemblé, all executed with the foot of a master and with the figure following a perfect regularity.

"But you dance like an angel, Celeste!" exclaimed the young officer. "Where did you learn that?"

"Through the keyhole, when the dancing teacher came to teach the young ladies"

After the minuet, the courante.[102] It was charming to see them, a pleasure for the eyes, pearls of sweat on their

---

[101] A slow, stately ballroom dance for two in triple time, popular especially in the 18th century.

[102] Triple metre dance from the Renaissance and Baroque eras.

foreheads, Raoul a little pale; Celeste as red as a cherry. Raoul's hand squeezed the trembling waist of his companion. They stopped, out of breath. They had not talked of love but the hour had passed.

Raoul picked up a beautiful piece of chiffon and put it in Celeste's hands.

"I don't lack anything but that," she exclaimed, laughing and fanning her face. "Here is Cinderella completely disguised as a princess... If we nly had a fairy godmother with her carriage, we culd leave for the Governor's Ball."

Raoul didn't have time to answer. They heard the sound of a carriage rolling on the stones of the road outside. At the same time the corridor door opened and a woman dressed exactly like she was the evening before, the Witch of the old windmill of the Wolf's Den, appeared on the threshold.

Celeste stepped back as if she had just seen a ghost. Raoul couldn't keep from trembling. The Witch, standing at the doorway, said in a soft and serious voice:

"That's good! You have kept the rendezvous." Then she turned toward Celeste: "Daughter, here is your fairy godmother. You carriage waits below. Both of you, go. You are expected at the Ball of the Count of Toulouse."

And she took them by the hand. They found all the doors open, but Celeste, noticed that they were following a way she had never before taken. It was a staircase that seemed to go directly to the countyard. The last door turned on rolling hinges.

Raoul and Celeste found themselves before a carriage bearing the Rohan arms drawn by four magnificent horses. The Witch, or her ghost, had Celeste get inside and took a place beside her. Then she put a pair of pistols in Raoul's hands, saying:

"Mount up, young officer! You will gallop close to the carriage window. The forest isn't very nice tonight."

And to the coachman, she said:

"To Rennes, to the Governor's palace, and don't spare the horses!"

PART THREE: COUNTESS ISAURE

I. Night Adventures

After Celeste's departure, the boudoir of the young Feydeau ladies remained empty. When the carriage with the Witch and her young companion arrived at the bottom of the hill, the Milller Woman leaned out the carriage window and looked toward the Chateau.

"Whip up your horses, Josselin," she shouted to the coachman. "It is time!"

The coachman gave a couple of vigorous whips to his team. The coach went like the wind, down the road already illuminated where the cavalcade had passed. Raoul, however had imitated the Witch. The Rohan manor was elevated almost vertically above the place where they were. A black mass with its pointed towers was clearly detached from the milky azure of the sky where the Moon was rising. Only one window was lit in all the extent of the dark facade. It was the boudoir window.

Raoul believed that he could distinguish moving shadows on the granite balcony.

"Can you see them, my lady?" he asked, leaning toward the carriage window.

"Be careful of what's ahead," the woman in a peasant's hood answered. "The danger is no longer coming from the manor house."

The road descended right to the ford of the Vache, located toward the middle of the Valley in the center of a little plain, half moor, half fallow land, where nothing grew except a few apple trees. The forest was before and after it; it was really like a vast clearing. The ford served as a passage for carriages and animals. From there to the Pont Joli, there was about a half league of countryside.

As they approached the clearing of the ford, Raoul returned to the carriage window and said in a low voice:

"Look! Look!"

His finger pointed to a prairie to the right which went on to become part of the brush near the Wolf's Den. The Moon lit with its vague and confused rays a truly fantastic spectacle. A peasant from Southern Brittany would have believed it was All Hallows' Eve when it was thought that no grave remained closed in the cemeteries, and where the immense, interminable line of the dead rolled out its mute rings on the moor, bringing with them the mystic stone that, each year, augments the number of Karnac's standing stones.

But those who had seen the cortege of the spirits on the night of Halloween, had said that all the ghosts wore their white shrouds over their shoulders. The procession that Raoul saw was large, long, but it could hardly be seen on the dark grass. It was like an army of black demons stampeding. Their walk made a dull sound. They did not speak.

"I saw it," the Miller Woman replied.

Celeste covered her face and retreated at the very back of the carriage. The Witch took her hand that she squeezed against her heart.

"Don't be afraid, child, as long as you are with me," she said.

That voice reached into the depth of Celeste's soul. Ten times she had wanted to ask by what miracle the Miller Woman had escaped the fire at the windmill, but she didn't dare.

The strange procession that cut across the prairie in a zig-zag, had seen the carriage. The head of the procession increased the pace, and suddenly a large circle formed around the ford. There were no shouts. That silence was frightening.

"Friend Raoul," said the Witch, "we must negotiate."

.

"With a pistol, *Morbleu!*" interrupted the young officer. "Trust me, my good lady. I will smash the head of the first two and my sword will do the rest!"

"I don't say that that would be impossible," the Miller Woman replied, "but the fathers of those who are facing you served your ancestors... Push on ahead and ask them if they will let the Rohan carriage pass."

Raoul spurred his horse forward, thinking far more about what he had been told about his ancestors than the present danger.

"Good people!" he shouted from a distance, "let the Rohan carriage pass, I ask you."

"What is your name, you French puppet?" insolently asked a hunchbacked fellow who seemed to be the leader of the band.

Raoul was now close enough to distinguish the dress and the shape of those nocturnal travelers. They were the Wolves, there was no doubt about it. Their usual attire was the skin of a nanny goat and a wolf mask.

"My name is not important," the young officer answered. "This is a Rohan carriage; will you let it pass?"

"And what if that was not our intention?" the leader asked again.

Raoul saw him bring forward his carabine, which was on a shoulder strap, and he heard the tic-tac of a weapon being armed. But the Wolf didn't have time to put it into action. An unusual cry—one that the people from the city had never heard—rose in the silence of the night, a cry that admirably imitated that long, gloomy, lamentable howl that belonged to the European wolf and the African jackal.

"Peace, Yaumi!" said several voices. "Those are our people. You can see that very well!"

"And who commands here?" shouted the handsome Cobbler, striking the ground hard with the butt of his musket. "Is it so difficult to learn how to howl? I want to see who's in that carriage."

The carriage was now but several feet away.

"Look at the coat-of-arms," Raoul said.

While they were negotiating, the resrt of the procession was still advancing. There was now a veritable army in the vicinity of the ford. The handsome Cobbler placed himself in front of the horses, which had halted.

"Move!" said the coachman. "You are doing a sad chore here, cousin Yaumi!"

"Move!" repeated Raoul, jumping forward, pointing his sword at the leader of the Wolves.

But, the crowd was already pressing around him. A strong boy jumped on the croup of his horse and grabbed him. The handsome Cobbler had trembled at the sound of the coachman's voice.

"If Vincent, my boy, was here!" he grumbled. Then he added to himself: *The game is too risky. Better wait for another opportunity.* "You should have talked earlier, Josselin, old man," he continued aloud. "I would have been sorry to have put a bullet in your body."

There was a great shout in the crowd.

"Josselin! It's Master Josselin, the son of Dame Michou Guitan." And a thouand voices asked: "Have you found our good young lady in Paris, Master Josselin?"

"We will talk about that another time, my friends," the coachman responded. "Move!"

"Move!" Yaumi repeated.

There had been no need for that order, The Wolves had already willingly arranged themselves, forming two long chains on each side of the ford. If anyone approached too close, it was to try to touch the hand of Dame Guitan's son. The traveler, Julot, the one who had discovered Paris, struggled like a devil to show that he was close to Master Josselin. He roughly threw on the ground the good fellow who had hoisted himself in the croup behind Raoul, and that fellow, when free, outran both of them to put himself ahead of the carriage.

Cousin Yaumi carried courtesy to the point of conducting Master Joselin through the two lines of Wolves.

"Since when, my friend," he asked him in a low voice, "have you been wearing the Seneschal's livery?"

"Since the Seneschal and you have become a pair of rogues," Josselin replied.

"I've seen a woman inside," replied Yaumi. "Is our good young lady going to dance at the Governor's Ball?"

"Our good young lady is too far away for you to betray her, cousin," the coachman replied. "As for the one inside, you wouldn't dare look her in the face."

"Tell the truth!" exclaimed the handsome Cobbler. "I have guessed it, my man! You're carrying the Countess of Toulouse, the Governor's wife. Good for you! But just beware of a big devil with sun-burned skin who is also riding along the road tonight, and whose name is Don Martin Blas."

"Thank you for the advice!" said a voice from the carriage window.

The handsome Cobbler stopped short and his legs trembled as if someone had struck him on the head. Then he recovered and rushed to the carriage window. He saw that dark hood that always hid the face of the Witch. And her voice continued:

"You didn't earn your blood prize, Yaumi. You have to do it all over again!

Those who were around Yaumi held him up. Without that, he would have fallen backward. The coachman touched the horses with the whip and they began to gallop again, preceded by Raoul, while the last of the Wolves shouted:

"*Bon voyage*, Master Josselin!"

The curious Wolves who questioned Cousin Yaumi about the cause of that sudden discomfort got nothing for their trouble. At the back of the carriage, poor little Celeste, half dead with fear, didn't dare open her eyes.

"The danger is past, dear one," said the Miller Woman, kissing her. "Don't think any more about that, and prepare your soul for happiness. Tonight, you will see your mother!"

The Wolves went across the prairie and stopped at the edge of the woods, which began again two hundred steps from there and only stopped at the gates of Rennes. There still exists at the end of the Thabor walk, in front of the Rennes Botanical Gardens, a giant oak tree that three men holding hands could not encircle. Tradition maintains that, at the time of King Louis XV, that oak marked the extreme edge of the Rennes forest. Nowadays, it takes three good leagues from Thabor to arrive at the first thickets.

Yaumi took with him a dozen men who never left him and who were in some way his bodyguards. He had already used them for his expedition against the old mill at the Wolf's Den, swomething that the remainder of the olves did not know. They were a few scoundrels without faith or law.

"Boys," he said to the biggest of the men, "I'm going to walk a little ahead to reconnoiter the way. Don't go any further ahead until I come back."

He started, in fact, in the direction of Rennes, but after five minutes, he suddenly turned and lost himself in the underbrush.

"Let's go, my lovelies," he shouted. "If we arrive on time, each of us will bring back his full load of écus."

The coalmakers of the foresrt of ennes, even today, let their little horses graze freely in the clearings. They are tiny, having no more in common with real horses than small terriers have with bif mastiffs. You can see them walking in a line, their heads low, sadly ringing the little bells hanging around their necks. When when one knows how to spur them, they can rise as fast as any regular horse, just like Rocinante once is supposed to have done.[103]

Yaumi and his twelve men re-entered the prairie at another point, each riding a small horse, and they left at a gallop, aftwer having removed the tiny bells. They rejoined the Vesvre Valley, passing without stopping before the Rohan manor house, taking the road that led to Vitré, then to La

---

[103] In *Don Quixote.*

Gravelle, the border between Brittany and France. There the handsome Cobbler dismounted and set up an ambush among the rocks.

II. Magloire's Supper

It was a night of adventures. Now, we must explain the vision that Raoul and the Miller Woman, before turning around, had seen, or believed that they had seen, in the lit boudoir of the Feydeau young ladies—these moving shadows.

The Witch and Raoul hadn't been mistaken. That gentleman from Spain who had thrown himself so resolutely into Breton intrigues, Don Martin Blas, was not, it seems, without servants. On his return to Rennes, he had sent his valet to the Cygne-de-la-Croix Inn, located in the rue Nantaise, outside the walls, and, a short time later, his valet had brought back six strong-arm men, who spoke the French of the Pyrenees and were built like true mountain men.

Martin Blas shut himself in their company. Toward dusk, they were seen leaving on horseback by the Croix-Rouge road that led into the forest.

Martin Blas' last words had been these:

"The carriage has only a six-man escort that you will easily disarm if you take them by surprise. As for the manor itself, it has no kind of defense. You will put a short ladder against the balcony. Madame the Countess of Toulouse and the young girl must be treated with the greatest courtesy, but under no pretext must you stop on the road before having reached Laval, where my carriages are stationed. I will join you there tomorrow. And then, we take the road to Spain!"

We will immediately say that the henchmen recruited by Don Martin Blas could not recognize the Princess, although her normal itinerary could have been to go through the forest. Just that morning, Beauvilliers, the gentleman of the Count of Toulouse who took care of her, had received in Laval a note frm the Baroness Saint Elme warning him and suggesting that he take another road.

As a consequence, Beauvilliers, without saying anything to the Princess, had turned left after leaving Laval to rejoin the road from Angers, by which Madame de Toulouse had arrived in Rennes at about ten o'clock at night, at the time the Ball was about to start.

"And she had only time to freshen up a little," said Madame de la Roche-Aynard at the end of her letter to Duclos, who speaks of that fact in his third appendix.

That left the manor. Don Martin Blas' armed valets had valiantly scaled the balcony, following their orders. They found a large number of chiffons in disorder, boxes of handkerchiefs, powder boxes, all that was necessary to make a pretty woman. Only the pretty woman in question was missing. As they were searching conscientiously in the neighboring cabinets and right into the corridor, the door that opened on the interior courtyard opened. The wheels of a carriage sounded on the pavement of the courtyard.

Our six men had done their job. They thought it prudent to leave. Here is, however, why the Rohan Manor was awakened and turned upside down at eleven o'clock that night.

Upon leaving the Royal Steward and the Seneschal, who had appointed him State Courier, our friend Magloire was taken to the kitchens by a valet who had been told to satisfy all his desires. They asked him what he wanted. He wanted everything that could be eaten, and everything that it is possible to drink. To satisfy that manifest desire, the valet covered the table with a multitude of cold dishes that would have been enough for a supper of ten men with ordinary appetites.

Magloire sat down and tied a napkin around his neck. We despair of expressing by mere words the pure, limitless joy which filled his soul at that moment. He regarded the plates aligned in front of him like a good father loving all his children equally and not knowing which to embrace first. He had to decide, however. A shoulder of mutton with its jelly had the honor of his first caress. It was the jelly that determined him. He had loved jelly since his childhood and that old affection carried him through a venison pâté, a tongue of Bréal, a smoked ham from Morlaix, and a dozen other delights.

It is very true that our first impressions are the most durable!

"What is your name? he asked the valet, his mouth already full.

"Hervé," the valet replied.

"That's not a proper name for a valet," Magloire observed. "My valet, who is a gentleman, is named Lafleur. He doesn't risk anything! I will wash his head properly on my return."

He watched the valet on the sly.

"Do you recognize me?"

"No," Hervé said.

"*No*? Can't you say, *No, Sir*, you rascal?"

Hervé bowed and poured him a glassful of wine. He was an old scoundrel of a valet, grown moldy in antichambers, a liar, a thief; the Seneschal liked them that way.

"I beg your pardon, sir," he said seriously. "Does ththise gentleman have a title?"

"Do I have a title, you scoundrel?" Magloire shouted again. "I have more than two hundred to choose from. I occupy an important position. Call me Baron, if you wish."

"I would gladly do so, Baron," said Hervé,, who kept a straight face and did not laugh.

"I like you," Magloire said. "When I return, I will dismiss my own valet and hire you in his place."

Saying that, he dropped the shoulder of mutton for a little capon that had lost but one wing at the supper of the day before. Hérvé thanked him and filled his glass again.

"When I think," exclaimed Magloire, swallowing all the white wine and eating another wing, "that today, I was mistaken for an apprentice baker from the rue Vasselot in Rennes! Someone named Magloire. He must be all right, that young man, but I find it astonishing that a good-for-nothing like that can resemble a person of my quality and nobility. Listen here, you wretch!" he said, continuing, eating the small scraps of the capon, "come forward... closer...."

And when he had him very near him, he whispered in his ear:

"I am the one who is Sidonie's lover."

He then put his nose back in his plate, giggling.

"Ah!" said Hervé. "Monsieur le Baron is her lover."

"What Baron, you wretch?" exclaimed Magloire, who had already forgotten his new title. "I told you it was me!"

"I heard clearly what Monsieur le Baron told me."

"Good! Good!" Magloire grumbled. "I have so many titles that I confuse them. Yes, I'm the one who seduced her."

Hervé pinched his lips with an air of admiration.

"That's going to help my reputation in Paris, won't it?"

"It certainly will!"

"A young gentleman who knows how to charm Sidonie with his words!" Magloire continued, becoming animated. "Sidonie, the only daughter of a duke and marquis, prouder than the King, with a coat-of-arm as long as the arm and as innocent as the flower of the field! I mean Sidonie, not the old man... More drink! That cider is really nice, isn't it?"

"It's a claret from Bordeaux, Monsieur le Baron."

"I said it's really nice, but I'm accustomed to drink better... Still, pour me some more!"

He was beginning to have a little trouble seeing, but that didn't keep him from making a formidable hole in the venison paté.

"They don't eat very much in this house," he said after having finished his plate. "If you had seen how we ate in my father's house... Ah! What a fine man! Oh, my!" he interrupted himself, "I've just put a grease stain on my doublet."

"That's too bad, Monsieur le Baron," said Hervé.

"I like you, Hervé! I'm going to tell you the history of this doublet... This morning, when I got up, I was in a hurry... I knew that the State absolutely needed me, so I jumped out of bed and I called out, 'Lafleur! Lafleur! You triple scoundrel!' No answer. Then I picked up the first piece of clothing I found under my hand. It belonged to Lafleur. I didn't notice that until two or three hours later... Pour me another glass... And then there was not enough time to retrace my steps..."

What he loved about the paté, that young and shameless Magloire, was the crust, the deep waffle crust, fawn-colored or the color of brown-gold in its grooves. His stomach was completely at its full capacity, but nevertheless he still wanted to eat a good-sized piece of crust.

"Pour some more to drink!"

Hervé, obedient and mocking, filled his glass.

Magloire's face, under his yellow hair, was as red as blood; his eyes were bulging. He soon wanted to hug Hervé, then to beat him. Sidonie was no longer enough for him. He needed regiments of wild girls. On that occasion, his imagination rose to prodigious heights of stupidity. He invented two or three stories that were so crass that even Hervé, who was himself a sordid scoundrel, wanted to knock him on the head.

"I am wicked!," Lagloire shouted, trying to swallow still more mouthfuls. "It means nothing to me to commit all the evil deeds of the guiltiest criminals! Ah! Ah! The two old fellas were afraid of me. I am more of a rogue than they are! Pour me some more to drink! I'm going to make a splash at the Court."

He fell while trying to shove a big piece of apple pie into his mouth.

"Lift me up, you scoundrel," he said to Hervé.

But the valet pushed him under the table with his feet and closed the door to the kitchen on him.

Magloire began to snore like a canon. The heads of these happy idiots are made so that they cannot die of apoplexy. All of this took place while the Feydeau young ladies were getting ready, about an hour before the departure of the cavalcade.

Hervé, who had his instructions, went down to the stables, saddled a horse, and was soon galloping on the road to

Rennes. The goal of that ride was to find a young adventurer named Raoul, to whom Hervé was to cleverly tell that little Celeste was going to be kidnapped that same night in a rented carriage, and that her kidnappers would go through the Saint-Julien woods at midnight near the Steward's chateau.

Another courier, also dispatched by the Seneschal, had just left for the Wolf's Den with a letter for the handsome Cobbler, Yaumi.

Hervé found with no trouble Raoul's domicile, an attic room located across from the Feydeau townhouse. But there was no one there, and the people in the house couldn't tell him anything more, except that young Master Raoul had been seen in the city that day dressed in thes uniform of an officer of the Conti Regiment.

Hervé then left to go talk to the various stations manned by the Conti soldiers. He managed to learn that the new young officer had been placed in command at the Mordelaise gates So he went there, but Raoul had already left to go and see Celeste, riding toward the Saint-Martin bridge.

Our valet was then obliged to return to the manor since his tasks for that night were not yet done. He had to put Celeste into a carriage with Magloire, the so-called State courier, and send them both to Paris.

It is not necessary to tell the reader why Hervé could put only Magloire into that carriage. Magloire, awakened with a start, and thrown into the rolling carriage, went back to sleep, being incontinent on the cushions.

"This strange fellow is dead drunk," Hervé said to the Rohan grooms. "God knows what is going to become of the message that he's carrying."

"Who else is in the carriage?" the other valets asked, because Hervé had taken care to close the carriage windows.

Instead of answering that question, Hervé shook his head with an important look and grumbled between his teeth:

"Those are the secrets of the Seneschal."

Some minutes later, everybody knew—or thought they knew—that little Celeste was in the carriage. Too bad for Magloire if he was no longer there at the first way station.

The carriage left at a full trot with two men on horseback as escorts. Under the bushes that extended near the Feydeau chateau, a half-hour from there, the two riders serving as escorts, were killed with shots from a pistol, as was the coachman of the carriage. The shots had come from somewhere under the foliage.

Yaumi and his bodyguards rushed out of their hiding place. The carriage was rummaged, then broken into pieces in order to find the six hundred thousand écus of the Steward. But there was nothing inside except Magloire, half-dead with fear.

The capture of Magloire, State courier, was the only result of that bloody intrigue so laboriously set up by Polduc; the scheme that was to deliver him from all worry about the Rohan heirs.

Magloire, searched for anything of importance, was then tied to a horse and taken into the underground realm of the Wolf's Den.

Historic cities are usually rich in monuments. By an unusual fate, the Breton Capital of Rennes has nothing that can speak highly of its past grandeur. While Rouen, its opulent and splendid rival, spreads out its almost inexhaustible marvelous treasures to the charmed traveler, Rennes, poorly located in the middle of a gloomy basin, bathing the feet of its grey houses in the dormant and troubled waters of the humble river Vilaine, can hardly show anything, but a passable church that has a few good features and several beautiful paintings, and a City Hall, original if not grandiose. Its modern edifices, it should be said, are as unfortunate as its old ones.

She's like a frumpy housewife who doesn't want, or know how, to embellish her appearance with jewelry. Inside its walls, the city is calm and pleasant. Outside, the neighboring countryside is thin and flat. A rather nice river runs through some pleasant prairies, flowing towards a horizon that is narrow without being high, like a nice frame to an mediocre painting.

However, at the times we're talking about, Rennes was, perhaps, after Paris, the most brilliant city in the kingdom, just as Brittany was the most important province of France. It was only given to Princes, and under the "reign" of Cardinal Mazarin,[104] it was Queen Anne of Austria, mother of Louis XIV, who had wanted to hold it herself. The King, of age and grateful to the Cardinal, wanted to give it to him, but Queen Anne refused, saying that it was the most beautiful jewel in her crown.

However, it had always been a difficult post for a Governor. Brittany couldn't become accustomed to being a part of France, and there was, in the lower classes as well as the middle class and the nobility, much rancor against Paris, the conqueror. Since the death of the previous King, difficulties had only grown more severe.

The nobility, agitated and hostile, was indignant about the peace; the middle class revolted about the tax, and the common people greeted tax collectors with torches and pitchforks. Rennes was the permanent home of a small *Fronde* where transparent intrigues often grew violent. We don't even want to try to describe the political situation of that rich, noble and elegant society that didn't know which way the wind was blowing. We used the word *Fronde* on purpose.[105]

That little civil war during the minority of Louis XIV was not more complex, involved, or inextricable than the agitation that reigned in Rennes and Brittany under the regency of Philippe d'Orléans. There were a least a dozen parties. People were in two or three parties at the same time.

---

[104] Jules Mazarin (1602-1661), born Giulio Raimondo Mazzarino, Italian cardinal, diplomat and politician who served as the chief minister to the kings of France Louis XIII and Louis XIV from 1642 until his death.

[105] See Notes 41 and 76.

The Cellamare Conspiracy, that had been able to provide an outlet for all the concentrated anger and discontentment of gentlemen land owners, had never been greeted except with defiance by the city's nobility. There were intrigues—that was a fact. A state of revolt was almost declared, but a plan or a goal—nothing! It was that war that could not be pinned down, that fantasy rebellion, that the Count of Toulouse, Governor of Brittany, had been called to put down. Perhaps no better doctor could have been chosen to take the pulse of a Province afflicted with such fever. Gentle, calm, pious, thoughtful, the Prince had arrived in Rennes with thoughts of peace and of pardon.

Another man might have wanted to bend Brittany harshly to his will, but Brittany doesn't bend; it breaks, as the saying went.

III. Before the Ball

It was in the City Hall, in the Presidental salons, that the City and the Parliament had decided to organize the welcoming festivities for the new Governor. The King's Lieutenant had imposed an urban tax to underwrite the magnificence of that ball, the impact of which would be felt all the way to the Court in Paris.

The Prince was liked. The middle class willingly contributed. That evening, Rennes was like a reflection of the Louvre or Versailles. From the Lebât chateau, where the Count of Toulouse made his home, right to the Presidial, across the Palais Square, the rue Royale, the rue d'Estrées, and the Place d'Armes, a route of honor had been laid out between two ranks of pilasters filled with greenery and flowers which had been woven into beautiful garlands. The houses were illuminated and were strung with lights on each side. The street disappeared under a thick layer of rose petals and green boxwood.

The garrison of Rennes was stationed to the right and left waiting for the Count's escort, which was to be composed of three hundred gentlemen on horseback. The City Hall, illuminated from end to end, displayed the portrait of the young king, Louis XV, in a niche under the clock, and was so bright that it seemed to be on fire. On the square, a forest of Yew trees ablaze threw out waves of light and of smoke. Behind the hedge of the guards on foot, the citizens waited, dressed in their best clothes. There was an enormous crowd; it filled the three squares, went down to the river by way of the Baudrairie, and rejoined, on the other side, the Saint-Sauveur Church the Jacquet field and the Rue aux Foulons.

The populace had been waiting for a long time already at the moment we crossed the squares to enter the Presidial, but that night, it was in a good humor, and far from complaining. People sang, it laughed, gossiped, only stopping from time to time to shout: "Long Live the Count of Toulouse!" and "Long Live the King!" The name of the Regent was never mingled with those shouts. The preceding year, the people had pulled down the sign from the Rue d'Orléans to replace it with its former name, Haute Baudrairie.

The vestibule, full of servants, commanded by the baillifs, was decorated with Flanders' tapestries on all the walls, and velvet on all the pillars. There were also abundant flowers on the stairway, where each step seemed like a flower bed. Perfumed candles burned between the flower pots.

There was already a crowd in the salons, even though the ballroom was not yet open. The ladies had been seated as soon as possible, and the dignitaries pretended to talking rapidly among themselves so that their impatience could be hidden. That the populace below waited was acceptable; but to make the King's Lieutenant, a Coetlegon, the President of the Estates, a Duke of Retz, the President of Parlement, a Lachanlotais, the Archbishop, a Noailles, the Seneschal and the Royal Steward, and so many others, wait was inconceivable! The Royal Father of the Count of Toulouse had once said that being on time was the politeness of Kings. Contrary to that maxim, so proud and otherwise so correct

Monsieur de Toulouse had no excuse, except that of being a simple gentleman.

In any event, there was no more bad humor among the highly placed than among the low. They were almost all Frenchified Bretons from Combourg , the son of the former League member, to Chateaubriand, who had forgotten his ducal origins. Old partisans of the Count of Toulouse were feted, and all those who could claim any kind of relationship with the Noailles raised their head higher, because Madame la Contesse de Toulouse was a Noailles.

The Archbishop held court; so did the President of the Estates. In a corner, Marshal de Montesquiou could be seen chatting with some country squire from Morlaix or Hennebon. And the country squire was embarrassed.

There was two centuries of such courtesan madness. Laporte, Portmanteau Ordinaire of Queen Anne of Austria, recounts, in his curious memoirs, that during the disgrace of the two queens, after the execution of Montmorency,[106] the courtesans, passing through the Courtyard of the Chateau of Chantilly, where Anne lives, to pay their respects to King Louis XIII and the Cardinal, didn't dare raise their eyes toward the Queen's apartment, for fear of having to bow to her.

Don Martin Blas, the Spaniard, was the center of a circle, dressed as a prince, wearing around his neck the sash of Ferdinand the Catholic. Achille- Feydeau de Brou flitted about near the ladies. The Seneschal de Rohan-Polduc had

---

[106] Henri II de Montmorency (1595-1632), is a contemporary gentleman of Louis XIII. Admiral of France, Viceroy of New France and Governor of Languedoc, he participated in the wars against the Protestants and defeated the fleet of Benjamin de Rohan, Lord of Soubise, in front of La Rochelle in 1625. Marshal of France in 1630, he intrigued with Gaston d'Orléans, brother of the King, against Cardinal Richelieu. Sentenced to death for the crime of *lèse-majesté*, he was executed in Toulouse on October 30, 1632.

monopolized the Viscount of Rieux, Lieutenant Colonel of the Conti REgiment, who had not given up his usual gaiety, and laughed in his face with resolute enthusiasm.

The two Feydeau young ladies, separated by the black silk dress of the hapless Zoé des Étangs du Ronceroy de Kerméléon, were standing, fanning themselves, yawning, and trying to see themselves in the mirrors, and doing their best to attract the attention of the gentlemen. They were bored to death and deserved some kind of prize for the length of time they had managed to keep smiling.

"Monsieur, my worthy cousin," Alain Polduc was saying to the Viscount of Rieux, "what should I make of what I am hearing everywhere? That the vacant officer post has been given to a young, unknown man?"

"He! He!" replied the Viscount. "Don't worry, Monsieur de Polduc, I know that young man. What are they saying, if you don't mind, about the Wolves in your region?"

"Nothing good, cousin. Have you heard about a certain local witch who was calling herself the Miller Woman?"

"He! He! Certainly, Monsieur de Polduc. What about her?"

"Something frequent when the Wolves are being discussed, Monsieur—a murder!"

Rieux shook from head to toe and stopped laughing. He seized Polduc's arm so hard that the Seneschal stifled an exclamation.

"If you have done that, Polduc," he said between clenched teeth, "as God is my witness, you can start writing your will."

He turned away, leaving the Seneschal livid and trembling.

The flute-like voice of Achille Feydeau was heard saying:

"Some successes with the ladies... A great knowledge of French poetry... The assiduous frequentation of the Court... All that should diminish your astonishment, my beautiful ladies… The King did me the honor of speaking to me and he said:

" 'Monsieur de Brou, would you do me the honor of reciting your last madriga to mel?'

"I demurred just as much as was necessary and I began thus..."

Rieux had reached the door where he found La Grève d'Hunieres, the Captain of his First Company.

"I am giving you five minutes to bring me news of Countess Isaure, nephew," he told him. "Get a horse and come back quickly!"

Rieux called all of his officers his nephews. La Grève was already at the bottom of the stairs; two seconds later, he jumped in the saddle in the rue de l''Horlage, that fortunately the crowd had not yet blocked.

"Yes, gentlemen," pronounced Dn Martin Blas, in a grave and sonorous voice in the middle of his circle, "I had the honor of reaching an understanding with His Excellency the Cardinal. From the moment that Spain could no longer count on the help of the brave Bretons, everything is finished... The King, my master, only wanted one thing: to safeguard the freedom of the young King."

Two or three hands timidly touched his shoulder, then mysteriously moved on so many closed mouths. Martin Blas' eyes searched for the Seneschal, who sent him a rapid nod. The Spanish conspiracy was in the process of being renewed in these magnificent salons of the Rennes Presidial.

"When I had finished reciting to the King that weak and light product of a muse that perhaps could have flown much higher," continued Achille Feydeau, turning his gold box between his fingers weighed down with rings, "His Majesty turned to Racine,[107] who was at his side, and asked:

" 'What do you think, Apollo?'

---

[107] Jean Racine (1639-1699), French dramatist, one of the three great playwrights of 17th century France, along with Molière and Corneille.

"Monsieur Racine was always a little jealous of me. It's characteristic of *genus irritabile*... I believed he nodded without answering; he was that irritated; but the King motioned to me with his hand and said:

" 'Au revoir, Monsieur de Brou. I have rarely met poets of your ability.' "

The Chevalier de Talhouët, the brother of the decapitated man, came in at that moment. He went straight to Montesquiou. A few brief words were exchanged, then the Marshal said:

"Monsieur, I have no accounts to give to anyone for the things that I did by the order and for the service of the King."

That was the fourth duel that the Marshal had refused that evening. Each of the four decapitated gentlemen of Nantes, had found, belatedly, an avenger. Talhouët had been the last. He turned around and asked in a loud voice,:

"Has the Count of Toulouse come in yet?"

And when he was told he had not, he added:

"That being so, I will not be disrespectful to His Highness by doing this."

And he struck the cheek of the Marshal with his glove. The latter touched his sword. Talhouët took him under his arm and they left. That noble and beautiful race of the Talhouëts was unlucky. Before Rieux could summon his men to stop the duel, the Chevalier and the Maréchal had already drawn swords under the lantern in the rue de l'Horloge. Talhouët fell against the wall with a sword blade through his heart. The Marshal returned to the ballroom, somber and cold as before, and resumed his conversation with the squires of Pontivy and Quimper.

La Grève came back to tell the Viscount of Rieux that Countess Isaure was at her townhouse and was soon to arrive. Rieux found his lost smile again. He came to slap Polduc's shoulder and said to him gaily:

"*Morbleu*, cousin, you've had a narrow escape!"

"I believe I know better than anyone," Achille Feydeau said, responding to a question of one of those ladies, "why our beautiful Countess is not yet at her post. The noble Isaure has no secrets from me.... Ah! Ladies! Why those smiles?"

No one was smiling. Feydeau continued:

"The day is not purer than the friendship that binds us!"

"Gentlemen," announced the King's Lieutenant, who had entered by an inside door, "the absence of the Governor has a reason that must be explained to you. His Highness was expecting Madame the Countess of Toulouse this evening and she has not yet arrived. An accident is feared."

Don Martin Blas smiled proudly.

"Aren't your Breton roads safe?" he asked between high and low.

Rieux had his eyes on him.

"Nephew," he said to Captain La Grève, "you see that handsome man over there? Don't let him out of your sight. I have an idea that we will have business with him later!"

His eyes encountered that of Don Martin Blas and he began to laugh so heartedly that the Spaniard's black eyebrows frowned, thinking that he was being mocked.

At the moment when the King's Lieutenant had pronounced the word "accident" in relation to Madame de Toulouse, Martin Blas had sent two rapid winks to the Royal Steward and the Seneschal. Both of them rapidly closed their eyes.

"To return to the anecdote that I promised you," Feydeau took up again, "and that was unfortunately such a great scandal at the Trianon, Mademoiselle de Beaumesnil, the niece of Monsieur de Colbert, had shown some attraction for my person at the time of the festivities for the crossing of the Rhine...."

But those ladies would never learn the end of that anecdote. There suddenly arose a great noise in the drawing room; then such a commotion that it was thought that the upsetting news brought by the King's Lieutenant was immediately going to have a happy outcome. To see the crowd, formerly so calm, push each other and struggle, the gentlemen form a line, the ladies leave their seats and stand on tiptoes to get a better view, no one had any doubt that the Governor and his wife had finally made their way into the vestibule. A number of voices were even heard saying, 'Their Highnesses! Their Highnesses!"

An expression of worry and of curiosity was painted on Don Martin Blas' serious face, but he did not budge at all. The Steward and the Seneschal, on the contrary, went toward the door. The groups that were obstructing the main entry parted at that moment, and one saw enter not the Governor with his wife, but the Duke de Retz, First President of the Province of Brittany, holding on his arm a woman of royal bearing, wearing jewelry, whose face disappeared under a mask of black velvet. Such masks were in fashion then, even at the King's Court.

What's more, the appearance of Their Serene Highnesses wouldn't have produced a greater effect in that noble assembly than the appearance of that woman. She must have been marvelously beautiful because an expression of envy darkened the faces of the women all at one time. What could be seen of her person excited admiration. Her blond hair fell in opulent rings onto shoulders so pure and so firm that they seemed to be sculpted of Greek marble. Her tall figure had the majestic grace that queens desire. She was a Queen indeed, the Queen of beauty!

A thousand mouths pronounced the name of Countess Isaure, and there was only respectful smiles and enthusiastic homages as she passed by.

Behind the Duke of Retz, came the old Abbot of Dandeau, La Meilleraie, Champlatreux, son of President Molé, the two Lavals of Montmorency, who had followed their Prince, the Marquis of Ploeuc, a great Lord of Southern Brittany, Göezbriant, Malestroit, Chateaubourg. d'Andigné, Montméril, all Breton gentlemen, Guitaut, a courtier from Paris, Fosseuse, Brigadier of the King, and Sancy, Councilor of the State, and a few more like that. That was the Court of Countess Isaure.

Passing in front of the Viscount of Rieux, she held out her hand, that the happy soldier kissed without laughing.

"Where is that Spaniard?" she asked in a low voice.

Rieux, without any trouble, pointed a finger at him.

The Duke of Retz felt the arm of the beautiful Isaure tremble under his. Don Martin Blas devoured her with his eyes. Countess Isaure walked straight to him, and her white hand pushed aside the Royal Steward, who seemed to want to put himself between them.

"Such familiarities," murmured Achille Feydeau, "will finally compromise her!"

Monsieur de Rieux stood next to him when he said that; you can imagine how much he laughed!

Countess Isaure, however, left the arm of the Duke of Retz and thanked him with a gracious smile.

"I am told," she said, while approaching the Spaniard, "that Don Martin Blas wishes to be introduced to me."

The Spaniard bowed deeply. A deeper paleness covered the bronze of his cheeks while he answered:

"Madame, I have ridden four hundred leagues for that."

IV. Tête-à-Tête

Don Martin Blas interested the assembly a great deal. Different gossip about him floated about. The ladies found him handsome. The men were astonished that his first visit had been to the Rohan manor house. A large number of them thought that he was a secret emissary from the Court charged with clarifying the conduct of the Count of Toulouse. Others believed that he was a secret envoy from the Court of Spain

We can't say enough that it is impossibled to judge the idea and passions of that time according to our own criteria; interests were divided; parties were sometimes in accord, other times at war; only the Government remained on the hot seat.

The King remained above those perry conflicts, surrounded with real or simulated respect that never changed, evenin the middle of all that hubbub of intrigues and battles.

People conspired then as we reason today. People followed some great Lord by sympathy or by alliance. They followed him blindly up until the day they left him to follow another. This was not called treason, and we wouldn't be able to define today what they called then honor.

Even those people who had dipped into the schemes of Cardinal Alberoni who sought to give the King of Spain ha controlling hand over the affairs of of France believed themselves to be the best patriots in the world. They would surely have poured out their last drop of blood for the young King Louis XV that they said had such great hope.

Order did not exist. Rules had yet to be drafted. Each person went into political life like a myopic man straying into the cohue, bumping into this, being hit by that, and having no other concern but somehow finding his way through. The Wolves of the forest of Rennes may well have been the wisest conspirators of that time. They had a precise and clear, if not very high, ovjective. That goal was to pay less taxes on tobacco, and no taxes at all on salt. Assuredly, in that resoect, they were well above all the other conspirators.

Countess Isaure, having dismissed with a gesture her cortege of honor, took Don Martin Blas'arm; that gesture gave him a new and unusual relief.

"Do you wish to speak to me alone?" she asked.

"Ardently, Madame," the Spaniard replied.

"Come then."

She walked toward the gallery that ran along the rue de l'Horloge and which has today vanished because of new construction made during the Empire. Passing in front of the Steward's daughters, Countess Isaure pointed out the Premier Presudent La Chalotais, who was talking to the two young ladies.

"Do you know what they are talking about?" she asked."

No," replied the Spaniard.

"That man is telling the teo Feydeau young ladies that they will be recognized tomorrow as the daughters and heirs of Rohan."

Don Martin Blas turned his head and said:

"That matters not at all to me."

Countess Isaure stopped to stare at him.

"Let's do it quickly, Madame," said the Spaniard. "I have other businesses to attend to."

Countess Isaure began walking again. The gallery was empty because the curious crowd was massed in the entry salon where Monsieur and Madame de Toulouse were supposed to pass by first.

Countess Isaure sat down on a couch. Her emotion, that she didn't want to show, but which was great, wouldn't have allowed her to remain standing. She motioned to Don Martin Blas to sit down beside her.

Instead of obeying he went to look for a stool and sat in front of her.

"I am waiting for you, Monsieur," said the Countess, controlling her voice as well as she could.

There was no misunderstanding. That was the opening of a battle. The beautiful Isaure did as our French Guards did at Fontenoy; they shouted, "Shoot first!"[108]

Don Martin Blas was a moment before answering. There were beads of sweat on his forehead.

"Don't you want to take off your mask, Madame?" he finally said.

---

[108] The Battle of Fontenoy was a major engagement of the War of the Austrian Succession, fought on 11 May 1745, outside Tournai, Belgium. A French army of 50,000 under Marshal Saxe defeated a Pragmatic Army of 52,000, led by the Duke of Cumberland. Louis XV was present and thus technically in command, a fact he later used to bolster his prestige. At the beginning of the battle, Lord Charles Hay, captain of the English Guards, is reported to have stepped forward and shouted: "Gentlemen of the French Guards, shoot!" Grenadier Lieutenant d'Anterroches, allegedly replied, "No, sir, we never shoot first." Be that as it may, French popular tradition has only retained the quote: "*Messieurs les Anglais*, shoot first!"

His voice was trembling. He was answered only by:

"No, Monsieur."

However, seeing a movement of anger that escaped the Spaniard, the beautiful Isaure added:

"For reasons that have nothing at all to do with you, Monsieur, I insist that my face remain covered."

The Spaniard seemed to have great difficulty keeping his calm gravity. Despite that covering of tan that the sun had put on his cheeks, he changed color several times. It seemed that he was forcing his eyes to remain lowered in order to hide the brightness of his gaze.

"Madame," he continued, after some seconds, trying hard to get control of himself, "do you know me?"

"I believed that I knew you," Isaure answered without hesitating, "but I was wrong."

"Are you Baroness Saint Elme?"

"That, Don Martin," said Isaure, instead of answering, "seems very much like an interrogation."

"It's up to you to tell me, Madame," Martin Blas slowly pronounced, "yes or no, if I have the right to set myself up as your judge."

"You don't have the right to do that, Monsieur," she replied in a resolute and almost haughty voice.

But her heart was beating rapidly under the gold lamé of her blouse and Don Martin Blas saw that very well. He was silent again; then he continued:

"Would you please explain the meaning of those words: *I believed that I knew you, but I was wrong.*"

"I would do so with pleasure, Don Martin."

"I am listening."

"Is your conscience as much at peace today as it was yesterday?"

"I am listening," the Spaniard repeated.

"Do you have to be told what you have done during the last twenty-four hours?"

"I am listening," Don Martin Blas repeated for the third time.

"In the last twenty-four hours, you have tried to take a daughter away from her mother, and a wife from her husband."

Don Martin Blas smiled bitterly.

"You don't want to be judged, Madame. So don't judge me!"

"I'm reporting facts."

"As they have been reported to you."

"Such as I know them myself... I thought I knew you... A soldier and a gentleman... I was wrong, because I see before me the accomplice of murderers!"

"Name these murderers."

"Polduc and Feydeau, who have tried to kill a woman... A woman, do you understand? At the very hour when you were seated between them in the boudoir of those two girls want to be called the Demoiselles of Rohan."

"And it was that conversation that your spies overheard?"

"That one, one other in the same place, and yet another one elsewhere."

Martin Bas frowned.

"Have you hoped to fight against me?" he asked between clenched teeth.

A proud smile under Countess Isaure's mask could be guessed.

"I have fought against those stronger than you," she said.

"And can one know what you believe my plans to be, Madame?" asked the Spaniard.

"Before acting out your little comedy to frighten the Royal Steward," responded Countess Isaure, "you had a long and secret meeting with Polduc... You, Morvan de Saint-Maugan, the ally of Alain Polduc!"

The Spaniard, made a quick movement of surprise when he heard himself called by that name, but he did not interrupt the Countess.

"You," the Countess continued, "You, whose honor and happiness Alain Polduc killed! During that conversation, the true goal of your coming to Brittany came out. You seek to kidnap the Countess of Toulouse and the daughter of Valentine de Rohan."

Don Martin Blas bowed coldly, then sat straight on the back of his chair.

"You did well, Morvan de Saint-Maugan," continued Countess Isaure, whose soft voice became almost deep and masculine, "to drop the name of your father, who was a Breton and a gentleman. Breton gentlemen do not attack women. You did well to take another name to commit an infamous act."

"Madame!" Don Martin Blas, pale, exclaimed, before adding, looking down in spite of himself: "I have been outraged, deceived, band roken. I want vengeance. I will avenge myself!"

Thus spoke Martin Blas, or Morvan de Saint-Maugan. The hot sun of Spain had not been able to thicken the olive mask that now covered his male face to hide that horrible emotion that struck him at that instant.

"Then take vengeance on the man who outraged you," replied Isaure, who seemed to become greater as Morvan became more troubled. "Avenge yourself on the woman who deceived you!"

"I told you then at that time, and I am telling you now, Valentine," he said in a troubled voice, "I will not take vengeance on you."

He had a smile full of bitterness.

"You are pardoning the mother," she said, "but you taking her child away, and you are striking a saintly woman, innocent of all that you have suffered."

"Valentine! Valentine!" exclaimed Saint-Maugan, "it is not up to you to defend the Countess of Toulouse, who hates you, and, without me, would have shown it cruelly tonight."

"I know that the Princess hates me, Morvan, but I am defending her.

Saint-Maugan shook his head and said, without lifting his eyes:

"You are defending her in vain, Madame. She is doomed. I have been waiting fifteen years!"

"And what were you waiting for?"

"For the Count of Toulouse to be married."

He lifted his head. His eyes burned like two flames among the livid pallor of his features.

"I had a woman whom I adored," he said, letting his agony explode, "a woman in whom I believed as I do in God. I had a master whom I cherished more than a brother and for whom I would have given all my blood, down to the last drop... My heart and my woman were taken from me, and, according to your own words, Madame, my honor was taken with my happiness. And the assassin was my master!"

"Blind fool!" murmured Countess Isaure.

"What could I do?" continued Saint-Maugan. "Kill him? That was my first thought, and I remembered that beautiful and terrible law of our ancestors: An eye for an eye... An eye, they said. Me, I say, a heart for a heart! I will torture the soul of that man as he has tortured my own soul. I want him to have my sleepless nights and my fevered days. I want his honor to perish at the same time as his happiness... and I wish that, standing facing him, my sword in my hand, I can say to him: 'Here I am. This is me. I am avenging myself.'"

Saint-Maugan rose. Isaure imitated him.

"Blind fool!" she said for the second time, putting her hand on his shoulder.

With the other, she took off her mask. Saint-Maugan stepped back, dumfounded.

"Oh!" he said. "You are beautiful! No woman was ever more beautiful than you, but I don't love you anymore, Valentine de Rohan. No! In the name of God, I don't love you anymore!"

Countess Isaure smiled. It was that smile that prostrated at her feet the noble youth of Brittany as if before an idol.

"But I still love you, Morvan. Since that first calumny that fell on me, many other calumnies have come. When you asked me to give you an account of those fifteen years, I will accept you as my judge. Now, I'm going to give you the only proof of affection that is in my power. Valentine de Rohan, since I am taking back that name for a few minutes, does not want her husband to dishonor himself. Morvan de Saint-Maugan, the cowardly machinations of Don Martin Blas have failed, because of me. My daughter is free and safe."

"What are you saying?"

"The wife of the Count of Toulouse is in the care of her husband!"

"That can't be!" shouted Saint-Maugan.

"Look, and believe your eyes!"

Saint-Maugan followed his extended finger which pointed to the open door of the gallery. Through that door came a great murmur that almost dominated the sound of the triumphal march composed by Lully after the Battle of Corfu.[109]

Saint-Maugan could see the Count of Toulouse climbing the stairs, holding the hand of the Princess, his wife. And when Their Serene Highnesses were seated, he could see a young girl, radiant with beauty, conducted by M. de la Germondaye, Councillor of the Parliement, the Prevost of the City and the Aldermen, was bringing the keys to the city on a plate of chiseled gold.

That was Celeste.

V. The Insult

Assuredly, Don Martin Blas was roundly surprised by that double apparition. But what can be said of the stupefaction of the two Feydeau young ladies? They had had joyful souls because the President of the Chalotais had just told them of the happy disposition of the Parliament toward them; then, they rose, like everyone else, at the entry of Their

---

[109] *March for the Turkish Ceremony* by Jean-Baptiste Lully (1632-1687). This march was requested by Louis XIV after a Turkish ambassador had visited Paris.

Serene Highnesses. Agnés thought that the Princess was badly dressed; Olmphe was in the process of finding fault in her coiffure when, figuratively, the Head of Medusa appeared.

Celeste—yes, their Cinderella—appeared, carrying her golden plate in the midst of all those dignitaries! Their Cinderella! Was that even possible? Such an honor granted to such a girl! To that little unfortunate girl had gone the golden apple of beauty![110] The Feydeau young ladies in disbelief rubbed their eyes until they were almost bloody.

"She's wearing my rose satin skirt, the insolent girl!" Mademoiselle Olympe said aloud.

"And my velvet blouse," Mademoiselle Agnès added in the same tone.

Agnès and Olympe were girls to make a fuss when they saw, at a distance, the Seneschal, who, gloomy-eyed, with a worried expression, motioned then to remain quiet.

At the same time, Monsieur de Rieux approached them, laughing like the good man that he was.

"Hush! Hush!" he said. "Behave, my pretty girls. "How much could those chiffons be worth?"

Agnès and Olymhe, revolted, were going to answer despite the Seneschal's instructionsbut Mobsieurde Rieux took out of his pocket a jewelry box that he opened. Inside were two identical rings, each with a diamond as its stone.

"Mademoiselle de Rohan doesn't want to owe you anything," he said, suddenly taking that haughty tone that he had when he ordered his men around, "and she's asked me to offer you this as compensation."

He bowed, turned around and disappeared.

If a flash of lightening had struck between Olympe and Agnès, you couldn't have seen them any paler or any more trembling.

---

[110] Allusion to Eris' Golden Apple and the Judgment of Paris who chose Aphrodite over Hera and Athena from Greek mythology.

At that moment, Achille Feydeau, putting his arm under that of his son-in-law, asked anxiously:

"What does this all mean, Seneschal?"

"My dear father-in-law," answered Polduc, "I don't know. I sense a storm coming, but I don't know where it's coming from... The Devil is here... Unless that is the hand of Valentine..."

"You had taken your precautions very well, Madame," Don Martin Blas said to the Countess. "You win this point, but I warn you that I will win the game."

Countess Isaure put her mask back on.

"So you don't want the peace that I am offering you, Monsieur?"

"I want that young girl and Madame de Toulouse."

"Good-bye, then!"

"Good-bye! And may everything that happens here fall back on you!"

Countess Isaure returned to the Ballroom, where she soon found a good part of her Court. The rest were at the feet of the Princess.

Marie-Victoire-Sophie de Noailles,[111] widow of the Marquis de Gondrin, Brigadier of the King's Armies, and presently Countess of Toulouse, was then twenty-five years-old. Her marriage, initially secret, had been made public by the intervention of the young king himself, despite the Philipppe d'Orléans' reluctance. She had all that sweet and somewhat austere beauty that was, somewhat later, to inspire Louis XV with the only platonic passion that he had ever been known to have.

Very different from the Duchess of Maine, her lively and worried sister-in-law, the Countess of Toulouse had very quickly understood that her husband's character forbade her to become involved in the field of politics. She limited herself to be pleasing and doing good, tasks in which she succeeded admirably. Countess Isaure was only just when she said of her,

---

[111] See Note 92.

"She is a saint."

But even saints feel compelled to using claws when they are still on Earth and become jealous. Now Madame de Toulouse had known for a long time that there was in Brittany a woman that her husband had once loved. Furthermore, she knew that the return to favor that had recalled her husband to the Government of Brittany was due to a woman. She knew that so well that her counsel had been for him to refuse the post, and without Abbot Fleury's intervention,[112] the Prince would have asked permission to remain in his retirement.

She had only been in Rennes for one hour, but already malicious tongues—promped by the Seneschal—had pointed out Countess Isaure as having been her rival, at least in the past. There was, in fact, a story that had spread through the fêtes and the streets of Paris. Countess Isaure was frequently absent. A Breton gentleman recounted that, even on the very day of his marriage, the Count of Toulouse had ridden in a hired carriage with Countess Isaure between Paris and Saint Germain. Madame de Toulouse had asked if that Countess Isaure was beautiful. I leave it to you to guess the answers. Madame de Toulouse had asked questions about her morality. On that, they looked down and let out deep sighs. It was a shame, they murmured, to see such creature under the same roof as that of Her Highness.

It was with the intention of striking a great blow that Madame de Toulouse had entered the Ballroom. If she had been less good, and more accustomed to rage, she would have used more measure. Cruelty is an art that must be learned like everything else.

Nobody knows how terrible a hatchet can be in the hands of a novice. From her entry, Madame de Toulouse's eyes had

---

[112] Claude Fleury (1640-1723), Church historian and jurist. From 1672 to 1705, he was tutor to the sons of the Prince of Conti, then to the Count of Vermandois, then sub-tutor to the grandsons of Louis XIV. From 1716 to 1722, he was also the confessor of Louis XV.

searched for that bold adventurer who, she supposed, had come to defy her. Her first idea had been to have her evicted by the officers, but a double incident happened that only increased the heat of her anger and tripled her desire for vengeance.

She opened the Ball with the Vice-President of the Estates because the Duke of Retz was lame in his right leg. That man, who belonged to the illustrious house of La Houssaye, never left his chateau at La Roche-Bernard, and this was unable to show him Countess Isaure, whom he did not know.

As she was returning to her seat, Don Martin Blas came to pay her his respects. The Princess had seen him at Court in Paris, and didn't suspect what the Spaniard had attempted against her that same night.

"With whom is Monsieur de Toulouse talking over there?" she asked him.

Martin Blas pretended not to understand.

"A masked woman?" the Princess added.

"She is the most beautiful of the beautiful," the Spaniard replied, "but she has more than one name."

"Tell me just one of them."

"The first time that I came to Brittany," Martin Blas said in a restrained but caustic voice, "His Highness, the Count of Toulouse, was already Governor... I am speaking to you, Madame, about many years ago... That woman's name was then Valentine de Rohan."

"Is it possible?" exclaimed the Princess, who almost snatched her arm from La Houssaye to take that of the Spaniard.

"Very few people here know her under that name, however," Martin Bas continued coldly, "but, Monsieur de Toulouse and I, we can't be mistaken."

Madame de Toulouse looked straight at him.

"And what name does that woman use at present?"

"She is called Countess Isaure," replied Martin Blas, who bowed and took his leave.

The Princess was near her chair; she sat down there. The shock was too great. For an instant, her thoughts fell with her courage, but anger again took the upper hand. She said to Montmorency-Laval, who had come to kiss her hands:

"Would you please go tell Monsieur de Toulouse that I wish to speak to him?"

Montmorency hastened to obey.

Behind the throne of the Princess, they had set up a folding stool for Celeste, confused and not knowing where so many honors came from; she almost believed that it was all a beautiful dream. She was enormously waited on. Some people said that Monsieur and Madame de Toulouse had brought her from Paris. Others told her real history, embroidering it. The Steward and the Seneschal were besieged by a crowd of curious people who naively asked them how they had discovered the birth of that charming young girl. They asked:

"Is it really true that she served in your household as a chambermaid?"

One never saw two men more embarrassed than the Steward and the Seneschal.

Another group crowed around Mademoiselle Agnès and Mademoiselle Olympe to ask the same questions. The poor girls were in torture.

There was just one shout in the salons:

"She is so pretty! She is delightful! She is adorable."

The older men found that she absolutely had the Rohan bearing and features. The young ones didn't go so far to look for their motives for admiration. She was an astounding success.

However, the message confided to Montmorency-Laval had a result that Madame the Countess of Toulouse didn't expect. It was the new Governor himself who, taking the hand of Countess Isaure, conducted her toward the stage to present her to the Princess, his wife.

Until then, although certain members of that noble assembly were being worried for themselves, although there were muted passions and intrigues in play, assuredly nothing announced that the celebration would be troubled by tragic events. On the contrary, what a layman would have guessed might happen next would have been closer to comedy.

However, from the moment that Madame de Toulouse returned to her seat, some mysterious discomfort seemed to spread throughout the ball. There are such things as premonitions. Those are to the spirit what those dull warnings that always precede serious illness are to the body.

The festivities were slow. Enough laughter was heard through the accords of the orchestra. The dance went on. Everything seemed to be as desired. But the joy, the spirit, the fever of the Ball, was absent. It would seem that, without being aware of it, all the men in their handsome uniforms, all the women dazzling with their jewels, felt a weight on their heart.

Just at the moment when the Governor, holding Countess Isaure by the hand, opened his mouth to make the presentation, the Princess moved disdainfully. No one heard the words that she spoke, but everyone saw her pale cheeks and her beautiful eyes with dark circles under them.

Countess Isaure untied her mask.

If the reader remembers the facts recounted in our Prologue, he will not be surprised that, until this day, the Rennes nobility had never attached the name of Valentine de Rohan to the charming face of Countess Isaure.

Valentine de Rohan had spent all of her youth in the most complete retreat, and the handsome Saint-Maugan, during the imprudent game that decided his fate, had to almost become a hermit in the forest in order to surprise the beautiful recluse. No one knew her, except the tenant farmers of her father's domain, and some rare neighbors who had occasionally encountered her in her rides across the thickets.

The role that she had taken at Rennes was therefore easy to sustain. Only one man could be difficult to deceive: the Seneschal, who as Master Alain Polduc had been part of the Rohan household and seen Valentine almost every day. \

We already know that he had had some suspicions. But does that commonplace truth have to be added: women are clever. Valentine had done a lot to deceive the Seneschal. To the extent that he had found a trail, Valentine, on the look-out, had taken countermeasures.

Could the Seneschal, clever and prudent, stake everything against Countess Isaure on the faith of a resemblance, when Baroness Saint-Elme threatened him from one side and the She-Wolf from the other, one from the Court in Paris, the other from the Wolf's Den in the forest of Rennes! And not mentioning the itch of the old mill, whom the Seneschal thought he was well rid of.

Alain Polduc was suspicious—that's true—but that was all.

The fact of Countess Isaure being unmasked could not produce in the salon any more effect than bringing out that admiring murmur to which she had become accustomed. She responded to the Princess in a calm and perfectly respectful voice. The Princess frowned and Toulouse was seen to turn pale in his turn.

What was happening on that stage? Everyone looked curiously at it, but none so strongly as the Steward, the Seneschal and Don Martin Blas, all reunited together in a corner of the room.

Suddenly, the crowd, so calm before, oscillated like the sea. A sentence had dropped from the stage. Those nearest had overheard it. It was already passing from mouth to mouth. The Princess had said:

"Have you dared to come here to defy me, Madame?"

VI. The Invasion

Countess Isaure had been insulted; That's what everyone had understood.

A few words, pronounced by the Governor in a timid and conciliatory tone, escaped the most attentive years. But they heard Countess Isaure's reply, that was made in a calm and distinct voice;

"Monseigneur, I beg you not to defend me."

You could have heard a pin drop in that vast salon, just a moment ago filled with so much noise. It was again the voice of the Princess that filled the silence.

"Then I shall be the one to leave!"

It was guessed that she had requested that the Countess be asked to leave the Ball, but that the Count had refused to do so.

Countess Isaure's attitude, despite being publicly outraged, was still as calm and and respectful as ever. It was assumed that the Governor was trying to talk to his wife and ask her for at least some good reasons, since the Princess responded bitterly:

"Because the place of an honest woman is not where she is exposed to meeting such creatures."

Anger had raised the voice of the Princess, in spite of herself. We said that she went too far because she didn't know how to behave badly. Her last words reached the most distant corners of the room.

Behind the chair of Madame de Toulouse, the distraught, but still charming, little Celeste was seen to rise. She, who, only moments ago, had lowered her eyes so timidly, who wouldn't haven't dared to murmur, however low, the least word, Celeste—our poor Cinderella—looked around the room with flashing eyes. Then, in a loud voice that anger didn't allow to tremble she asked:

"Is there no gentleman here?" she asked.

If everyone's stupefaction could have been any greater, the answer that Celeste's cry solicited would have carried it to its greatest height. The door had just opened, the outside door, and a young man, whom no one knew, who wore gracefully the uniform of the Conti Regiment, just entered the salon. He went through the crowd like a knife thtough butter and mounted the first step of the stage.

"I am waiting," he said, "for any man's voice to be lifted to uphold the accusation that has just been made against Countess Isaure."

Polduc squeezed the Steward's arm and whispered.

"Seek no further. Rohan has just spoken twice!"

The Count of Toulouse turned around.

"Good, my nephew! Good! Good!" said Rieux.

Raoul bowed before the Governor.

"With regard to His Highness," he said without backing down. "Respect closes my mouth, but if there is someone here who will repeat these words, I am declaring in advance that he is a liar and a coward!"

The Princess, ready to faint, fell back onto her seat.

Countess Isaure looked at Celeste and Raoul, one after the other, with happy tears in her eyes.

"What is your name, my friend?" Toulouse asked gently.

"I do not know," replied Raoul, "but there are people here who do know it."

Polduc turned his head away.

Countess Isaure leaned over toward the Governor and said a word into his ear. Monsieur de Toulouse bowed gravely, and, as if all the astonishment should be exhausted, he was seen holding out his hand to the young officer, saying:

"Madame the Countesse de Toulouse, with better information, grants you her pardon."

Without those words, according to what we have said, according to the fever that reigned at that time, it is possible that Raoul's challenge would have been repeated twenty times. But what more could be done in the presence of the Governor's words? In the salon, however, there was a man who was acting for himself. Don Martin Blas pushed aside the crowd and came to place himself in front of Raoul.

"I support and repeat the words of Madame the Princess, my young companion," he pronounced in a loud voice.

"You!" exclaimed Raoul.

"Me! And I say like her: The place of an honest woman is not where she is exposed to meeting such creatures!"

"Go on, nephew! Go on!" shouted Rieux as loud as he could.

But Raoul didn't need any encouragement. His hand, that held his glove, was already raised to strike the Spaniard in the face, when he felt himself stopped from behind.

It was Countess Isaure who had stopped him..

"Peace, Raoul!" she ordered with that sovereign authority voice that she knew how to use just as much as the woman seated on the throne. "That man is a fool. That sword that hangs on his side no longer belongs to him! Peace! I command you!"

That was no longer a Ball. Each person tried to get closer in order to hear and see better. It was truly a theater. There were no box seats, but a fevered crowd, The action was on the stage.

Don Martin Blas threw Countess Isaure a look of defiance. The Princess was suffocating behind her fan.

"I will deal with you forthright" said Isaure to the Spaniard, without losing her calm. "Madame," she said, turning toward the Princess, "God has granted me today the joy of doing you much good in exchange for the evil that you wanted to do to me, but for which I forgive you, because you were abused... I fstill ear for you, but I hope for my part that I will have the opportunity of serving you again."

A tear came to the Princess' eyes, not because of what her alleged rival had said, but because she believed Toulouse had abandoned her.

We said earlier that the Count of Toulouse was a gentle and wise man, not at all like the hero of a romance novel.

Such a character would have chosen justuice over his wife in tears. But Toulouse did nothing of the sort and tried instead to console his wife in tears. Let justice take care of itself! Madame de Toulouse kept from that incident a grudge that lasted for the rest of her life.

Having spoken as we reported, Countess Isaure, who seemed here to be the real princess, descended the steps of the stage, and called the Viscount of Rieux by his name.

"Present, by all the Devils," he said, beginning to laugh. "Present!"

He nudged shoulders going through the crowd, saying on the way: "I knew this time would come!"

Countess Isaure took a sealed parchment from her bosom. She broke the seal and gave it, opened, to Monsieur. de Rieux, who read it:

"*From His Royal Highness, the Duke d'Orléans, Regent of France, I hereby order the immediate arrest of Don Martin Blas.*"

He then looked with astonishment at Countess Isaure.

"What about the others?" he murmured.

With a nod of her head, she told him to remain silent. The Spaniard, however, surprised, but not disconcerted, had drawn his sword. It was certainly not to turn it over.

"To me, Conti!" shouted Monsieur de Rieux.

Raoul, Captain La Grève and several other officers made a circle around him. Martin Blas looked around the room to see if he could hope for defenders. His eyes fell on the clock, and he smiled.

Countess Isaure caught that glance and that smile. She focused her attention on Polduc and Feydeau, who were at the other end of the room. The Steward seemed profoundly beaten down, but the Seneschal, his ear glued to a half-opened window, was listening with all his might.

"Your sword, Señor Cavalier," Rieux was saying at that moment.

"Come and get it, Colonel," answered Don Martin Blas, taking the *en garde* position.

The attention of almost everyone was entirely on that woman whose life had always been a mystery, who remained there, in the Governor's palace, despite the bjections of the Governor's wife, and who had hidden the Regent's orders in her bosom. A cloud came over her beautiful forehead. She seemed to be listening to sounds that no one else could hear. For the second time, she called Monsieur de Rieux by his name.

The Colonel, leaving Martin Blas, went to her immediately. After she had spoken some words to him in a low voice, he stamped his foot and rushed toward Raoul, whom he seized roughly by the collar.

"Who told you to abandon your post, you little wretch!" he shouted.

Celeste began to tremble. Raoul had told her at the Rohan manor that that crime was punishable by death according to military law.

Poor Raoul stammered. Monsieur de Rieux shook him, but while shaking him, he said very low:

"Nephew, when I signal to you, take Madame de Toulouse in your arms and run to the Horloge Gallery. Thank God, it won't take you very long to become a Captain."

Raoul lifted his astounded eyes toward him.

"Did you understand?" asked Monsieir de Rieux.

"Yes," Raoul answered.

"Listen to me... If she cries out, if she weeps, that's none of your business... It's a matter of life and death." And he added roughly in a loud voice: "Boy! I wouldn't give six écus for your skin."

"Relax, comrade," Martin Blas shouted to Raoul, "in two minutes, it will be too hot here for anyone to think about those silly things."

Two minutes was a lot of time, more time than was needed to bring Martin Blas down, but they didn't have two minutes.

As Monsieur de Toulouse was asking "What is it?" a musket discharge toward the Champ-Jacquet was heard. The whole Ball shook as if an electric shock had lifted the floor of the salon. The Steward let out a girlish cry. Polduc crouched, sensing that this was the crisis.

A great clamor followed the musket discharge. Then the ushers on guard broke into the room, shouting:

"The Wolves! The Wolves!"

"Is now the time?" Raoul asked de Rieux.

"Don't move!" was his answer.

"Well, Colonel," said Martin Blas, joking, "you don't want my sword any longer?"

Monsieur de Rieux smiled broadly.

"Pah!" he said. "This was supposed to be a masked Ball, after all. Those who are coming are wearing theirs, that's all!"

There was, however, a general scattering. Men and women were dashing toward the exit when suddenly there was a terrible uproar outside. Broken windows fell with loud noises, and a wave of hairy faces inundated the room. Fifty Wolves had just entered through the door leading to the Gallery de l'Horlorge.

"Now!" shouted Rieux in the middle of the silence, because gentlemen and ladies had stopped talking.

The Wolves in their nanny goat skins silently slid aming all the satin and velvet dresses.

Raoul, hearing the signal from his superior, crossed with one leap the steps to the stage. He picked up the body of the fainted Princess. La Grève pulled away the Count of Toulouse. As if by magic, the officers of Conti Corps had assembled. Naked swords opened a wide gap in the crowd.

"Shoot! Shoot!" shouted Martin Blas.

But a hand of steel was placed over his mouth.

Yaumi, wanting to obey, adjusted a pistol that he had in his hand. He fell, his face struck by the pommel of a sword. Monsieur de Rieux hadn't wanted to use his blade.

"Aren't you happy, you scoundels?" he asked like a very happy man. "Except for those two over there," he added, "you can have all the rest."

VII. Change On Sight

That was a strange spectacle, one it is not often given to an author to describe. Through all the doors, through all the windows at the same time, a black swarmof Wolves had invaded the room. Everyone that the Presidial contained at that moment had been made prisoner without any resistance, and the great clamor that was heard outside proved that their army controlled all the exits. But those poor people, stunned by their own victory, timid at first, faced with all those splendors, didn't try to hold their captives, whose ransom would have been worth all of the Province of Brittany. Among the gentlemen who were there, some seemed to have some authority over the invaders. Among their number was Monsieur de Rieux.

We may well wonder, how and why?

At that time, as we have said, even a man's best friend could never know exactly where he was or where he was going. At best, where he came from. The Viscount of Rieux was a Breton, a brave man and a man of intelligence; that is all that can be said. Let's also add that the pommel of his sword had left on the face of Yaumi, the handsome Cobbler and alleged leader of the Wolves, a deep and bloody imprint, and that Yaumi had not breathed a word about it. So perhaps he was a Wolf himself, that cheerful Monsieur de Rieux, Lieutenant Colonel of the Conti Regiment. What is certain is that, seeing his behavior, Polduc and Feydeau didn't dare to act in a hostile manner. Don Martin Blas, on the contrary, had said:

"For my part, I want the Countess of Toulouse and that young girl."

Rieux, always in a good humor, had answered:

"The Countess of Toulouse, no; but the little girl, God gave her to you before us, friend Morvan."

And going toward him, Rieux shook his hand with an ironic air.

"*Palsambleu!*" he added, "You have become greatly tanned in fifteen years! Without your accent fron the region of Carentoir, which you haven't lost, my old companion, only the Devil knows if I would have recognized you!"

Thanks to the Viscount of Rieux, and a few others, the Wolves did not insult the guests of the Governor; but each one had to leave a little something in the hands of the conquerors, and not one of the ladies left with all of her jewelry.

Soon, under the stream of lights that the large mirrors still reflected and the gold of the high moldings, everything grew darker. In the place of those sparkling dresses that just a while ago filled the Ballroom, in the place of that shimmering crowd glittering with silk, diamonds and flowers, the light from the chandeliers and the girandoles was absorbed in the dull, heavy fur that formed the clothing of the Wolves.

What's more, from instant to instant, the crowd grew. Everyone wanted to see what was going on, but the greater part of the army was still outside. While the real guests managed to steal stolen away, using the rue de l'Horlorge, more Wolves were still coming up. And each newcomer entering into that bright sphere was equally dazzled. If they had been attacked in that place, they could not have defended themselves. They were all seen, such as they were, to be astonished and as if numbed by shock. Most of them didn't move. A few moved about as if the floor burned the soles of their feet.

The ones who had demanded ransom of those fleeing, in the corridors or in the stairs, did not show off their trophies. On the contrary, they hid them carefully under their nanny goat skins. Evidently, in that unknown and fearsome place, they were afraid that some avenger would come up out of the ground to reclaim them. During several minutes, at the most, satins, lace, precious stones, were mingled with the heavy rags of those rebels from the forest. Little by little, the last lady, escorted by the last gentleman, passed the threshold of the low door that opened onto the rue de l'Horloge. Achille Feydeau and the Seneschal went out with the others in order not to compromise themselves and also to escort Mesdemoiselles Agnès and Olympe, who were searching for a convenient place to faint with effect.

One of the last to leave, his sword in his hand and his head high, the Marshal of Montesquiou, said:

"If I still governed the Province, I would make those scoundrels dance without violins!"

Perhaps he would have done as he said, although the peasants of Rennes had once proved to him, in the town of Pacé, that they were not so easy by killing a hundred and fifty men from the La Fertéé Regiment. Because there were still battles when blood flowed abundantly. However, the idea of the Revolution had not taken root in any head, most of all not there. But it can be said that it was already a revolution, ignorant of itself, that blindly took its first hesitant steps.

On leaving the Presidial, almost all the gentlemen had a smile under their mustache. They had been chased away; but if they were beaten, it was by the fault of France. They were a little like those weak fathers who are amused even by the most terrible mischief of their children.

Apart from those who, secretly. had *entered*, or wanted to *enter the forest*, most rejoiced at that slap given to the full face of their conqueror. The city was taken for good and all. Everyone knew that the garrisons were barricaded as well as the Hôtels Saint-Georges and Peése, where the cadets were quartered. The Military School of Kergus was under guard. The Chasseurs of the Conti Regiment had been taken prisoners outside the Mordelaises Gates. The Intendance soldiers had put down their arms. The shots that had been heard fired were fired into the air by the city watch. It was a victory, but it was also a betrayal.

Of all the noble assembly that, only an hour before, had filled the grand Presidial room, there soon remained only two men and two women: Countess Isaure and Monsieur de Rieux on the one hand, and Don Martin Blas and little Celeste, who was dying with fear, on the other. Countess Isaure had put her mask back on.

A wolf, distinguished from his companions by his tall stature, approached her.

"Let the Palais of Monseigneur be safe from attack," she said to him in a low voice. "Leave the aides and the tax collectors to Yaumi... Let Jouachin, with a troop of Rohan men, take charge of the prison... Here is a list of the prisoners to be released..."

323

She gave him a paper. The Wolf pushed aside the crowd, left and soon returned. In his absence, there were loud acclamations outside.

Seeing a movement from the pretended Spaniard to get closer to Celeste, Monsieur de Rieux came to put himself between them nicely.

"You have been told that you shall have the child, my cousin," he said, rubbing his hands, "but do you think your men are going to stay there with their arms crossed? The Ball isn't over yet closed, *morbleu*! Let's carry on!" Then with a voice of thunder. he shouted: "Hola! Orchestra! Carry on!"

The dark crowd trembled, then moved about grumbling, for thart Greek word, *orchestra*, wasn't known to the Wolves. It was as if Monsieur de Rieux had invoked the cannon or the flag! The blades of all the swords came out. Each one believed that had been a call to arms. But the orchestra struck a cord, and all the Wolves showed their black teeth to laugh, not to bite.

The orchestra, seated in a gallery rotunda, six or seven feet from the floor, had not been able to flee with the ladies and gentlemen. They had found themselves captives from the very beginning, and the virtuosos of which it was composed, having nothing else to do but be brave, had hidden behind their chairs, hoping not to be seen. Monsieur de Rieux's order made them come out from their holes: the very pale violins were seen; and the bass violins, moved to tears, took their places and set up their instruments again.

A great burst of laughter made the windows of the Presidial tremble. That was the ice breaking moment. At the first note, the Wolves dropped the timidity that accompanies every debut in the world. They fnow felt at home, as we shall soon see.

"Come on, Signor Fontana," said Monsieur de Rieux to the conductor, "let's start with a *courante*."

Signor Fontana lifted his baton to begin. There was immediately in the salon a stamping of wooden clogs. The orchestra did its best to dominate that thunder, but fifteen hundred pairs of heavy wooden clogs on a good oak floor, that's a powerful tool! They were set in motion. There were no women at all, but what gaiety! Ah! What gaiety! Of the three thousand shoes, you could count fully fifteen hundred clogs of coal-makers. I leave you to guess the color of the dust that was raised!

Don Martin Blas pulled his hat down over his eyes; Monsieur de Rieux put his embroidered handkerchief in his mouth. He laughed to his heart's content.

"Eh! Josille!" shouted Julot, the traveler, who had put a lace veil on his head, "I'm going to show you what I saw the Duchesses in Paris do: they balanced this way; they balanced that way. Pelo! Lend me your fan!"

Pelo, who had put a bunch of white roses on his wolf-skin mask, lent him his stolen fan. Julot, the traveler, tried to mimic the dances of the Duchesses in Paris. Everyone wanted to add something to his attire. He was soon wearing a heap of ribbons, attached haphazardly, three or four mantillas, and just as many scarves. Several hands at the same time attached plumes, knots of velvet, and garlands snatched from pillars. They put around his reddish neck a pretty collar of swan's feathers.

Proud and serious, Julot the traveler certainly saw that they wanted to honor him, and he conducted himself in a manner worthy of the favor of which he was the object. He used the fan on all the faces that surrounded him, and thus had a large circle around him. He began to dance in that circle, imitating in his fashion the Princesses of the Court of the Regent.

The orchestra was playing with desperation. The wooden clogs, furious with joy, made an infernal stomping. Those who were in the salon shouted to manifest the enthusiasm of their pleasure. Those who were outside were shouting to enter. It was a terrible bacchanal, and Monsieur de Rieux had never been so amused!

When the exhausted orchestra finally called for a truce, and when the cloud of dust had dissipated a little, a slight change in the position of our characters had occurred. Perhaps that had happened purely by chance?

Celeste was still seated on the stage, but Countess Isaure had now taken her place beside her. Monsieur de Rieux remained alone at the bottom of the steps. As for Don Martin Blas, the crowd had seized him in such a way that it kept him immobilized in one of the doorways that let out onto the Place d'Armes. He was so perfectly surrounded by the crowd that pressed on him from every direction that he couldn't even make a movement to reach his sword.

The stentorian voice of Monsieur de Rieux was again heard:

Refreshments are being served!" he shouted at the door of the grand gallery, where several valets, totally frightened, had shown up.

This time, Julot, the traveler, had never seen anything like it, even in the great city of Paris. As soon as the Wolves had learned the way to the kitchens, there had been a coming and going of plates of food, and soon some were even thrown aside as superfluous. More Wolves came in, their arms full of bottles, cakes, pâtés, preserves, all that had been prepared to fill the noble stomachs of the gentlemen and the ladies of the fête.

They drank—It was a benediction! Every mouth had its swallow, so much so that there was a silence filled by the happy sound of all those bottles in the process of being emptied. The fortunate who had found a place in the Ballroom showed their good will. Many bottles and much food were thrown out the windows and the crowd camped on the Place d'Armes had its part of the festivities. Champagne, Bordeaux, Chambertin... The Wolves could now brag that they had tasted all these fine wines at least once in their lives!

Then the dance started again, frenzied this time because the orchestra had been told to play the famous *Ronde du Tabac*. The farandole began at the foot of the stage and continued through the vestibule and the stairs, right to the

Place d'Armes, that it crossedwith much shouting, to form its line again right up to the steps of the Salon des États.

After the farandole had finished, another change took place in the Ballroom. Countess Isaure and Céleste had disappeared. We find them again in the neighboring gallery, with Raoul, who had had returned, his hair disheveled, his forehead covered with sweat and blood, but wearing on his torn uniform the insignia of a Captain.

Raoul had saved Madame the Countess of Toulouse, and it was the new Governor himself who had attached with his own hand the insignia of his new rank.

That tall Wolf who had left an hour earlier with the list of prisoners to be freed and the orders of Countess, came back at that moment. Under his mask, that he removed to wipe off the sweat running down his cheeks, was the frank and good face of Josselin Guitan.

"Everything is done," he said.

It was two a.m. The Wolves had done other things than dancing, eating, and drinking. The prison of La Petite Motte had been forced open. Fourteen gentlemen and a greater number of people of common birth who were still detained for rebellion, having been part of Cellamare Cons[iracy, had been set free.

The tax rolls had been shredded; the safes of the tax men looted; their offices burned to the ground.

The townhouse of Marshal de Montesquiou was located rue de Bourbon. The back of it opened onto the Square of the City Hall. Some twenty gentlemen were assembled there, all French and enraged at their misadventure. The Marshal proposed taking up the sword and wading into the middle of these rascals; but the folly of that enterprise was all too obvious: twenty men against three or four thousand! There were peasants from at least thirty parishes there.

After an hour or two, the Marshal's companions came to the windows of the opposite façade, from where they could see the broghtly lit salons of the Presidial. They became even

327

angrier. They gathered all the muskets that they could find in the Marshal's house, loaded them, and just as the Wolves, who had eaten their fill, started to dance again at the sound of the violins, a well-directed round of fire laid out a dozen of them on the floor. Don Martin Blas' hat was pierced with a bullet.

"Uh-oh!" exclaimed Monsieur de Rieux, showing his whole body at a balcony, " that Marshal is a real kill joy. Turn off the chandeliers," he commanded on reentering the room.

The instant afterward, a profound obscurity had replaced the shining lights of the celebration. The Wolves, terrified, went down the grand staircase pell-mell. Don Martin Blas, half suffocated, finally freed himself, swearing to himself that he would take his revenge.

In the staircase, the handsome Cobbler whispered to him:

"The young lady will be at the Wolf's Den tonight."

"I want her!" replied the Spaniard.

As he came out on the Place Armes Square, he felt his arm being squeezed. Countesse Isaure, masked, was near him.

"Monsieur de Saint-Maugan," she said to him, "I wish you no harm... You can still take flight... For that, I give you an hour!"

VIII. The Wolf's Den

The murderous musket fire by the guests of Marshal de Montesquiou had been the signal for retreat, or rather for flight. The Wolves were hard campaign soldiers, but those thousands of eyes that the houses opened onto the streets justly frightened them. Each of these could turn into a murderous window through which they could be fired upon.

The Wolves were poorly armed. Everything had to be brought out for that memorable expedition. Most of them had only their pitchforks. Muskets were rare. Montesquiou, in his *Relations des Troubles de la Bretagne*, affirms that a single regiment could have easily massacred all that human cattle. All probabilities indicate that he was right. Monsieur de Montesquiou adds that the Breton nobility covered themselves with shame during that event. His mistake begins here. The Breton nobility were in a position even more excusable than that of the French Princes and the nobility of France during the minority of Louis XIV. The Breton nobility regarded themselves as wrongfully conquered. There was still Breton patriotism. To clarify that idea, what would you say today about a Polish city that would play a similar turn to its Russian occupiers? Assuredly, no one would pronounce the word shame. Only under Louis XV did Brittany become French at heart. And Monsieur de Montesquiou, despite his incontestable valor, was one of those who contributed the most to prolonging the hatred against the French.

The firing was not renewed. The crowd of Wolves, growling low, went into the streets that led to the Rue de la Croix-Rouge. The Saint-Georges gate was open. The crowd passed through. It was taking prisoners; at least, two gentlemen, who were marching in the center of a group, didn't seem to be doing it of their own free will. They were Steward Feydeau and Seneschal Rohan-Polduc.

"My good men," Polduc was saying, "Is this my recompense for all that I have done for you?"

Achille Feydeau added, his hand on the pocket that contained his gold box:

"You are compromising us, my children. Henceforth, we can no longer be useful to you."

A tall fellow, who seemed to command this escort answered:

"We are following the orders of the She-Wolf."

That was the first time the name had been pronounced since the beginning of the expedition. It didn't moderate the fright of either father-in-law or son-in-law.

In the middle of another group, Don Martin Blas was on horseback. He had wanted to pass by the Château de la Tour Lebât in order to see if a surprise attack was still possible, but the grills had been raised and the orders of the officers in the Courtyard could be heard. Madame de Toulouse was henceforth protected from all attack. Don Martin Blas had to abandon his plans.

But as that same moment, here's what was happening in the Château. The Princess, broken by emotion, had just sent away her women. She was kneeling in front of her prie-dieu searching for, but in vain, peace in the usual orison. Fright, anger, the supposed abandon of her husband, filled her heart. She could think of nothing but that.

"That woman!" she said to herself. "That miserable woman!"

Madame de Toulouse's bedroom opened onto a little suspended gallery which made a balcony in the Chapel of the Tower. It was there that the family of the Governor usually heard Mass. As the Princess was absorbed in her prayers, she heard a noise coming from the direction of that chapel. She raised her eyes, trembling, because her body and her mind were equally shaken. The cracking of a piece of furniture gave her goose-bumps, exiled as she thought herself in that terrible country of wild beasts and revenants. But disposed as she was to fright, what she saw surpassed even her own fears. Countess Isaure stood there, majestic and immobile in her proud beauty, in front of the door to the chapel.

Who had let her in? How had she gotten there?

In her first reaction, Madame de Toulouse went so far as to fear an assassination. In the middle of her flight, that night, she had lost her string of diamonds, which was of great value and, for her, priceless, because it was a gift from her friend, the young King.

Countess Isaure was holding that string of diamonds in her hand. Without saying a word, she placed it on the night table of Madame de Toulouse. Then she slowly walked across the room. The Princess wanted to call for help, but her cry stopped in her throat.

Countess Isaure took her hand, that she kissed.

"Come!" she murmured.

Madame de Toulouse's hand was as cold as marble.

She followed the Countess, moved by some strange magnetic force. Sleepwalkers move as she did. The Countess opened the door of the chapel. Something assuredly strange at that hour of the night, a somber light, was shining inside. But she saw something even stranger. What that light showed was two resin torches which were burning on the altar, on both sides of the tabernacle. Two men, wearing nanny goat skins but unmasked out of respect for the holy place, were holding their torches high, casting their light on the silver crucifix which crowned the tabernacle.

Countess Isaure extended her hand toward the divine symbol of redemption.

"By the living God," she said, "I swear that I am innocent of the accusations you have lodged against me tonight, Madam."

"Take your revenge, then," stammered the Princess, who fell to her knees.

Isaure kissed her hand for the second time.

"I am already avenged," she murmured, "since you owe me your life and your honor."

The torches were extinguished.

The next day, Madame de Toulouse wanted to believe that she had dreamed it all—but the diamond necklace was there.

Abbot Manet in his erudite and curious studies on the soil of Northern Brittany,[113] speaks of the Druid caves located on the left bank of the rover Couesnon and its subsidiaries for a great distance, principally around the town of Fougères. According to him, those underground grottos are partly natural and partly dug by the hand of men. Most of them were not useable from the time of his youth, following interior cave-ins.

---

[113] François Manet (1764-1844), priest and a scholar of history and geography. He published *Histoire de la petite Bretagne ou Bretagne Armorique* (E Caruel, 1834) and a study on the bay of Mont Saint-Michel (1829), rather discredited today.

He affirms, however, having gone across, South of Saint-Aubin-du-Cormier, vast subterranean passages that no longer existed when he wanted to visit them again in 1820. The crumbly soil had fallen away by itself—that's his opinion—following the earthquake that shook the Rennes region the year of the death of King Louis XVIII.[114] Those caverns, after having hidden the mysteries of the Druids, and covered up human sacrifices within their eternal shadows, served as a retreat for the Bretons vanquished by the Saxon invaders. It was there that the wives and daughters of the subjugated Rhedons, when the great King Meriadoc was obliged to commandeer one hundred thousand English virgins to give as wives to his warriors.[115]

The deplorable fate of the seven hundred ships that were commandeered to transport that immense cargo of love is known. Thrown off course by the storm, they ran aground at the mouth of the Rhine and the Cologne Cathedral possesses authentic relics of eighty-nine thousand virgins. Added to eleven thousand noble virgins, that adds up to the round figure of one hundred thousand young ladies.

---

[114] 1824.

[115] Conan Meriadoc is a legendary British leader credited with founding Brittany. His story became a dominant founding myth for the Bretons for hundreds of years, and he appeared as a founder-figure in several genealogies of Breton aristocratic families, including the Rohans. In the 15th century the Bretons used his story to establish precedence for the Breton aristocracy over the Kings of France. Its political impact declined with the Union of Brittany and France in 1532. However, in the 17th century, the Rohans used their supposed descent from Conan Meriadoc to seek status as "foreign princes" at the French court; King Louis XIV recognized their pedigree, but denied their foreign status.

Later, the grottos became the hideout for criminals, so much so that Francis Ist of Brittany[116] ordered their destruction. From the beginning of the wars between Brittany and France, the grottos gave asylum to partisans of independence. They served, notably, under the League, to the vanquished soldiers of Guy Eder, Baron of Fontenelle.[117] It was there that "Ironfoot" Rollan[118] passed in review the troops of the Breton Brothers during the first years of the reign of Louis XIV.

The Wolf's Den, located on the estate of Rohan-Polduc, almost at the center of the forest of Rennes, was the principal and the best known of these caves. Tradition maintains that those winding galleries, tangled like a skein of wool, once extended as far as the hills of Fougères. A tunnel that led to Vitre was allegedly filled in by Rollan himself because of the flooding of the Vilaine during the winter. But thousands of other galleries still exist, among them can be cited the deep one that goes under the lake of Paintourteau.

Here, it is no longer the obscure scholar who lends his testimony, encased in a dusty book, but the charming, elegant, and brilliant Marquise de Sévigné, annoyed at being from Brittany, and receiving with distaste the money of her tenants. Receiving them, however, but not giving them anything in return. The dear Marquise, exiled to Rochers, tells her daughter, along with a somewhat chatty thousand kisses, that there is a cave under her lake, at the center of which there is a

---

[116] Francis I (1414-1450), Duke of Brittany, Count of Montfort and titular Earl of Richmond, was the son of John V, Duke of Brittany and Joan of France, daughter of King Charles VI of France.

[117] Guy Eder de Beaumanoir de la Haye (1573-1602), also known as La Fontenelle or *Ar Bleiz* (the Wolf in Breton), French nobleman, Seigneur of Le Vieux-Bourg, Saint-Gildas et Leslay, and a warlord active in Brittany in the late 16th century.

[118] See Note 51.

big rock. A drop of water falls every two minutes on top of that rock. That drop of water, falling that way for centuries, has cut into the stone a small round hole about two inches deep. They say that the water found there is good for curing eye infections.

Madame de Grignan,[119] the daughter of the adorable Marquise, had beautiful and good eyes. She preferred that someone write her to tell her about the arrest of Monsieur the Prince or the unbelievable marriage of the Grande Mademoiselle.[120] At the beginning of the 18th century, when our story takes place, the Wolf's Den was a great deal more limited, if not in reality, at least in the use that was made of it. It was like one of those gigantic manors from the middle ages, where the family, when it grows smaller, only uses but one wing, while the rest is allowed to fall into ruins. The Wolves used it to store weapons, but the caves, such as they were, could only hold but a portion of their numbers. Besides, that army didn't live there. There was scarcely in the cave, in ordinary times, but a thousand malcontents, irremediably

---

[119] Françoise-Marguerite de Sévigné, Countess of Grignan (1646-1705), French aristocrat remembered for the letters that her mother, Madame de Sévigné, wrote to her.

[120] Anne Marie Louise d'Orléans, Duchess of Montpensier, (1627-1693), nicknamed *La Grande Mademoiselle*, was the only daughter of Gaston d'Orléans with his first wife Marie de Bourbon, Duchess of Montpensier. One of the greatest heiresses in history, she died unmarried and childless, leaving her vast fortune to her cousin, Philippe of France. After a string of proposals from various members of European ruling families, including Charles II of England, Alfonso VI of Portugal, and Charles Emmanuel II of Savoy, she eventually fell in love with the courtier Antoine Nompar de Caumont and scandalized the court of France when she asked Louis XIV for permission to marry him, as such a union was viewed as a *mésalliance*. She is best remembered for her role in the *Fronde*, bringing Lully to the Court, and her Memoirs.

compromised. The others remained in their houses or their farms, voluntarily joining the expeditions, but protecting their idebntities behind their wolf masks.

The current Wolf's Den, as it was used the handsome Cobbler and his merry band of men, was composed only of a large gallery bordered with smaller canes that they called "rooms." Most of these were damp and uninhabitable. Only the gallery and the grand chamber had a clean floor that could be used for sleeping. So men slept there, pell-mell on straw. The women had their retreat elsewhere, under the ancient Pond of Muys.

It was a Rohan who had first opened the caverns to Bretons who were revolting. It was a Rohan who had organized their association and who had given them the name of Wolves. A Rohan was the born leader of the Wolves of forest of Rennes. Whether it was some bizarre imagination, or a ruse to throw off the searches by the French authorities, the men had given a feminine name to the general of that dark army: the She-Wolf.

Her scepter was the sword of Duke Pierre of Brittany, kept at the Rohan manor. Her authority was supreme and uncontested.

It is very important to note this: the power of that mysterious autocrat, whatever her sex, did not depend on the caprices of prestige. It did not have as its foundation those fantastic beliefs that so tyrannically dominate the Breton soul. Beyond all superstition, beyond all traditional or legendary influence, the power of the She-Wolf was much more grounded in reality, since it originated in a material fact. At the hour of danger, the She-Wolf held in her hand the life or death of her people. Here's why:

The Wolves knew only one entry to the place where their weapons were kept, even though public opinion counted three at least, and perhaps more. Only the She-Wolf possessed the secret of Rohan. Only the She-Wolf could open the other exits.

Yaumi, the handsome Cobbler, had put all his efforts for years into discovering at least one of the other exits, but all his diggings had remained fruitless. Some poor devils buried under a cave in; that was all he had achieved.

Toward the west, on the side of Rennes, the grotto presented a wall of flaky rock which had no discontinuity. Towards the east were the chambers, and beyond them, many galleries. It was there that they had probed. They had managed to find a secret transversal gallery, but it was blocked at both ends by a mass of heavy rocks that seemed to have been rolled there by the hand of man. Beyond was a chasm. Yaumi himself had descended into that hole. Fifty feet down, he had found a rapid and deep torrent.

Toward the north was another enormous precipice. A stone thrown into it returned a dull and far-away sound, as if it had fallen into the very bowels of the earth. From the moment when it left the hand, right up to the one when it finally gave a sound on touching ground, one could count up to one hundred.

Toward the south was the only known entrance, the door through which the Wolves went in and out, the famous door that was forever be hidden from the people of France by the thick bushes of the forest Unless there was an act of treason, it was almost impossible to discover that opening. It was about three hundred feet from abandonedcauseway of the old pond of Muys. A little stream from the Vesvre formed a miniature waterfall, falling from a mossy rock above, and stopped between two giant, lonely oaks. On leaving the fall, the stream flowed in a straight line for about ten feet before disappearing into the mossy ground. The earth *swallowed* it, as they said in Brittany, to regurgitate it a quarter of a league beyond, right at the edge of the forest, where it rejoined the Vesvre.

The first bush of a sense thicket was found under the waterfall. The naked shape of a grey rock was seen here and there. As there was no high forest in that place, the tufts of brambles died, from year to year, burned by the sun. One of those tufts, to the left of the rock, was false and hid the stone door of the Wolf's Den's caves. Even if the brush was moved by chance, that wasn't enough. It was still necessary to push the rock aide and lift the ancient grill of the draw bridge of Rohan, that had been placed inside. Any assailant would have found himself facing a black hole, exposed to the fire of an invisible enemy.

Yaumi had long tried to find one of the other entrances that would have made the security of this underground fortress perfect, but he hadn't been able to keep his promise. The She-Wolf could have, but probably didn't want to. What's more, there was not in the Wolf's Den a single man who could brag that he had seen her face. Josselin Guitan was reputed to be her right hand man, and that conveyed the idea that Old Rohan, if he was still alive, or, if not, his daughter remained depository of that big secret.

But Old Rohan and his daughter had disappeared from the country a long time ago. As for the authority of the handsome Cobbler, it somewhat resembled that of Philippe d'Orléans over the beautiful country of France. The handsome Cobbler had made himself master. He was obeyed. He had his own henchmen. However, the major part of the Wolves only followed him while waiting until they could do better. *Rohan does not die*, says the proverb of Tréguier. It was always hoped that the old throne would be occupied again someday.

Once past the grill, one descended some thirty slippery steps, cut with a spade in clay soil, and one found himself at the threshold of a first square room, whose ceiling was supported by worm-eaten wood.

A second less high stair led to the kitchen, which was level with the rest of the grotto. That kitchen was an irregular room more than a hundred feet long and twenty or thirty feet wide. A chimney, similar to those of Breton farms, made of masonry, was located at its far eastern end. The hearth chimney emptied into an unexplored gallery from which there was a constant current of air. It never smoked. Evidently that gallery communicated with the outside. But where was the opening? Yaumi had spent entire weeks exploring the bushes outside. The smoke came out nowhere.

Beyond the kitchen was the big dormitory, then the rooms, among which was distinguished the one where they took counsel. In that one, located facing the cuisine, the same phenomenon happened: the hearth devoured its smoke.

IX. Dame Michou Guitan

It was three o'clock in the morning. All the men from the Wolf's Den were in Rennes. Only women were found there, except for the guards at their post and our poor friend Magloire, State courier, taken prisoner by his enemies.

At the head of the women, there was naturally Dame Michou Guitan, virtual queen of the female population therein. She was in the process of boiling immense marmites, to feed the men of the expedition. To the left of the chimney, nice big girls, suntanned like Atlantic sailors, were heating the oven where they were going to bake. The Wolf's Den wasn't a paradise for women. Yet the men found them good at every enterprise. The girls stirred the faggots in the hot fireplace and smoked their pipes peacefully.

"Mark my words," Dame Michou Guitan was saying, a big spoon in her hand, "they're going to come back famished and beaten, the poor fellows! As usual, and I'm not lying. So long as there isn't a good Christian to tell them: 'Go right! Go left!' it will always be the same thing."

"Have you seen your boy, Dame Guitan?" asked Nielle, one of the bakers.

"Well! My little girl," replied Dame Michou, "my boy isn't a little kid that can be led on a leash, isn't that right? He does what he wants."

"I meant no affront," began Nielle.

"Of course! Of course! But I tell you," said Dame Michou solemnly, "the less we talk about these affairs, the better it is."

"About what affairs?" asked a half dozen of the women baking, coming forward, their bonnet turned backward and their pipe in their mouth.

338

Dame Michou Guitan, without taking hers from between her teeth, took out of her pocket her vast supply of tobacco and opened it. Those who sniffed tobacco put it in their nose in powder form. They would have wanted to use it in their ears, because their opposition to the tax increased the natural passion of those half-savages for those gross stimulants. All the politics of the place was about tobacco.

"You will see, my little children," Dame Michou pronounced gravely, savoring her smoke. "You will see shortly something new; and remember, it's me telling you that! When my boy chats with me, it's not to be repeated. That's what's true... But something's being prepared."

"What? What? Tell us, Dame Guitan!"

"Yes, it's simmering. Ah! Ah! That makes me laugh, you see! That bowlegged Yaumi is going to go back to his wooden clog."

"You don't like him, do you, Dame Michou?"

"Who? That Cobbler from the back of the Sangle? I care as much as that about him, my little doves."

She shook the cinders from her pipe to fill it up again. At that moment, behind the oven, they heard a low sound. The bakers lent their ears. Dame Michou turned a deaf ear.

"Bring me that stupid fellow there!" she commanded, lifting her voice more than was necessary. "It's shameful to see a big do-nothing like that stretched out like that when poor women are working!"

The big stupid fellow was Magloire, who was lying on the floor in a corner. They went to get him, which prevented hearing a second noise which seemed to come from the chimney. Old Dame Michou had a loud and prolonged coughing fit. Cathos, Nielle, Thurine, Scolastique and other bakers were around Magloire, who was pretending to be dead. Jacquelle and Fancille joined them and all with one voice shouted:

"Stand up, fellow!"

Magloire played deaf.

Two bakers and two girls cooking marmites took him by the legs and the arms.

Magloire immediately began to let out painful cries. Dame Michou, who was all ears trying to analyze that mysterious sound whose weak echo seemed to come even from the walls of the cavern, shouted in an angry tone:

"If you cry out like that, you're going to be thrown into the bottomless hole!"

Magloire moved about convulsively between the arms of those carrying him, but he no longer said anything.

Dame Michou started again to listen. The noise had ceased. Cathos and Nielle were holding Magloire's arms; Jacquette and Fancille were holding his legs. They came and dropped him at the Dame Michou's feet. She examined him for a minute with a disdainful expression.

"That thing," she said, "looks like a scarecrow with straw on top!"

That allusion to the color of his hair greatly displeased Sidonie's lover. He sat up on his rear end and passed his hand coquettishly through his yellow locks.

"They're blond, don't you see, good woman!" he shouted.

The choir of bakers and those making marmites, began to laugh and shouted with one voice:

"Isn't he a strange little man! Lord! Is he ugly!"

"Ah!" said Magloire, "that's not the opinion of all the ladies!"

"The scrarecrow speaks," said Dame Michou, who was examining him as if he were a strange animal. "What's your name, scarecrow"

Sidonie's lover drew back an instant, then he began to be poetically plaintive.

"It's going to make you break out in tears to hear the story of my misfortunes! I am the most cruel example of all those who have seen themselves persecuted by the rigors of fate."

On my word, it didn't take that much to excite the interest of Nielle, Cathos, Scholastique, Fancille, Thèrese, Thurine, and Goton. They were already wiping their eyes, these good girls, with aprons that had no memory of washing.

Magloire let his head fall on his chest. Then, straightening up, with a sad expression, he began:

"The truth is, my dear ladies, that I have been the victim of every misfortune from the earliest age..."

Instead of following that epic, whose debut showed so much promise, Magloire suddenly threw his yellow head backward and remained with his mouth wide open, watching the hole in the hearth. A gnome, a fantastic being, came out of it at that moment, holding in its hand a long pole, at the end of which was attached a pack of seeds, or grains of thistles.

That sort of brush was black with soot; the gnome also.

"Grincette!" shouted the girls, "Grincette, thechimney-sweep!"

Grincette jumped with one bound into the middle of the group, which dissipated to avoid any dangerous contact. She was a little girl about twelve or thirteen years-old, sickly, deformed, unwelcome, but in whose eyes, as brilliant as two diamonds, shone an intelligent and wicked face. Grincette's function was to unstop the chimney pipe daily, because it was constantly clogged by dirt and gravel that fell from some unknown place. High protection had been granted her by Dame Michou Guitan. Grincette came to stand behind the stool of that good woman.

And while those curious girls pressed that eloquent Magloire to continue with his story, a few rapid words were exchanged between the sweep and Dame Guitan.

"Well?" asked the good woman.

"Well, she just went by," replied Grincette.

"Alone?"

"No, with a little young lady, as pretty as can be."

"I thought I had heard her!" murmured Dame Michou Guitan, who that time took her pipe out of her mouth to make the Sign of the Cross devotedly on her silver rosary.

"We are going to hear some news. Only, may the Holy Virgin protect us!"

"And then? Then?" shouted the girls around Magloire, former State courier and presently a victim of fate.

One can be a fool and cunning all at the same time. Magloire was such an example. He saw very well that stories of true or false escapades would be badly received. What was necessary here was to touch the heartstring.

"My name is Edmond de Philidor. I owe my life to two noble families, one from my father, and the other from my unfortunate mother, who died in the flower of her years in mourning and in tears."

Two bakers dried real tears. Those good girls always have tears ready... Just the name Edmond de Philidor had tickled their tear glands.

"Poor mother," murmured Scolastique.

"Hush!" said the others.

"Of course," Magloire continued, "those who hurt my mother and finally plunged her into the depths of the tomb are people high in society, but I have sworn to avenge her and I will dedicate myself to that, even to the death!"

"That's good, that! Bully for you!" they all shouted with one voice.

Magloire, despite his position, and the color of his hair, was reaching rapidly the level of hero of a romance.

"Well!" he continued, "all the splendors of proper families who have beautiful fortunes and an income, surrounded my cradle. My wet nurse was a middle-class woman... my father was a duke, a marquis, and a baron with clothing and stockings of embroidered silk. I remember it well; I still see it with my own eyes.... My father! My poor father, who, one night, was passing near the river at the end of Saint-Cyr, when fourteen masked men grabbed him. They threw him in a sack, and spelled the end his days at the bottom of the river."

"Just like that!" groaned the choir of bakers.

"All that to get their hands on his fortune!" continued Magloire. "You have his orphan before you, that they also persecuted with their lies. I was raised by my uncle, who took care of me until I could fly with my own wings. There was no one in the neighborhood as studious and as learning as I... I won all the prizes and encouragement at the College of Toussaint—you can ask all former little comrades there. But my enemies had sworn my death before my eighteenth birthday..."

The circle closed around Magloire.

"My uncle was sick in bed," he continued, "with a bad sweat that had come back, and a fever such that my aunt no longer knew which saint to pray to. It was then that I made the acquaintance of Sidonie, whom my enemies used to make me fall into their trap!"

"Who is that Sidonie?" demanded the bakers.

Magloire lifted his eyes to Heaven. He was once again going to transfigure Sidonie.

"The beauty of the angels!" he said, "with a milk-white complexion, the fresh colors of the spring time rose, the queen of our gardens, the figure of a wood nymph, the graces and everything else of Venus... The best education, knowing how to read and write... The god of love pierced my heart with his arrows as soon as I saw her—and reciprocally. It seemed to me that she was taken with my natural advantages... Therefore we agreed to a rendezvous at the corner of the rue Vasselot at eight o'clock in the evening."

Here, Magloire stopped. He had a circle of open mouths around him. Never had Nielle, never had Fancille, never had Felicite, nor Mathurine heard such a touching story.

"I bet," someone said, "that something is going to happen at that rendezvous."

Magloire gave an enormous sigh and continued:

"The rendezvous took place yesterday at dusk. I still have goosebumps from it, although it wasn't courage that I lacked. I had been waiting for Sidonie for a short while, when the scoundrels who had murdered my father came out of an alley and put me in chains. They threw me into a carriage with a cloth in my mouth, and they shouted to the horses: *Gallop!*

"I was still unconscious, my good ladies, when, in the middle of the forest, the Wolves attacked the carriage. They mistook me for someone else. They beat me, although I am a native Breton, and they brought me here as their prisoner. How my poor dear aunt must be worried."

Magloire covered his face with his hands and wept at the thought of his aunt.

"He must be set free, that young fellow," said Thurine.

And all the young girls shared her opinion.

Dame Michou Guitan, since the beginning of the story, had chatted in a low voice with little Grincelle, who was describing a beautiful lady and a pretty young lady that she had encountered in the part of the cave lost behind the stove and its chimney. Grincelle was not at all astonished by that encounter. The women bakers, however, and the marmite cookers, were already plotting the charitable enterprise of reuniting young Edmond de Philidor with his weeping aunt. But suddenly, there was a great rumble in the direction of the entry to the grottos.

"Hide me, my good ladies!" exclaimed Magloire, frightened.

X. The Handsome Cobbler

There was no longer time to hide Magloire. The Wolves rushed back into the caverns. They were drunk with their victory and were speaking all at one time, recounting their great accomplishments in the conquered city. All that din was at first favorable to Magloire, who huddled behind the oven, waiting for an occasion to revive the tender interest of his protectors. But there was a Wolf from the rue Vasselot. The Wolves came from everywhere. That Wolf immediately recognized Magloire and called him by his name. When Thurine, Catiche, Fancille and the rest learned that Magloire was not named Edmond de Philidor and that he was an apprentice baker, they became terribly angry. The oven, at a very high heat, was almost called on to roast Sidonie's lover. Catiche hit him with a shovel; Fancille with a broom. Thurine, Félicité, Goton, and Scolastique regretted the tears they had shed. Finally, Grincette, a true demon, used her teeth and nails on the upside-down patient.

Fortunately, there were other things to do. The suitors of those young ladies had brought back the spoils of their enterprise, and in there, they found a good number of bottles of brandy. Another Ball was going to begin. Magloire's life was spared. He was only condemned to work as a baker under the sovereign orders of Dame Michou Guitan, and was proclaimed a slave in perpetuity, his sentence to begin immediately. While the young ladies drank, shouted and jumped about, Magloire, despite his gentleman clothes, his alleged noble birth, and his poetic misfortunes, was obliged to bake the next day's bread all by himself. None of his fantasies had succeeded. That was almost enough to turn him into an honest man!

Soon the grand gallery where the Wolves were assembled to celebrate their triumph was filled with a cloud of tobacco smoke, so thick that the crowd could barely be seen. There were savage shouts and great bursts of drunken laughter. The girls went about like bacchantes, a pipe in their mouth, wearing already jewelry stolen from the Presidial Ball on top of their rags. The men, crazy, twice as drunk, embraced or beat each other. They no longer felt that weight that, despite themselves, had oppressed them when they were among the splendors of the Hôtel de Ville. They were in their home; their heavy clogs felt comfortable on that earth covered with black dust and mud.

"Ham! Ham!" as their descendants still shout in fairs: "Ham, brandy and tobacco!"

Very salty ham, brandy that scratches the throat, tobacco that speeds up the heart! The three delights of the Breton paradise! How many people preferred that to the Church's Heaven!

The council chamber, a large room whose sides had been dug out with a shovel, had a higher ceiling than the rest of the caves. A dozen tree trunks served as columns, and topped with large beams placed in stacks, supported the ceiling. There was, at the far end, twenty or thirty logs already stripped of their bark that acted as curule seats[121] for the Wolves' "senate." At the back, facing the opening of the grand gallery, one could see the stiff and dull folds of the old silver cloth tapestry that we already mentioned in the first pages of this story. Once, it had served to separate the Rohan armory where Alain Polduc and Dame Michou Guitan had established their rival quarters and the main staircase of the manor. That was what was pulled back to show Count Guy responding to the call of his tenants in distress. Now it was used to hide a kind of invisible sanctuary where, in spite of the jokes of the handsome cobbler and his damned henchmen, no Wolf dared to enter, except with fear. It was forbidden to lift the drapery, but everyone in the caves knew what was behind it. Behind it, there was a niche, or a rotunda, in the center of which was placed that old family throne which in the past had ornamented the grand Hall of Rohan.

It was there, according to legend, that the She-Wolf had appeared to their ancestors. It was there that she would return if the denizens of the Wolf's Den were ever fated to see her again.

Yaumi had done what he could for fifteen years to destroy the prestige of that closed sanctuary. But there was there something legendary, and he had wasted his time. Precisely because she was invisible, the She-Wolf appeared to the imaginations of her savage subjects as one of the great dreams of Breton mysticism. She was no longer a mortal being. She was the personification of the ancient Ducal power; she was the very embodiment of Breton nationalism.

---

[121] A chair noted for its uses in Ancient Rome where it was a symbol of political or military power.

While the smoky feast was going on in the gallery, a serious synod was taking place in the council chamber. Yaumi, Steward Feydeau, Alain Polduc and Don Martin Blas, were gathered there in a dark corner, chatting in a low voice. Before entering, the handsome cobbler had had a conference of another type. Grincette, that little female devil that we have seen come out of the chimney, had made her report to him. The good Dame Michou Guitan believed that she could trust Grincette whom she had raised, but the fact was that Grincette loved her somewhat less than brandy.

And Yaumi had given her some brandy.

Behind the chimney of the kitchen, thought the handsome cobbler on reaching the council chamber. *If I were not too fat, I could go through that pipe to see for myself... I have always had an idea there was an entry there, because the chimney draws... But I have looked, I have probed... All in vain! This is not the time to do that chore. I have to strike somewhere else.*

In the room, the Steward and the Seneschal were seated next to each other; they were speaking with vivacity. Not far from there, somber and mute, Don Martin Blas leaned back on the wall of the grotto.

Yaumi approached the Steward and the Seneschal.

"Here, you scoundrel!" said Martin Blas, as if he had called a dog.

His contracted face showed, written in readable signs, that he shouldn't be contradicted at that moment. However, Yaumi didn't obey.

"My good man," Alain Polduc said to him, "the few hours that will pass from now until the opening of the Parliement are worth a lifetime for us. Your fortune is made if you can get us outside of here tonight."

Yaumi took a seat on a stool and said nothing. Martin Blas took a step toward him, his hand on his sword.

"You deceived us, you miserable wretch!" he said. "You swore to us that you were the master here!"

"I am the master," the handsome cobbler replied.

He passed the back of his calloused hand over his forehead covered with cold sweat and continued:

"The proof that I am the master is the fact that all three of you are still alive."

"But we are still prisoners," Polduc objected, "so you are not the master."

"You are prisoners because I wished it," said Yaumi.

Martin Blas's sword came halfway out of its sheath.

"You," said the handsome cobbler, who looked at him straight in the face, "I don't need you. You are the one who wanted to come... What did I promise you? That you would find here Countess Isaure and Cinderella? I didn't lie. Cinderella and Countess Isaure are here."

The Steward and his son-in-law exchanged a rapid glance.

"I want to see them," the Spaniard continued. "This instant."

"For my part, I don't want that," the handsome cobbler replied coldly. "I am the master here! Leave your sword where it is and, believe me, don't get too close, because if you trespass, you will see that our muskets' bullets are hard enough to break a gentleman's head... At this moment, there are four good pairs of eyes watching you, Monsieur the Ambassador of the King of Spain, and your forehead is in the sight of four reliable guns that have never missed their marks!"

Involuntarily, Martin Blas looked around him.

Yaumi began to laugh.

"Look at that," he continued, pointing to the bloody scar that the pommel of Monsieur de Rieux's sword had left on his face. "I had just to whisper one word to have the head of the one who marked me like this blown off. But I said nothing... nothing!" Then he added with a movement of pride: "Yes, I am the master, the master of others and of myself!"

His fawn-colored eyebrows frowned and his eyes shot out a flash from their dark depth.

"You will see her, your Countess," he continued, still with a disdainful tone, "but this time, will you have the heart to take your revenge?"

"What does that matter to you?" Martin Blas asked haughtily.

"No," continued the handsome cobbler as if speaking to himself. "She is too charming... He won't avenge himself!"

His hairy head disappeared between his hands, and he convulsively pressed his forehead. Evidently, that man was no longer in control of himself. His head was shaking. He had one grand plan, or perhaps madness was stalking him. Or still yet, he had hidden his hand for fifteen years and no one had guessed his intentions. When he uncovered his face, he was very pale and his eyes were shining.

"I am the master!" he repeated, as if to affirm his own conviction, "but I can do nothing against her, because she has a talisman... Didn't she go through fire and water? I put a silver bullet in my musket the day that I shot at her at the Cross of Mi-Forêt! I, who can kill a running hare at three hundred feet. I was fifty feet away, and I found my bullet at the same spot where she had been kneeling before the image of Our Lady."

"Then, it's really true that you tried to assassinate her?" asked Don Martin Blas, whose gaze left Yaumi to focus on the Steward and the Seneschal.

Polduc limited himself to making a very small shrug of his shoulders, and the Steward murmured:

"Don't you see that he's just mad as a hare?"

"It's you," suddenly shouted the handsome cobbler, whose pale lips were lined with foam. "It's all three of you who have deceived me... It's you who have lied to me, gentlemen that you are! You promised me to get rid of that woman, but she scares you! I'm all alone," he interrupted himself. "The war is between the two of us... It's necessary to strike—even if she is untouchable and invulnerable, I must strike... I will be the master. If the rock that I want to shake falls on my head, then everything is over! But what would death matter?"

He stopped talking.

In the neighboring gallery, the sounds of the feast increased with the warm vapor that the feverish crowd put off.

"All that is well and good, my good Yaumi," said the Seneschal, "but we offered you a fortune."

The handsome cobbler let out a dry and strident laugh.

"A fortune!" he repeated. "What would it have cost me to loot your two chateaux, my two gentlemen? A fortune! Ha! I am richer than you... because all that you have is already mine, if I so wish it. There is only one thing that counts: to be the master here. That's worth all of a man's blood. The rest is nothing!"

He stopped and closed his two big fists to threaten the Heavens.

"You'll see!" he shouted in a strangled voice, "that's a curse, you'll see... There is only one weapon that can kill that damned woman: her secret, and I have it! But the day that I tell her true name, the forest will tremble, and all those wild beasts here will tear me apart with their teeth."

His speech was short and broken. Jerky convulsions pulled at his facial muscles.

"And her power," he continued, suddenly standing, "do you know where it lies? I have spent days and nights looking for those damned entrances... If only I could say, I, too, know the secret of those entrances, nothing could resist me... Her power is there. I'm going to take it away from her... her power! I'm going to know as much as she does!"

He stood up in the middle of his three companions.

"You want to be free, don't you?" he asked them briskly.

Only the Steward and the Seneschal answered. They wanted, indeed, to leave the caverns at any cost. Don Martin Blas had different views.

Yaumi seized the Seneschal's arm and drew him to the other end of the room. They chatted a minute very low and with great animation.

Don Martin Blas had taken a seat and was thinking.

The Steward was following with a worried eye the conversation of his son-in-law with the handsome cobbler. From time to time, he had recourse to his gold box, but that was no longer with the grand manners and triumphant grace that we so justly admired in the boudoir of the Feydeau young ladies. He hardly took the trouble now to shake the lace around his neck. Alas! What good was that? That terrible night had completely washed the color from his face. The white, the red, the blue, all had disappeared. The unhappy Achille Feydeau was back to his natural self, with deep lines crisscrossing a sallow, pallid skin, and too few gray hairs springing fron under his wig. He had a pocket mirror which showed him the extent of his misfortune. He felt that discomfort, that sense of shame, that same confusion of the fox of the fable that had had his tail cut off. If he wanted to be free, it was to restore his former glory.

What's more, he saw immediately that his son-in-law and the handsome cobbler understood each other extremely well. Polduc rubbed his hands together and tapped on the Yaumi's shoulder in a very friendly manner.

It was at that point that Achille Feydeau had the courage to leave his place and to approach them. When he was close, he heard Yaumi speaking, and here's what the Wolf said:

"In an hour, everything can be done. Only pay close attention to the cavern's entrance... In any event, I will give you a guide... The Conti soldiers followed us as far as the ford of La Vache. They should be camped in the clearing. A gallop will send them to the Poond of Muys where they will find, Thank God, a big load of rocks... Let each man carry a stone and the entry to the Wolf's Den will soon be shut."

"This isn't a trap that you're leading us into, my boy?" asked the Seneschal, who was beginning to reflect.

AchilleFeydeau was now all ears.

"No," the handsome cobbler replied, "this is not a trap. You have your affairs, and I have mine, that's all."

"But how will you save yourself?"

"If I don't know everything, I know a lot," Yaumi replied with a certain repugnance, as if he ceded only to the need of his questioner for guarantees. "I know where Countess Isaure is at this moment... I know that she has with her a young girl that she would save at the peril of her life. When she is told: 'The entrance to the den has been shut,' she will certainly find another exit."

"Ah!" the father-in-law and the son-in-law said at the same time.

"And I who will be behind her without her knowing it," the handsome cobbler added, "and I will learn her great secret... I will be the master at last!"

"But then," the Seneschal began, "Countness Isaure would be..."

He didn't finish his sentence because Yaumi's hand was rudely put over his mouth.

"Don't say it! That word would wake up a terrible echo here."

"And you will let her leave?" Polduc asked.

"If my sword is not made of butter, no!" replied Yaumi with unusual energy.

"You will swear to that?"

"Yes."

"On your eternal salvation?"

"On my eternal salvation!"

"Done!" said the Seneschal, who held out his hand to Yaumi.

"Done!" said Achille Feydeau, from whom no one had asked anything.

"Wait five minutes for me here," continued the handsome cobbler. "I'm going to get rid of that man."

He went straight to Don Martin Blas and said:

"I am ready to take you to Countess Isaure."

The Spaniard rose without answering and the two men left together.

XI. Mother and Daughter

It was a kind of masonry cell whose walls were covered with a serge tapestry. It had a single door that opened onto a narrow, dark corridor from which came a large current of air that violently agitated the flame of the lamp. In that cell there was a couch and some stools. Lying on top of one of them was a folded country woman's dress in brownish homespun. At the bedside table, there was a big *Book of Hours*. A strange confusion of sounds and of voices could be heard, the same noises and the same voices that could be heard throughout the caverns.

The sounds of the musical instruments that animated the dancers in the gallery arrived perfectly distinct, as did the serious chatting of Dame Michou Guitan, who was undertaking the subterranean education of the unfortunate Magloire.

When there was a sudden clamor in the gallery where the Wolves were celebrating, the walls of the cell shook. The corridor situated outside the door was cold, but not damp. There was a violent wind that carried away with it the bitter smoke odors.

The reasoning of the handsome cobbler on the subject of that displacement of air that favored the draw of the chimney in the kitchen was not rigorously accurate. In large caves of a vast extent, with the only difference being in the levels, the temperatures can determine the continuous currents of air.

There were two women in that cell: Countess Isaure and Celeste. Both were still wearing their Ball dresses. The Countess was seated at the foot of the bed. Celeste was kneeling near her. The Countess, leaning forward, was holding Celeste's head pressed against her heart. Their beautiful blond and brunette curls were mingled.

A painter would have searched a long time before arranging more graciously two such ravishing creatures. They both had similar smiles; they were admiring each other; they adored each other; they wept.

"My mother! My mother!" Celeste was saying, making it her delight to repeat that word. "Is it possible that God has sent me so much happiness?"

"My daughter," Isaure said. "My darling daughter."

There were kisses without an end.

Then Isaure started talking:

"Let me tell you, Marie—because your true name is Marie, and your infancy was pledged to the Holy Virgin, Mother of God. Let me ask your pardon for having left you alone for so long, unhappy and abandoned; we were outlaws... I want you to know all that."

"But you are too beautiful and too young to be my mother!" Celeste interrupted.

She stepped back, laughing and crying.

"Beautiful," she said again. "Beautiful as the Saints of Heaven! My mother... My mother..."

And more kisses... They never stopped, insatiable as they both were for that divine happiness that thy had been waiting for for such a long time. Then Countess Isaure took on a very grave tone.

"My silly girl," she scolded, falsely severe, "will you not listen to me?"

"Only if you talk about yourself... I wish to hear nothing that is not about you, dearest mother, then I will listen to you."

"About me and about you, Marie... You, isn't that still about me? Do you remember what the Miller Woman told you that day in the ruins of the old windmill? Your destiny was decided that day. Your mother's efforts brought back to Brittany the only man who could bring peace and concord here—the Count of Toulouse. You are smiling because his coming was paid for by a battle. You are still very young, little girl, for me to explain to you the strange games of the various factions. Everyone gained at that battle, Marie, and you more than all others. That will be the last fight, if God helps us. There has been only two days since you were told your good fortune, and tomorrow you will become the wife of a great lord."

"Tomorrow?" repeated Celeste. Then she added, blushing and smiling at the same time. "But Raoul is still only a Captain."

"What was he only yesterday?" said the Countess. "Don't you believe the Miller Woman's predictions?"

Celeste devoured her beautiful hands with kisses.

"It was you, my mother; it was you!"

"Yes, it was me! And how many years it was before arriving at that first joy! But I don't know where to begin my story, Marie, my beloved daughter. We have only a few minutes and I have so many things to tell you! Fortunately, the Witch furthered my work the other day. First, I want to explain to you why you were brought up by the hands of the enemies of your family. It was at a time when there was no ground under my feet: my father was a prisoner; Josselin Guitan, the only servant who had remained faithful to me, had gone away, dying from a wound that he had received while serving me... I was alone and I had to leave for Paris. A voice told me that salvation was there.

"I knew that the traitor, Alain Polduc, and his father-in-law, the Royal Steward Achille Feydeau, were looking everywhere for my daughter and the son of my brother, and I knew why they were looking for them. God inspired me. It was during my prayer to Our Lady of Mi-Forét that the idea came to me to place the poor child right in the center of the enemy camp. How could Polduc and Feydeau suspect so much audacity? Besides, I was thinking that I would only be away from you for a few weeks... I was carrying with me a key that would open all the doors in Paris to me. But political figures don't decide anything in one day. I worked for ten long years.

"But what does it matter now, Marie, since you are here in my arms, since I can kiss your sweet forehead, and see your sweet smile?"

Celeste took both hands of the Countess and pressed them against her heart.

"What about Raoul?" she murmured.

"Ah! My rival?" said the happy mother, laughing. "The one you love more than me."

"Oh, not more than you, mother!" Celeste exclaimed.

"I am not jealous, and I love him almost as much as you do... God is good and Providence shows itself in all this. I had said to myself: The man my daughter will love and who will love her will be happy. Every obstacle will be removed from under his feet. As low as fate has placed him, he will rise, sustained by an invisible hand, right to the Ducal throne where my fathers sat. I said that in my pride, but God, who normally punishes pride, sees with a clement eye a mother's love, because that is not pride, but love. Raoul's happiness has been to love you. My own love is that Raoul loves you, because Raoul is the son of my brother César, and in serving my mother's love, I also fulfilled my duty at the same time."

"Raoul! My cousin!" exclaimed Celeste. "And then what is our name, mother?"

"Didn't you already guess it, Marie? Very often, yiu must have heard your own story told. But for you, poor child, it must have been stories of the old days, legends... If you have sometimes shed tears upon hearing of the last days of Rohan, as they still tell it in the forest, that's because you have a good heart."

"Oh! I cried very much!" said Celeste.

"You never suspected at all," continued Countess Isaure, "that the child asleep in the arms of Valentine of Rohan, driven out and cursed, that was you."

"Me!" exclaimed Celeste, very pale. "I feared it, my mother, and I am trying not to believe it. I have been a poor girl far too long. That grand name of Rohan frightens me."

Countess Isaure pressed her, shivering, against her breast.

"If God pleases," she said, "that grand name of Rohan will be easy for you to bear in the future, dearest daughter... I have worked at that for an entire lifetime."

Her arms suddenly stopped holding tightly Celeste, who slid to her knees. Her face had changed expressions. She was listening, her eye staring and her head inclined. She rose without making any noise.

"Wait," she said.

Walking softly, she went into the dark corridor. Toward the north, ended in a dead end. That was the end of the caves on that side. Countess Isaure pressed her ear to the wall.

"They're here!" she whispered.

As she finished, the voice of Martin Blas, invisible, was raised from the other side of the wall. Countess Isaure heard him pronounce distinctly:

"You deceived us, you miserable wretch!"

Then came Yaumi's response.

Countess Isaure was on the other side of the wall of the council chamber. She turned toward the left and took a few steps in the darkest obscurity, and her hand, tapping, found a little wooden door. She tapped softly three times and asked very low:

"Are you there?"

"I am here," replied the voice of Josselin Guitan.

Countess Isaure, pensive, but calm, returned to the little cell where Celeste was waiting for her, trembling.

"We will have more time than I had thought," she said. "Don't be afraid, little girl. Your terrors of this night are not ended, but your mother is near you."

"Don't leave me anymore!" whispered Celeste, using the familiar "*tu*" for the first time.

That was worth a long and sweet maternal caress.

"Where was I?" continued the Countess. "I can't tell you everything because you wouldn't understand... Have you ever heard of Baroness Saint-Elme, Marie?"

"Never," the young girl replied.

"That's the name of an isolated and weak woman to whom God gave the power to prevent war between two great people. It was the name of a woman, who, without support or recommendation, knew how to acquire enough power over the Regent, Philippe d'Orléans, to extract a promise from him that not a drop of blood would flow in Brittany as a result of the

Cellamare Conspiracy... Despite it all, four heads fell at Nantes... The woman about whom I am talking does not, however owe God any accounting for it, because that was a cowardly murder."

The Countess' forehead was leaning sadly on her breast.

"Why don't you talk to me more about yourself, Mother?" demanded Celeste.

"I am talking to you about myself, child," answered Countess Isaure, straightening up, proud and serious. "I am talking to you about the hardest days of my life... Those were four noble heads... Talhöet, the companion of my childhood; Malestroit; de Poncallec, a true gentleman; and du Couëdic, who died kissing the feet of the Crucifix. For a long time, I haven't been able to close my eyes without seeing their martyred heads. Because I was the one who had exposed and revealed the secret relationship between Spain and Brittany to the Regent..."

"You, Mother?"

"For you, daughter. I do not repent for that. Those four fallen heads spared thousands of other lives... May God wish, child, that you never approach the throne, even to do good... There are fatalities there... The memories that one keeps all too often resemble remorse."

She fell silent. Celeste didn't dare question her any further.

"On my salvation," Countess Isaure continued, "on you, Marie, who is almost as dear to me as my eternal happiness, I swear that I acted according to my conscience! At that time, daughter," she interrupted herself, "I could have been great... But I only wanted to be a mother. Once already, your very beloved cradle had stood between greatness and I. Once already, I had shown your smiling sweetness to the son of Louis XIV, telling him, 'You certainly see that I can't be your wife.' And to the Regent of France, I could still say: 'Everything that I do, I do it for my daughter.' My daughter was the cherished star that guided me. When I was tired and discouraged, I got on my knees... I spoke of you to the Holy Virgin and to God.

"You consoled me for everything, Marie, my beloved, and, when, after many sleepless nights, I found again in some sad retreat my noble father, deprived of his reason, uttering your name saved my own sanity.

"My daughter, I had only you, but that was enough. How do you want me to tell you how much I love you, Marie, you who have been my talisman and my strength!

"You are weeping, child... Is that because you love me too?"

Celeste had no more words, but what words could have replace thed eloquence of her eyes flowing with tears!

"I have worked a great deal," whispered Countess Isaure, weak at that moment like the child at her feet. "And I have suffered a great deal! But what is that, Lord, compared to this delightful hour that your kindness has granted me? Marie! Here you are, mine at last. We will never again be separated."

"Is it true, Mother, that we will never part again?" exclaimed Celeste, who had a radiant smile through her tears.

Countess Isaure's hand caressed Celeste's beautiful unbound hair, and adored her in silence.

"Let me tell you!" she began again in that naive and happy tone that mothers use leaning over the cherished crib that contains their whole heart. "Let me tell you all that I have done for myself, Marie, or rather for you, my beloved treasure... Oh! I had to fight! Everything was against me. In Paris, I was Baroness Saint-Elme, followed by a thousand enemies, and supported only by the capricious passion of the Regent.

"At Rennes, I was Countess Isaure, because I had to know the strength and weakness of those myriads of intrigues that circulate around the Parliament; because I needed gold, and partisans; because, also, while working for you, I also wanted to save our poor and valiant Brittany, drawn toward its end...

"In the forest, I was Valentine de Rohan, or rather I wore another terrible and strange name that made me the Queen of the savage inhabitants of those caves; and I needed an army. And finally, in the ancient domain of my fathers, I was the Witch, the Miller Woman, in order to trace a mysterious and uncrossable circle around the retreat where I was hiding my father."

Celeste was almost lost.

"Good Lord!" she said. "And you were able to do all that without dying? My poor Mother!" Then, carried away by the strength of her admiration, she added: "My noble Mother! My saintly Mother!"

"I can tell you that I was only thinking of you!" Countess Isaure said softly.

"And I didn't know that!" the young girl exclaimed. "I was weeping only because of my own misery."

"Oh!" continued the Countess, "I would have given my own blood for each of your tears, Marie... I knew, day by day, what you were doing and what you were suffering... I, too, berated God, whose hand, in my opinion, didn't move fast enough... Time passed. Fear was growing in me that Alain Polduc might discover the secret of your birth."

"But why so much work, Mother?" Celeste couldn't keep herself from asking. "Why did you not take me with you? We could have fled to some unknown retreat... We would have hidden our happiness."

She interrupted herself, confused and almost frightened. She no longer recognized her mother's regard. Her mother had put her hand on her forehead. Her expression, that had become severe, suddenly changed again. She had a serious but sweet smile.

"Marie," she pronounced slowly, "we cannot flee. We cannot be happy anywhere but in our ancestors' house. You will understand that one day: we are the Rohans!"

XII. The Hostages

Hearing those last words, Celeste's pretty face took on an expression of pride.

"I understand now, Mother," she replied. "We are the Rohans. I ask your pardon for what I just said."

"My dear child!" murmured Countess Isaure. "An indulgent Heaven is taking vengeance for us by covering us with kindness. You are going to be reborn into a new life. For a minute, it was the heart of our fathers that beat in your chest. Look and admire! The hour of our victory sounded even at the very moment that Polduc was going to crush you. For tonight, you were supposed to be kidnapped..."

"Tonight!" repeated Celeste, who trembled.

"Tonight, that precedes a great day," continued Countess Isaure. "Everything comes to us at the same time. Toulouse is now Governor—he who owes me his life twice. His wife, rhe Princess, a poor abused woman, tried a public outrage against me that only increased my glory. Our enemies are here, under this roof, in my power. They had prepared their iniquitous work for tomorrow. We will be there tomorrow, strong and assured of our victory. What proofs were we missing still? The proofs of that double birth, an unimpeachable testimony that Raoul is César's son as you are Valentine's daughter... Well, yesterday, hear this, Marie, only yesterday, Count Guy de Rohan, from whom God took away his sanity fifteen years, ago, recognized me, his daughter. His mind suddenly cleared. The shadows that obscured it were suddenly torn away... He said, kissing me on the forehead

" 'Valentine, take me to the tomb of my son, César... Valentine, I bless you. Valentine, please forgive me!'

"Rohan will speak!" she continued with sudden warmth. "Rohan promised. And when Rohan comes to say: 'This is the son of the son that I cursed; This is the daughter of the daughter that I chased away,' who then will dare to doubt the word of Rohan?"

361

There was silence. Countess Isaure had retreated inside herself, and Celeste, overwhelmed, dazzled, lost, tried to clear the confusion in her mind.

"But," she suddenly asked, "what about my father? You haven't mentioned my father."

A cloud came to darken the Countess'beautiful face.

"The first person that you will see tonight, Marie," she replied in a changed voice, "will be your father."

Celeste lowered her eyes under her gaze.

"When he arrives," Countess Isaure finished in a voice of grave authority, "remember that you owe him respect and love!"

At that same moment, Yaumi was introducing Don Martin Blas into a side passageway parallel tothe council chamber which terminated in a heap of rocks. Yaumi climbed up on these rocks that seemed to have been left there by chance, and pressed his shoulder against the wall of the tunnel, that gave way under his effort.

Martin Blas followed him. He saw a second corridor that plunged into profound darkness, but which eventually led to a fullu lighted room. Yaumi let him pass in front of him and said:

"They are there."

Martin Blas found himself alone in the corridor. He walked forward. He heard two female voices. His heart was beating violently, but it was with anger and hatred, because there was nothing in him at that time but thoughts of vengeance. But that hate and that anger were still expressions of love.

On arriving in front of the door, he saw the mother and the daughter, a charming group aureoled by a halo of sweet tears and smiles. He pressed both his hands against his beating chest. He recognized his wife and his daughter, the woman that he had once adored, and the child toward whom all of his soul was directed. What happiness was reunited there, under his hand! What precious treasure which he was forbidden to touch.

They were beautiful. The light from the lamp played about their foreheads, which were touching. Martin Blas had to find some support against the wall of the gallery. His legs were giving way under the weight of his body. That beautiful young girl was the blonde angel that he had kissed in the past in the mysterious cradle, above which Valentine, attentive and smiling, was watching. These far-away days were reborn. He was suffering. He wanted to die.

The sound that he made when touching the wall of the subterranean corridor awoke the attention of Countess Isaure, who abruptly rose.

"Come in," she said. "Come in, Monsieur de Saint-Maugan, I was expecting you."

Saint-Maugan saw a challenge in those words. He drew himself up to his full height.

"Marie," Countess Isaure added nevertheless, "stand up and greet your father."

Saint-Maugan entered, his forehead pale and his eyebrows frowning. Celeste glanced at him timidly. She recognized him as the man who had insulted her mother in the Presidial salon.

"Him!" she exclaimed. "He is my father?"

She fled to the other end of the cell and covered her face with her hands.

Saint-Maugan smiled bitterly.

"You have warned her against me," he said, "but I was expecting that. But it's my turn now, and I want my daughter to judge between her guilty mother and her dishonored father!"

Meanwhile, Yaumi had returned to the counsel room, to talk again to the Steward and the Seneschal.

To reach the entry of the Wolf's Den, it was necessary to cross the great gallery where the peasants of the forest were celebrating their victory.

The handsome cobbler no longer had that braggart and mocking tone that we had heard before. His head hung on his chest and only a bright shine in his eyes told what energy was left in him.

"Are you afraid, my friend?" Polduc asked him.

"No," replied the handsome cobbler coldly. "I'm betting my life on a single card, that's all."

"Whst about ours?" asked Achille Feydeau.

"Yours?" repeated Yaumi. "I need you.... Othewise... Let's go, my brave gentlemen!" he concluded. "We don't have time to chat. Will you do what I told you?"

"We will," replied both father-in-law and son-in-law.

"But you," added Polduc, "just remember your promise."

"Let's go," commanded the handsome cobbler, "and try to act like men along the road!"

He went first into the gallery. His presence was greeted by a grand acclamation. Yaumi was not an ordinary man. The Wolves had great confidence in his intelligence and his resolve. He had many enthusiastic partisans.

"The handsome cobbler! The handsome cobbler! A drink to his health, boys and girls!"

The dance stopped. They circulated jugs of brandy and crocks of cider. The Steward and the Seneschal were the object of attentions that didn't reassure them much. Polduc, however, put up a bold front, but Achille Feydeau was beginning to find the situation tiresome .Yet, they had only taken the first steps.

"To your health, Cousin Yaumi!" shouted Josille, who could hardly stand on his legs.

The traveler, Julot, had made the conquest of both Catiche and Scolastique, whom he was parading proudly one on each arm.

"What do you want to do with these two birds of ill omen, Cousin Yaumi?" he demanded in passing.

"Shut up," replied the handsome cobbler, "and be careful."

"Don't irritate them," whispered Polduc in his ear.

"I know how to deal with them," responded Yami. "The danger is not for the present," he said low. "Drink, dance, my children," he continued aloud; "I'm working for you."

"And what are you doing for us with your hands in your pockets, Cousin Yaumi?" was heard from all directions.

"My opinion," added the old tenant farmer, Jouachin, "is that those two there who are with you don't work very often for us poor people."

Then others said:

"Hang on to them, Yaumi. They're worth more money than you!"

A tall fellow that they had gotten out of the Petite Motte prison that night, where he had been locked up for having assaulted a tax collector, came to light his pipe by that of the handsome cobbler.

"You aren't going to dance a *rigoton* with us, Steward?" he asked.

"My good fellow," stammered Achille Feydeau, "at my age..."

He must have felt very low for him to show in this way his surplus years.

"Go ask the Seneschal to dance, Javotte!"

"Fanchon, help the Steward twirl!"

Despite those cries that were resounding from all directions, followed by long bursts of laughter, nothing came to stop the progress of the three associates. Everything up to now had been only noise. Without seeming to do anything, Yaumi was still coming down lower and gaining ground. He was already halfway down the path of the entry to the cave. No one thought that he wanted to let the two prisoners escape.

While he was walking, the handsome cobbler began a ploy that most of the crowd didn't notice at all. Every time he saw one of his die-hard henchmen in the crowd, he casually lifted the index finger of his right hand to the corner of his mouth. The fellow immediately came out of the crowd and joined him. He assembled a half-dozen men in this way. The others were lost in the crowd and hadn't seen him.

The handsome cobbler, it seems, thought he needed all his people, because he tried to see over the heads of the crowd, and locate the missing ones. Unfortunately, his legs were too short and stocky. As he passed by, he spotted Grincette, who was behind a pillar, crouching on the ground, sucking on a half-full glass of brandy. Yaumi whistled softly while pretending not to see her. The little girl trembled and drew in her head like a grass snake that is being disturbed. Without any other visible communication between her and her master, she took off her wooden shoes and slipped into the crowd, looking for the others. A moment later, all the of the handsome cobbler's henchmen were fully united around him.

The dance had started again. Yaumi was still gaining ground. He was no more than twenty-five feet from the entry.

"Oh!" Dame Michou Guitan suddenly shouted to him as he passed by the kitchen door, "you're in good company there, cobbler! Didn't you tell those two puffed up rogues that once one has entered the Wolf's Den, one never leaves it, except feet first?"

"I have organized things as I think best, my ood woman," responded Yaumi.

Dame Michou had perhaps stroked her plate too often that night to stay fully awake. But the sight of her former foe, Alain Polduc, revived a whole world of bitterness in her.

"Hear this, you traitorous scoundrel," she said to him, coming out from her den to put her trembling fist under the Seneschal's nose. "You won't leave here alive; I'm the one who's telling you that!"

Polduc was paler than a corpse. As for the once seductive Achille Feydeau, he shivered with fever. Magloire, who had been obliged to leave his fancy clothes to put on the simple and traditional dress of bakers, saw, in his turn, the father-in-law and the son-in-law.

"Ah! Jesus Christ!" he shouted in his most piercing voice, "they're are the ones who are the cause of all my troubles. Those two are the most perverse of all the old scoundrels. They seduced my inexperienced youth with strong drink. Let me go, my good lady. I want to take my revenge on the oldest one."

Saying that, he placed his oven scoop under the eyes of the Steward, who moved backwards, making the cries of the peacock.

Yaumi, furious at seeing his progress halted for so little, wanted to grab Magloire by his throat, but Dame Michou put herself bravely between them.

"He's mine," she said. "I forbid you to touch him."

We know that Dame Michou Guitan was a robust woman. Since she had lived at the Wolf's Den, her mustache had grown a half longer.

"Make room, Good woman!" said Yaumi, who was becoming uneasy.

Dame Michou looked at him askance.

"Make room?" she repeated. "To go where, my good man?"

"He wants to let them escape," said Magloire, guessing correctly purely by chance.

Dame Michou's face became scarlet. She took a step, not backward, but forward. Camped thus, she completely barred the way.

This is bad. Very bad, thought the Seneschal.

"We are lost, my son-in-law," sighed Achille Feydeau in a tone of desolation.

That was almost the opinion of Cousin Yaumi

"The Devil! You shrew!" he shouted in fury. "Do I have to answer to you?"

At the same time, he pushed her roughly to one side.

There was a long, dull murmur from among those present. A hundred voices were heard repeating:

"That's the mother of Josselin Guitan!"

And the murmur grew closer and closer, becoming a growl, rumbling from one end of the immense gallery to the other.

"Yes!" shouted the old woman, raising her voice. "I am Josselin Guitan's mother, who has been struck because she suspecs foul betrayal. Help me, good Bretons! Help me!"

"Forward!" shouted Yaumi to his henchmen. "Forward!"

The Seneschal and the Steward pressed against him. Yaumi's henchmen forced an opening in the blink of an eye, and our three associates reached the exit in one bound.

Magloire, however, had time to give the Steward a master blow on his neck with the cake server. He bragged about that for the rest of his life.

The stone which blocked the door was rolled away. Yaumi pushed the son-in-law and the father-in-law outside, saying:

"There are horses under the Causeway. Ride like the wind! And bad luck to you if you betray me!"

The stone fell back. The Steward and the Seneschal were outside.

It would be impossible to paint the tumult that followed that act of violence. Those people, three-quarters-drunk, mist of whom didn't know what had just happened, all rushed at the same time to the back of the gallery to see what was going on. The musical instruments fell quiet; the songs ceased. A growling like thunder filled the cavern. Those who knew and those who didn't know shouted all at the same time, some accusing Yaumi, others defending him.

Betrayal was talked about here and there; this word floated above all the din in the cavern; but the main complaint seemed to be the blow struck to Dame Michou Guitan, who was Old Count Guy's condidente; and no one present had forgotten at what cost she had helped the tenant farmers of Rohan in distress. It was she who, on that famous day of Saint John—his last day at the manor—had obtained from the Count that he return to his poor vassals half of their land payments. To strike Dame Michou, was almost the same as to strike the venerable memory of Rohan.

Yaumi heard all that fracas of menaces and clamors. He remained near the stone entrance to give the two fugitives time to reach the Pond of Muys. The hardest part was done. He was not afraid. It was in fight like these that he had won his authority, by keeping his head cool and his superior force at his side. He believed himself able to dominate all that tumult.

But suddenly, there was a new and stronger shout. Yaumi heard that they were saying:

"There he is! There he is!"

He turned around. Josselin Guitan was there. He was embracing his mother.

XIII. The She-Wolf

The handsome cobbler turned pale. However, he said:

"Greetings, Josselin, my boy. I tried to be of service to your good mother by advising her not to get involved in what doesn't concern her. I brushed her a while ago in passing by and I regret that action, because one should always show respect to the old. But old women should not stand in the way of men going about their work."

Josselin Guitan left his mother and came to stand facing Yaumi.

"And what work were you doing?" he asked in a cold and severe tone.

"As for that," replied the handsome cobbler, "we don't have to argue, my boy. I command here, isn't that true? I don't have to ask advice from anyone."

He glanced around him to look for agreement. The core of scoundrels who were surrounding him agreed with him and a dozen drunks joined them.

But Josselin never drank.

And the greater part of the Wolves remained silent and attentive.

It was a trial that was taking place. Yaumi realized that at once, but did not tremble. When it came to making speeches, he was very good. The Wolves had let themselves be taken in a hundred times by his savage eloquence.

"You command here on the condition that you obey," answered Josselin Guitan, "since the Rohan domain is now underground. You must ask advice and render accounts. Pay close attention to me, Yaumi. I am not talking to you about what you did to my mother. I am telling you this: Yaumi, you are a traitor, and I'm going to wait for you in the council chamber!

He turned his back, going through the crowd, that let him pass, bowing their heads out of respect.

While going through the gallery, he was choosing the judges who would, in a short while, pronounce for him or for Yaumi. Each time that he pronounced a name, the designated Wolf followed him. He had the right to choose seven of them. A similar right belonged to the accused.

Yaumi hesitated for an instant. At the moment when Josselin turned his back, his knife came half-way out of its sheath, but the look of the crowd stopped him. They were not with him,

I must preach to them, he thought. *Without that, I'm lost!*

Meanwhile, time was passing, and to gain time was essential, because Yaumi was counting on the terrible trick that he had set up when he had organized the flight of the Steward and the Seneschal. He got ready in his turn, calling the men that he wanted as his jurors from right and left. Josselin was already in the council chamber, his seven jurors seated on their stools to the right of the silver drapery. Those selected by Yaumi took their places to the left. The veiled niche therefore found itself in the center.

That was the custom and that was a symbol. The tribunal of fourteen was supposed to be presided over by the She-Wolf herself, behind the drapery. The crowd came into the council chamber behind Yaumi and those who couldn't come in massed behind them in the gallery.

Josselin and Yaumi stood facing each other like two fighters in the ring.

"What do you accuse me of, Josselin Guitan?" asked Yaumi.

"I accuse you of having betrayed Brittany and your brother Wolves."

In those caves, that were so noisy before, you now could have heard a mouse scuttle.

Yaumi shrugged as if he didn't deign to answer that vague accusation.

"And what are you asking?" he questioned in a provoking way.

"Your death!" replied Dame Michou Guitan's son in the midst of the most profound silence.

"Do you remember that among us," said the handsome cobbler, without losing his assurance, "a false accuser pays the same price as the innocent he accused!"

"I do remember that."

"The death that you are demanding for me, do you accept it for yourself?"

"I accept it."

"Speak, then, my boy... I am not so wicked as you. I promise that you will be pardoned."

There was a small movement in the circle that surrounded the tribunal. That movement was in favor of Yaumi.

"You have betrayed us," Josselin continued, however. "We had two prisoners here and you set them free."

"Our true hostages," replied Yaumi, "were the Count of Toulouse, Governor of Brittany, and the Princess, his wife... I was not the one who set them free...."

A second louder murmur proved that he had again scored a point.

"You are guilty of betrayal," Josselin continued. "Those two hostages of which I am speaking, Alain Polduc, Seneschal of Brittany, and Achille Feydeau, Royal Steward, had been entrusted to you by she whom we all obey. I am the one who brought you her orders."

With a rapid glance, Yaumi took a survey of the room. Without mentioning any name, Josselin Guitan had just invoked an invisible and supreme authority. He had alluded to

371

their mysterious leader, just the thought of whom inspired veneration and fright. It was the *noli tangere*, the Holy Ark that bo one was permitted to touch! But it was also an opportunity for him to strike the first blow of his hammer to on the sacred idol.

The handsome cobbler took a step toward the inside of the enclosure. His pose becane more solemn, his accent more grave.

"Enough of this deceit. Josselin Guitan!" he shouted. "I would have left you in peace out of respect for our dead masters who loved you; and out of pity for the white hairs of your mother. But you have gone beyond what is acceptable, my boy, and it is I, now—do you understand, all of you?—it is I now who accuses you in front of everyone, and who says to you: Josselin Guitan, you have betrayed Brittany and your brother Wolves."

"Silence! Silence!" was heard from every direction.

Each man held back its breath.

"Listen to me closely, my children and my friends," continued the handsome cobbler, who was, when he wanted, an effective orator. "Here is someone who, for ten years, has pulled our strings as if we were a bunch of puppets... He told himself: 'These are simple minds, poor peasants. I'm going to deceive them and make myself their master. I'll create some kind of phantom and place it behind that curtain and turn it into a scarecrow... For that's what the She-Wolf is...' "

At that name, the crowd trembled, and Yaumi felt it, but he had now burned his bridges and had to carry on.

"Yes, the She-Wolf," he repeated, raising his voice.

"Are you going to insult Rohan?" old Jouachin, who was among the judges, exclaimed.

"Let him; let him talk," Josselin Guitan ordered.

And the crowd, already half-way won over, perhaps, repeated:

"Let him talk!"

The crowd was afraid, but those emotions were dear to it. They expected some great event. Their hearts jumped, beating

372

in a thousand breasts. We are telling the truth. The masses love to tremble more than they do to drink and dance.

"The She-Wolf," the handsome cobbler repeated for the third time, made confident by his success, because, after all, that feared name had not made the roof of the cavern crumble. "Will you believe me?" he continued. "If Rohan's daughter existed, do you think that she would have protected Toulouse, who sent her father die in exile?"

"No! No!" came from every direction.

"Do you think that she would have left Alain Polduc in the manor of her ancestors for ten years?"

"No! No!"

"Do you think she would have let ten years go by without showing herself to her vassals and her servants?"

"No! No!"

"I told you she was a scarecrow, a phantom, behind which that man there (here, he pointed at Josselin) was hiding, plotting to first subjugate us, and then to sell us to the French—as he would have subjugated us without me—as he would have sold us without me!"

"Answer, Josselin Guitan, answer!" shouted several voices.

And as Josselin kept silent, the Judges also said:

"You must answer!"

The case for the handsome cobbler seemed as much as won.

However, a number of eyes were still fixed with terror on the silver drapery. What was behind that veil that could not be touched, except at the cost of one's life? The thought of a miracle was in everyone's mind. And everyone, without completely believing in it, represented to himself the grand figure of the She-Wolf behind that mysterious drapery.

Yaumi knew them and understood this. He wanted to strike one last, supreme blow.

"Him? Answer?" he shouted. "I defy him! Tell him to show you the She-Wolf. The time for lies is past. I have crushed his grand words beneath my heel. I have blown away his phantom. What does he have left? There he stands, mute, the true traitor... It's I, my friends, I who is going to answer in his place, for I amthe one who is going to show you what the She-Wolf really is."

"Wretched man!" shouted Josselin, who saw Yaumi take a step toward the drapery.

Blood stopped in every man's vein. The fourteen judges stood up involuntarily at the same moment.

"The She-Wolf!" the handsome cobbler continued with insane bursts of laughter, because he had become drunk with his own words, and the effort he made to conquer his terror had gone to his head. "Ah! Ah! The She-Wolf! Ah! Ah! You're going to see what the She-Wolf is! An old arm chair that's turning moldy in an empty niche. Ah! Ah! Take a good look! Here! I'm touching the veil! Look closely and see if death strikes me!"

His face was marked with red and livid blotches. He was daring, but terror still made his teeth clack.

With a convulsive gesture, he pulled aside the drapery.

The Wolves saw what he had foretold: an empty niche with an antique armchair. But that didn't last very long. Suddenly, there was an explosion. No one knew where it came from. All the Wolves fell down with their face against the ground. When, after a long silence, they stood up again, at the voice of Josselin Guitan, the silver drapery had been closed again. Only Yaumi was not standing up. The lighting had struck him.

The profound stupor caused by that event was still going on, when a new catastrophe came to shake the crowd violently. A dull noise of an inexplicable nature originating from the entry of the caverns had been heard for several moments. Scouts were sent to investigate; a musket discharge was heard outside. The sound of it resonated under the vaults as a solemn signal of death. For all those who were there, it was like the trumpet of the Last Judgement. Yaumi the traitor had been punished, but the effect of his betrayal still lived.

Two of the torch carriers returned and they didn't call to arms. Their fellow scouts had remained there, dead behind the entry grate.

"Let's put down our guns and take up our rosaries," said one of the survivors. "The Conti soldiers are there, filling the entry of the Wolf's Den with rocks

For several minutes, there was a somber silence, then there was a cry of rage. And an impetuous flow of men dashed toward the opening; but it was too late. The last rock had been placed, blocking the last fissure. Behind that wall that couldn't be crossed, the cruel laughter of the Conti soldiers could be heard.

You could have then said that the crowd had turned into an immense pack of wild beasts trapped behind the iron bars of their cages. They all prowled up and down without seeing, mechanically testing with their hand the walls of their prison, searching for new exits, but always coming back to where they had started, discouraged, desperate, perhaps even mad. Some of them became delirious, and began the orgy again. Others, huddled in a circle, told each other, in a lamentable voice, the horrors of the death that was to come: death by hunger in the dark and impenetrable shadows, because the lamps would soon to be extinguished, and all the food soon used up!

The women were weeping and wringing their hands; there were loud bursts of laughter. Joyous songs among the concert of sobs were heard. Madness is contagious; madness rose in every head. Some women and some men, very few, had gathered around Dame Michou Guitan, who was praying at the top of her voice.

An hour passed; a century of a horrible length. There was some with black hair who turned white during that awful hour. Sunken eyes and wrinkled cheeks were seen. Young people slumped their shoulders like old men.

I'm telling you, it was like a century! When Dame Michou Guitan had finished reciting her rosary, she rose and came into the gallery.

"God is good, children," she said. "Appeal to him first of all."

Every knee flexed. After a short prayer, she said:

"Follow me!"

She went to the Council Chamber, where Jossselin no longer was. Yaumi, whom they had pushed into a corner, showed some signs of life. But no one even looked at him.

"Remember, children," Dame Michou Guitan continued, "in the past when you were in trouble, to whom did you appeal, after God?"

"To Rohan," answered some voices.

"But, said some other desolated voices, "Rohan is dead. He can no longer hear us."

"Rohan does not die!" gravely pronounced that old woman, who seemed to grow taller in the middle of that sagging crowd. "Remember again, when Rohan was too far away to hear you, I came to you, and I told you: 'Children, let's all shout together, and let all our voices make only one shout!' "

"That's true, isn't it?" murmured the unhappy poor, like little children whose smile shines through their tears.

"Why don't we do now as we did in the past?" continued Dame Michou Guitan. "We have prayed to God; now let us call our master!"

She placed herself in the center of the circle, and in a shouting voice, shouted:

"Rohan!"

A feeble echo responded.

"Rohan!" she repeated.

They had extinguished all the lamps with the exception of just one to relight the other lamps, leight being almost as necessary for life as bread.

A light seemed to appear behind the silver drapery.

"Rohan!" Dame Michou called for the third time.

As she did that, the entire crowd joined with her, because hope had returned into their hearts thanks to that belief in the marvelous that always lives in every Breton's heart.

The name of Rohan, repeated in a chorus, made the ceilings shake.

Miracle! The drapery opened of itself. In the lighted niche could be seen, seated on the antique throne, her hand holding the great sword of Duke Pierre of Brittany, a woman, beautiful as the Madonna, whose radiant forehead is crowned with stars. She was wearing on her shoulders a long ermine cloak, the Ducal Cloak. Everyone recognized Valentineof Rohan, as beautiful and young as in the happy times. There was no knee that did not bend, not a forehead that did not fall to the earth before the supreme power of the She-Wolf.

She silently extended her hand toward an exit that appeared to the left of her throne.

No one had ever seen that exit before!

That was life for all those condemned to death! The secret of the exits belonged to Rohan! And Rohan had never failed to answer the appeal of his vassals in distress.

An hour later, the Wolf's Den was deserted. Profound silence reigned there, interrupted only by a few dull, periodic moans. It was the handsome cobbler, who had some trouble giving up his last sigh. He had tried to drag himself out of his corner to follow his former companions, but his strength was no longer there. Fate has cruel jokes for the ambitious of all kinds. That exit for which he had searched for so long, and the knowledge of which would have given him supreme power, he had finally discovered it—but, alas, at the hour of death!

As he already felt the first spasms of agony coming, he heard the sound of footsteps in the deserted gallery, and a man carrying a lantern in his hand came out of the shadows. He seemed to be uncomfortable guiding himself through the cavern's maze.

"That's the council chamber," he was saying to himself, trying to throw light on the wall to find out where he was. "Here is the drapery... So they went out this way... If I can just get to clean air, I will still have my revenge, even if I die for it."

Yaumi was not the type of man to die passively:

"Hey! Monsieur de Saint-Maugan," he shouted as loud as he could.

Don Martin Blas turned around quickly on hearing himself called by that name.

Yaumi made and effort to sit up. Martin Blas ran to him and tried to to dress his wound.

"Many thanks, Monsieur de Saint-Maugan," the handsome cobbler told him. "You're better than your actions would indicate. I'm going to render you a service before taking the final plunge. A good deed, that always helps when one is dying."

His breathing began to whistle in his throat.

"Tell me," he continued, "I have often mocked those who say their last prayers, but you wouldn't have a crucifix on you, by any chance?"

"No," answered Martin Blas. Then reflecting a moment, he added: "I have a relic,"

An expression of naive joy spread over the features of the agonizing cobbler.

"Lend it to me," he said. "My dead mother was a good Christian. With your relic and her prayers, I will at least go to Purgatory... Ah! Ah!" he added suddenly, "you have kept that for sixteen years! I saw it once around the neck of Mademoiselle Valentine."

And as the Spaniard blushed, he said:

"You did a good thing. She too is a Saint!"

"What!" exclaimed Martin Blas. "You're the one who is telling me that!"

"There is a scoundrel without any guts who doesn't deserve a pardon," replied Yaumi, whose voice was becoming weaker. "It's Alain Polduc, who gave me money to lie to you. Valentine Rohan was as pure as the angels of God... and the day that you surprised her..."

He stopped. His hands clinched. Martin Blas leaned over him, holding his breath.

"Yes, and...?" he asked.

"And," Yaumi finished, making one last effort, "the Count of Toulouse had asked her for her hand, but your wife showed him the cradle and the child inside, and replied: 'I am married to the man that I love.'"

Yaumi's head fell back heavily on his chest. Nevertheless, he still had time to say:

"There it is, one good action! With the relic and the prayers of the poor old woman... With that, one can get by."

He was dead.

Morvan de Saint-Maugan stayed near him, immobile, like a man struck by lightning.

PART FOUR: VALENTINE DE ROHAN.

I. The Tombs

It was one of those cold foggy May mornings that make Brittany's flowers bloom; the mist didn't rise very far off the earth; the sky was clear; and the Sun's rays played hide and seek through the wavering tops of the trees, where the young tender leaves were turning green.

Two horsemen were following on foot the path that borders the Vesvre, passing under the arcade of the Pont Joli. One of the two, who was in the strength of age, was mounted on a good, stocky horse from Léon. You would have recognized him easily by his brilliant uniform. It was the cheerful Monsieur de Rieux, Lieutenant Colonel of the Conti Regiment.

The other, a great deal younger, wore the rich riding habit of a gentleman. He handsome, proud, and seemed happy to be alive. His mount was expensive. That was our friend Raoul, who had seen much happening since the night before.

"Ah! Well! My nephew," said the Viscount de Rieux, "are we beating about the countryside? I'm told you refused to obey the Major's orders!"

"Absolutely, my dear Colonel..He ordered me to close up the entry to the Wolf's Den, near here..."

"Hum! Hum!' coughed Monsieur de Rieux.

That was perhaps the effect of the morning mist.

"I told the Major," Raoul continued, "as you would have done yourself, I'm sure, that I was a soldier, not a mason."

"That's good, my nephew."

"That I was willing to go in by force, pistol in my hand, into the den of the revolting peasants, and give him a good account of myself, but that moving boulders seemed to me unworthy of a soldier and a gentleman..."

"I know the formula," de Rieux interrupted. "Eh! Eh! Perfect! But the Major walled up the cave anyway?"

"After I broke my sword over my knee."

"I know the gesture," interrupted again Monsieur de Rieux, sarcastic. "One needs suede gloves to do that, otherwise you cut yourself. And tell me, who had revealed the entry to the Wolf's Den to my worthy Major?"

"I saw the Royal Steward Feydeau and Monsieur de Polduc arrive on horseback...."

"On their own horses?'

"No, on little coalmen's horses."

"Good! Good! Get used to not dooting the I's and crossing the T's for me, nephew. That will go faster. And so?"

"And so, I returned to Rennes."

"And the Governor had you summoned?"

"Yes. At four o'clock in the morning."

"And then?"

"And then, he said to me: 'Colonel...'"

"Ah. So it's really true then?"

Raoul made a movement of proud impatience.

"My dear Monsieur Raoul," the Viscount de Rieux began again, "I'm treating you as if you were still my little *cornette*, but you have earned all your promotions to the rank of colonel in twenty-four hours. That's fast! Pardon me! I won't do it again."

"Colonel!" exclaimed Raoul, "you are my first and my dearest protector. If you change tones with me, I will never see you again in my life."

Rieux held out his hand to him and shook his strongly.

"Brave little heart!" he said affectionally. Then, taking back that movement: "All right, nephew," he added, laughing, "I promise to make fun of you just as before."

"All Right! Where was I? Ah, yes! The Governor said to me: 'Colonel..' But I interrupted him to observe that I wasn't even a captain anymore.

'I know!, I know!' he answered, 'but you have reacted as a true gentleman, and I honor you for that, so you are now Colonel. Madame the Princess thought that you might accept from her hand the command of the Flanders Regiment, which she has arranged for you.' "

"That dear Princess!" said the Viscount.

"Me," continued Raoul, "I objected because I don't have a single penny to pay for that commission. The Governor pinched his lips and answered me with haughtiness:

" 'In the house from which I come, and which Madame de Toulouse has entered, we have the right to give gifts to gentlemen!'

"I bowed very low, and an instant later, Madame de Toulouse, with enchanting grace, gave me the commission of Colonel of the Flanders Regiment."

They turned onto the winding road that bordered on the smaller road where our friend Magloire had had such a bad scare. There was a large clearing among the bushes where stood the ruins of the old windmill.

"The Aldermen of Rennes,'' Monsieur de Rieux grumbled, "pay a reward to those who remove mad dogs. Who will rid us of that cowardly scoundrel once and for all?"

A man came out of the bushes and crossed the road. In passing, he lifted his peasant's hat.

"Would that be you, Josselin, my brave fellow?" asked de Rieux.

"I am on my way to doing just that, Monsieur le Vicmte," answered Josselin Guitan.

"My nephew." suddenly continued Monsieur de Rieux, stopping in the very middle of the road, "we are going to see some strange things today... I have for a long time thought myself a clever politician; I confess this naively... Now... Now, I am persuaded that clever politicians are asses, and I renounce being part of their brotherhood. We live in a time when everything happens by ricochet. You leave for the east; you arrive in the west. Monsieur du Maine has done that notably. He left for the Louvre and is likely to arrive one of these days at Pignorol[122] or at the Bastille. The straight line is a pure invention of the mathematicians, and the only way to decently conduct oneself is to put a blinfold over one's eyes when one doesn't have the luck to have been born blind... Do you understand what I'm saying, nephew?"

"Not really, Colonel."

"So much the better! Here you are, a Colonel at twenty, just for having broken military law. I, who am talking to you, I have been a Lieutenant Colonel for twelve years, and my name is de Rieux."

"The fact is..." Raoul began.

"Be quiet, nephew," interrupted the Viscount, "you're going to say something stupid. I found on my bedside table this morning my commission as BrigadierGeneral of the King's armies. I think that was a recompense, first of all, for having placed a scatterbrain like youtself in charge of the Mordelaises Gates, and next, for having let the city of Rennes be taken by a troop of badly-dressed scoundrels, when I had ten times more boys than necessary to defend it."

"It was a recompense for your bravery, and your well-known loyalty," said Raoul, "and allow me, General, to first to congratulate you..."

---

[122] a.k.a. Pinerolo. Italian town conquered by the French in 1630. An impressive fortress was erected there by architect François Levé in 1666. It also served as a state prison. Nicolas Fouquet, disgraced superintendent of finances of Louis XIV, was transferred by d'Artagnan from the Château de Vincennes to Pignerol after his trial and died there in 1680. The Duke of Lauzun was also imprisoned there for 10 years. Pignerol's most famous prisoner was the Man in the Iron Mask. France agreed to hand Pignerol back to the House of Savoy under the Treaty of Turin in 1696, with the conditions that its stronghold's fortifications be demolished and that Savoy withdraw from the League of Augsburg.

"Well! Well! Those are nice words. Let's move on, nephew. I'm too old; and you're too young... the whole story is there."

He spurred on his horse, which picked up a resounding trot. He asked, as if to break off the previous conversation:

"Who gave you an appointment at the Rohan manor?"

"Countess Isaure," Raoul replied.

"By letter?"

"By courier. I knew in advance that I was supposed to meet you and take orders from you."

"And do you also know what we are going to do at the Rohan manor?"

"Not the least in the world. What about you?"

"I?" replied Monsieur de Rieux, finding again his gaiety, that had, for a moment, been subdued. "I know that we are going to have a good laugh, nephew. Let's ride!"

They arrived at the top of the hill. At the first bend in the road, they found themselves facing that bizarre construction that, in spite of restorations and recent changes, still constituted the old Rohan Manor. The front lawn was ahead of them. To their right extended the grove of chestnut trees that played such a role in the prologue to this story. Above the chestnut trees, they could see the profile of the famous granite balcony.

As Raoul turned his horse's head toward the gates, Monsieur de Rieux said to him:

"That's not the way we're going to enter."

Raoul knew the other way better. Monsieur de Rieux and he went around the trees and soon found themselves on that little knoll, transformed now into a small garden, where Alain Polduc had, in the past, surprised Morvan de Saint-Maugan leaving Valentine's quarters.

Raoul halted his horse in front of the balcony.

"Dismount, nephew," commanded Monsieur de Rieux.

"And onward to the attack, right?' questioned Raoul, laughing.

He pointed with his finger to the granite balcony that he had scaled the night before.

"Not to the attack," replied Monsieur de Rieux.

The horses were tied in the chestnut grove. Since they had arrived at the Château, they had not seen a soul alive. It would have seemed that it was abandoned. Only the window to the Feydeau young ladies' boudoir was open, as it had been left the night before.

When Raoul and Monsieur de Rieux went down into the ditch, the dogs in the interior court yard started barking. That was all. No one showed themselves.

It will perhaps be remembered that, the evening before, when she was on the balcony, after the departure of the Feydeau young ladies, Celeste had been frightened by a vision. She believed that she had seen two dark shapes slip through and disappear into the ditch at the foot of the walls. It was a tall man and a woman whose appearance resembled that of the Miller Woman.

Our two companions went directly toward the place where Celeste's vision had disappeared. There was a little gate there, located at ground level. Monsieur de Rieux put a key into the lock. The door turned on its rusty hinges and revealed a stairway cut into the rock.

"Enter, Nephew César," he said, uncovering his head, and in a voice that was both sad and serious at the same time.

Raoul looked at him, stunned.

"Come, I tell you, into the house of your ancestors," repeated Monsieur de Rieux, who bowed. "Come in, César de Rohan-Polduc!"

Raoul's whole body trembled and he turned pale. He crossed the threshold. Monsieur De Rieux and he descended the stairway in silence. At the end of some twenty steps, their feet reached soil. They were in a huge subterranean room with an arched ceiling and comprised of a central nave between two rows of low sides, like a cathedral. The grandeur of the Rohans was all in the past. Their domain, as Josselin Guitan had said, was underground.

Two long lines of tombs in black granited from Pen-March were located along the low sides, each bearing one or two couched statues, the heads on a marble cushion, the feet placed against the symbolic greyhound. At the vault, a lamp was hanging by three long iron chains.

Monsieur de Rieux and Raoul, both standing with their head uncovered, remained for a moment in the middle of that nave.

"It seems that we are the first to arrive at the rendezvous," murmured the Viscount, looking around him.

Nothing moved between the two perspectives of aligned tombs. Raoul had taken the hand of his brave companion.

"You have just said some words," he stammered, making vain efforts to hold back his emotion, "that have put my heart in great mourning and great hope... In the name of God, Viscount, please explain yourself!"

"There is one tomb missing here, nephew," replied Monsieur de Rieux, in a shaking voice, because he was also emotional. "Nephew, you are the one who will put it here... Your father sleeps in the small cemetery at Noyal, and there is only a poor wooden cross over his grave."

"My father!" Raoul repeated. "Am I to believe....?"

"He was my friend, nephew... My friend and my cousin trice over, by Rohan and Combourg... The first time I touched your hand, I had tears in my eyes."

Raoul threw himself at Monsieur de Rieux, who held him against his chest. Then, stepping back, he said:

"Oh! That's enough of that, my boy... I believe that you will be a good gentleman.... If you became, like so mny others, a confirmed scoundrel, that would be very sad."

He drew him toward the side that was to the right of the door.

"Look," he continued, pointing to the first tomb, "and rejoice if you like past glories... Here is the statue of Saint

Winoch,[123] your earliest ancestor. Legend has it that he converted the giant Corseult, my earliest ancestor. You can see that Rohan and Rieux have been cousins for a long time, which hasn't kept them from cutting each other's throat on fifty occasions."

Raoul hardy heard, and he certainly didn't understand.

"I... I..." he repeated without knowing what he was saying, "the heir of Rohan?"

And everything that had happened to him during the last two days overwhelmed his imagination with a sort of sudden violence. It was like a short novel with many lightning-like twists and turns, that seemed almost like an impossible dream. He had left Rennes only two days before, poor, obscure, without a name, without resources. The previous evening, Countesse Isaure had told him, speaking of a poor orphan like himself, humble like him, just as poor as him:

"*To love her, that will bring you luck!*"

And happiness had come, every happiness at the same time, a deluge of happiness: wealth, rank, a name, everything that could be desired when one has only a cape and a sword, is young and full of foolish dreams! And on top of those accumulated felicities, the dearest of all: happy love! Celeste loved him. Celeste was going to be his!

If you could know how much that good little Raoul was afraid of waking up! While he was plunged with delight into that triumphant dream, Monsieur de Rieux took him from

---

[123] Also Winnoc or Winnock (c. 640-c. 716/717), abbot or prior of Wormhout who came from Wales. St. Winoch is generally called a Breton, but was more probably of Welsh origin. He is said to have been of noble birth, of the same house as the kings of Domnonia. Some sources state that his father was Saint Judicael. He may have been raised and educated in Brittany, since his family had fled there to escape the Saxons. Winnoc eventually traveled to Flanders, to the Monastery of Saint-Omer, and was soon afterwards sent to found a priory at Wormhout in Northern France.

tomb to tomb; he told him the names of all those noble ladies and brave knights. They were now almost in the center of the low side, in front of the tomb of Guiomar de Rohan, who took to King Louis XI the challenge of François de Bretagne in the Monastery of Mont Saint-Michel, when they both started trembling, hearing a veritable sepulchral voice that was speaking from the deep shadows of the colonnade. That voice was saying:

"Whoever you are, did you come to tell me that the hour has come?"

Raoul opened his mouth to question.

"Silence," said Monsieur de Rieux. "That's Count Guy, that God has struck with insanity—your grandfather."

Raoul knew the story of that terrible night when César de Rohan had died, crushed by the paternal curse. His blood turned to ice in his veins.

"Will he pass by today?" repeated the voice. "Is he going to pass by today, the enemy of the Bretons? Is Philippe d'Orléans, Regent of France, going to pass by?"

Monsieur de Rieux and Raoul looked around, but didn't see anyone. They stepped forward again. When they were at the end of the colonnade, they saw the statue lying on the last tomb move.

"Approach," said the voice, and they saw the lips of the statue move. "I'm trying out the place where I will rest tomorrow."

When Raoul and Monsieur de Rieux were very near the tomb, they recognized that the figure lying on the stone was, in fact, an old man with a long white beard, whose almost diaphanous thinness was frightening to see.

Monsieur de Rieux remembered that, a long time before the events of our story, Rohan had had this tomb built, exactly like those of his ancestors. The heraldry, *de gueules à neuf macles accolees d'or*,[124] was embossed in the marble. The

---

[124] Nine yellow lozenges over a red background.

cushion was on one end; at the other, the crouched greyhound guarded the statue.

The old man raised himself up on his elbow and looked at the new arrivals. His eyes were glazed and fixed. Their sunken and greatly enlarged orbits comprised half of the face.

"You are de Rieux, you," he said to the Viscount. "Your father was a Breton... The other... The other..."

He began to tremble, and his poor bones without flesh made a sound against the stone of the tomb.

"The other one," he stammered, "oh, I see him often!"

He let himself fall back his full length. His lips were moving and murmuring a prayer in the form of an exorcism. Then, suddenly, his madness returned.

"Which of you has come on behalf of Orléans?" he asked, his strength returning. "Has he accepted my challenge? Does he still have a drop of warm blood in his veins?"

"My noble cousin," said Monsieur de Rieux, "we are going to take you back to your bed so that you can get some rest... You will need all your strength for that great battle."

And turning toward Raoul, who was petrified with stupor, he added:

"That man will be dead in an hour."

II. The Agony of Rohan

Raoul had had joys even beyond what he had desired. He was now learning to suffer unknown agonies. A tragic element was now entering his life, which until then had been so care-free. He was feeling for the first time the deep sadness that seemed inseparable from all grandeur. That man had killed his father and his mother; yet he was his grandfather. That man, so violently struck by the Hand of God, could make him feel only a sentiment of respectful pity, but his whole being had been turned upside-down. The tranquil quiet of his lonely adolescence had vanished. Raoul was being reborn to the fatalities of Rohan, and its disastrous past fell on his shoulders like an overwhelming burden.

Monsieur de Rieux had taken the old man's arm and felt his pulse.

He was thinking of Valentine, that noble creature who had fought so valiantly and for such a long time; Valentine, whose supreme hope was going to be disappointed just at the moment of victory; Valentine who was counting on that dying man who was already slipping into eternity.

The hand of Count Guy, damp and icy, fell back onto the marble as soon as Monsieur de Rieux released it. He opened his eyes at the shock, and seemed astonished to see someone near him.

"Ah! Ah!" he said. "Why are you waking me so early in the morning? Are we going hunting before the lamps are extinguished? Call Remi.... My old Remi... But isn't he dead? Call his son, the other Remi..." he interrupted himself, then went on: "I want the hunt today to be at the back of the Sangle. If he disappoints me today like yesterday, I'll get rid of him."

His eyes met Raoul's puzzled eyes. His features tried to smile.

"Is that you, César?" he murmured. "How was your night? And our dear treasure, Valentine? Give me your hand, César."

Raoul held out his hand. When the old man touched it, Raoul's whole body became cold; it was like touching a wet, cold stone.

The old man drew him to him and said in his ear,

"I dreamed that you were dead, César... My poor child. I was the one who had killed you, and I had aged twenty years. There is something strange about dreams!" he interrupted himself, rubbing his cold hands on the reverse side of his doublet, because he was shivering and his teeth clacked while he was talking. "There's something strange... Last night, I saw our Valentine with a little infant in her arms... That was her daughter. At the same time, our manor was crumbling, throwing great clouds of dust over the ruins. And a strong man from France was crushing our coat-of-arms between two rocks. A voice from among the stones was repeating: '*Rohan does not die; Rohan does not die.*' "

His eyes became haggard and he threw back his head, that rebounded on the marble cushion.

"But was that only a dream?" he repeated in a low voice. "Why are we among these tombs? César, my son, I can see that you have lifted the stone from your grave. What do you want from me?"

He closed his bluish eyelids. It was pitiful to see that gaunt, fleshless face, lost in the masses of that long white hair.

"My noble cousin," said Monsieur de Rieux, "those are foolish thoughts... Would you not like to recite with us the *Pater* and the *Ave*?"

The voice of the dying man was weaker and more and more indistinct. Still, instead of answering, he ssaid:

"Noyal is far from here. Why have you come all that way, César? Can a dead man move so far from his grave?"

His breath began to be caught in his throat.

"Who was it then who said, '*Rohan doesn't die!*'" he asked with a bitter smile. "Under this roof, there are only dead Rohans."

He made an effort to sit up, but he could not.

"Where are you?"

His thoughts could still be guessed by the movements of his lips, but his voice no longer came out. For one or two minutes one could see that he was fighting against death itself. Monsieur de Rieux and Raoul both knelt. A great sigh swelled the old man's lungs, and for one last time his voice was lifted.

"If he comes by," he pronounced with a supreme effort, "if he finally passes by, that man, today, that Frenchman, the Regent, tell him that he is a coward, and that he has made me wait too long... Are you there? I can't see you any longer..."

"We are here." answered Monsieur de Rieux.

"Tell him that I am still going to wait for him... at the foot of God's tribunal!"

His arms were stretched out along the sides of his body. His blind eyes stayed wide open. There was a funereal silence.

An hour had gone by. The sun had risen outside and chased away the vanquished fog. In the tombs, things had changed. The tomb that had served as the mortuary couch for the last Count de Rohan was now surrounded with lighted candles. In addition to our two companions, still kneeling, there was an old woman and a priest who was reciting the funereal orison. They had thrown a shroud over the body. The old woman was Dame Michou Guitan. The priest was the Vicar of Noyal-sur-Vilaine.

Everyone had entered without hindrance, because the manor had been abandoned that same night. The Seneschal today needed all his servants.

The priest pronounced all the verses; Monsieur de Rieux, Raoul, and Dame Michou devotedly intoned all the responses. That was a lugubrious scene, but also a grandiose one. It had been a long time since Rohan, banished, had had so much pomp around him.

Suddenly, in the middle of the monotone of the Latin Psalms, a cry was heard and a dishevelled woman rushed into the cave. Behind her, Josselin Guitan was supporting the shaking steps of a young girl.

Valentine de Rohan—for it was she—crossed the tombs with rapid steps, and came to stand in front of the death bed of her father. She put her hand on his heart.

"You have waited too long, Madame," said Monsieur de Riux in a low voice.

The priest lifted his hand and wanted to continue his prayer, but Valentine silenced him with an imperial gesture. She placed her face against that of the cadaver and called him by his name. Everyone saw the cadaver tremble.

"Have the horses made ready, Cousin," she instructed Monsieur de Rieux. "My father must be in Rennes in an hour."

The people there looked at each other. The strength of the soul has its limits. Had Valentine, broken by this last blow, lost her reason too? As she saw that Monsieur de Rieux was remaining there, his mouth agape, stupefaction in his eyes, she repeated coldly:

"Do it!'

The Viscount stood up. The Count's body had again become still.

"It would take a miracle…" the priest pronounced very low.

Valentine replied in a confident tone:

"God owes it to us!"

Then taking de Rieux to one side, she explained:

"We have rummaged through the ashes of the old windmill. We have turned over each ounce of soil… The papers were burned. Only Rohan himself can be a witness. He must! I will it!"

There was a feverish fire in her eyes; but her voice was calm and her hand, that was squeezing that of the Viscount, did not tremble.

Some people believe that the human will, heated by passion and reaching heretofore unknown heights, can have supernatural power. At that time, that power did not have a name. In our day, magnetism produces miracles. And what is magnetism if not the prodigious power of the will?

Monsieur de Rieux bowed and left. When he came back, the old Count was sitting up. Valentine had her arms around him. He was groaning horribly and his white eyes no longer had pupils, but he was alive. And that returned soul, that had been snatched back from death itself, put some strength back in the cadaver. The battle was poignant.

"Father," Valentine said, warming him with her own warmth, and resuscitating him with her own life, "Father! Now is not the time to die!"

The old man moved about under his winding sheet. His knees hit one against the other and produced cracking sounds. The word sacrilege was on the priest's lips.

"Live! Live, Father!" repeated Valentine, desperately. "I will it! I will it!"

During a minute that seemed to be as long as a century, Count Guy remained in some sort of suspension between life and death. Then life gained the upper hand. His lips parted; he began breathing again. His eyes showed a vague light.

"I can see," he said. He added almost immediately, because he was conscious of what had taken place: "Will I have to die twice?"

He was right. In that short or long respite that death had granted him, he had found himself again, and a cloud no longer covered his thoughts.

"My beloved father," said Valentine, "look at these children that are here near you..."

She had taken Raoul and Celeste by the hand. They were both pale as if crushed under the emotion of that solemn hour.

"I recognize them," murmured Count Guy. "That's my son, but did I have two daughters?"

He passed the back side of his hand over his forehead.

"I must rest," he begged. "Have mercy! Let me rest!"

"You will rest, Father," replied Valentine, "but not right now. Time is short, and we need you."

The old Count closed his eyes.

"I need rest," he said again. "I could live... I sense that, daughter... if I have silence and rest..."

"Your brandy, Josselin," Valentine commanded.

Josselin Guitan had his flask full of brandy. Valentine took it and brought it near the lips of the old man, who pushed it away with his hand.

Monsieur de Rieux looked away.

"Have compassion on him, Madame!" exclaimed Raoul.

"Mother! Leave him alone! Leave him alone!" exclaimed Celeste.

Her horror made her shake from head to toe.

The priest made the sign of the cross.

Josselin remained immobile and mute.

Dame Michou Guitan interrupted her rosary to exclaim:

"Courage, young lady. Your ancestors are there, who hear you and watch you!"

Valentine threw down the gourd and knelt beside the stone bed.

394

"Father," she continued, "the Parliament is assembled. They are expecting us. The boy here is not César. The earth doesn't give back its prey after fifteen years. The girl here is not Valentine, and may God will that her poor heart never be tortured as mine is at this instant. The boy here is the son of César. The girl here is the daughter of Valentine. They have no name, Father. Only you can give them back what they lost because of you."

"What are the things of this world!" murmured the old man. "And what will a Rohan do on this land of Brittany, which is now only a province of France!"

"Father! Father! I am at your feet. I implore you..."

"Let me die!" said Count Guy, whose enlarged eyes were begging.

She seized him by the arms. Those who were there heard the old man, who was babbling in his profound decline, say:

"Do you want to kill me, Daughter?"

A murmur escaped from every breast.

Valentine turned around, commanding, inflexible:

"Leave us!" she ordered. "I must be alone with my father!"

Dame Michou Guitan took hold of the priest, who was going to reply, and drew him away, saying:

"That woman there is a saint!"

The others went away, their heart tight in their chests.

Valentine then remained alone with the old man.

"Look at me, Rohan," she said. "Me, that you chased away and cursed... Me, who was innocent as was your son, César, whom you killed... Look at me, Rohan, I am wearing these peasant clothes that I have worn for fifteen years to watch over you and protect you. Look at me, Rohan, and wake up! You have destroyed your own race! Yesterday, the son of your son had no home; Yesterday, the daughter of your daughter was a servant to the usurper. All of that because of you! Rohan! Rohan! You have been a bad father!"

"Mercy" stammered the old man.

"Mercy?" repeated Valentine, who covered him with her burning look. "That is what your vassals, gathered all around you, kneeling, in tears, said the day you condemned your daughter!"

The old Count covered his face with his hands. Valentine leaned over him.

"No mercy, Rohan. That word could only occur to you in a dream. You are asleep, My Lord! Wake up! God gives everyone an hour for forgiveness: that hour has come. Providence is allowing you to resuscitate your race... Stand up, Father!"

She was pressed against the old man. Her breath was burning him. She was speaking low, but her voice was as cutting as a sword. Something ardent and intoxicating flashed in her eyes.

"I will go," Count Guy said despite his exhaustion. "I will go, but give me time. I feel that I don't have the strength now... Tomorrow..."

"Today, Father. This very hour."

"What shall I say?"

"The truth."

"They won't believe me, Daughter."

"Rohan has never lied. Everyone knows that. What piece of parchment is worth the word of Rohan? Everything depends on you."

The old man tried a slight movement.

"I cannot," he said, overwhelmed and paralyzed. "On the honor of my name, I cannot."

Valentine was wringing her hands.

"We are lost!" she said, inclining her beautiful, discouraged head on her breast.

Dame Michou Guitan saw that; the others did, too. The others felt less weight on their heart; the terrible battle seemed over to them. But Dame Michou shouted:

"Courage, young lady!"

Then prostrating herself and kissing the earth, she continued with the passionate strength of her devotion:

"O, Lord Almighty, I promise you a candle bigger than the oak at Mi-Forêt, even if my boy Josselin has to beg along the roads! Holy Virgin Mary! I will make a pilgrimage to Sainte Anne d'Auray—and Sainte Anne was your mother—on foot, barefoot, without eating or drinking anything but bread in a sack and the water in my gourd. O Lord God! Take my blood! Take my life!"

She interrupted herself to finish, fool that she was, adding:

"Give me a hundred years of Purgatory, O Lord God, and let the son of Rohan keep the house of his fathers!"

The old man turned his head slowly. Valentine stood up to her full height. Hope was reborn in her heart. She took both the hands of the old man and kissed them.

"You do not know this, my beloved Father," she continued softly, "but I had the proofs... Documents... It is because of you that I lost them. They were in the old windmill, but theu disappeared when it was set on fire... Do you understand me, Father?"

Rohan made an affirmative sign with his head.

"When it was set on fire," continued Valentine, "by order of that scoundrel in whom, in the past, you had placed all your confidence, Alain Polduc... Nothing would have been easier for me than to go and fetch the box in which I was keeping them, but then, I would have had to leave you, Father, all alone, in the middle of the flames... And you were already very feeble!"

"Help me!" said Count Guy.

Valentine put her arms around his body, thanking God in her soul.

"Ah!" he exclaimed in a long cry of destress. "I still cannot! I am dying!"

"No, Father! No! You are not!" exclaimed Valentine, clutching him against her breast, while her flaming eyes galvanized his dying body.

"My strength is returning... I feel it... Do you feel it, Valentine? Stand up! Stand up, Rohan! Rohan cannot die before having done his duty!"

Count Guy's feet touched the floor. He leaned for a moment on his daughter's shoulder.

"You are right," he said.

Then, in a distinct and high voice, he ordered:

"Have my horse saddled!"

He pushed Valentine away and passed her without staggering amongst the amazed helpers. It seemed to be the walk of a phantom.

In that way, he reached the moats where Josselin Guitan held out the bridle of the horse to him. Count Guy mounted into the saddle, upright and rigid.

All along the road from the manor right to Rennes, he took the lead of the cavalcade.

III. Rohan Does Not Die

As soon as the Count of Toulouse knew about the extreme measures taken against the peasants of the Wolf's Den, he sent a detachment of his guards with orders to clear the obstructed entrance of the cavern, escorted by the city's firefighters.

He did that out of humanity, because he had an excellent and noble heart. But he also did it for politics. His personal opinion was that Breton resistance couldn't be overcome by terror. Such a massacre, with its hideous consequences, would have raised the entire province. Yves Kemper de Lanascol, squire of the Countess of Toulouse, was charged with leading the liberating workers. The Celtic harmony of that Southern Brittany name indicates the nature of the Prince's thoughts. He wanted to surround himself and his wife with true Bretons.

Lanascol was twenty years-old. He had, for the first time, a few weeks earlier, left the paternal manor. In parting, he had dried his mother's tears with kisses, and promised that he would earn honor. And all along the route, that he crossed on horseback, from the black hills up to the flat and cloudy basin of Rennes, he had shared his dreams between his beloved mother and the young girl who had captured his heart.

Yves de Lanascol enthusiastically recognized that here was an opportunity to earn honor! He kissed the hand of the Prince and jumped in the saddle.

My mother will be happy and Margeride will hear about me! he said to himself.

Alas! His mother was soon in mourning and Margeride took the veil. The death of the poor squire Yves Kemper de Lanascol is still recounted in the winter evenings in the Finistère. Legend says that he was handsome; and what he did proves that he was brave.

It was still night when he arrived with his troop at the Pond of Muys. The workers began work immediately, and as soon as they had a passage opened, Lanascol entered first, shouting: "Quarter!"

He came up against the dead bodies of those who had been killed behind the gates. They lit torches. The cavern seemed deserted.

Lanascol went through the grand gallery that was cluttered with debris from the earlier feast. He came to the council chamber, where the body of Yaumi, the handsome cobbler, was lying.

The opened silver drapery showed the niche and, next to it, the opening through which the Wolves had made their retreat. From that opening came confused and loud sounds.

"They are still there!" the soldiers said.

Lanascol, despite the prayers of his companions, showed his unprotected chest and shouted again that His Highness, the Governor of Brittany, was pardoning all the peasants who had revolted. He was not answered.

He said: "Forward!"

Everyone knew very well that those caves were filled with precipices. The troop hesitated. Lanascol seized a torch, brandished it above his head, and rushed into the opening

Barely ten feet from the opening, they heard a cry:

"Mother!"

Lanascol and his torch had vanished into a chasm.

Such was the sad news that the soldiers of Toulouse later reported in Rennes. That news spread like lightning in the noble townhouses, as well as in the huts of the poor. All of the Wolves must have died, right to the last one, all at the same time, into that bottomless precipice.

There were no more Wolves!

As can well be thought, neither the Royal Steward Achille Feydeau, nor the Seneschal Alain Polduc, had gone to bed that night. They were the first to get the news.

At daylight, Alain Polduc was in the office of his father-in-law

"Vanished, the whole army of Wolves!" he shouted. "We have won, my excellent father-in-law! Yesterday evening I certainly thought that we were doomed!"

"I did too!" answered Feydeau.

Being so close to the end of this story, we cannot consecrate a half-dozen pages to describing Achille Feydeau's negligé. We regret it. Just his dressing gown was worth a long poem.

"Ah! Father-in-Law!" continued Polduc, "when I saw Monsieur de Rieux apply the pommel of his sword to the face of that cowardly scoundrel, Yaumi; when I saw Countess Isaure defy everyone; and Don Martin Blas a prisoner in the midst of the clumsy nobodies..."

"I have done an act of contrition, dear son-in-law," Feydeau interrupted.

"As for me, father-in-law, I felt like riding straight to Saint-Malo and taking a boat for England."

"What?" said Achille Feydeau, with a movement of retroactive terror. "Had it gone right to that point?"

"My dear father-in-law," Polduc answered, "between the abyss and us, there was just the thickness of a hair."

"What about now, son-in-law?"

"Now, I repeat to you, we have won. I don't know how that happened, but it is certain that all those who were in these caverns are dead. Now, count them all: Yaumi, who knew so much and bothered us; Martin Blas, who scared us; Valentine, our Medusa; and probably her old father, if he was not already dead; and almost certainly her daughter... I am not even including Josselin Guitan and his mother..."

"Then my son-in-law," exclaimed Feydeau, enchanted, "we have nothing left to do but celebrate our victory!"

"No, father-in-law... That young man who saved the Countess of Toulouse yesterday is still across our path... Our Hydra still has one head. This morning, if you please, we're going to split ourselves into four and spend a million if need be, so that this evening, we will be definitely the masters and untouchable!"

"A million?" repeated the Steward.

"Maybe two, if that's what it takes. I have a list here of tall he people we have to buy... Pick up a pin, some paper, and let's go to work, my dear father-in-law."

It was eleven o'clock in the morning.

The "big one," as they still call the master clock of the Rennes City Hall, was striking the minutes of the only prolonged sound that announced the solemn deliberations of the Breton Parliament.

Now, this deliberation was the most solemn of all. The Breton Estates were assembled in an extraordinary meeting, on the order of the Prince Governor himself, who had called into session all four chambers of the Parliament.That had happened only once, at the vote of resistance against the subsidies requested by Monsieur de Mercoeur in the war against the Bearnais.[125]

---

[125] Philippe Emmanuel de Lorraine, Duke of Mercœur (1558-1602), French soldier and prominent member of the Catholic League. In 1582, he was made governor of Brittany by Henry III of France, who had married his half-sister. In 1588,

The matter on the agenda was the trial of Rohan. May it please the Lord that we do not claim to say anything against the judges of the Rennes Parliament, or against the gentlemen of the Estates! However, it is certain that the Viscount of Rohan-Polduc, Seneschal of Brittany, has found a way to usefully spend the two millions given by his father-in-law.

In the opinion of everybody, the lawsuit had been judged in advance. For the last fifteen years, the litigation had been pending. Alain Polduc had won; he could no longer be denied his rights.

So, when the two Feydeau young ladies left the townhouse in the carriage of their father, all the populace that had received a little portion in the two millions, began to follow it, shouting:

"God save Rohan and our beautiful young ladies!"

The whole town was still very excited by the events of the preceding night. Houses remained deserted. All of Rennes had gone out into the streets that bordered on the Palace Square ; the Square itself seemed a rolling sea of heads because of the crowd that filled it.

Mercœur became the head of the League in Brittany, and had himself proclaimed protector of the Roman Catholic Church in the province. He formed an alliance with Spain and continued to press for his independence from France when Henri IV became King of France. Henri IV was born in Pau, the capital of the joint Kingdom of Navarre with the sovereign principality of Béarn. Henri IV sent a force against him led by the duc de Montpensier. With the aid of the Spaniards, Mercoeur defeated the French at the Battle of Craon in 1592. However, the royal troops were reinforced by English contingents and soon recovered the advantage. The king marched against Mercœur in person, and received his submission at Angers on 20 March 1598. Henri IV assured his control of Brittany through the marriage of his illegitimate son to Mercœur's daughter Françoise.

The Palace, now the Court of Appeals, was a quadrilateral building, the southern portion of which was occupied by a great antechamber. Its three other sides were occupied by audience rooms that opened onto three interior galleries. The grand chamber, where meetings of State were held, took up the eastern wing. The decoration was magnificent. The ceiling was by Coypel;[126] the wall paintings by Jean Jouvenet.[127]

The wall coverings, imported from Flanders, had cost Honoré d'Albert, Duke of Chaules, the next to last Governor of Brittany, fifteen hundred thousand livres. That room, of a monumental aspect, was in every respect worthy of its high place and of the proud province of which it was a representative.

On that day, however, it was much too small, and the doors of the two adjacent rooms had been opened wide to enable a communication made necessary by the presence of the entire Parliement plus all the members of Estastes.

A double throne, placed in the center of the enclosure, was reserved for Their Highnesses. The President of the Estates was seated immediately below. On the right, three seats were reserved for Rohan and his adopted daughters.

The meeting started at eleven o'clock. President de Montméril read the report. At eleven-thirty, Their Highnesses entered through the Clerk's door, and Steward Feydeau immediately had a dais with the arms of the Bourbon and Noailles placed above their thrones.

The smile of thanks that the Prince Governor gave him was found to be too cold and too brief. Their Highnesses, on the contrary, sent a gracious and kind greeting to the Viscount

---

[126] Antoine Coypel (1661-1722), French painter, pastellist, engraver, decorative designer and draughtsman. He became court painter first to the Duke of Orléans and later to the French king.

[127] Jean-Baptiste Jouvenet (1644-1717), French painter, especially of religious subjects.

of Rieux, who had entered at the same time as they did, wearing his new uniform of Brigadier of the Armies of the King, and who took his post at the front door.

Achille Feydeau, who, until then, had been radiant, had a bad premonition and turned toward his son-in-law, who was waiting not far from Monsieur de Rieux with the two young ladies.

The Seneschal motioned to his father-in-law. Then, seeing that Feydeau was moving about on his seat as if its cushions were filled with thorns, he scribbled some words on his tablet, folded the note, and sent it by an usher. That note, found on Feydeau after the meeting, contained these words:

We are protected from every direction. There are two thousand of our men inside and outside the Palace.

As a matter of fact, Alain Polduc had, that morning, bought an entire army with him. But of all the traffickers, the most shameless thieves are those who sell themselves.

We must say how the compact crowd, massed inside the building, in the vestibules, and on the steps, was composed before recounting the strange scene that occurred that morning in the Palace. The crowd plays an important role in this last act of our drama.

Outside, on the Square, there was a kind of purge going on among the crowd. All along the little Rue Saint-Benoit, located under the windows of the grand chamber, along the Convent of the Capucins, and in the vicinity of the Square, there were peasants and tenant farmers from the domain of Rohan-Polduc and Feydeau. They had systematically pushed back the ordinary men and women from the streets of Rennes. Evidently, they had been posted there by design.

In the center of the Square, and on the steps, there were also peasants, but peasants from the forest, with fierce demeanors, and dark attires. Their sunburned faces were hidden under big straw or felt hats, from which their tousled hair escaped. They formed a tight troop. Their movements were made all at one time. They had pushed the Polduc tenant farmers to the back without saying a word, with just the weight of their mass. They went right up to the doors, touching the last ranks of the gentlemen who filled up the vestibule, the stairs and the galleries, even right up to the Estates chamber.

As noon rang on the City Hall clock, an unusual cortege was seen arriving on the Rue Saint- George, that had great trouble getting through. That was a country woman whose features disappeared almost completely under her hood. She was holding a young girl by the hand. Then there was an old man wrapped in a big cloak who was supported by a young man from the forest on one side, and by a young gentleman in a brilliant uniform on the other. Finally, there was an old woman, a pipe in her mouth and a rosary in her hand.

"Hola! Good people," said the first farmers at the corner on the Rue Saint-George. "You shall not pass, even if you were the King and Queen!"

"Make way!" replied the young gentleman.

The old man didn't open his mouth.

The country woman seized the arm of the man who had spoken and said:

"Did you see the fire at the windmill of the Wolf's Den, François Lequien? I passed through those flames. Those who try to stop me today should beware. For I am the Miller Woman!"

François Lequien snatched his arm away as if he had been bitten by a snake. He leaned over toward his neighbors and spoke. Soon, the words ran from mouth to mouth:

"The Miller Woman!The Witch!"

And in that crowd through which you couldn't have put a finger, a large opening suddenly appeared, as if by magic.

At that moment, in the Great Chamber, the First President De la Chalotais began speaking to sum up the claims of Master Polduc and the petitions of the young Feydeau ladies.

The country woman, the old man, the young gentleman, the man from the forest and the old woman entered the path that had opened for them. Everyone stepped back from them with terror. At the sight of the old man, the dead man walking, everyone made the sign of the Cross. What devilment had the Witch prepared?

After crossing the ranks of Polduc 's and Feydeau's vassals, the cortege saw themselves up against a new human wall: those long-haired men with their hats pulled down over their eyes.

"Make way! Make way!" the young gentleman said.

The men from the forest summed him up with an insolent gaze and began to laugh. Not one of them budged.

"Julot!" said the country woman in a low voice.

All those who heard it paid attention.

"Josille!" continued the country woman. "Francil! Benoit!"

Four strapping lads came forward with their head uncovered.

"Put this old man on your shoulders," the woman ordered, "and walk forward until I tell you: *Here!*"

A name, however, had again gone from mouth to mouth. It was no longer that of the Miller Woman. The Wolves said:

"It's the She-Wolf!"

Because those who were there were the Wolves of the Forest of Forest, whose lives she had saved only the night before. A wooden plank bridge thrown over the precipice where poor Yves Kemper had found his death had given them a way across. The last fugitive had, with a kick of his foot, pushed the plank to the bottom of the chasm.

That name—the She-Wolf—made all those somber heads, from one end to the other, waver. Soon, the pale face of the old man, whose hair was floating in the wind, was seen lifted above the lads' shoulders. The four porters found the road open everywhere for them.

On arriving at the foot of the steps, it was necessary to fight again. It was now the gentlemen who barred the way. The country woman unhooked the hood that had covered a noble and beautiful face.

"Gentlemen," she said, throwing back the full curls of her hair, while her humble disguise fell to her feet, "will you not make way for Countess Isaure?"

"*Par la morbleu!*" answered Cadet Laval, "if they don't, beautiful lady, then it will be necessary for me to use my sword, because I wish it! Everyone wishes it. Who, indeed, among the young nobility of Rennes would resist the most beautiful of the beautiful!"

The four Wolves carrying the old man passed through. They were asked no question, although each one could certainly tell that a strange event was going to take place.

Countess Isaure came after the old man, still holding by her hand the charming young girl that the gentlemen of the nobility recognized as the chosen one from the previous night. All of them had seen her carry the keys to the city on a golden plate. Behind the Countess and her companion came Josselin and Dame Michou Guitan. These last two, after they had gone across the vestibule, mounted the stairs and went across the galleries, stopping at the threshold of the grand chamber outside.

The old man, the two women and the young gentleman went in under the Flemish tapestry that decorated the main door. Monsieur de Rieux, who was there, said very low to Countess Isaure:

"Not yet."

At the same time, he detached the cord that held back the heavy curtain. Our cortege became suddenly invisible for the people who were in the room. President De Chalotais had just finished his summary, concluding in favor of the Seneschal and his two daughters. Many favorable remarks greeted his speech. But just as the Seneschal and his daughters started to rise, at a sign from the Major of Ceremonies, Steward Feyeau stopped his son-in-law. He had just received a note passed from hand to hand, and large drops of sweat ran down his makeup.

"We are lost!" he stammered.

Polduc shrugged his shoulders and ignored the warning.

Then, Monsieur de Rieux said:

"It is time!"

And he began to walk at the head of the cortege. When the dying but still handsome head of Old Count Rohan appeared above the other heads, a loud rumble was heard in the room.

Monsieur de Toulouse rose from his throne. The wig of the poor Steward sagged. He could no longer be seen: he had fainted like the old woman that he was. Polduc, however, went through the crowd, happy and proud. Those rumblings, he though they were for himself and was grateful. That name, Rohan, he naturally applied to himself and was thankful for the money spent by his father-in-law. He had not seen what was happening behind him when he arrived on the steps of the stage. Mademoiselle Agnès and Mademoiselle Olympe had already mounted the steps.

Suddenly, Polduc turned around because Monsieur de Rieux had touched his shoulder. At the sight of Rohan carried in that way, as if in triumph, the Seneschal's face became decomposed. He looked like a man struck by lightning. Countess Isaure passed in front of him, pushing aside the two Feydeau young ladies who were choosing their seats. When they asked her proudly by what right, she answered:

"These seats are for Rohans; these are not at all yours. Move away, girls!"

Then she added, sitting down beside her daughter:

"We are the Rohans!"

Raoul stood behind her seat.

The four lads had deposited the old man in the third seat, more elevated than the others. The rumbling had stopped. All emotion had been translated into deep silence. Something unheard of was then seen in the Parliamentary splendor. Their Highnesses the Prince Governor and his wife crossed the full length of the stage, walked in front of the woman that Madame de Toulouse had insulted only the evening before under the name of Countess Isaure. The Princess offered her her hand and kissed her on the forehead.

"Monseigneur," said Valentine, "this is Count Guy of Rohan, who is still an outlaw by Royal decree. I need him to speak here. Please extend you protection so that he can be heard."

"Rohan is here among peers," answered the Count of Toulouse. "I bring from Paris a Toyal Decree that gives him back his titles and estates." Then turning toward the old man, he added: "Speak, Count, you are free!"

A little blood mounted into the wrinkled checks of the old Breton.

"It is perhaps the Will of God," he murmured, "that Brittany become French... Bourbon!" he repeated, in a voice that was no longer of this world. "You are a noble Prince. I wish to testify before you..: This man is the son of César, my first born... This woman is the daughter of my daughter, Valentine... Both born from legitimate unions... Both Rohans... I so swear!"

He fell silent. The Count of Toulouse took a step toward him, his hand held out. But Rohan had done his duty. His last word had been his last breath. His death had saved him from that alternative: to shake hands with a Frenchman, or to refuse a loyal hand offered to the most loyal of knights.

He was no more. Rieux said:

"At least, he died restored to his rightful place."

EPILOG

In that session of the Rennes Parlement, César de Rohan and Marie, his cousin, were solemnly married. It was Madame de Toulouse that joined their hands in holy matrimony. When they left the Palace, the Prince Governor motioned from the top of the steps that he wanted to talk. Valentine was near him. The Wolves applauded from one end of the grand palace to the other.

"Good People," said the Prince, "the war between you and us is finished. The King (and he stressed the word King as if he had wanted to push aside the person of the Regent, who was odious to the Bretons) loves you and, because of that, he has sent me to you. I bring you forgetting of the past with the promise of better days, and for proof, good people, here is the son of your former Lords that the King returns to you... He was a Count. The King makes him a Duke... And to wipe away even the memory of the traitor who soiled for an instant the dwelling of your noble masters, the name of Polduc will nevermore be pronounced."

He took Raoul by the hand.

"This man here," he added, in the midst of the acclamations, "is now Duke of Rohan-Rohan."

They say that after that grand triumph, back in her townhouse, Valentine found on the threshold of her oratory Morvan de Saint-Maugan kneeling.

Feydeau and his two daughters had left for Paris at the end of the session.

Alain Polduc had disappeared. Here is what is told very low in the Forest de Rennes. Josselin had one day told him, swearing to it, "You will die by my hand."

Polduc's body was found in the Noyal Cemetery between the tombs of César and Jeanne de Combourg, his wife. The murderer was lying between his two victims.

410

In conclusion, we will add that Julot, the traveler, told about the marvels of Paris until the last day of his life and Dame Michou Guitan returned with honor to her position as housekeeper of the Rohan manor. The Memoirs of that time have only one gap. In spite of our diligent research, we were never able to discover if the romantic Magloire finally married his Sidonie.